NIGHT OF THE WHITE RAVEN

Ethan Miller

Earth Star Publications
Cedaredge, Colorado

FIRST EDITION
June 2006
Second Printing August 2017

Library of Congress Control Number: 2006904543

This novel is a work of fiction. The characters are all fictional, although there are names of people and places that existed at one time. Any similarity in names to real people is coincidental and unintentional. This book is suggested for a mature readership.

ISBN 978-0-944851-24-1

Printed in the United States of America

DEDICATION

I dedicate this writing to my wife, Annie, because of her willingness to stand beside me, encouraging me to finish and publish this novel. Her dedicated hard work with typing and corrections, and overseeing its publication, made this work possible.

Front cover art by the author

FOREWORD

From the moment I first met Ethan, I recognized him as a special man and knew in some way he would influence my life. I had no idea that he would one day become my husband, or write a novel. During the first ten years of our relationship, we spent winters apart with correspondence through letters. It wasn't until many years later that I realized this man was dyslexic and had difficulty composing a letter.

I have always been impressed by his wisdom, and the fact that he is, for the most part, self educated.

Over a period of twelve years, he worked on *Night of the White Raven*, laboriously writing, reading, rewriting, and revising again. His style may not win any praise from professional editors, but it makes no difference. He has written from his heart, and in his own voice, which those with whom he is acquainted will recognize and cherish.

He is a man born 130 years late, and has taught me—a city girl—the enchantment of life in the outdoors: camping, fishing, hiking, and cutting wood. I have learned survival skills from him, but more importantly, I've come to appreciate the mountains because of him. My memories are full of shared adventures with him in the wild, and the longing to return to the woods and the high country. Once you have experienced it, you'll agree there is nothing that can take its place.

Ann Ulrich Miller

1

Mom was standing in the doorway, tall and thin. Her long blond hair, mixed with a little white, hung loosely over the front of her shoulders. In the early morning light it shone like gold, even with the tears flowing down her cheeks. She was the most beautiful person I would ever know.

As I slid down off my mule, Mom came running and my two sisters and brother were right behind. My feet had no more than hit the ground and she threw her arms around me, pulling me close. Her cheeks, wet with tears, pressed tight against mine, and she whispered over and over, "I love you."

The two little ones—the twins—were holding fast to my legs. Frances had her arms around both Mom and me. She was crying. My own tears were mixed with Mom's as she hugged and kissed me over and over. "Nathan," she said, "please ... take care of yourself."

Finally, I pulled away, and wiped my eyes. Bending down, I hugged and kissed my sisters and brother, then stood and placed my hands on each side of Mom's face as her hands covered mine. I looked deep into her blue eyes and could see the hurt she was feeling deep inside, and I saw the love she was pouring out to me as only a mother can. I saw the happiness she was feeling for me, knowing I was doing something I wanted to do – knowing I was growing up. But it still wasn't enough to cover the hurt she was feeling deep inside, for she knew as well as I did that we may never see each other again.

It was on this sunny morning in the beginning of March that I rode away from the cabin that had been my home for the past fifteen years.

My life had begun in this log cabin, around 1803, and it was here that my father and mother staked out land that, in time, would become their farm. Our place was some distance from the settlement that had sprung up around Fort Pitt. It was here in this settlement that my father operated a gristmill where he ground grain into flour, grist and meal for the people in the settlement. He also supplied the garrison at the fort.

My father was stocky built with reddish-brown hair, a bushy beard the same color as his hair, and dark brown eyes. Dad wasn't quite as tall as Mom, but with a temper that had no match. Most of the time he was patient and understanding, and a good, hard-working father. But sometimes he drank too much. Drinking and his temper didn't go good together, and at such times the whole family suffered.

I was the oldest of four. I had two sisters and a brother. My oldest sister, Frances, was tall for her age, and as scrawny as a willow switch, with long, scraggly blond hair and beautiful blue eyes. She was the spit 'n image of her mother, and so much like her, she sometimes even acted like her. Frances was a very good girl, very patient and always willing to help. She had a lot of common sense for her age. I knew that one day Frances would be a beautiful woman, and make someone a good wife.

Then there was the twins, Abilene and Noel. Brother Noel, well ... he was a chip off the old block, stocky built like Dad, and looked like him with his reddish-brown hair and dark brown eyes, with about the same temper to go with it. Noel was very different from Frances and Abilene in his everyday moods. He was always picking on the others and wanted his own way in everything. He was so much like Dad that it was even funny. Sometimes I wondered what he was going to be like when he grew into a man.

Now Abilene! Well, well ... I guess she was kind of a different story. It was hard to tell about Abilene at such a young age. She didn't favor Mom nor Dad in her looks. Her hair was light brown and she had grayish-colored eyes. I think she was more like Mom in her temper, and more easy-going, yet strong-willed. She could hold her own in a scrap with Noel. I had no way of telling what she would be like when she grew older.

Our father worked from daylight until dark operating the mill, and Mom tried to farm and bring up four kids. There wasn't always a lot to go on. Dad's pay wasn't much, mostly bartering in grain or other things. For some reason I was never close to my father, and sometimes I think he resented this and blamed my mother. I knew he was always after her to let me help him work at the mill, even when I was about seven or eight.

For whatever reason she had, I never knew, but Mom would not let me go to the mill. She would simply say, "I have too much work around this place for that boy to do. Now that's that! I don't want to hear any more about it."

I think this is the reason I became a lot closer to Mom, and from an early age I knew Mom depended an awful lot on me—maybe too much. It was Mom and I who did just about all the work. Dad helped whenever he had time, but it seemed he never had much time—not even for us.

Mom was a very loving person, full of affection, hard-working, with a lot of patience, easy-going, and very understanding. She was a strong woman in both physical strength as well as strong-willed. Kind and gentle, you could say she was almost the opposite of Dad.

We had two cows, a few pigs, a dozen or so chickens, and of course our horses. I did most of the feeding, and Mom would let me do the milking sometimes. Dad would barter for hay and straw for the livestock and the grain we needed, so we would have enough to feed the animals during the cold winter months.

I wasn't long past seven. It was late spring, and Mom and I were doing the plowing. Mom was a strong woman, able to handle the plow. I would walk beside her and drive the team of horses. Frances was three then, and Mom made her stay at the end of the field and watch over Noel and Abilene, who were just babies, a little over a year old. We would plow from where they played to the other end of the field, then back to where they were. Then we would stop and rest. Mom and I would sit down on the warm ground, and Mom would hold and play with the two little ones. Then we would make another round.

Time after time we did this. I remember at the time how Mom was with baby and she would say, "Nathan, it won't be long until you have a new brother or sister."

It was days before we got all the plowing done, and more days went by before she and I got the planting done. At the time, I was too short to unhitch the horses. Mom fixed a place where we could pull the horses beside, and I could stand on and help her put the harness on and take them off.

It seemed like we had to go to church most every Sunday. Then after church, Dad always found someone to talk business with or he would go to the mill to work for the rest of the afternoon. Mom and the rest of us would go home. Sometimes, if it was a nice day, Mom would make something to eat and hitch up a horse in the buckboard and drive down by the river, where she would let me fish, while she sat in the warm sun and played with the little ones. Then she would holler, "Nathan, are you catching anything?" Sometimes I would say yes, but more often it was no.

After a while, she would holler for me to come, and we would sit and eat the things Mom brought along. And Mom would tell us stories of when she was a little girl in the old country. Mom was always very patient and loving with us. She never hollered at us the way Dad did, but when she did, we knew she meant it. I must say, Mom made for us a very pleasant home. It may not have been much, but it was home.

Both Mom and Dad said they came from the old country. I think it was Germany. Sometimes they would talk in Dutch or German. Even though I had to work hard, I would always love my parents, for it would come in handy later in life.

It was early summer when the baby came, and Mom and all the rest of us were very happy about the new baby. Mom had to stay in bed for a few days. Dad would leave for work early, so that left the milking and feeding of the animals to me. Noel and Abilene would stay with Mom, and I would take Frances with me. Frances couldn't do much, but she would try, and she always stayed very close to me, most of the time only a few feet away. She would say she was afraid of the big *moo-moos*... cows.

It wasn't long until Mom was on her feet again. Things went well the first three months, then little baby Jeanette became sick, and about three days later, she died. I could see Mom was heartbroken, for she cried and cried for days after we buried Jeanette by the church. Dad didn't say much, and he didn't seem to be much comfort to Mom. It seemed she stayed away from him as much as she could. I couldn't help but feel that Mom blamed him, and yet I knew she blamed herself most of all.

There was plenty of work to do during the summer and she buried herself in work. There was the tending of the different things we planted for food that would see us through the long winter. When they were ready, I would help Mom gather them and we would put them up in cans and store them in the underground root cellar, where they would keep quite well for most of the year. Other things went in there, too, like cabbage, carrots, apples—when we could get any—pumpkins, potatoes and squash.

By now, it was the end of fall, and before I knew it, it was winter and snow was falling. It was about then that Mom finally got back to being her old self. I was going on nine, and Mom decided it was time I started to school. She made arrangements for me to go to school half a day in the afternoon. In the morning, I had to help Mom with the work in the barn and house. Then, she would make me something to eat before I went to school.

When Dad found out I was going to school, he yelled at Mom. "Why isn't that boy helping me at the mill? And why aren't *you* teaching him?" It was as though she had nothing else to do.

Mom never gave in. She looked at him and said, "That boy is going to school, and that's it!" There was never anything said after that.

When I first started getting my schooling, our teacher was an older man whose name was Mr. J.C. Beckworth, who wasn't all that nice. He hollered a lot at the kids, but I must say, he made everyone listen, and we learned. At first, I didn't like going to school. I would sooner have been doing something else. I never told Mom, for I knew how much she wanted me to be schooled. It wasn't long before I came to like school and looked forward to going. It was here that I found other kids my age to talk and play with.

The years passed, and in the year I turned thirteen, it was that fall that we got a new teacher. Her name was Miss Lillie Martin. She was young and pretty, just seventeen. At least that's what people said.

It was that fall that I became interested in trapping. During the summer, I had been doing some work, helping this man and woman who went to our church. While cleaning up their barn, I came across some old traps hanging on a peg. The man saw me looking at them over and over. After a while, he asked if I would like to have them.

I looked at him and finally said, "Gosh, I sure would!"

The man taken them off the peg and handed them to me. "Here, boy, they're yours."

That winter, I set out to do some trapping. I must say I didn't do too well. It was toward spring when I finally caught one skunk and one 'possum. I didn't know how to skin them, and neither did Mom. I asked Dad if he'd show me how to skin them.

"I don't got time!" he hollered. "Now forget about that trapping and get some work done!"

I still had one afternoon of school left that week, and I was sure one of the kids at school would know how. I asked some of the kids and they didn't know. Finally, I asked my teacher. She said she didn't know either. Then she said, "Nathan, I heard of an old man who might help you." She told me where I could find him.

When I got home after school, I asked Mom if I could go see the old man.

She said, "After you get your work done on Saturday."

2

The next day being Saturday, I hurried and got my work done, then told Mom I was going to look for the man Miss Martin told me about. I started walking in the direction I was told, and I walked and walked. I had my skunk and 'possum in a sack, and they were getting heavy. It seemed like I walked at least three miles when I found the place. It was an old shack not far from the river.

I laid my sack down, and before I got to the shack, the door opened and this man came out with long gray hair. In a rough voice, he said, "Hey, young fella, what you want?"

I told him my name and that I was looking for someone to show me how to skin animals and put them up.

He looked at me awhile. "Where you live?" He spoke in broken English.

I told him.

"What your old man do?"

"What? You mean my father?"

"That's it."

"He owns the grist-mill."

"Oh! Come in, boy. They call me Old Joe." Then he turned and went back into the shack.

I didn't know if I should go in or run. My wanting to learn overcame my fear and I followed him inside.

"Sit, boy." He pushed a wooden box at me with a stick. I sat down. It was next to his stove. He sat on his only chair on the other side of the room. The place smelled a little bad, and the floor was just dirt, but then a lot of houses just had dirt floors. The stove was hot and he had something cooking in a battered-up pot. "Now... what was it you wanted?"

"I want to know if you will show me how to skin animals and put up the fur."

"Oh yes, that's it. What's it you got?"

"I have one skunk and one opossum."

"Is that it?"

"Yes."

"Where are they?"

"They're outside in a sack."

"How old you, young fella?"

"I'm thirteen."

"Kinda big for thirteen ... ain't you? You go school?"

"Yes."

"Now what was you come here for? Oh yes, you talking 'bout trapping. Yes, yes, how I do remember … remember those days when I would go out and do much trapping. Mind ye, that's all I do back then. I start in early fall through late spring. I catched much fur in them days, made good money too. I *did.*" Then Old Joe went into telling all about when he trapped. He talked and talked in his broken English. He told me how he did it, and what I should be doing, and all the while he talked he kept sticking wood in the stove.

By now it was getting hot in that shack, and the hotter it got, the worse the smell got. Finally, he said, "Let's go take a look-see at what's in that bag you have."

Boy, was I glad to get outside, not that I didn't want to hear what Old Joe was talking about. We went out and I got my sack of two animals and taken them to where he was standing by a big tree.

"Fetch it here, boy. Now, what your name again?"

"Nathan."

"Oh yes, that's what … Nathan."

I didn't know what to expect. He had these two pieces of wire wrapped around nails, about 14 inches apart, and they hung down maybe 10 inches.

"Well, boy, bring one of them critters."

I did as he asked. He taken the skunk by the back legs and looped a wire around each back foot. Then he got out his knife and showed me how to make each and every cut, and how to skin around the shoulders and head without cutting the hide. After he was done, he told me to do the next one. I did, and with his help I was able to get it done without ruining the hide.

Then he showed me how to scrape the fat and stuff off the inside of the hide. Next, he got two boards that were tapered at one end, then rounded. He told me to pull the hide onto these boards, and he showed me just how they should look when they were on the boards right, and how to fasten the hides to the boards until they were just about dry, then remove them and hang them until they were to be sold.

It was past mid afternoon, and I knew I should be getting

on home. I didn't like calling him Old Joe, so I simply said, "Mr. Joe, I need to be getting on home. I know Mom is wondering what got me."

"Okay, boy, leave animals' bodies. I take care of them." He handed me six or so more boards of different sizes. "Here, boy, take with you."

I put them in my sack with the two hides, and slung the sack over my shoulder, then reached out my hand to shake his. I asked Mr. Joe how much I owed him.

"Be on your way, boy, and don't forget ... come back, see Old Joe. I tell you more about how to trap."

"I will, Mr. Joe." I started the walk home, and every step I taken, I thought about what Mr. Joe talked about and showed me. I knew in my mind I would be back as much as I could.

It was late when I got home, so I went straight to the stable. I hung the two hides up as Mr. Joe told me to. I had just started to feed the animals when Mom and the other kids walked in. The first thing Frances said was, "What's that smell?"

Mom wrinkled up her nose. "Nathan, can't you put the skunk somewhere else?"

"No, Mom, this is the only place I have to put anything."

She knew that, and didn't say anything more, and went about milking. Mom always milked the cow while I did most of the other work. The only time I milked was when Mom wasn't able, and that wasn't very often. The other kids helped me, what little they could. Mostly they played. Frances did feed the chickens and gather the eggs.

We finished our work and went to the cabin. While Mom was getting supper, I carried six buckets of water in from the spring and filled the two wash boilers that were on the back of the stove to heat while we ate supper, so it would be ready for our baths later. Our cabin wasn't big, just two rooms down and a loft up. The kitchen was the biggest. It was where Mom did all the cooking and sewing, and where we ate and did a lot of other things. The little ones played in here when it wasn't nice to be outside. The room in the back part was Mom and Dad's room, where they slept. They did have a big wooden bed, wash stand and other stands in their room. There was one window in this room and the door from the kitchen, which was closed with a blanket. The kitchen part had two windows and the outside door, a cook stove and a fireplace. The kitchen table was fair-sized with two wooden benches. We did have four chairs, a work table and shelf on the one wall to put the kitchen things on. The loft covered a little more than the back room. This is where Frances and I slept. Shortly before baby Jeanette came, Mom and I filled another bag of straw and put it on the loft close by Frances for Noel and Abilene to sleep on. Each spring and fall, Mom would get them down and take them out to the stable and empty them out, then put new straw in, as she did hers and Dad's.

It was way past dark and Dad wasn't home. I knew Mom was worried, yet she didn't say anything. Mom put our supper on the table and sat down and said the prayer. We ate supper. We were all finished and Dad still wasn't home. Mom got up and told Frances and I to start the dishes. She went outside, but wasn't gone long when she came back in. She helped us finish doing the dishes, not saying anything.

It was getting later, and Dad still wasn't home. Mom got the wash tub and set it by the stove, where it was warm, and put enough hot and cold water in so that it was just right for bathing. Noel and Abilene got undressed and got in the water and started to splash each other. Mom yelled at them, and soon had them settled down and bathed. Then she told me to empty the water out. I did, and Mom filled it again. Next she gave Frances her bath. I was sitting at the table doing some school work while she was getting them all put to bed.

Taking some water and one of the tubs, she went into her room as she pulled the blanket closed that covered the doorway. She told me to take my bath while she was in her room. I got up from what I was doing, filled the other tub, and taken my bath. I was sitting there by the warm stove, playing in the water, when Mom looked out from behind the blanket and saw what I was doing.

"Nathan, get dressed!" she yelled.

I did, and put my night shirt on, then emptied my water.

Mom had her nightgown on when she brought her bath to be dumped. It was very late by now and Dad wasn't home. I was sitting at the table, looking at my school books, when Mom came over and sat down across from me.

"Nathan, where do you think your father is?"

I shrugged my shoulders. "I don't know." We knew he would stop once in a while and have a few drinks, and come home feeling good and do a lot of yelling, but he was never this late.

Mom sat and talked to me as if I was a grownup. She talked about school and what I wanted to do when I grew up.

She asked me about Mr. Joe and what I thought about him. "Do you like him?"

"Yes, he's okay."

"Are you going back to see him?"

"Yes, if you say I can."

"What did you talk about?"

"He told me about when he was a trapper and how he caught animals. He told me to come back anytime I wanted, and he would show me how to set my traps, so I can catch more animals… and how to fish."

Mom and I had some long talks before, but nothing like tonight. She was talking about all kinds of things, a lot that I didn't understand or know anything about. I knew the later it got, the more Mom worried. I knew things between them weren't the same since baby Jeanette died. As Mom and I sat there talking, I remembered long before the baby died, sometimes at night, when everyone was in bed sleeping, I would wake up and hear Mom and Dad laughing and making noises. I would lie there and wonder what they could be laughing about.

As Mom talked on and on, I remembered other things that happened, like one time before I was eight. One night I was wakened by the noise coming from their room, so I decided to see what they were laughing about. I got up very quietly and creeped down the ladder from the loft, just enough so that I would be able to see what they were laughing about. The lamp was burning in their room, and the blanket that hung over the door was open a crack. I was halfway down the ladder, and from where I was, I could see them on the bed. They were rolling around, and I couldn't possibly understand what they were doing or what was so funny. So, I crept back up the ladder and crawled back in bed.

I guess it was past midnight when Mom finally said I should go to bed. Getting up, I gave Mom a hug and went on up to bed. I heard her go to bed, and I noticed she left the lamp burning on the kitchen table.

I don't know how long I had been asleep when I was awakened by noises from the kitchen. I sat up, so I could see what the noise was about. Mom was standing by the table, still in her nightgown, and Dad was sitting on the other side. Mom was talking in a low voice, I guess so as not to make any noise. "Otis, where were you all this time?"

He barked back at her, "It's none of your damn business,

you bitch!"

I looked around, to see if he had awakened the other kids. Thank goodness, they didn't wake up. I could tell right away Dad was *drunk—very drunk!* Drunker than I had ever seen him. They argued for a while, Mom wanting to know where he was this late, and why he was so drunk.

Mom was turning to go back to bed when Dad yelled, "Shut up, you bitch, and make me something to eat!"

Mom turned around and said, "If you want to act like a pig, make it yourself, and go to the stable to sleep! You're *not* sleeping with me!"

With that, he staggered to his feet. "You damn bitch, I'll knock you on your ass!"

Mom yelled, "Go to hell, you drunk!"

With that, he hit her so hard across the face, it knocked her back against the wall under the loft. Before she could get up, I was down the ladder and to where she was. By now, the other kids were awake, crying and yelling for them to stop.

Dad grabbed her by the hair and was pulling her to her feet when I started pounding on him with both of my fists as hard as I could. He turned and hit me, sending me flying across the floor. He grabbed Mom again and pulled her to her feet. I was on my feet now, a little dazed, just as he was going to hit Mom again. I gave a run and a jump onto his back, knocking him off balance. I had my arms locked around his neck and held on for dear life, not knowing what was going to happen.

I don't know what happened next. He just fell down on the floor. I let go and got off of him. Mom was crying and yelling at him as she jumped up and ran to the other kids and pulled them close to her. I think Dad was too drunk to do anything else. He had gotten to his knees and crawled into his room and flopped on the bed.

I went up on the loft, where Mom and the little ones were. Putting my arms around her, I held her and the other kids tight as we all sat and cried.

Mom asked between sobs, "Where is he?"

I told her, "He crawled in and flopped on your bed."

We sat a long time, holding each other and the little ones. Finally, they went back to sleep. Mom and I listened, and after a while, we could hear Dad snoring.

Mom and I went down and looked in her room. Dad was lying on his back, sound asleep. Mom said to me, "Nathan, get the gun off its pegs and take it along up with you."

I went and got a drink of water, then got the gun. "Mom, what are *you* gonna do?"

"I'm going to sit at the table and rest," she said.

"Mom, come up with us."

At first she said no. When I insisted, she said she would. I handed her the gun and waited until she was up and settled down. I blew out the lamp and made my way up. As I lay down next to Mom, she pulled me tight to her as she sobbed.

I don't know how long Mom cried after I fell asleep.

3

It was mid morning when Mom finally stirred and wakened me. The other kids were still asleep and that was unusual for them. Mom got up and went down and changed into her clothing. I dressed and went down and got a fire going in the stove while Mom fixed something for us to eat. It wasn't long before the little ones were down and dressed. Mom put the things on the table and we sat down and ate.

We were all finished eating when Dad got up and came out. He stood there, looking at us for a few minutes, then walked over to the stove and poured himself a cup of coffee and came to the table and sat down. Mom and I had gotten up and cleaned the table off. She told the other kids to go out and play. Soon they were all outside. Mom fixed Dad a plate of food and set it in front of him. She then sat down at the opposite end of the table and I went over and stood beside her. She put her arm about my waist and pulled me close. She sat there a few minutes, looking at him. I could tell she was nervous. Dad was eating slowly, I guess not knowing what to expect.

Very calmly, Mom said, "Otis, I want you to understand a few things. I want you to listen very closely to what I have to say to you, because I won't be telling you again. Do you hear? I and the children forgive you for what you did to us last night, especially your son here and myself. If it wasn't for him, it's no telling what you may have done. If you ever hit me again, I promise you, you'll not be going to that damn mill ... or anywhere else, for that matter."

There was silence for a moment, and then she said, "One more thing. Don't ever come home drunk or be with another woman. If you do, just go to the stable and sleep with the animals, because you won't be sleeping with me, or in this house. Do I make myself clear?"

Dad got up and went to the stove and poured another cup of coffee, then came sat down where he had been sitting. He sat there, sipping at his coffee, and looked at Mom, not saying anything. In fact, he hadn't said anything since he had gotten out of bed. Finishing his coffee, he got up and went out to the stable. It was Sunday, and Mom figured he would go to the mill. She watched out the window, but he never left.

Even though it was late, the animals had to be taken care of. Mom and I went to the stable to do the work. We were surprised to see he had done the milking and had most of the other work done. Mom picked up the pail of milk and went back to the house. I stayed and helped Dad clean the stable up some, and we fixed things that was in need of fixing.

We worked most of the afternoon in and around the stable. Things were looking pretty fair. Next, Dad went to the house and started cleaning up the outside. Anything he saw that was in need of repair he got to it and fixed it. He never said anything all afternoon, just when he needed me to help. We worked hard until dark, when Frances came and told us that supper was on the table.

We went in and washed, then taken our places at the table. Mom had cooked a good meal of ham and potato pot pie. There wasn't much talking while we ate. Now and then, I could see Dad sitting there looking at Mom, like he wanted to say something. I could sense he really wanted to talk to her, but his stupid German bull-headedness wouldn't give in.

When we finished eating, Mom got up and cleaned off the table. Frances and I got with doing the dishes, and the other two kids were running around, hollering and picking at each other, as usual. I looked just in time to see Dad had lit a lantern and was on his way out.

After he closed the door, Mom said, "I wonder where he's going." It wasn't long before we heard him splitting wood. Mom looked at Frances and I, and said, "I wonder what got into him," and went on getting the other two washed up for bed, then Frances.

Soon they were all in bed. Mom taken a basin of water and went to her room. I got myself washed and went to bed. It wasn't long and I heard Mom coming up. She brought along an extra cover and laid down next to me. That was the only place there was any room for her. In a whisper, she was telling me about sending Frances to school since she was now seven, then she asked if Dad had said anything about last night. I told her that he hadn't, and the only time he'd talked all afternoon was when he wanted me to help him do something.

It wasn't long before we heard Dad come in. He washed, then dumped the water out. After checking the fire in the stove,

I could see by the light that Dad picked the lamp up from the kitchen table and went into his room. I don't know what his reaction was when he saw Mom wasn't there, but there was nothing said.

The next morning, Dad was up early and went to the stable. He had most of the work done by the time Mom and I got there. Mom taken the milk and went back to the house. I helped Dad finish the work, then we went to the house. Mom had breakfast on the table and the other kids were eating.

After Dad was through eating, he went out and hitched the horses to the plow and started in plowing the field, even though it was fall. He plowed till mid morning, then unhitched the horses and turned them out to eat. He stopped by the house, got some water and something to eat, then went to the mill.

Mom didn't say anything. She looked at me and told me to get ready for school. She said, "Frances is seven now, and it's time for her to be schooled. I'm taking her over to the school to talk to the teacher."

School wasn't all that far away. Mom and us kids walked. Once there, Mom talked to the teacher about Frances getting schooled.

Miss Martin and Mom had talked in the past, but this time there seemed to be a closeness between them. They would talk and laugh. When Mom was ready to go, she told Miss Martin that if she wasn't doing anything, come next Sunday afternoon, that she was to stop for some talk.

Miss Martin said, "I think I will."

4

Time passed quickly. Dad had spent more time at home these past weeks than he had in … hell, I couldn't remember. When Saturday night came, Mom moved back to her own bed.

Miss Martin came to visit on Sunday, not long after we got home from church. Dad had just gone to the mill to do some work. It was that time of year when the trees were full of their beautiful colors, and as the warm fall sun shone, it made them even more brilliant.

"Miss Martin, come along in and sit," Mom said. "Would you like something to drink?"

"Well, what do you have?" Miss Martin took a seat at the kitchen table.

"Coffee or milk?" Mom replied.

"Milk, if you please."

"Nathan, run out to the spring house and bring in some cold milk." The spring house was built into the bank beside the house and was walled up with stones on all four sides, except for the doorway. The roof was made of heavy logs, then covered with ground. The spring was walled up in one of the back corners with an overflow that allowed the water to run into a long wooden trough and out a spillway at the opposite end. The water was maintained at a desired depth. Milk and anything else that was to be kept cold was placed in crocks and set in the water. The cold spring water flowing through the trough kept things cool. From here, the water flowed down a wooden ditch under the ground to the stable and into a big trough, so the animals would have water for drinking.

Upon my return from the spring house with the milk, I was about to enter the cabin when I heard Miss Martin say to Mom, "Nathan is quite a young man for his age."

"Yes," Mom said. "I think so. I don't know what I would do without him helping me around here."

"I take notice that …" Miss Martin stopped whatever she was going to say as I entered the cabin and handed Mom the milk. I then went back outside.

During the winter, we used a lot of wood for cooking and heating. After finding Frances, I asked her to stack the wood on the wood pile as I split it. We had been working for some time when Mom and Miss Martin came out, and Mom asked me to look at the meat she put in the oven to roast and make sure it didn't cook dry, and if needed, to add a little water. And if I would, keep an eye on the other children, she added. "Miss Martin and I are going for a walk."

The two of them went past the stable and down towards the stream in the meadow. I went back to splitting wood. Now and then, Frances and I would go in and look at the roast. Every time we looked, the better it smelled. We knew we were going to have a good supper. Noel and Abilene were playing, like always. They played well together when Frances left them alone, so I made sure she stayed with me all afternoon.

When it was time to go do our barn work, Frances and I taken Noel and Abilene to the stable. We had just started with the work when Mom and Miss Martin walked in. Frances had taken the milk pail and was going to try and do the milking, so Mom taken over while Miss Martin stood close by and watched Mom as she milked the cow. After Mom finished, she took the two little ones to the house to get supper started. Miss Martin said she would stay and help Frances and me finish up the work. She stayed, but didn't do anything besides follow me around.

It was almost dark as we walked to the house. When we came through the door, the smell of Mom's cooking made me even more hungry. Mom was putting things on the table when Dad walked in.

"Otis, I'd like you to meet Miss Martin, the schoolteacher," Mom said. She explained how Miss Martin was staying to have supper with us.

Dad said hello to Miss Martin, then went and washed before supper.

When everyone was seated, Mom said the prayer. Then things got passed, and while we ate, Miss Martin, Mom and Dad never stopped talking. When everyone was through eating, Mom and Miss Martin did the dishes, and Dad told the rest of us to go and get washed and ready for bed.

I heard Mom ask Miss Martin, "Would you like to stay the night?"

"Why, I would, if you don't mind," Miss Martin said.

"Of course not."

It wasn't long before Mom told us kids to get up to bed. I stayed sitting where I was. The other kids went up on the loft to bed, and Mom looked at me. "Nathan, that means you, too."

I grumbled.

Dad said, "Go, boy!"

I said good night and went up to bed. I lay there, listening to the adults talking, wondering where Miss Martin was going to sleep. I don't know how long they talked, for it wasn't long before I fell asleep.

I didn't know what to do when I awoke in the morning and saw Miss Martin sleeping next to me, so I just lay there. It wasn't long before I heard Mom quietly calling Miss Martin. Slowly, the schoolteacher sat up and looked around as if a little puzzled about where she was. I closed my eyes and pretended to still be asleep. Then she got up and went down.

I lay there for a little while, then got up and dressed and went down to the kitchen. Mom had breakfast ready and had fixed herself and Miss Martin a plate and set them on the table. She told Miss Martin to sit. I fixed myself a plate and sat down.

"Where is Dad?" I asked.

"He already went to the mill. He had a lot of work to do."

After they were through eating, Miss Martin told Mom she had to go if she was going to start school by nine o'clock.

After Miss Martin left, Mom told me, "Miss Martin thinks you're doing very good with your reading, spelling and numbers."

As the weeks passed, I noticed Miss Martin seemed to find things for me to do after school. Frances always waited for me, and we would walk home together. Miss Martin was spending more time at our place. Every few weeks she would walk home with Frances and I after school on Friday, and stay until Monday morning. She always carried this red and green plaid satchel with clean clothes. I always thought it was the ugliest satchel I ever saw.

Miss Martin and Mom had become very close, and when Miss Martin was there, she and Mom would spend most of their time together, always laughing and talking. Miss Martin helped Mom with the work around the house, and did some of the cooking and baking. They were always doing something. Now and then, I would see them hugging each other.

I spent most of my time outside or in the stable, where it was warmer. As winter dragged on, it got to the place where Miss Martin would come to the stable and milk the cow while Mom stayed at the house and got our meals ready. Often, she would help Frances and I take care of the animals. There were times when she would chase after one of us and, when she caught us, she'd pull us down on the hay and start tickling us. She did this mostly to me, and when she had me down, Frances would pile on top, knocking her flat on top of me. Then she'd lay there, holding me down. We had lots of fun. She was the only one that ever played with me like this.

Sometimes in the evening, when supper was over and it would be cold and dark out, Miss Martin and I would sit on the floor by the fireplace, where it was warm, and play checkers or sometimes she would read by the light from the crackling fire. There were times when we could hear the wind howling outside. Sometimes it would be snowing. There were times when Mom and Dad would also sit nearby. Mom would knit and Dad would play with the kids. I didn't know then that I would remember those times as some of the best times in my life. Now, whenever I look back over that part of my life, I can see how happy it was.

Every chance I got, I'd go to talk to Mr. Joe. We would sit and talk. He would tell me everything he knew about living off the land in the wild. He told me the best ways to catch fish and how to hunt. Mostly, he told me how to trap. He would always say to me, "Boy, if you know how to read signs of animals, you be able trap them, and if you can trap them, you can survive anywhere."

He made sure he planted this in my head by telling it to me over and over, so that I would remember. On days he was feeling good, we would go to the woods or fields, sometimes to the river or a creek that was nearby, and he would have me tell him the different tracks of the animals I saw. He would tell me, or sometimes show me, how and where to place a trap or snare. I learned a lot that fall and winter, and my fur catch was also a lot better.

It was early spring, and Mr. Joe told me it was time to sell my furs. He decided to go along, to make sure I got the best price. When the next Saturday came, I taken my furs, tied them on one of the horses, and rode to Mr. Joe's place. He was waiting and told me to go and bring one of his mules. They weren't far, so I ran to where they were feeding in a field and caught one and led it back to Mr. Joe. He had a hard time getting on the mule and wouldn't let me help him. Finally, he made it on, and we rode off toward town.

We went to the general store, where the owner bought

hides and furs. Mr. Joe didn't get off his mule. Instead he told me to go in and tell the man to come out. I went into this building that smelled terribly and asked the man if he was the one that bought furs.

"I am," he said.

"Mr. Joe says for you to come out," I told him.

The man looked at me a little funny, then followed me out. When he saw Mr. Joe he yelled, "How did you get on that mule, you old buzzard?" He walked over to Mr. Joe and shook his hand. "It's good to see you out and around, Joe. What can I do for you?"

Mr. Joe stroked his beard. "My young friend here has furs he'd like to sell. He asked where he should sell them. I told him you was the best buyer around, and won't take advantage of him. You hear what I said?"

"Yes! Yes!"

"Well, don't stand there. Take a look!"

I got the furs from my horse and handed them to the man. He looked each one over twice, turning them this way and that, touching and feeling them. I was thinking, *what's he doing all that for,* when he said, "I'll give you ten dollars."

Before I could say anything, Mr. Joe said, "Try again."

The man looked at Joe, then at me. "Okay, I'll go fifteen."

Mr. Joe cleared his throat and said, "Now, that's better!"

The man handed me fifteen dollars. I thanked him and jumped up on my horse. As we rode off the man yelled, "Take care, you old buzzard! You hear?"

We rode back to Mr. Joe's place. Once there, he slid down from the mule and told me to take it back to the others. I did, and when I returned, I asked Mr. Joe, "Are all the mules yours?"

"They are, but I don't know why I keep 'em."

"How much do I owe you?" I asked.

Mr. Joe thought a moment, then said, "If you carry that heap of wood in for me, we call it square."

I carried the wood into his shack and piled it where he told me. He had poured me a cup of tea and told me to sit. I sat on a box and he handed me the tea.

As I sipped my tea, Mr. Joe said, "Nathan, as you can see, it's hard for me to get around. Would you be interested in buyin' two of my mules? You can have any two you want."

I didn't know what to say. "Gee! I ... I ... I would have to ask my mother."

"Okay, boy, fair enough. You have your mother come and

take a look-see. If she likes them, I will give you good price."

I finished my tea. "Thanks a lot, Mr. Joe! I must go now."

I went out and jumped on my horse. Mr. Joe stood in the doorway as I rode off and waved. I waved back. When I got home, I put the horse in the stable and ran to the cabin to tell Mom about what Mr. Joe had said about the mules.

Mom listened, then looked at me. "Nathan, what in the world do you need mules for?"

"Mom, I could use them when I check my traps, and haul wood. They could be helpful around here."

"Nathan, I don't see why you would need those mules. They'd just be more work!"

"But, Mom! Would you just go and look at them?"

"Well ... maybe sometime. I'll see."

Several weeks passed and Mom didn't say anything, so one day after school I asked her if she would go and look at the mules. "Mom, I promised Mr. Joe that you would."

"We can't go this weekend. Miss Martin is coming."

"Oh, heck!" I cried. "Mom, can't she sleep someplace else besides with us kids?"

"Why would you say that?"

"Because ... because I ... us kids don't like ... don't like her sleeping with us, that's why! She bothers me... I mean, us ..."

"Nathan, quit that! She has nowhere else to sleep, so quit griping."

When Friday came, Miss Martin walked home with Frances and I. She helped us with the work that evening. Saturday morning, after she did the milking, her and Frances went to the house and I stayed and did some work around the stable. Come noon, I went to the house for something to eat, and Mom and Miss Martin had just finished baking bread and cinnamon rolls. They had made a big pot of stew as well. I ate a couple pieces of jelly bread with a mug of milk and was on my way out when Mom told me to hitch up the buckboard.

"Why?"

"We're going for a ride."

"Where?"

"Just do it, Nathan!"

I went and did as Mom said. I taken the horses and buckboard to the house. Mom, Miss Martin and all the kids were waiting. As soon as I stopped the horses, they climbed on board. "I'm not going," I told Mom. "I have work to do."

"Yes, you are. Get on."

"But, Mom ..."

"Get on!" she commanded.

Reluctantly, I climbed up and sat on the back with my feet hanging down. I wasn't happy about going. Taking the reins, Mom told the horses to getty-up and they started off.

"Mom, where are we going?" I asked.

"Just be still for once, will you? You'll see soon enough."

I sat there as we bumped along, paying no mind where Mom was going. Before I knew it, we were at Mr. Joe's place. I looked around.

"Mom, what are you doing?" I had almost forgotten about the mules. I jumped down and tied the horses to a post as Mom and Miss Martin got down. Mom told the other kids to stay on the buckboard.

"Go and get Mr. Joe," Mom said.

Before I could, Mr. Joe came out the door.

"Mr. Joe, I've come to look at the mules," Mom told him.

"That's fine! Boy, you know where they are. Go fetch them for your ma—all of them!"

"Yes, sir!" I ran to the field where the mules were feeding and rounded them up, then led them back to where Mr. Joe stood.

Mom said to Mr. Joe, "As you know, I'm Nathan's mother, and this is the schoolteacher, Miss Martin."

"I see," he replied. "Well, you look them over and I'll let you have any two you want."

Mom and Miss Martin walked over and looked at the mules. Mom asked how old were they.

"Ma'am, the gray and black ones is five. Old white, she's ten or eleven."

Mom turned back to look them over more, then said to Miss Martin, "What do you think?"

"I don't know much about mules, but I must say, they look real fine."

Mom turned back to Mr. Joe and said, "How much are you asking?"

Mr. Joe stood, looking at Mom as though he were thinking. "Well, ma'am, if you're buying them for the boy, they're five dollars each."

"What! Five dollars! You mean... *five dollars each?*"

"Yes, ma'am. If it was anyone else besides the boy, they'd be twenty apiece. As you can see, ma'am, they're good mules."

"Mr. Joe, you've got yourself a deal." She fished in her pocket and pulled out some money and handed it to Mr. Joe. In the meantime, Miss Martin had gone back to the buckboard and stood there. Mom asked Mr. Joe if he had a basket and a pot.

He looked at her, squinting his eyes. "What you want it for?"

"Would you please bring them?" she asked.

Mr. Joe shook his head and grumbled the whole way into his shack.

Mom motioned for Miss Martin, and she picked up the basket they had brought and carried it to Mom. When Mr. Joe came out with an old basket and a pot, Miss Martin held the basket while Mom opened it and taken the bread, some rolls and a pie out. She put them in Mr. Joe's basket. Then, she took a pot out of the buckboard and poured the stew into his pot.

Mr. Joe just stood there with his mouth hanging open, I guess not knowing what to say.

Mom looked at him and said, "Nathan is thirteen now. I knew he wanted the mules, and Miss Martin and I thought it would be good to bring you something nice."

He stood there, looking at the things in the basket. "Thank 'ee, thank 'ee, ma'am, thank 'ee!" He cleared his throat. "Now which two mules you want, the gray one and black one?"

"Is that okay?" Mom asked.

"Yes, ma'am! Very good choice, ma'am."

"Mr. Joe," Mom said, "Nathan has told me a lot about you, and the things the two of you talk about, and I'm very thankful for the things you've done for him. If it would be all right, I'd like to stop by sometime for a talk."

"Yes, ma'am. I would like that, ma'am. Oh yes, ma'am, you come by anytime!"

Mom thanked him and climbed up on the buckboard and sat beside Miss Martin. I untied the horses and handed Mom the reins. Then I asked Frances if she wanted to ride one of the mules.

"I sure do!"

I helped Frances on the gray mule, and I jumped on the black one. Mom had started for home. I waved to Mr. Joe as Frances and I followed behind the others.

5

In no time we were home, and I helped Frances down and taken the mules and put them in the pasture while Mom taken the kids and went in the house.

Miss Martin was waiting for me when I returned. I led the horses to where we kept the buckboard, then she climbed down and helped me unhitch the horses. After putting the horses in the pasture, I went in the stable to start the evening work, and Miss Martin came along and helped until it was time to do the milking. When we had everything done, we went to the spring house and strained the milk into crocks and put them in the water trough to keep cold. We covered them and took the milk pail and went to the house, where Mom had supper almost ready.

The house smelled so good from all the baking they had done earlier. Miss Martin and I washed and taken our places at the table. Just then, Dad came in and sat at his place. Mom gave thanks and we began eating.

Mom and Miss Martin were talking with Dad when Mom said,

"I bought Nathan two mules today!"

Dad stared at Mom. "You did *what?*"

"You heard me the first time."

"Two *mules?* Well, we'll just see about that!"

Mom said, "That's enough talk. I don't want to hear any more about it."

Maybe it was because I was hungry, but I think that was the best stew, bread and rolls Mom ever made.

After the meal was over and put away, Mom and Miss Martin sat by the fire and talked while they did some knitting. Dad was at the table doing numbers—something to do with the mill, I guessed. All the while the little ones were running around playing, I sat by the fire, half-listening to what was being said and thinking, *Dad isn't happy about the mules. Will he be mad and make Mom take them back to Mr. Joe?* It was making me sad, thinking maybe I wouldn't get to keep the mules after all, and the sadder I got, I wanted to say something, but knew better.

Finally, I went to bed. It wasn't long before Mom told the other kids to go to bed. Once they were settled down, everything got quiet, and soon I heard Miss Martin coming up. She lay down on the other half of my mattress. She always changed into her nightgown before coming up.

She knew I wasn't asleep. After a few minutes, she whispered, "Nathan, what's wrong?"

"Nothing."

"Then why aren't you sleeping?"

I didn't answer.

"I know something's bothering you." She rolled over closer to me. "Tell me what's wrong."

In a whisper, I asked, "Do you think Dad will make Mom take my mules back to Mr. Joe?"

She reached over and put her arm under my head and pulled me close to her. "No, I don't think so. I don't think your mother will let him do that." She then pulled me even closer, until my head was tight against hers. "Come tomorrow, I think everything will be all right. Now why don't you try and go to sleep?"

She didn't move away, and I don't know how long she held me like that. I finally felt her move her arm and roll over. I opened my eyes just enough to see it was getting light. I went back to sleep, and the next thing I knew, Mom was telling us to get up.

"It's Sunday and there's work to be done before church!" she called.

Miss Martin was already sitting up. Jumping up, I saw her staring at me, and then realized my night shirt had somehow shifted up around my waist, and I was standing there with nothing on from my waist down. I pulled my shirt down as quickly as I could. I was extremely embarrassed. She smiled and said, "It's okay."

Hurrying, I pulled my pants on and grabbed my shirt and went downstairs. Mom told me to go help Dad with the work. I put my shirt and shoes on, grabbed my coat, and was out the door.

I helped Dad finish up the work. He had already done the milking, so there wasn't much left to do. I taken the milk and went to the spring house, and was done taking care of it when

Dad came and asked if I was done. I said I was, and we went to the house. So far, he had said nothing about the mules, and I was glad.

Mom and Miss Martin had breakfast on the table and were eating. The other kids had already eaten and were getting dressed for church. Dad and I washed, then filled our plates and sat down to eat. Mom told us we'd better hurry if we were getting dressed for church.

I said, "I'm going like I am."

"Nathan, you can't go looking like that," Mom said.

"Mom, if I have to change clothes, I'm not going!"

"Boy, I don't know what I'm going to do with you. Now get dressed!"

"Mom, if I go, I'm going like this!" I insisted. "And besides, I don't know why I must go to church anyhow."

Mom looked at Miss Martin. She didn't say anything, just dropped her head. Mom looked at Dad.

He said, "Don't look at me. He's your kid. You won't let me have any say other times, so don't ask me now!"

I could see Miss Martin shaking her head at me. "Okay, Mom, to make you happy, I'll change." I went and changed my clothes, then everyone got on the buckboard, and we were soon at church.

When we returned home from church, Mom and Miss Martin made us something to eat, and afterwards Dad went to the mill. As close as I can remember, everything went as usual, and the time passed quickly.

It was late April, a Monday forenoon, that I was working in the stable and Dad came in, saying something had broken at the mill. He yelled at me to get the horses hitched to the wagon. I could tell he had been drinking, so I didn't say anything. I ran and got the horses and hitched them to the wagon. I was bent over, hooking the last traces to the singletree, when Dad started cursing at me for not helping him at the mill. He picked up a thick leather strap that was lying on the wagon and started beating on me. I was knocked to the ground next to the wheel, on my belly. I put my hands over the back of my head as he rained blow after blow over my back, butt and legs.

"I'll teach you, boy!" he screamed. "I'll teach you! Damn you!"

I was crying and yelling for him to stop. Finally, I got a chance to roll toward him. I hit both his legs and knocked him down. Then, jumping up, I ran for the house. Once inside the door, I slammed it shut and barred it.

Mom came running. "What happened? What's after you?"

Still crying, I told her what had happened. Soon we heard the horses and wagon going. Mom told me to take my shirt off, so I did, and she looked at my back.

"Oh, my God! Go in my room!"

"Why?" I sniffed.

"Just do as I say. Frances, take the two little ones out and play." Mom got a basin of hot water and soap while Frances taken the little ones and went outside. "Now get in there and get undressed. Lay on the bed," Mom ordered me.

"Mom, must I?"

"Nathan, if those welts and cuts get sore, you'll wish you had."

"Oh, Mom ..."

"Git!"

I taken my shoes off and went in and got undressed. I lay on my belly on her bed.

"Are you undressed?" she called.

"Yeah."

She brought the basin of hot water and set it on the wash stand, then took a rag and soaped it good. Then she washed my back, butt and legs while I buried my face in the covers, so she couldn't see my tears.

While she washed my backside, I could hear her sobbing. When she was done, she dried me off, then rubbed some ointment all over me. After she was through with that, she asked me again what had happened.

I told her everything, just as it had happened, and what Dad said.

She put a thin piece of linen over me, and told me to lie there the rest of the day. Mom kept Frances home from school, since I wasn't going to be with her. Mom came often and checked on how I was doing. She would rub more ointment on me. I dozed off and on all afternoon.

The last time I awoke, everything was quiet. I knew it must be getting late and they all had gone to do the barn work. When I tried to get up, I found I didn't hurt too bad, so I sat on the edge of the bed and slowly got myself dressed. After putting my shoes on, I went to the stable. When I walked in and Mom saw me, she almost had a fit.

"Get back in that house right now!" she yelled.

I walked over to where Mom was and put my arms around her and laid my head on her shoulder. "Mom, it's not that bad. I'll be all right," I said.

Mom was angry. "Just wait until that bastard gets home. I'm going to lay into him!"

"Mom, please, just let it go," I begged.

"How can I?"

"Please, Mom, will you? Will you, Mom? For me? I don't want another fight like the last time. Dad was just mad because you won't let him take me to the mill so he can put me to work, so he wouldn't have to hire someone to help him." I sighed, then said, "I'm glad you never let me go, because I know what would happen. That's the reason I never wanted to go."

She hugged me and didn't say anything, just went back to her work. I pitched in and did what I could. After we finished the work, we all went in, and Mom soon had supper on. There wasn't much talking while we ate. Frances and the two little ones looked like they were scared.

After we were through eating and everything was cleaned up, it wasn't long before Mom told the other kids to wash and get dressed for bed. I said I was going to bed.

"Just wait. I want to put more ointment on you."

"Mom, I'll be okay!"

"You just mind me. I know what's best, do you hear me?" She rubbed my backside, then I went to bed.

I had to lie on my stomach to sleep. I don't know how long Mom stayed up. I never heard Dad come home.

I awoke early the next morning and was unable to go back to sleep, so I quietly got up, got dressed, and slipped out the door and went to the stable. I lit a lantern and went and checked to see if the horses were in the corral. They were. It was too early to start my work, so I gathered hay on a pile and was sitting on it, wondering when Dad got home and daydreaming.

I don't know how long I had been sitting there when Mom walked in. She looked around, then saw me and came over and sat down beside me.

"How do you feel this morning?" she asked.

"I'm okay."

"Then why are you sitting out here so early?"

"I don't know. I couldn't sleep, so I got up and came out here, so I wouldn't bother everybody. Where's Dad?"

"He just left for the mill."

"When did he get home?"

"It was late," she said.

"Was he drinking?"

"I don't know, I couldn't smell anything. I was in bed when he came in and didn't get up. He made himself something to eat, then came to bed."

"Did he say what happened at the mill?"

"No. I didn't talk to him last night, nor did I talk to him this morning." After a short silence she asked, "What are you going to do now?"

"I'm going to do my work."

"Nathan, I want you to go back in the house."

"Mom, I'm okay! I'll do my work."

"Then at least let me help you."

We did the work, then went to the house and Mom fixed some breakfast. While we ate, Mom didn't have much to say. I could tell she had something on her mind. I thought it best not to say anything. The other kids had just gotten up. Mom made them something to eat.

I said to Mom, "I'm going to the stable."

She looked at me and asked, "What are you going to do out there?"

"Oh, I don't know. I'll find something to do." I could tell she didn't approve.

I went anyway. Then I decided to get my mules in and play around with them a little. I gave each one a good brushing and trimmed a little off their hoofs. After finding some leather strap, I worked on repairing some bridles so they would fit each mule. I had two belly straps that I fastened the stirrup to, and a sheepskin to sit on I used the sheepskin so it would be easier on the mules, since I didn't have any saddles.

It was going on noon when Mom came and asked if I was going to school. I said, "No, and I'm not going the rest of the week."

She didn't say anything. I was sure she understood. She asked, "What are you making, and what's that you have on your mules?"

I tried to explain what I was hoping to make.

"Oh, I see." She started out of the stable, then turned around and came back. "Nathan, are you planning on leaving home?"

"No! Why? Why do you ask that?"

"Because I'm your mother, and I think I should know

what you're up to."

"What makes you think I'm going to leave?"

"Because you wanted your own mules, and I know you bought a musket and pistol with your fur money."

"Who told you that?"

"Never mind."

"Frances did!" I yelled. "Frances told you, didn't she?"

"Yes, Frances told me she saw you cleaning them."

"So!"

"And she also told me you have some other things hid away."

"So!"

"I think you better start explaining what it is that you're up to."

"Mo-om! Mo-om! I'm not up to anything, and I'm not going anywhere. I just want to have my own things. I know if Dad saw me with a musket, he'd get mad and take it away. Mom, when it's time for me to be on my own, I wouldn't go without telling you."

"I hope so," she said. She started to leave, then turned around. "I'm going in to get the others something to eat. If you want something, come in."

"Okay, Mom." After a while, I went in. Mom had made sandwiches and gave us milk to drink. Then she got Frances off to school.

When Frances was leaving, I told her to keep her mouth shut about why I wasn't going to school. While Mom and I were eating, we talked about getting the ground ready for planting. It was getting close to that time of year again.

"Mom, do you think I should start hauling the rest of the manure out and put it on the part that isn't plowed?"

"When you are better."

"Mo-om! I'll be all right. Don't treat me like a baby!" I finished eating, then went to the stable. I had finished what I was doing, so I hitched the horses to the skid, then loaded it with manure, and led the horses as they dragged it to the field, then unloaded it and scattered it over the unplowed ground. After that I went and got another load.

By the end of the week, I had the manure all hauled and the stable cleaned. I didn't see anything of Dad since the first of the week. He was up and gone before I got up, and I was in bed when he got home. Mom hadn't said much about him all week. It was Friday and Miss Martin came along home with

Frances after school.

I didn't want to see her, because I knew she would ask me what was wrong that I didn't come to school all week. So I stayed away from her as much as I could, and when she could have asked, she never did. Maybe Mom had said something, I don't know. I knew after working with the manure all day, I needed a bath, so right after supper I asked Mom if I could bathe in her room. She told me to go ahead, so I taken some hot water and a tub and went in Mom's room and taken my bath while they cleaned up the supper dishes. Then I put on my night shirt, which came to my knees, and taken my bath water and dumped it out and put the tub away. I told Mom and Miss Martin good night and said I was going to bed.

"Nathan, are you feeling all right?" Mom asked.

"Yes, Mom. I'm just tired." I lied a little. I wasn't that tired. I just didn't want to answer any questions. I went up on the loft and crawled in bed. I wasn't asleep when the other kids came to bed. Once they settled down, I fell off to sleep.

I didn't hear Miss Martin come to bed, but sometime during the night I was awakened by her hand moving over the back of my legs, up over my butt and back. I lay still, not moving. I knew she was feeling what was left of the welts on my backside. She moved her hand from under my night shirt, then I felt her move closer, and soon she was sleeping. I fell off to sleep, too.

6

It was light out when I awoke. When I went to get up, I felt my night shirt was up around my waist again, so I pulled it down and slowly got up, so as not to waken the rest. I got dressed and went down, then went to the stable. After the work was done and breakfast was over, I told Mom I was going to see Mr. Joe.

Mom grumbled awhile, then said, "Go!" I left without saying anything more.

I spent all day with Mr. Joe, talking and helping him cut some wood. It was getting late, so I told Mr. Joe I would see him again and left.

I made it home just in time to do my work. While we were eating supper, Mom asked how Mr. Joe was, and wanted to know what we talked about. I told her everything, and how Mr. Joe told me how to make skunk fat and how to use it when a body gets sick. I just finished eating when Dad walked in. He went and washed up, then sat down to eat. I got up and put my dishes on the sink, then went out, not saying anything.

The days were longer now, and it would be a little while before dark. I was by the stable, petting and talking to my mules, when Frances came out.

"What are you doing?" she asked.

"Frances, do you want to go riding with me?"

"Oh yes!"

"Then go ask Mom if you can."

She ran back to the house and asked. Mom said she could go.

I had put my new belly strap and sheepskin on the mules, so we could try them out. I helped Frances on one of the mules, and I climbed on the other one. I kept close to Frances, just in case she had any trouble. As we rode, we found the mules were gentle to ride as well as to handle.

We rode until it was just about dark, then went back to the stable. After getting Frances down from the mule, we taken everything off and put the mules out to pasture. Frances was so excited, she ran to the house and told everyone.

By the time I got there, she was raving about how she'd ridden the mule all by herself and how gentle the mules were. Abilene and Noel were sitting at the table, eating a roll that Mom had just taken out of the oven.

"Why can't *we* ride the mules?" Noel hollered.

"I wanna ride Nathan's mules!" Abilene cried.

"Hush now!" Mom finally got them settled down by telling them she would think about it.

I had gotten some rolls and milk and sat at the table eating. Frances was still following Mom and Miss Martin around, telling them how she rode the mule.

Finally, Mom told her, "Frances, if you want a roll, you'd better get it." Frances then settled down and got a roll and came to the table.

Miss Martin brought rolls and coffee for herself and Mom. They sat down across from me. After they talked awhile, Mom started telling me about Miss Martin wanting to help with the planting. They were excited about their plans of putting in a big field of different kinds of vegetables.

"What do you want with that much vegetables?" I asked them.

"Just wait and we'll tell you," Mom said. They then told me again about the different kinds of vegetables they wanted to plant. "And if they do real good, what we don't need we can take to town and sell."

"We know it's going to be a lot of hard work," added Miss Martin.

"So we're asking you if you would help us," Mom said. "With three of us sharing the work, it shouldn't be too bad. Once school is out for the summer, Miss Martin can stay here, except on the days she has tutoring to do."

Miss Martin said she would arrange her tutoring so she could do it all on one or two days. "Will you help?"

"I'll help," I said. "Since we're planting anyway, I guess we can do a little more." I listened a while longer as they kept talking. Finally, I got up from the table and went and washed, then got ready for bed. I didn't see Dad, but I think he was already in bed. I said goodnight and went up to the loft.

Soon Frances, Abilene and Noel came to bed, and then everything was quiet. I could hear Mom and Miss Martin still talking. Miss Martin was telling Mom that she ran her hand over my back last night when I was sleeping, and she could still feel the welts.

Mom said, "I know, and I don't know what to do about it. He doesn't want me to say anything, because he doesn't want another fight. I don't know why his father beat him like that. He's such a good boy, and will do anything I ask. Rarely does he sass me, and when he does, I feel he has good reason. I know he is very strong for his age, and sometimes that worries me. He works too hard, and that worries me! He has a peculiar being within him that I don't understand."

"He's not like the other children around here," Miss Martin said. "In fact, he's not a child!"

"Well, sometimes I have a feeling he's not one of us, but another creation."

"Yes, sometimes I get that feeling, too. I can see in school how much difference there is in him from the other children his age. He's so mature."

"Lillie ..."

"Yes?"

"You're the only one I have to talk with," Mom said. "And ... I don't know ... I don't know how to say this, but ... but I'm kind of worried about Nathan."

"Why?"

"I get feelings at times that he's thinking about leaving."

"Well ... uh, where would he go?"

"I ... I don't know. I don't have any idea. I just get a feeling."

"Virginia, what makes you think this?"

"As you know, he wanted mules, and I know now he taken his fur money and bought a musket and pistol, and I don't know what else he may have hid away. I asked him, and he said he's not going anywhere. And then said, 'When I do, I'll tell you, Mom.' "

I soon fell asleep and didn't hear Miss Martin come to bed.

7

On Monday morning I started plowing the rest of the field. I was big enough now that I could handle the plow good, and Mom didn't need to help. I would plow until it was time to go to school. I worked every morning, and by Thursday, I had finished the plowing. Most of the ground that had been plowed earlier was dry enough that I would be able to start harrowing come Friday. I knew it would take a lot of harrowing to get the ground knocked fine enough with the old spike-tooth harrow, to where we would be able to plant.

Frances and I went to school in the afternoon. School went as usual. The afternoon passed quickly, and it was time to go home. Miss Martin told Frances and me to stay after school. We did, and helped her clean up the schoolhouse. When we were through, she grabbed her satchel and other things she would need for the weekend, then the three of us headed for home.

As we walked, Miss Martin asked me when we could start planting.

"As soon as I get the ground knocked fine," I said.

"As soon as tomorrow?"

"Maybe. Maybe so. I don't know."

She asked us what we wanted to do when we were done with school.

Right away Frances said, "I want to be a teacher, just like you. How old must you be to teach?"

"Well, this is my second year here, and I'm nineteen," Miss Martin said.

"How did you get the job teaching here?"

"Well, it's like this. I was born and raised in Philadelphia and started to school when I was six. By the time I was 16, I was asked to help teach, so I taught that whole year. Then I was asked if I would come here and teach, because Mr. Beckworth was getting too old to teach. So I said I would. That fall, just before the new school year started, I turned 17."

Frances asked, "Don't you miss your mom and dad?"

"No, Frances." She hesitated before telling us that her mother and father died when she was very young. She had no family, so she was taken to a church school for girls, where she lived until she came here. "The last year and a half I spent at the girls' school, I was taught how to be a teacher. The people here paid for me to come here and teach. They pay me so much a month, and give me that one-room cabin behind the school house to live in."

By this time, we were home. Frances and Miss Martin went into the house. I went to the stable and got the horses out of the corral and hitched them to the old spike-tooth harrow, and headed out in the field and went to work, breaking up the ground. It wasn't long before Frances came running and wanted to ride on the harrow with me.

"No!" I told her.

Then she wanted to ride on one of the horses. I thought that would be all right, so I helped her on, and placed her where she could hold onto the horse's collar. I don't know how many trips we made back and forth across the field when Miss Martin came and told Frances that Mom wanted her. So I got Frances down and she went running off for the house.

"Nathan, your mother said you were to keep on harrowing, if you want to. The rest of us will take care of the barn work." She turned to go, then hesitated. "But before I go, I would like to ride with you a couple of times."

I had a couple of wide planks fastened on the back part of the harrow that I stood on. I told her to get on beside me. She did. I hollered for the horses to get up, and they started off with a jerk that made her lose her balance. She almost fell off and grabbed my arm and managed to gain her balance. She wasn't very big—5'1" maybe—105 or so pounds. Hell, I was a lot bigger than she was at 5'11" or so. She held onto my arm, and put her other arm around my waist, and rode like that a few rounds. Then I handed her the reins.

"What do you want me to do?" she asked.

I told her how to stand and which rein to tighten to make the horses go right or left and how to stop them. After she got the hang of it, I stepped off and walked. We made a few rounds like that, then I stepped back on and taken the reins as she held onto me. Once we got close to the house, I stopped so she could get off, then I kept harrowing and she headed for the stable to help with the work.

It was getting dark as I finished harrowing. I taken the

harrow to the stable and unhitched, then put the horses in their pasture. On my way to the house, I stopped by the water trough and washed. The rest were already in the house. Mom and Miss Martin were giving the kids their supper, so I sat down and they handed me my plate. As we ate, Mom asked if the ground was ready to plant.

I said, "I think so. I think we can plant in the morning."

After everyone was done eating, Frances and Miss Martin did the dishes and cleaned up while Mom got Noel and Abilene ready and in bed. While Mom was doing that, I went outside and sat on the makeshift bench by the spring house. I was enjoying the stillness of the night, even though the spring air had a chill to it, when I heard Mom, Miss Martin and Frances. The moon was just peeping over the distant horizon, and they could see where I sat and came to sit with me.

They talked about planting the next day as the moon rose higher and higher. Their talk drifted to other things. Dad still wasn't home from the mill. Finally, I said good night and headed for the house. Mom told Frances to go with me, so Frances came running, and we went in. Frances stopped to wash as I went to bed. Soon I heard her getting in bed, too, and before I knew it, it was daylight out.

I had grown so used to Miss Martin sleeping with us that I got over my bashfulness about her being there and would get dressed, whether she watched me or not. I heard her stir just as I turned to go down. She was pulling her nightgown over her head. When I went down, stopping to put my shoes on before going to the stable, I could see Dad had already gone to the mill.

There wasn't a lot to do in the stable this time of year, except to feed the hogs and chickens. The cows were in at night, then put out to pasture during the day, until it got warmer. Then they would stay out all the time.

I had just finished cleaning out the manure from where the cows were tied when Miss Martin came in to do the milking. I was through with my work, so I stayed and talked with her while she finished the milking. Then, I took the milk to the spring house and put it in to cool.

As we entered the house, we saw Mom had breakfast on the table. While we ate, Mom told us, "As soon as we are through eating, we're going to get at the planting. Frances, you do up the dishes."

"Oh, Mom!"

"Frances!"

"I'll give her a hand," Miss Martin said, "while you get everything ready. It won't take long."

"Okay, then. Come, Nathan, let's get at it."

I went to the shed and got the push plow out, to see if it would work. To my surprise, it wasn't too bad. A little grease on the wheel axle and it would do. The push plow had two handles, a small V blade behind a large wheel, which made for fairly easy pushing. I didn't know where Dad got all these things, or what he was going to do with them. He had them all piled in one corner of the shed.

Taking the plow, I headed for the field, where Mom and the two little kids were. Mom had all her plants that she had growing in her bedroom since sometime in late February. I had plumb forgotten about them. I asked Mom where she wanted me to start.

"Right here! Start and go along the edge like this."

"Okay."

Just then, Miss Martin and Frances came running out to where we were. Mom said, "Make one row, then we'll know how far apart they should be." She wanted them wide enough apart so we could use the hand cultivator and a horse between the rows.

"Okay, Mom, I'll make them as straight as I can." I started, and by the time I got to the other end and looked back, I thought I did pretty well. I taken the plow back to Mom and the rest. They looked at me and burst out laughing. I looked at them. "What's so funny?"

"Look!"

I turned and looked. From where they were standing I could see what was so funny. I had to laugh myself. The row was so crooked that a snake would have made a straighter path. "Well, Mom, maybe we'll be able to get more in each row if they're a little crooked."

Then they *did* laugh. Mom said, "Go fetch one of them long ropes."

"What you want that for?"

"I'll show you. Now get!"

I ran to the stable and got the longest rope I could find and taken it back to Mom. "Now what?"

She tied a small rock on one end and told me to take the other end and go down the row I had made. I did, until the rope was stretched out. "Now pull the rope to you."

I did. As the rope was pulled over the loose ground, it left a mark. "Now what?"

"Go to the end, then we'll make more marks, so you can follow with the plow."

After we made a few rows, Mom told Miss Martin to help me. We marked all the rows while her and Frances put in some of the plants. Then I finished the rows with the plow, and Miss Martin went and helped the others. After I finished, Mom told me what seeds she wanted planted next, and where.

By noon, they had all the plants in the ground, and I had some of the seeds planted. Mom said, "Come, let's go get something to eat." Everyone headed for the house. I stopped by the overflow from the spring house and washed. The rest followed. Mom and Miss Martin got right to making sandwiches with butter and honey, and some with left-over ham from breakfast. They poured each of us a mug of cold milk and themselves some coffee.

As soon as we were done eating, it was back to planting. I was hoping we could get everything planted, for tomorrow after church I planned on going to see Mr. Joe.

It was late afternoon when we finished. Miss Martin said, "That's the biggest garden I ever saw. Now all we need is a good soaking rain."

"Nathan, take the plow to the shed. Come, Noel, Abilene. Head for the house. Frances, grab that rope and bring it with you."

"Must I?"

"Go, Frances!" Mom hollered.

She came running after, pulling the rope. I put the plow and rope away and went to the stable. Soon Miss Martin came to do the milking.

"Your mother's making supper and getting Abilene and Noel bathed."

Frances helped with the work, and soon we were done and went for supper. Mom was still working on supper and getting the little ones bathed. Frances and Miss Martin pitched in and helped Mom. I figured I had enough time to bath before supper. I asked Mom if I could use her room, taken the tub and some water, and went to bath. By the time I was through and the water dumped, the rest had already started eating.

After everyone was done and things cleaned up, Mom put Noel and Abilene to bed. Miss Martin went to take her bath. Mom hollered at me to help Frances get water for her bath. I did, then went up to my bed. I could hear Miss Martin emptying her and Frances' bath water, and soon Frances came to bed.

I guess Mom was bathing when Dad came in, for I heard Miss Martin ask him if he wanted supper. He said he did. I could hear her getting Dad's supper from the stove, and her and Mom telling him about the garden.

I was tired from the day's work, and soon fell asleep.

8

The next day being Sunday, we all had to go to church and, like always, it was tiring to sit there and listen. I could never understand how anyone could sit and listen to all that stuff that didn't make any sense at all. I knew better, but didn't know if anyone else did. Besides, I wasn't supposed to talk about church.

Once home, I asked Mom if I could go to see Mr. Joe and maybe fish with him. Dad wasn't going to the mill, like usual, so right away he hollered, "Boy, you aren't going anywhere. There's work to be done around here!"

I looked at Mom. She turned to Dad and said, "I said he could go, and that's it."

"I don't understand why you let that boy hang around that old Indian!" Dad yelled.

Mom stared at Dad, then said, "Maybe that old Indian treats that boy like someone, not like some animal he *owns*."

Miss Martin spoke up, "Nathan, can I go with you?"

"I don't know! Why would *you* want to go?"

"Just to go."

"Well ... I guess it's okay." I hadn't meant to sound annoyed, but I had planned on going alone.

Then Frances hollered that *she* wanted to go.

"I don't think so," Mom told her.

"Why not?" Frances whined.

"Let her go, Mom. I'll take care of her," I said.

"Take her and go!"

I was going out the door when Dad hollered, "Why don't *all* of you go?"

Frances and Miss Martin were right on my heels. We went to the pasture, and I caught the two mules, then helped Miss Martin on one. I then jumped on the other and pulled Frances up behind me. We started off while Frances and Miss Martin chattered the whole time we rode.

Once we got to Mr. Joe's, I jumped down and tied the

mules. Mr. Joe came out of his shack to greet us. "Who are these young ladies you bring to see old Joe?"

"This is Miss Martin, and that's my sister Frances. They were here before, when Mom bought the mules. Remember?"

"Oh! I see."

"When I said I was coming to see you, they wanted to come along. I hope you don't mind."

"Oh, not at all. Come."

We followed him to his shack. Mr. Joe sat on a bench outside by the door and told us to find something to sit on. We found some old wooden boxes that were suitable, and sat on them.

Mr. Joe and Miss Martin hit it off right away. In fact, they did most of the talking. That was okay, for most of what they talked about he had told me. Like being a boy growing up, what nation of Indians he came from. Miss Martin was very interested in what he told her and asked him a lot of questions, so much that I can't remember what all. We talked a long time, and Frances was awestruck and didn't say anything.

I saw it was getting time to leave and told Mr. Joe we must be going.

"Okay, boy! How are the mules doing?"

"Just fine."

"When do you plan on leaving?"

I looked at him. "Leaving? What do you mean?"

"Oh, I just wondered. I know you will before another summer comes, or maybe passes."

"See you later, Mr. Joe. Come, Frances."

Miss Martin asked Joe if he could read.

"I do some," he said.

"Good, when school opens, I'll see that you get something to read."

"Oh, thank you, miss."

Frances and I were at the mules when Miss Martin caught up. I helped her on the mule, then jumped on mine and reached down and grabbed hold of Frances' hand and pull her on up behind me. We waved to Mr. Joe and headed for home.

Frances and Miss Martin weren't as chatty as before. We were almost home when Frances asked me, "What was Mr. Joe talking about?"

"What do you mean?" I asked.

"He asked you when you were leaving."

"I don't know what he's talking about!" I saw Miss

Martin look at me, but she didn't say anything.

Once we got home and the work was done and supper over, I said goodnight and went to bed. The other kids were already sleeping. I lay on my bed, thinking about what Mr. Joe had said. *How would he know? He couldn't know! No way!* Unless he was one of those Indians others talked about that speak to the spirits and know what you are thinking. Or did Mom... or Miss Martin... say something to him? *No!* Was that why Miss Martin was spending so much time at our place, that I wasn't told to help with housework?

I was lying there wondering, when it dawned on me that the rest were talking about Mr. Joe. Mom was asking Miss Martin what she thought about Mr. Joe. I listened while Miss Martin told them she thought Mr. Joe was a nice man, and she was impressed with his knowledge about life, his beliefs, the white man, his life growing up, how he came to speak English.

"I could feel the goodness come from his heart by the way he talked. I could feel deep within that he thinks Nathan is the greatest friend he ever had. I think Mr. Joe's a wonderful man!"

I heard Dad say, "Oh, hell, you don't know what you're saying. He's taken you in with those tales of his. He's nothing but a lazy old Indian who knows nothing besides how to steal."

Mom shouted, "Otis, damn you! You know that is not true!"

I heard Miss Martin come running up the ladder and crawl in bed.

"Otis, what the hell's wrong with you? Damn you!" I guess Mom went to her room, for everything got quiet. Miss Martin lay only a few feet away. I could hear her sniffling. I knew she was hurt by what Dad had said. She moved closer and, in a low voice, whispered, "Nathan, are you sleeping?"

"No, not now."

"Why?" She moved closer. "Why? Why is he that way?"

"I ... I don't know."

She reached over and taken my hand. "Do you mind?"

"No."

"Hold me, will you?"

I held her hand, not answering, and I let her talk.

I was almost asleep when she said, "Are you listening?"

"Yes."

"What did Mr. Joe mean when he asked you when are you leaving?"

"I don't know! I was lying here wondering the same thing

when you came running up to bed. Why? Did you or Mom tell him something?"

"No, not me. I don't think your mother did either."

"Miss Martin!"

"Nathan, wait! Let me say something first."

"What?"

"We are friends, aren't we?"

"I think so."

"It would make me feel good if you called me Lillie instead of Miss Martin all the time."

"Do you mean that?"

"Yes!" She squeezed my hand. "Now, what were you going to ask?"

"Lillie, do you think Indians can talk to spirits like some people say?"

"I don't know."

"And tell what white people are thinking?"

"I don't know. Why?"

"I just wondered."

"Do you want to talk about it?"

"Maybe. But now I want to sleep."

Weeks had passed since we planted the field. Everything was growing nicely, and so did the weeds. It seemed we hoed and cultivated every few days. As time passed, our garden looked even better. Some things were big enough for us to use. Mom would have to start canning soon.

I was able to see Mr. Joe every week, and Mom would fix things from the garden for me to take to him. The time I spent with him passed quickly.

A few weeks passed when I noticed he was trying his best to teach me everything he could, so that I could survive on my own. "Boy, someday you may need to know this," he'd say about whatever he was teaching me at the time.

One day he asked me if I could come see him two times a week, and I said, "What for?"

"I need teach you Indian talk."

"Indian talk! What for?"

"Someday it come in handy and may even save your life."

"Why do you say that?"

"Believe what I tell you," he would say.

"I'll try." I didn't know how I would be able to go see him twice a week. I knew there was lots of work to be done, but I asked Mom anyway.

The first thing Mom said was "No!" I kept asking. "Boy, what on earth for?"

"Mom, he just asked me if I could come."

"To do what?"

I lied a little. "I don't know. He just said we have things to do."

After some talking, she gave in.

In the meantime, things from the garden had to be put up and canned, and every other day Lillie, Frances and I would get up at first light and do the work, then after breakfast load the vegetables in the wagon, hitch the horses and drive to town, going from house to house, selling our vegetables or sometimes trading. Other times, the trading post would take some, or we would drive to the fort and sell. I can remember the people at the fort not being very nice. They would take things and not want to pay. Some of the army men would say unkind things to Lillie and sometimes Frances, or grab at them. We only went twice, and that was enough.

In the meantime, I would go see Mr. Joe one evening of the week, and then on Sunday. He started teaching me his language and sign talk. As things progressed, he would teach me other Indian languages he knew. When I would start to lose interest, Mr. Joe would look me in the eye and say, "Boy, you learn sign talk, you be able get along and make friends with most tribes. Learn their ways. There are many."

9

Summer was coming to an end, and we had most of our work done. Dad never helped much with work all summer. Now he would be busier than ever with fall coming.

One evening, Mom and Lillie sat and figured up how much we had made from the vegetables we sold. We were all surprised to learn we did very well. Mom kept the most, and gave us each three dollars.

Frances and I said we were keeping ours for Christmas. Mom said that was a great idea. She, too, would save hers.

"I think I will, too," Lillie said.

With the coming of fall, the days were growing shorter and cooler. School would open before long. Over the summer I had grown quite fond of Lillie, and I no longer saw her as my teacher, but as a very close friend. After the work was done in the evening, she and I would sometimes go for a walk or maybe take Frances fishing. Sometimes we just sat and talked. Mom liked fish and was always happy when we went fishing and came home with a nice catch. Sometimes Mom would go, but mostly she stayed home with Noel and Abilene and her knitting or sewing. There was always something to be done.

In the meantime, I continued seeing Mr. Joe. So far, he had taught me enough so that we could talk by hand signs. I had learned enough words in his language that I was able to understand some of what was being said.

Where our place was located, it was wild and untamed. Around the cabin and other buildings was an open area with cleared fields and a meadow, with a stream flowing through it. At places along the stream it was thick with alder and other bushes.

Beyond this clearing, it was heavily wooded. There were no neighbors, and there were always tales of Indians waiting in the thick woods to attack. On occasion, we did see them passing through the meadow, but rarely did any stop, and when they did, it was always to trade for something.

Since we lived not far from the woods, we had our hands

full with wild animals that came around the buildings, mostly small animals like skunks, raccoon, opossum and other critters. Occasionally, a cougar came around, and we had our share of bear. It was their frequent presence that led to many hair-raising experiences over the years.

One such experience I will never forget had taken place one cold evening late in the fall, not long after dark. Mom and I were sitting by the fire, playing a game of checkers. The other kids had gone to bed, when all of a sudden we heard this terrified noise coming from our animals in the stable.

Mom jumped up. "Come, we better take a look!" She grabbed the musket and handed it to me. We always kept the musket loaded.

After Mom lit a lantern, we stepped out in the cold night. It was clear and starry crystals of white hung heavily in the air. Everything was covered with a heavy frost. Mom held the lantern as high as she could, in order to cast more light out in front as we slowly made our way toward the stable.

As we drew closer, we could hear the noise coming from the area of the corral. Just as we rounded the corner of the stable, out from the darkness of the corral came a large bear, charging straight at us.

Mom yelled, "Shoot! Shoot!"

I had taken aim and pulled the trigger. The flash from the muzzle blinded me for a split second. Right then, Mom and I were knocked to the ground.

Jumping up, we realized the beast had run over us. Mom was still holding the lantern and, fortunately, it hadn't gone out.

I reloaded as fast as I could.

"Did you hit it?" Mom cried.

"I don't know!"

Looking around, Mom saw some blood. Looking closer, we found a trail of blood and followed it a short distance. It headed toward the meadow. "We're not going any farther," she said.

"Mom, I think I see something lying out there."

As she held the lantern to see better, we saw the bear turn and charge.

Taking aim, I fired. Again we were knocked to the ground.

Jumping up, I reloaded, then realized Mom was still lying there, holding the lantern up, and the bear was lying across her legs. I made sure the animal was dead, then laid the musket down. Grabbing hold of the bear's feet, I pulled and tugged until Mom was able to pull free. I helped her up, then asked, "Are you hurt?"

"No, I don't think so. Just scared!" Her dress had a tear, where a claw had hooked in and ripped it. Other than splattered with blood from the bear, she seemed all right. "Nathan, are *you* all right?"

"I'm fine!"

Putting her arms around me, she pulled me close. "Thank God. That was close! I'm sure glad I gave you the gun. I don't know what would've happened if I had had it."

That was my first bear. Little did I realize it wouldn't be my last.

We went back to the cabin and got on our coats, then brought knives and another lantern out to where the bear lay, and started the process of skinning, and once we were through, we put the hide up, so nothing would get it. Tomorrow we would ready it for tanning.

Shortly after we got in the house, Dad came home. Mom told him what went on. He didn't say much as he finished his supper, just "I'm glad you'se got the damn thing."

School wouldn't be starting until most of the families had their work done for the coming winter, and that wouldn't be for a few weeks or more. So as soon as the morning chores were done, and I had breakfast, I grabbed my musket and headed out. I was used to Lillie and Frances going with me once in a while, but lately it seemed anytime Lillie knew I was going somewhere, she made sure she was ready to go.

After checking my traps and skinning anything I caught, we would spend the rest of the day fishing or hunting. There were times when we would ride along the river for miles and hunt ducks and geese. A few times, we rode in the woods that surrounded our place. One direction we rode seemed to have no end. Rarely did we see anyone.

One day, we were following a few deer, and they led us deeper and deeper into the woods. I had no idea how far we rode. The trail was well used and easy going. The first thing we knew, we were at the edge of a clearing that was fair sized. We rode on, and before we knew, we were surrounded by a half dozen Indians.

We sat there, side by side, not moving, not saying anything, just looking at them. I whispered to Lillie to stay close. They, too, just stood, looking us over, not saying anything, not making any moves toward us, just looking. I didn't think they were hostile or we wouldn't have been sitting there.

I raised my hand in a gesture of peace. They didn't move, just looked. My mind was moving faster than blowing wind. By all the tales I'd heard about them, I could see us being stripped naked and tied to a post and burned alive, or chopped to pieces and eaten, maybe even made into their slaves. On and on my mind went. I didn't know what Lillie was thinking. I only could imagine.

Finally, after what seemed forever, the one standing in front of us raised his hand in peace, then spoke in broken English and Delaware. He wanted to know where we had come from and what were we doing there. And he wanted to know if that was my woman.

Answering the best I could in Delaware and English, and with my hand signs, I said, "We're from the settlement. We're hunting. I think we lost our way." Then I added, "This is my woman." I was afraid to tell him otherwise.

Then he asked, "How come you hunt with squaw and not braves?"

"I'm all alone," I told him. "I have no braves. Squaw do skinning!"

"Ugh!" They moved closer, and Lillie moved even closer to me. They touched our mules, our clothing, my musket, but mostly Lillie—squeezing her arms, legs, back, breasts and anything they could. Lillie stayed calm. I think she was too scared to move. "How ye know talk Delaware?"

"My friend Old Joe that lives by the river taught me," I explained.

"Oh! Friend! Yes! Ye go there?" He pointed back the way we had come.

Then something went wrong. One of the braves grabbed me and yanked me to the ground, and another one grabbed Lillie. We lay there as they held their weapons, ready to strike. Lillie started gasping and crying.

Just then, something caught my eye. Against the bright blue of the afternoon sky, something white flashed over us. It lasted only a second, and then it vanished. It looked like the braves were getting ready to strike us, when suddenly, the leader stepped over us, shoving the two braves away from us. He held his weapon high, as if to strike them if they came any closer. He was talking so fast, I couldn't understand much of what was being said.

Two other braves stepped forward and pulled us roughly to our feet, then helped us on our mules. One handed me my musket.

All the while, the leader never stopped yelling at them. Turning to us, he yelled, "Ye go! Ye go! Ye go!"

I yelled at Lillie. "Get going!"

She pulled the mule around and headed off. I raised my hand in peace, swung my mule around, and kicked it into going, racing after Lillie. After I caught up with her, I slowed her down and let the mules walk. I let Lillie take the lead, so I could keep watch out behind, to make sure we weren't being followed. All the time I kept my musket ready. We never stopped until we reached the meadow, then rode to the stream, to let our mules drink and rest.

Getting down, we drank from the stream, too, then sat down to rest. We sat in silence for some time. Finally, Lillie said, "Nathan, were you scared?"

"Yes! Damn scared! Were you?"

"God, was I ever! I just knew we were going to die! I could see all those terrible things happening to us flash through my mind. At first, I thought you might shoot."

"No, I had no intention of shooting. First, there was no way we could've had a chance. Second, this is *their* land, not ours. We are *stealing* their land. I *know* this! That's why I wouldn't have shot them."

"Instead, you stayed calm and didn't panic."

"I tried."

"Nathan, you were very brave!"

"So were you."

"What do you think happened?"

"I don't know. Things happened too fast, and their leader was talking so fast that I couldn't understand much. I think those two braves wanted our mules ... and maybe you, or maybe they thought we were following them, I don't know. All that matters is we got out alive."

"Yes, I know! Nathan, I didn't know you could speak in their language or use sign language. Where did you learn it?"

"Mr. Joe is teaching me."

"Is that what you do when you go see him?"

"Most of the time, lately."

"Why did you want to learn?"

"I didn't!"

"Then what?"

"Mr. Joe said I was to learn it, that it may come in handy or save my life someday. I guess he knew what he was talking about. Lillie, do you remember when I asked you if you thought some Indians could talk to spirits and know what other people were going to do or what was going to happen?"

"Are you asking me if Mr. Joe knew this was going to take place, and that's why he wanted you to learn their language?"

"Yes! I think that's what I mean. I just don't know!"

"But Nathan, it does make you wonder. Ask your mother."

"Oh! No! No way! And don't you tell anyone what happened today!"

"Why?"

"Because then they won't let me go anywhere on my own."

"Don't you think your mother and dad would be proud of you?"

"I don't know! And besides, then everyone in church or school, or wherever I go, will be asking me all kinds of questions. So don't say anything, will you?"

"I think I understand. I promise I won't say anything."

"Thanks." After a minute, I said, "Lillie, when we were lying on the ground back there, did you see some sort of a white bird fly over?"

"No! Why?"

"I did, and I think the leader did, too. Right after it passed over is when the leader jumped over us and protected us!"

"What are you saying?"

"Never mind, I'm not sure. Come on, we must get going." I helped her on the mule, and we headed for home, getting there in time to do the stable work.

Later that evening, Mom asked where we had been all day. I told her we were following some deer, and before we realized it, it was getting late, so we hurried back as fast as we could. Mom looked at me, then at Lillie, but said no more.

10

School had now started, and Mom made sure Frances and I attended school most of the day. Frances was now helping me check my traps in the morning, so I could get done before school. We left the skinning and putting the fur up until after school. Frances was catching on to trapping really good. I continued going to see Mr. Joe every week for my lesson. According to Mr. Joe, I was doing very good. He continued to broaden his teachings, and Lillie continued coming to our place almost every weekend. Dad was busy at the mill, as always.

One Sunday at church, the man who bought fur told me beaver and muskrat would be paying the most, so I concentrated on trapping mostly those and was doing good. In just a short time, Christmas would be here. Frances, Lillie and I had gone to the settlement shortly after we had gotten our money from selling vegetables, in hopes of buying what we wanted for Christmas. Instead, we found there wasn't much to be had. We asked around and, finally, found a woman who agreed to make the things we wanted. After asking her how much it would cost, we found it was more than we had. But after talking it over, I told her I would have the rest of the money and pay her two weeks before Christmas. The lady was very nice, saying she would accept that. Now all I needed was to catch enough fur to make the rest of the money we needed.

When two weeks before Christmas came, all three of us went into the settlement and sold my furs. Were we ever surprised when we got more than enough money needed to pay the lady for the things we ordered. Then I gave Frances half of what was left for her help with the trapping. We taken our things to Lillie's place, then went home.

It was the Friday before Christmas now, and school would be out at noon. I had been taking the mules and sled to school for the past few days, due to the snow being too deep for Abilene and Noel to walk. Mom and I kept the sled partly filled with straw and feed and blankets. I would stable the mules in the building by the teacher's cabin and put their blankets over them and give them feed. This worked out nicely, since Lillie was spending Christmas with us.

After school let out, I went and hitched the mules in the sled while Frances helped Lillie with the cleaning and getting Abilene and Noel bundled up for the cold trip home. As Lillie gathered her things, I carried Noel, and then Abilene, to the sled, and put them on the straw and covered them with one of the horse blankets. Lillie and Frances brought the things we were taking, stowing them on the sled. Frances crawled under the blanket with the other two kids, and Lillie climbed up, helping me cover the seat with the other blanket. Then, sitting as close as we could, pulling the blanket up over our shoulders and legs, I hollered to the mules, and we headed for home.

Once there, I stopped and let the kids off, giving Frances Lillie's satchel. They all headed into the house. Driving to the stable, Lillie and I unhitched the sled and put the mules in the stalls, then we hid the presents.

Mom and the others spent the rest of the day baking and making other things for Christmas dinner. After I ate something, I went to the stable and did some things I wanted to do. Since Lillie was spending Christmas with us, and Dad had invited this young man that was working at the mill for him, named Isaiah, Mom told me to invite Mr. Joe, too, which I did the last time I saw him.

That night while Mom was bathing, I ran to the stable and brought the presents in and taken them up on the loft, where we slept. Since it was Christmas Eve, and the work was all done and everyone was cleaned up, we all gathered around the fireplace, eating goodies and listening to Mom and Dad tell stories of what Christmas was like in the old country, when they were young and growing up. Shortly after they quit telling stories, everyone went to bed.

I was lying on my stomach and had moved so I could look down from the loft. With the lamps all out, it was dark, except for the light from the fireplace. Lillie lay not far away, and I could hear her stirring and could tell she was restless.

"What's wrong?" I whispered. "Why are you restless?"

"I don't know!" Rolling on her stomach, she crawled beside me. "Why aren't you sleeping?"

"Oh, I was just lying here, thinking and watching the flickering light from the fireplace as it reflects across the rafters and the room."

She was lying close to me. I don't know how long we lay there, talking and watching the firelight. She told me this would be the first real Christmas she ever had, that the church home she grew up in didn't have Christmas, just a dinner and that was all. "The people who were in charge were very strict with us kids. There was no warm, loving feeling like there is here with you."

"Didn't they treat you'se good?"

"Most of the time they did. Mostly, if we did something they didn't like, we got sent to our room without anything to eat, and if we did something they thought was really bad, we got a strapping … and a good one at that!"

She stopped talking and everything was quiet. We were lying there when we heard this noise. At first, we didn't know where it was coming from. It got a little louder, then we could hear it was coming from Mom and Dad's room. Lillie rolled onto her back and started snickering.

I reached over and put my hand over her mouth. "What's so damn funny?"

She stopped then, not saying anything. Then, we heard someone checking on the fire. Lillie quickly scuttled back to her bed, and I did too.

The next morning, I slept late, as did everyone else. Sitting up, I could see it was going to be a nice Christmas day. Lillie stirred, opening her eyes. "It's so quiet! No one's up!"

Dressing quickly, I went downstairs. After checking the fire, I grabbed my coat and went to the stable to do the feeding. It was cold and there was a lot of snow, yet the sun was shining so nicely. I knew then Mr. Joe would be coming. I was almost through feeding when Dad came to do the milking. Finishing up, I went to the cabin. Mom hollered, "It's too late for breakfast, just have some milk and a roll."

I cleaned up, grabbed a few rolls, then sat at the table to eat them. Over a bed of hot coals in the fireplace, Mom had this big turkey we raised on a spit, and the other three kids were taking turns turning it over as it cooked. Lillie sat at the table, getting potatoes ready to cook. As I ate, we talked and soon Dad came in. After cleaning up, he gave Mom a hug and patted her on the behind a few times. Lillie looked at me, turning a little red in the face.

A little past noon, Mr. Joe rode up. I went out to greet him, then stabled his mule. Before I got out of the stable, Isaiah rode in and we stabled his horse, then went to the house. Mom and Lillie had prepared a big dinner and had everything on the table.

After everyone was seated, Mom said a prayer, then the food was handed around. Dad, Mr. Joe and Mom did most of the talking. Dad seemed to enjoy talking with Mr. Joe, even though he was Indian. I mostly listened, as did the other kids. One thing everyone agreed on was the dinner was the best anyone could ask for. I could tell it made Mom and Lillie very happy to know everyone enjoyed the meal.

I had noticed Mom asking Lillie if she would sit across from Isaiah. She did, but didn't seem too happy about it. Her and Isaiah didn't have much to say, they just answered what was asked and didn't seem too comfortable with each other. Isaiah was maybe bashful or uncomfortable, I don't know which. I knew there weren't many young, unmarried men their age around the settlement, so I think that is why Dad invited Isaiah, hoping he and Lillie would hit it off and maybe start courting.

After dinner was over and put away, Mom gave each of us a present. She had fixed a nice basket of food for Mr. Joe, and one for Isaiah. Long underwear for Dad, stockings and sweaters she had knitted for Noel and Abilene, a coat for Frances, and for Lillie a feather quilt. Mom had made everything over the past year and, with Lillie's help over the summer, had made me a sheepskin coat like Dad's, except longer. It reached below my knees, and was split up the back to the seat, with a high collar that came over my ears and could be buttoned over the face. I was so happy with my coat.

Lillie motioned to Frances, and she went up on the loft and handed down the presents we had gotten. Noel and Abilene gave each one their present. A new sweater for Dad and one for Mr. Joe. Abilene and Noel got gloves. Mom got a new blue dress, like the one she talked about. Frances and I gave Lillie a new fur muff. Dad and Mr. Joe really liked their sweaters, but Mom was really thrilled with the dress. She couldn't believe we had taken our money and put it together to have her dress and the other things made.

The rest of the afternoon was spent listening to the elders telling stories, especially Mr. Joe. Even though Dad didn't care for Indians, he sure was taken in by Mr. Joe, and was all ears as Mr. Joe unraveled tale after tale about his life.

It was now getting toward dark, and Isaiah said he had to be going. Mom told him not to be in a hurry, and she would warm up leftovers and he was to eat before he left. As he was eating, I got my coat and headed to the stable to do the feeding. As I left, I heard Lillie tell Mom and Dad that they were to stay in and she would go do the milking, and she told Frances to come along and help.

Lillie was milking when Isaiah came and got his horse and led it outside and climbed on, then hollered goodbye and rode off.

Looking at me, Lillie said, "He's sure strange!"

We finished the work, then went to the house. Mom had supper on the table. Everyone else was through eating, and Mom had Noel and Abilene helping with the dishes. Mr. Joe said he must be going. Dad told him, "No, it's too dark. You stay here tonight."

"I'll be all right," Mr. Joe said.

"No! You're staying!"

"All right, I'll sleep in the stable."

"If that's what you want ... but you can sleep in here."

"No, the stable will be fine," Mr. Joe said.

"Suit yourself. Do you play checkers?"

"I have been known to play a little," Mr. Joe said. They sat at the table and played checkers while the rest of us sat around the fire, talking and watched. The little ones went to bed. It wasn't long before Mr. Joe said he had enough and was going to bed. I don't know how many games they played, but they came out with a tie.

I walked with Mr. Joe to the stable, and got him some horse blankets to wrap himself in. He curled up on a pile of straw, and I left a lantern burning very low, and left. When I returned to the house, everyone was in bed. I blew out the lamp and climbed up to bed.

The next morning after breakfast, Dad asked Mr. Joe if he would go to church with us.

"No thanks, I better be getting on home," Mr. Joe said, and thanked us for everything. Then he went and got his mule, and headed for home.

The rest of us climbed on the sled and covered up with blankets. Dad drove us to church. Church was the same old dull, boring thing, and seemed to last forever.

Later that afternoon, Dad went to the mill to check on Isaiah. He was back by dark, and the rest of the evening we sat around the fire, playing games and reading some books Lillie had brought.

11

It was back to school, and before long it was early February. A thaw had come, and I was able to recover the rest of my traps. I hadn't caught anything due to the deep snow.

It was a Saturday afternoon. I was in the stable, putting my traps up, when Dad rode up. As soon as he walked in, I knew he had been drinking. He got down from his horse, cussing everything about the mill. I stayed out of his way, and kept on with what I was doing, and didn't say anything. I could see he was looking for something and couldn't find it, all the time cussing.

Suddenly, he stopped and picked up a whip, and started beating me and cussing me. It was warm in the stable, and I had taken my coat off. This left me with little protection as the whip bit into my backside, from my shoulders to my knees. He had me cornered with no way out. It didn't matter which way I turned, the whip bit harder and harder, until I fell to the ground, curling up in the corner, which helped ward off some of the blows. He stood there, looking down at me a few seconds, then turned and went to his horse and rode off.

Gathering myself up, I grabbed my coat and limped to the house, barring the door behind me. Everyone came running. Mom yelled, "What's after you?"

With tears streaming down my face, I said, "Dad beat me again!"

Then Mom saw the blood coming through my shirt. "Damn that bastard! I'll kill him yet!" she yelled. "Lillie, get some warm water and soap, and help me get him cleaned up."

Mom made me get undressed and lie on her bed. As Mom and Lillie were cleaning the cuts, I could hear them sobbing. Between my own sobs, I said, "Mom, I swear to you now, this is the last beating I'll ever take from him, and I will no longer call him Dad."

Again, Mom made sure I wouldn't get any infection in

the cuts. I don't know how many beatings I had taken from him, but this was by far the worst. This time they would leave marks that would remain the rest of my life.

While I laid on Mom's bed, Mom or Lillie would come and rub ointment on my backside, and make sure I was comfortable. It was getting dark when I got the strength to get up. Pulling my nightshirt on, I went to the kitchen, and Mom yelled, "What do you think you're doing?"

"I must go to the outhouse, Mom." After getting my shoes and very carefully pulling my coat on, I slogged my way to the outhouse, then on to the stable, where I got my pistol from where I had it hidden, then returned to the house.

Mom and Lillie had supper on. It hurt too damn much to sit, so I stood while I ate. Later on, I taken my coat, with the pistol tucked inside, and climbed up to my bed. Lying on my stomach, I drifted off to sleep and never heard the rest of them coming to bed.

Something woke me, and I could see a lamp was still lit. Then I heard Mom talking to Dad. Then I heard him say, "Shut your damn mouth, bitch! I'll do as I damn please! That boy needs a good going over once in a while! You don't ever hit anyone in this house! Damn you, woman, you want the shit knocked out of you?"

Grabbing my pistol, I crawled to where I could see. As he stood up, I pointed the pistol at him. At the sound of it being cocked, he looked up, then yelled, "Damn you, boy! What the hell you think you're doing?"

Calmly, I said, "You ever hit Mom again and you're dead. And that goes for the rest of the kids. Today you beat me for the last time. You ever try it again, and I'll blow your damn head off ... I mean everything I said! Do you hear?"

I felt Lillie crawl up beside me and lay her hand on my arm. "Nathan, don't!"

He just stood there with a shocked look, his mouth open, his face turned white. Sitting back down at the table, he buried his head in his hands, not saying anything.

Mom said, "I think you better do some serious thinking about what you have done to this family, Otis. I'm telling you now, do us right, or you won't be living here! Do I make myself clear?"

Lillie was tugging at my arm to move back to my bed. I moved, neither of us saying anything. I lay on my stomach with my hand on my pistol, and finally fell to sleep.

I healed quickly, and was able to do things in a few days. All the while, no one had said anything or brought up what went on, and our lives stayed much the same.

The next time I saw Mr. Joe, I told him what had happened. Looking me straight in the eye, he said, "Friend, it's time," and said no more.

It was early March, and I had just turned 15. I knew the time had come. Mom knew, too, without me saying anything. In the evening, she would sit and mend my clothes, making them ready. All the while, I said nothing about my leaving, and I don't know that she did either.

It was a few days after my birthday when I made my things ready. That evening, Mom didn't have much to talk about while we ate our supper. I don't know if she had told Dad or not. I had gone to bed before he got home, and the next morning, when I got up, he had already gone to the mill.

As I rode toward the house, Mom was standing in the doorway, tall and thin, her long hair hung loosely over the front of her shoulders. In the early morning light, her blond hair, mixed with a little white, shone like gold, even with the tears flowing down her cheeks. She was the most beautiful person I would ever know. As I slid down from my mule, Mom came running, along with my two sisters and brother. My feet no more than hit the ground when she threw her arms around me, pulling me close. Her cheeks, wet with tears, pressed tight to mine, and she whispered over and over, "I love you. Please take care."

The two little ones were holding fast to my legs. Frances had her arms around both Mom and me, crying. My own tears mixed with Mom's as she hugged and kissed me. I finally pulled away, wiping my eyes. Bending down, I hugged and kissed my sisters and brother, then stood and placed my hands on each side of Mom's face as her hands covered mine. I looked deep into her blue eyes and could see the hurt she was feeling deep inside, and the love she was pouring out to me as only a mother can. I saw the happiness she was feeling for me, knowing I was doing something I wanted to do. Knowing I was growing up, but still it wasn't enough to cover the hurt she was feeling deep inside, for she knew as well as I that we would probably never see each other again.

With my thumbs, I wiped the tears from her eyes. I pulled her close, kissing her lips. "Mom, take care of the little ones and Dad, but most of all, take extra care of yourself, and please don't worry about me as you know I'll be taken care of. Mom, you're the best mother I could ever have asked for. But now I must say goodbye. Mom, I love you! Bye!"

Turning, I taken the few steps and swung up on my mule. Mom taken hold of my hand, tears still filling her eyes as it did the kids'. "Frances, take care of your mother and help her." Then, kicking my mule, I rode off, looking back one last time. I waved and knew I couldn't look back again.

I rode to Lillie's cabin, tying up at the stable, then knocked on her door. When she opened the door, she was startled to see me. "Come in! What happened? Is there something wrong?"

"No. No. I just stopped to say goodbye."

"What! You're not leaving?"

"Yes."

"You can't! What about the rest? They need you!"

"I know, but it's better if I go now before something happens."

"Must you?"

"Yes. I made up my mind that night not so long ago."

"Damn you! You can't! I'll miss you too damn much! Shit!" Tears filled her eyes as she threw her arms around me. Sobs came from deep inside. Looking up into my eyes, she said, "Nathan, please, don't go and leave. You're the only close friend I have."

"I know… as you are to me. But the time has come for me to set out on my own. You know that."

"Where will you go?"

"I think I'll head west." Pulling her close, I held her until she stopped sobbing, then kissed her goodbye. As I turned to leave, she held onto my arm, still shaking.

"Will you write?"

"Yes, if I can."

Returning to my mules, I headed off to see Mr. Joe.

As I rode up to his shack, I saw his mules tied up outside. As I stepped down, he came out the door, carrying a bundle of things. Looking up, he said, "You're late."

"What do you mean?"

"Don't stand there. Come give a hand with this."

"Where do you want it?"

"Where do you think? On my mule!"

"On your mule?"

"That's right, on my mule! Damn it."

"Where are you going?"

"Where do you think?"

"Damned if I know!"

He always looked me straight in the eye when he said something that he meant. "With *you!*"

"With me! What the hell are you talking about?"

"Yes, with *you!*"

"But... why?"

"The time has come."

"What about your place? I thought you liked it here."

"There's nothing here."

"What about your friends?"

"You're it," he said. "The rest will go on living."

"Well?"

"Well, what?"

"Well, what if I don't want you with me?"

"You will."

"If that's what you want to do, then, let's get going!"

12

After several tries at getting up on his mule, Mr. Joe made it. "Which way?" he asked.

"Downriver."

"Are you sure?"

"Yup."

"I'll lead. I know the way."

"The way to where?" I asked.

"To where it is you want to go."

"How do you know where I want to go?"

"I know. I know you want to go to the big river and the place you can cross to go west."

"Have you been there?"

"Old Joe knows the way. I take you. I am your friend."

"How far are you going with me?"

"Don't know. Maybe stay with you where you go."

"But why?"

"Maybe you need me, friend."

He led the way, not staying close to the river at all, but a good distance from it.

I said, "Mr. Joe, why ain't we staying close to the river?"

"Many trails along the river. Too close. No good. We travel here, far from water. Many whites and Indians travel close to water. Good trail, many bad people. They steal all you have, even clothes you wear. Maybe you see many pony soldiers, too. They are very bad, not like Indian. They catch Old Joe, they hang him maybe. Old Joe and you keep very close eye out for bad people and pony soldiers."

All morning we moved at a slow pace, stopping often to listen and look out ahead and back down the trail. The trail we were on was heavily wooded and fairly dense. Mr. Joe would stop every time he heard a sound, even if it was off in the distance, or if it didn't sound natural or right.

I was growing impatient and annoyed with him. I wanted to move faster, making more distance, covering more ground.

When midday rolled around, Mr. Joe said, "We rest now."

"What did you say?" I asked.

"We rest now."

"That's what I thought you said! But why?"

"Listen, boy, Old Joe knows. Mules know they need rest and to eat. We rest now." He found a small clearing some distance off the trail, where the mules could feed and the sun shone through.

Getting down from my mule, the first thing I did was stretch and yawn.

Mr. Joe put his hand to my mouth. "No, not good. Quiet!" He had his long musket in hand and a pistol stuck in his waist band. Stepping closer, he said in almost a whisper, "Keep long gun in hand all the time."

"Why? I hear nothing, and I don't see anyone around."

"You don't know. Listen to Old Joe, you stay alive. Three riders come."

"Where?"

"Maybe a long distance, maybe a mile, maybe two or three they come. You learn to be quiet, you live long."

"All right, I'll be quiet, but how do you know three riders are coming?"

"Old Joe know. Old Joe feel when things not right. Talk low. Talk soft when on trail. We find stuff to eat now."

"I have things in my pack to eat."

"Save for later, when needed. Nathan, when you can find food, save what you have for time when you can't find anything to eat. Be wise like brother, the beaver, and watchful like mother, the owl. Come now, I show you how to find things to eat."

"Where?"

"I show. Come!"

I followed beside him as he looked around the small clearing, picking this kind of plant or that one. He found mushrooms and told me which ones we could eat and showed me the ones that were poisonous or would make you sick. Turning over rocks or anything that lay on the ground, we looked for grubs, beetles, worms, anything. When he said, "Quit. Get the mules," I did, and he motioned me to follow.

I led the mules to where he was. Taking his mules, he led them into a thicket. I followed. We tied the mules again, and he motioned me to follow, leading me back towards the trail. We were only fifty feet or so from the trail now. Looking around, he spotted a tree that had blown down. I followed as he made his way to where it was and crawled into the thickest part. Once in there, he whispered, "Don't move, and keep your gun at ready."

Whispering, I asked, "What are we doing?"

"Riders. They come now. Getting close now. We watch to see if they stay on trail and go their way. Quiet."

I didn't see or hear anything, but sure enough, no more than two or three minutes passed when I heard someone talking. Then there they were, coming into view, three of them. At first, through the thick brush, it was hard to make them out, but as they passed directly in front, we were able to see it was three pony soldiers. They weren't being very quiet, doing a lot of talking. One of them was doing a lot of bitching about having to ride this trail.

"There's nothing here, we haven't seen a damn buddy the past month. This damn trail is the roughest we have to ride. It's hell on my ass! That asshole of a sergeant, damn him! He always assigns us this hell trail. It's the worst one there is. Hell trail … that's a good name for it. Damn him, damn his fat ass! I wish someone would kick his damn balls off!"

"Quit your bitching, shit brain, and be quiet. I don't want to hear another word from you!"

"Yes, Corporal."

That was the last we heard. They were out of range. I couldn't believe they passed so close and never looked our way. They just bounced along, like they were going to a Sunday school outing. We lay where we were, until Mr. Joe was sure they were far enough away, then we crawled out from our hiding place and returned to where the mules were, leading them back to the clearing. There, we gathered up our plants and mushrooms and returned to the trail.

Mr. Joe taken the lead once again as we continued on our way. We rode for some time before stopping at a small stream to let the mules drink. After taking on some water ourselves and relieving our bodies, we continued, this time walking, leading our mules to give them a rest, and to keep ourselves from getting too stiff. The trail was very rough now, and I soon realized why the pony soldier was doing all the complaining.

Mile after mile, we followed this trail. By now, there was only an hour or so of light left, when Mr. Joe stopped and waited for me to come up beside him. In a low voice, he said, "Boy, we will make camp up there," pointing to an outcrop of huge rocks.

"For the night?" I said. "Up there?"

"Yeah. Up there we be safe."

"All right, if that's what you think."

He led the way. It was several hundred yards up, and very steep. Once we reached the place, we wound our way through the rocks, until we found an open area where the animals could feed, and we would be out of sight of anyone passing on the trail.

Once we had the mules unloaded and everything stashed under a rock ledge, where we would be spending the night, Mr. Joe said, "Come, boy, let's go and see if we can find something to eat."

"I'll go shoot something for us."

"No, boy! No shoot! Not good to shoot gun! Make too much loud noise. Hear long, far distance. We hunt with this." He pulled out his bow from his pile of things.

"You're going to shoot with that?"

"Come, Nathan, you see. I show you how. You learn patience."

I followed after as he scouted around, looking for something to shoot. Half an hour passed and we didn't see anything. I said to Mr. Joe, "Now what do we do?"

"Be patient, boy, and always think the best. We find something."

We kept on moving quietly through the trees, looking for signs. We had been searching for some time when we saw where the leaves were all rooted up.

Looking at Mr. Joe, I said, "Pigs were here."

"No, boy. Turkey. Turkey!"

"Yeah, that's what it is, turkey scratching up leaves, looking for things to eat."

"Two, maybe more. Leaves not dry. Fresh, not far away. Be very quiet. We follow. Maybe find." He led the way, and I stayed very close behind him, and kept my eyes searching all around, hoping to see them. The light was fading, and then the trail ended. We were standing there, searching every foot of ground, hoping to find the trail again, when we heard a noise.

Looking up, we spotted a turkey roosting in a tree, no more than twenty feet off the ground. Mr. Joe pulled his bow back, taking aim, and then let go. I heard the arrow make a thud sound, and the bird tumbled off its perch.

Mr. Joe watched as the bird hit the ground, making sure it didn't move. He stood, searching the trees for more. A few minutes passed, then I saw him pull his arrow back and take aim again. It was now so dark in the woods, I could hardly make out where the bird was. Then, I heard the bow snap forward, and a thud as the arrow found its mark. The second bird fell from its perch.

After gathering up the birds, we saw that neither one was very big. We headed back to camp. After cleaning our birds, they were put over the hot coals from the fire we had started earlier.

Mr. Joe said, "Boy, go get some of your snares. There's a little light left in the open. If we set them, maybe we'll catch something for tomorrow."

After getting six snares set, we returned to see how the birds were coming along. By the looks of them, they had a lot more roasting to do. After filling a pot with water from a nearby spring, I held it out for Mr. Joe, who threw a handful of coffee mixed with dried dandelion root into the water. Then he hung it over the fire to cook. We sat by the fire, watching as the birds roasted, keeping them turned. We could smell the coffee as it began to boil. Neither one of us had much to say. I guess we both were lost in thoughts of our first day on the trail, and my first night away from home.

I was sitting there, feeling alone and maybe having second thoughts, when Mr. Joe said, "Here, boy, have some coffee." Then he said, "Feeling alone, huh, boy? Unsure of what you wanna do? Thinking about home?"

"No! No!" It was just like he knew what I was thinking. "Well, maybe some ..."

"I thought so."

Taking a sip of coffee, I said, "I'll be all right after I have something to eat."

"The birds look like they are finally done," Mr. Joe said.

"Yeah, they do."

We each taken one. Pulling it apart, we started chewing on them, as well as the dandelion and watercress we had gathered earlier. It wasn't a supper like Mom cooked, but I was hungry, and it tasted damn good anyway. I was glad we cooked both birds, for in no time we devoured them.

"Hand me your cup, boy, and I'll give you more coffee."

I did, and he filled it. We sat and talked, watching the fire burn down, until it was just hot glowing coals. He asked me a lot about my family, then wanted to know why my father beat me.

I said, "Who says he beat me?"

"I know he has."

"How do you know?"

"Well, boy, I guess I shouldn't be saying, but I think it would be all right now. Boy, you see, the teacher came to see me. What's her name?"

"Miss Martin."

"That's it. Well, she said she brought me a book to read, but I knew she had something else on her mind. We talked for a while, and I could see she was becoming nervous and restless. I said, 'Miss Martin, you want to tell Old Joe what troubles you?' She sat, looking at me for a spell, tears in her eyes. Then she said, 'Mr. Joe, I should not be telling you this, but I'm very worried about Nathan. I know he's your friend.'

" 'What is it, girl?' I said. Then, she said she was over at your place a few weeks ago. Then, she went on to tell me how your father beats you when he is drinking, and told me everything else that went on that night. Old Joe just listened, not saying anything. Then she said, 'Mr. Joe, what can I do? I'm very worried about Nathan. I'm afraid he might …' I said, 'Miss Martin, I don't think you have anything to be worried about. As you can see, Nathan's a big boy for his age, and I think he can take care of himself if need be, and I'm sure he would never do anything to harm his father. I think what he did was to put a scare into his father.'

" 'I sure do hope you're right. I think a lot of Nathan. I must be going before it gets dark. I thank you for listening and putting my mind somewhat at ease.' Then she left."

I sat there, staring into the glowing coals, waiting to see what else he had to say, but he said nothing more. I waited a few minutes, then said, "I'm turning in."

"I think I will, too, boy."

13

The next morning, Mr. Joe was up at first light and got a nice fire going. "Come, boy, get up. Let's go see what we caught."

Crawling out from under my blankets, I hurried to the fire to get warm. Looking around, I could see everything was white with frost. After pulling on my heavy coat, we went and checked the snares. I was surprised when I saw we had caught four rabbits. After they were cleaned, we put them over the fire to roast, then packed our things, loading them onto the mules.

After the meat was done and the fire put out, we taken our meat and ate it as we made our way back to the main trail. After riding for an hour or so, it became clear the trail was just as rough as the day before. It was late morning when we came upon a fair-sized stream. After looking it over, Mr. Joe said, "What you think, boy?"

"I don't know. Looks awfully damn swift to me."

"Maybe too damn deep to cross also. Boy, we could go downstream and find us a bridge, but the chances of pony soldiers seeing us would be much greater. The other thing we can do is ride upstream until we find a place to cross. I guess that would be the best thing to do," I said.

Mr. Joe led the way as we wound our way upstream. This trail was easier to follow and not so damn rough. We rode for miles without finding a place to cross.

It was past mid-afternoon by now, and I was becoming more restless and disappointed with the headway we were making. Yesterday's slow going was bad enough, but now no damn place to cross. Feeling down, I was having second thoughts about Mr. Joe. Why did I agree to let him come along with me? He was old and moved slowly, taking his good old time. I was in a hurry, and wanted to move as fast as I could. Looking out ahead, I saw he was a good ways in front and had dismounted. I hurried my pace and rode up to where his mule was tied and got down. He had already walked over to the stream and was standing, there looking it over.

Turning towards me, he called, "Bring the animals, boy."

I led all the animals over to where he was standing.

"Nathan, I think we can make it across here. Take a good look and see what you think. Do you think we can make it?"

"Don't know, but I think it's worth a try."

"Yeah, boy, I think so." Taking hold of the bridle on each mule, he told me to wait there. He led them into the cold, swift water, staying in between his animals. The farther out he waded, the deeper it got. I was becoming worried and thinking the worst. What would I do if the swift water swept him away? How would I be able to help him? Then I saw he was over halfway across, and the water only came up to his waist. I could see it was swift, the way he was holding onto his mules. Once he was safe on the other shore, I taken ahold of the bridle on my animals and led them into the water, just like he did.

Damn, was it ever cold! My feet, then my legs, were instantly numb. I knew now why Mr. Joe hung onto his mules with both hands. I did the same, and was soon on shore where he waited. I was shivering from the cold water.

"Damn cold, huh, boy?"

"Damn if it ain't!"

"Boy, we must find a place to spend the night and get a fire started, so we can get warm and dry our clothes."

Still shivering, I said, "Damn! Better before we freeze!" I was cold, tired and feeling down. Leading our mules, we went to search for a place to spend the night. We didn't need to go too far before we found a place that the animals could feed and a good spot that would shelter us. We let the animals go, and got a fire started. Once it was going good, we taken our shoes off and placed them as near the heat as possible, to dry. Then we sat as close as we could, letting the heat from the fire chase the chill out of our bodies. At the same time, it dried our wet clothes.

After my clothes were dried and I was feeling warm again, I told Mr. Joe I was going back to the stream to see if I could catch us some fish.

"Good, me could eat some fish, boy. You have things for catching them with?"

"I do."

On my way to the stream, I gathered worms and grubs from under rocks and logs that lay along the way. I was so busy with my fishing and with the noise coming from the stream that I never heard Mr. Joe coming, until he was almost beside me.

The first thing he said was, "You catch fish?"

"Yeah."

"How many?"

"I think fourteen, maybe." I looked over to where he stood, and saw he had killed three birds.

"I think maybe that's enough fish. Rain coming. We better go and get shelter made."

"Okay. I'll clean the fish first."

"Sure. I clean birds, then we go."

"Yeah."

Once we were back at camp, it didn't take long to get a shelter up, using a large boulder for one side and some dead trees for poles, then using the extra canvas we had. It made a good shelter. It rained most of the night, like Mr. Joe said.

Not long after daylight, the sun peeped through the clouds, and it wasn't long before it cleared and we were making our way along the trail once more. This was a different trail now, and we were no longer close to the river. Once when we stopped, I asked Mr. Joe why we were not going back closer to the river.

"No need. This will go to the right place."

"How do you know?"

He looked at me and then said, "Boy, you trust Old Joe. He knows."

Mounting up, we rode off, staying on the same trail. We rode and walked the rest of the day, only stopping for the night or when we had to. We followed this trail, mile after mile, and day after day. It was a trail that led us up steep embankments, so steep that our mules were barely able to make it. It took us across rocky flats and led us through streams that were so deep, the water came almost to our necks, and was as cold as ice.

The days turned into weeks, and soon the weeks all blended together. I didn't know what day or week it was, and when I thought about it, it didn't really matter. All that mattered was we were headed in the right direction—at least I hoped so. We rode and we walked for miles over some of the most beautiful green meadows, and I thought of Mom and home. We traveled through woody areas and marshes, and I thought of Lillie. I don't think there was anything that we hadn't crossed.

14

As the days passed, the sun became warmer, and that also brought warmer nights. There were days while riding that I found myself wondering if I had done right by myself in letting Mr. Joe come along with me. I wondered where he was going, and why. Why did he just pick up and leave? Leave his shack and his few friends, and decide to go with me? I wondered how he knew I was leaving, how did he know when? I couldn't understand. It made no sense to me, and he never talked about it. All he would say is, "You understand soon enough."

We had been riding all morning, and now the sun was high and it was warm. The last while, we had been taking turns riding lead, and it was my turn. I was out front a hundred yards or more. I had rounded one bend in the trail, and was just rounding the second one, when I glanced back and caught a glimpse of Mr. Joe coming. I hadn't gone but a short way when a man and woman stepped out from behind some bushes and onto the trail.

The man pointed his gun directly at me and demanded that I get down. I was scared shitless, not knowing what to do. I knew what they were after, and I wasn't about to give anything up, so I started making signs with my hands. I hoped there weren't others that may have gotten Mr. Joe, and hoped he would be able to hear what was going on. I just sat there. Then the man again yelled, this time louder.

"Damn your ass! I told you to get the hell down! You hear?"

I kept making signs with my hands.

Then the woman said, "He's just a boy, and I don't think he can talk."

They were no more than twenty feet away when the man handed the woman his gun and said, "Shoot the bastard, if he tries anything."

"But he's just a boy!"

"I don't give a damn. If you know what's good for you, you'll shoot!"

She held the gun on me, and he made only a few steps in my direction when I heard the sound of a bow. The arrow flew past and stuck in the ground a few feet in front of the man's feet. He stopped dead.

I heard Mr. Joe's voice, loud and clear in his broken English. "Put the gun down or the next one goes through your heart!"

The man turned towards the woman and yelled, "Shoot, damn you, shoot!"

But she had already laid the gun down. The man made a run to pick it up. Just as he reached his hand out, an arrow went through it, and the man gave out a yell in pain. Then he yelled at the woman to get the gun.

Jumping from my mule, I ran toward her, just as she bent to pick it up. I gave her a hard shove, and she went rolling. Grabbing the gun up, I stepped back. Mr. Joe had come out of the woods with his pistol in his hand.

When the man saw Mr. Joe was an Indian, he went into a ranting, cussing fit. "You son-of-a-bitch, stinking, filthy no-good savage! Look what the hell you did to my hand!" He walked to where Mr. Joe stood, with his other fist raised, ready to strike.

Mr. Joe reached out and grabbed hold of the arrow that was still sticking through the man's hand, and gave it a twist. The man went down and hit the ground, yelling and cussing in pain.

The woman gathered herself up and went over to where he lay groaning. She tried to help him, but he just cussed all the more.

I moved closer to Mr. Joe and asked, "What are we going to do with them?"

He didn't answer. He just stood, looking at them. Finally he said, "Well, as I see it, they hang thieves. But these two are too dumb to be thieves. They didn't steal anything that we know of, so we can't hang them."

The woman gave a big sigh of relief. The man lay there and continued cussing Mr. Joe. The woman said, "Shut your damn mouth. You got us into this, so shut up, or I'll go with *them!*"

"No way. Don't even think about it, woman. No way," Mr. Joe said.

"Mr. Joe, what do we do with them?" I asked. "Let them here?"

"Yip."

Mr. Joe looked at the man and said, "You won't follow, will you?"

The man didn't answer, but the woman said, "No."

Mr. Joe knelt down in front of the man, looking him in the eyes. "I said you won't be following, will you?"

The man didn't answer.

Mr. Joe reached out his hand to grab the arrow.

The man flinched backward, yelling, "You stinking savage! Get out of here! No, I won't follow, so let me alone. Take that whore with you! If it wasn't for her, this wouldn't have happened!"

"You're lucky. The next time, you die." Mr. Joe stood up, put his hand on my shoulder, and said, "Come, boy."

"What do I do with their gun?"

"Shove the barrel down in the ground. By the time she gets that arrow out of him, and his hand fixed, then clean the ground out of their gun, we will be long gone." He then left to fetch his mules.

I mounted up and waited. Mr. Joe soon came, and as we rode away, he stopped and looked down at the woman, then told her what plants to gather from the woods, to put on the man's hand, to make it heal. "The best thing for you is stay here for a few days, so hand gets better. You hear? If you don't, you be sorry."

Mr. Joe taken the lead as we rode away. Neither of them said anything. Once we were far enough out of sight, he led us off the trail and into the tall timber, where we wound our way among big trees. We stayed there until we came to a stream. The stream was wide and shallow. There, Mr. Joe swung us south, right down the middle of the stream. We stayed in the water for a mile, maybe more. Finally, we came to a place that was very rocky. Here, we left the stream and once again headed west.

As time wore on, I would think back over the days and what we came through thus far. Even though I was 15 now, and ready to be on my own—so I thought—I soon came to realize that I didn't know a damn thing about being on my own out here in the wild, away from home. I was coming to appreciate Mr. Joe more and more, and was downright glad he was with me as the weeks passed. I finally came to realize, by the things he had me do, and the decisions he would have me make, that he wasn't making this trip for himself. No, not at all. Not at his age. Not with his health. No, instead it was all for me. He was making this trip for me, to teach me what it was like living off the land. He was teaching me to survive in an environment that was harsh and cruel, sometimes so unforgiving that one mistake—*any* mistake—may very well be your last.

15

Day after day, as we rode, I was haunted by my thoughts —the thoughts I had earlier about Mr. Joe moving too slowly, or being old and being overly cautious. I knew now he was doing it for my good. He was the teacher. He knew I had to learn, in order for me to go it alone and survive. It was no different than being in school with Miss Martin as the teacher —only this was a different classroom and a different subject.

From time to time our journey would take us close to a settlement and, if we were low on supplies, I would ride into the settlement and purchase what we needed. Joe would never go with me. Somehow he knew what might happen if he were to ride into some of the settlements.

As we traveled, we saved the hides from the animals that were taken for food. They were later sold or traded for supplies when stopping at a settlement. Our supplies were mostly beans, pork fat or a slab of bacon. If there was enough money, I would get some flour or each of us a loaf of bread. Always we rode miles away from any settlement if we planned to stop for the night. And if I were stopping at a settlement, Joe always looked for a good vantage point, where he would be able to watch me going and coming. That way, he made sure I wasn't being followed.

It was the middle of the month of April that Joe said he figured seven or eight weeks before we would reach the big river. We had been riding for several days since Joe told me this. We were moving alongside a hill, just below the ridge, when we spotted a small settlement nestled among tall trees in a valley far below. A stream ran close by.

We sat among the rocks, where we were well hidden, and watched for half an hour or more. We could make out an army post on the outskirts of the south side. There didn't seem to be much activity of any kind. We were in need of supplies, so we talked it over and decided I would backtrack a long ways, so I would be out of sight, and then drop down into the valley and ride in from the east. Joe would continue on west some four or five miles, and find a spot to wait until I caught up.

It was after midday when I rode into the settlement. Heavy clouds hung over the valley. It was very hot, and sweat rolled down my face. My shirt was soaked and stuck to my back. The air was heavy. It felt like a rain storm was in the making. There were buildings on each side of the street, but most looked like they had been boarded up for some time.

As I rode along the street, a very strange feeling hung over me. It made me uneasy. I had a feeling of being watched. This was not a place to be riding alone. It was too late now. My long gun lay cradled in my arm. I had my pistol tucked in my waistband and my shirttail hanging out covered it. I kept on riding, letting my eyes take in both sides of the street. I saw there were very few people, and the ones I did see paid no mind.

Strange place—very strange. I kept riding, and finally I came to an emporium store, stopping at the hitching post. I stepped down and tied up my mules. After a good look over, I walked up the steps onto the porch, then into the store. My long gun lay in my arm.

The only person I could see in the store was a middle-aged, fat, bald man working behind the counter. I walked over to where he stood. He didn't say a damn thing, just stared. I looked him in the eye and said I would like to buy some grub, twenty pounds of beans, a slab of bacon, ham hocks, and—if he had any bread—two loaves. He never taken his eyes off me.

"You got money?" he asked.

"I do! How much for the grub?"

"Three dollars."

After laying three dollars on the counter, I watched the man slowly go and gather the things I had asked for. He never turned his back on me once. I could sense something very wrong. After placing my order on the counter, he wrapped the meat in heavy paper, then nodded. I tossed my knapsack to him, and he shoved everything into it and picked up the money.

Picking up my sack, I turned to leave, then heard him say, "Which way you headed, young man?"

Turning my head a little toward him, I said, "West."

"West? To where?"

I then noticed another man standing just inside the doorway and to one side. He wasn't real tall, but had a very muscular build. "To the big river," I answered.

"What are you going to do there?"

"Work."

"Doing what?"

"On the river, for my uncle. Hell, if I don't soon get there, he'll be a-coming looking for me," I lied. I put my finger on the trigger of my gun and walked past the man in the doorway, and out onto the porch. I stopped and listened a few seconds, then heard one of them say, "You let him go?"

I hurried to where the mules were tied. After putting my things on the pack mule, I mounted and rode on west out of town.

Along the way, I saw a saloon, a gorge house and, off to one side in the distance, a small army encampment. As I rode, I kept my eyes on anything that moved and never taken my finger off the trigger of my gun. Again, I saw people. Again, they acted and seemed strange as I rode by. The place was giving me the spooks. I could tell something wasn't right.

I knew I would have to ride four or five miles west out of the settlement before I would dare head north to find Joe. I was sure he was watching from somewhere along the ridge, and I would have no trouble finding him. After rounding a bend in the road, I stopped and got down to piss and listen. I walked back to where I could see if anyone was following. I watched and rested for a while, and when I was sure I wasn't being trailed, I mounted and continued on for another mile or so before heading north.

I was almost to the ridge when I found the trail. Getting down, I led my mules and looked for any marking Joe might have left, and checked for his tracks. I hadn't gone far when I found his mark and knew he had gone by. Jumping back on my mule, I started after him, knowing he would find us a place for the night. I had no idea how far I had ridden when I noticed other fresh tracks that covered up some of Joe's. Getting down, I looked them over, and saw the tracks were made by shod horses. Checking closer, I was able to make out two different sets of tracks. I didn't like what I saw.

Jumping back on my mule, I followed the tracks and, to make it worse, the trail headed into a woods that was thick with tall trees. I knew it wouldn't be long before it would be dark here among the trees. I hadn't gone far when I saw what looked like more tracks. Stopping, I got down and taken a closer look. In the fading light, I was able to make out yet another shod horse track. That made the third one. *Now what the hell is going on?* I wondered.

I walked along the trail, trying to figure out what happened. It didn't take long for me to figure it out. There were three others riding with Joe now, and I had a feeling it wasn't for the good. Dark had closed in as I rode on. I had gone a piece farther when I got a whiff of wood smoke. I wasn't sure of my thoughts now, so I stopped and slowly slid down from the mule. Taking hold of its bridle, I led my mules, taking one or two steps at a time and listening—listening to every sound, keeping my long gun at the ready as I slowly made my way along the trail.

Slowly, slowly, I inched my way through the dark, not knowing what lay ahead. I didn't know who was leading who, me leading my mules or the mules leading me. We just topped a rise when I caught a glimpse of light. I was able to make out a very faint light flickering in the distance. I knew right away it was someone's campfire.

Moving a bit closer, I could tell it wasn't a fire Joe would make. It was now dark here in the woods, and I tried to see through the darkness and figure out what to do. I just knew something wasn't right. Deciding not to go on and take a chance, I led my mules several hundred feet off the trail, where I tied each to a small tree. I checked my pistol and long gun, and started the slow stalk towards the campfire. When I was within 200 feet or so, I got down on hands and knees and crawled, creeping inch by inch, foot by foot, feeling with my hands out in front of me for anything that might make a noise or alert whoever may be at the campfire.

Finally, I came to a tree that had fallen some years before and was mostly decayed. I crawled along the rotten trunk on the blind side. I was able to get within 30 feet of where three men, dressed in gray army uniforms, were standing around the fire. I crawled under a bush that had grown up among the rotten wood and lay watching, but didn't see anything of Joe.

Then, one of the men said, "I wonder what gotten the other one. He would have shown up by now, don't you think?"

"Yeah, I reckon so," the others said.

Then, one of the men moved and I saw Joe. His arms were pulled back and tied behind a tree. A rope was wrapped tightly over his chest and around the tree, up over his shoulders, binding him to the tree.

As the soldiers talked, one of them said, "Let's hang him right now, and let him for the buzzards."

The other two said no, they had to take him back to the post in the morning and let the sarge do the hanging, to show the townspeople that they mean what they say.

After throwing more wood on the fire, one of them pulled out a bottle and passed it around. "I wish that other son-of-a-bitch would show up. Then we would have the two of them for the sarge," one of them said.

I lay the short distance away, not moving. Thoughts were racing through my mind, not knowing what I should do. I knew I didn't stand a chance against the three of them, if I tried something. I realized my only chance was to wait—wait until they went to sleep, or got drunk and fell asleep.

Just then, I felt something on my legs. Knowing what it was, I froze, not daring to move. I felt it crawl up over my ass onto my back. I was paralyzed, and stopped breathing as the snake slithered up over my shoulder, across my neck and head. I could tell it was large as it crawled over onto the rotten wood, and then disappeared into the darkness. Slowly, I taken in a breath of air, and finally got up enough nerve to raise my head.

A few minutes earlier, the men were cursing about something, but I couldn't hear what. Peering over the log now, I saw them all sitting around the fire. One had a stick and was poking the fire as they passed the bottles of whiskey around. They weren't doing much talking now, just drinking. I could see they were getting drunk.

It wasn't long before the one I taken to be in charge said, "We better get some sleep. Frank, you take the first watch."

"Why me?"

"Damn you, Frank! Because I say so. You hear me?"

"All right … asshole!"

"What did you say?"

"I said all right!"

"You better have!" He and the other soldier moved back away from the fire, and unrolled their bed rolls and lay down.

The one called Frank threw more wood onto the fire, then sat down and reached into his bed roll and came out with another bottle. He put it to his mouth and took a long pull, downing a quarter of it in one slurp.

As the fire blazed up, I could see Joe was tied—rather, hanging there on the tree head down—I didn't know if he was alive or not. It was a warm, very humid night, and I could feel it wouldn't be long before it rained as I lay there on the damp, musky, rotting wood, waiting. Sweat rolled down my face. I didn't know why they kept such a big fire, except for light.

While I kept a close watch on the one called Frank, I put a plan together in my head. I knew what I must do, but I would have to wait for my time. The other two were snoring now, and Frank had leaned back against a tree. As I watched, I would see his head drop and he would jerk it back up, rub his eyes, and take another slug from his bottle. Finally, his head stayed down.

I watched a while longer, and saw Joe's head move a little. He knew I was there, and he was telling me it was time. I made my move, working my way into position. It wasn't very far to crawl before I would be behind the tree Frank was leaning against. As I crawled along, I found a rock about the size of my fist. Keeping it in my hand, I crept up behind the tree. Frank just sat his bottle down. As his head bobbed back and forth, my left hand clasped over his mouth, pulling it back. At the same time my right hand came down hard with the rock on the side of his head. He went limp. I held him there, until I was sure he wouldn't fall over.

Then, reaching down, I pulled his pistol out, then the knife he carried. Kneeling low behind the tree, I watched and waited to see if there was any movement from the other two. There was none—just the sound of the them snoring. Taking the knife, I crept over to the closest one, and placed my left hand over his mouth and nose. I sank the knife deep into his chest and held him down until all movement stopped. The other man slept a good 20 feet away. After watching for any sign of movement, I slowly crept over to where he lay. His back was towards me. Reaching with my right hand, I did as I had the other, and plunged the knife into his back, and held him until he didn't move. Moving my hand from over his mouth, he gasped, and in a whisper said, "You son-of-a-bitch," then went limp.

Looking around, I saw the one called Frank was still leaning against the tree. Getting up, I went over to where he was out. Taking his pistol, I started to place it in his right hand, then saw he was left-handed, by the way he wore his holster. Putting it in his left hand, I placed the end of the barrel under his chin and squeezed the trigger. The right side of his head disappeared. I let him fall on his right side, then placed the rock under his head, and laid the bloody knife down beside the empty whiskey bottle.

Shaking badly now from what I had just done, I made my

way over to Joe, trying not to throw up as I cut him down. He blinked his eyes several times, then went limp in my arms.

Half carrying, half dragging, I got him over by the fire and laid him down. Getting one of their canteens, I held his head up and poured a little water into his mouth. He swallowed it. I kept giving him more until he had enough. Then I let him lay back down, and sat beside him, trembling, and looking at what had taken place as tears rolled down my face. Finally, I pulled myself together and could see it was getting on toward midnight. I knew I had to keep on moving. I checked Joe, and could see he was still breathing, but hadn't come around very much.

Standing up, I looked around for their horses. Hearing them, I made my way to where they were, and found they had tied Joe's mules with theirs. Taking hold of their bridles, I led them over by the fire and tied them up, then went looking for my mules. I had some trouble, stumbling around in the dark, before I found them and led them back to the fire.

I tried getting Joe up, but he didn't want to move. After throwing wood on the fire and letting it blaze, I could see why Joe didn't want to move. The three soldiers had badly beaten and tortured him. It looked like they had used burning hot sticks, by the way he looked. His face, arms, chest—and his pants—had burned holes in them.

Looking over at the dead bodies, I no longer had any feeling of sorrow for what I had done. Now, all I wanted was to get the hell out of this damn place. Moving Joe's mules in closer to him, I kept pleading and begging for him to sit. Finally, with my help, he did. I had already gotten his coat and slicker. After getting his coat on him, I taken his hands and pulled him to his feet. Joe wasn't a big man, so I didn't have much trouble getting him on his mule. Once there, I put his slicker on him, and secured everything. Grabbing the reins to Joe's mule, I was about to jump on mine, when I heard a *whooshing* sound overhead.

I looked up in time to see a white bird fly off above us and into the darkness. Jumping on my mule, I didn't think anything about it as I kicked the animal into moving. I felt drops of rain start to fall, and yelled at Joe's mules to get moving. We started off into the darkness.

I kept Joe and his mule reined in as close as I dared. A steady rain came down now, and I was damn glad for it, even though I was soaked to the bone. I knew the rain would cover our tracks, and that would be most important now. It was so damn dark, I couldn't see where the trail was. Knowing our mules could see a hellish sight better than I could, I gave them their head and kept prodding them on, knowing they would follow the trail.

I stopped from time to time to check on Joe and give him water. I found his slicker was keeping him fairly dry. I could tell he was hurting badly by the way he rode, all slumped over, barely hanging on. At times, I wondered how he did. I knew there was nothing I could do for him, and decided the best thing to do was to keep pushing on. *Pushing on to where?* I didn't know. I couldn't think of nothing else, except to keep moving, putting as much distance between us and that town as possible.

We rode throughout the night, and I could tell by the way the mules were acting that they were wearing down. It wasn't light yet, when the mules stopped dead in their tracks, and wouldn't move. Jumping down, I pulled on their bridles, but they stood fast. Then I thought I heard Joe.

Going to his side, I could hear him mutter very weakly, "Go north, boy."

I told him okay. Walking ahead a piece, I found the trail split three directions. Returning, I checked on Joe, and asked if he wanted anything. He shook his head no. I said, "Okay, Joe, hang on."

I got back on my mule, and nudged it a little. "Let's go, Curse."

We taken the north trail, and before I knew it, we were climbing. I had to get down and walk, in order to save the mules, knowing there was no way but to let Joe ride and hope for the best.

16

I had no idea how far we had come, or anything else, for that matter. I was beat. My body wanted rest, as did the mules. Yet, I knew there was no way. I must keep moving. The trail seemed to have leveled some, and I could tell we were higher.

Stopping to rest the mules as well as Joe and myself, I dug in my pack and came up with some of the bread I had bought earlier. I tried getting Joe to eat some, but he refused, shaking his head. I stood there beside Joe and gulped down the bread, along with some water. With my arm around him, I finally got him to drink some water.

My shoes were soaked. I was soaked. I was covered with mud to my ass. I was so damn tired and beat, I was shaking. I just knew I couldn't go on, yet I knew I must. And to make things worse, flashes started running through my mind of what had happened earlier.

The rain was still coming down as I grabbed hold of the two lead mules and forced myself to push on. I was crying, tears running down my cheeks, along with the rain. I felt happiness because of the rain, and yet so alone—so alone and scared—afraid of what might happen to Joe. Afraid from the flashes going on in my head of what I did, what I got myself into.

It was beginning to break light now, and it felt so good to see where I was going. I saw the trail was just below a large, rocky ridge. I knew I had to find a place to hole up, and see how bad Joe was, and for us and the mules to rest. The rocky ridge was some hundred yards off the trail, and looked like it might be a good place to find a hideout.

I was keeping my eye on the rocky ledge, looking for a way up there, and wasn't watching the trail. Hearing a noise out front, jerking my eyes to the trail, I was just in time to see a very tall Indian step out of the bushes onto the trail 40 feet in front of us, scaring the hell out of me. I froze, not knowing what to expect. Staring at him, I saw he had no weapons and was motioning me to come. I stayed put, slowly reaching for my pistol, then he spoke.

I knew enough to know he was speaking Cherokee, and wanted us to come with him. He would help us.

Slowly, I walked toward him, keeping my hand on my gun. When I was in reach of him, he taken hold of Joe's mules and looked Joe over, then said something I didn't recognize. Then, the bushes beside the trail opened up and were held back by five more braves. He led Joe and his mules through the opening and said, "Come, boy, I help."

I followed, not knowing what to expect, and too tired to give a damn. After passing through, the bushes were let back in place and all tracks covered. The others caught up with us. Two ran up beside Joe, to steady him with their hands. One taken hold of my mule and the other two took ahold of my arms, helping me and hurrying me along. It was like going through a big hole in the bushes. They were so thick overhead that hardly any light came down through. I had no concept of how far we had come when, suddenly, I realized we were under a very huge rock ledge, maybe 150 feet long, 70 or so feet deep, and four times as high as I was.

We were taken to about half its length, where a hot bed of coals lay close to the back wall. It was hot and dry under here, with not much light. Four of the braves carefully taken Joe down from his mule. As the tall one gave the orders of what to do, they prepared a bed between the fire and the wall, and lay Joe on it. Getting some of their blankets, they covered Joe.

The tall one came and motioned for me to sit by the fire. "Take shoes off. They dry," he told me.

I did as he said. Taking them, he placed them by the fire, then walked away. I stood so the heat from the fire would dry my clothes. Even though it was very warm, the fire felt good. I watched as the tall one motioned and spoke in Cherokee. Soon they taken our pack mules and unloaded them, putting everything against the wall close to Joe, then taking anything that was wet and laying it out to dry.

At times, I was able to make out some of what was being said. The tall one pointed to two of the others and said, "Go watch." The two walked away from where I stood. I soon saw them disappear into a crevice in the rocks. Later, I was to learn they had a place up higher, where they could watch the trail, to see if anyone was coming.

The tall one had gone and sat down by Joe, and was talking and chanting to him. I was so damn beat that while I stood there, letting my clothes dry, I nodded off and damn near fell into the fire. After that, I decided I'd best lie down, even though I didn't want to. My clothes were fairly dry, so I gathered up my bed roll and lay it out a few feet from where Joe lay, with my head towards his, hoping I might hear what was being said. Instead, I fell asleep before my eyes closed.

It was sometime in the middle of the night that I awakened and had to pee. Sitting up, I looked around and was bewildered at first, not knowing where I was, until I saw one of the braves sitting by the fire, his head down as though dozing. Then I remembered where I was. As I stood, the brave's head jerked up. He watched as I walked off into the bushes. As I stood there peeing, I could feel a fine, misty rain still coming down. Upon returning, the brave motioned me to the fire, where he handed me a bowl of meat and broth and some kind of meal cake.

Sitting down by the fire, I began eating. He sat and watched every move I made. When I finished, he motioned with his hand and asked, "More?" I motioned, "No. Enough." The light from the small, flickering fire bounced off the rocks in back, and was just enough that I was able to see the other braves bedded down here and there.

I got up and went to Joe, and knelt down beside him. He seemed to be breathing good and felt warm, so I moved over to my bed roll and lay down. The brave watched until I covered myself up, then he lay down and pulled his blanket over him. I lay awake with thoughts running through my mind, remembering that it was early the morning before that Joe and I had broken camp and how, in that short amount of time, everything changed so much. I had barely stopped moving, with nothing much to eat, for more than a day, until I laid down here somewhere around midday.

Thoughts of the soldiers, Joe, the rock, knife, pistol—all raced through my mind—and now this. Were these Indians helping us, or did they take us captive? It was too much. I was so tired that I drifted back to sleep.

It was late morning when I opened my eyes again. Looking around, I saw braves here and there. After sitting up, I crawled over beside Joe. He opened his eyes, then reached out and taken my hand and said, "My boy." Then his eyes closed.

Placing his hand down beside him, I stood up and looked for my shoes. They had been placed on top of my things. I walked over and pulled them on and, feeling they were dry, then headed for the bushes to relieve myself. Returning, a brave motioned me to the fire, where he handed me a bowl with more meat and broth and more meal cakes.

Sitting down, I ate, then he handed me a bowl of hot tea and motioned for me to drink. I put it to my mouth and tasted it. It was so damn bitter, I almost gagged. He motioned to drink. I drank it as fast as I could, then got up and went and sat on my bed roll, close to Joe, and watched him. I could tell he was asleep, but his breathing came in jerks and was very heavy.

After sitting a while, I noticed the brave who had been taking care of me was watching. Finally, he came over and sat down close to Joe and me. Looking at Joe, he did some kind of ritual, then turned to me and said, "I Chief Long Feather. You! What name called?"

"Nathan," I answered.

"You white?"

"Yeah."

"You and chief friend!"

"Yeah. His name is Joe."

"No! White man name! He Chief Golden Eagle!"

"Chief?" I said.

"Yeah."

"You … Chief … good friend?"

"Yes."

"You … Chief … make long journey to-geth-er?"

"Yes!"

"You name?"

"Nathan."

"Na-t-h-a-n. Chief not good." Then he said, "Chief Golden Eagle mighty medicine man."

"How come he never told me?" I wondered out loud.

"Chief … he too many proud. He not tell!"

"Where was he, Chief?"

"Long time ago past, he Chief in Iroquois n-a-t-i-o-n. Delaware, Wyandot, I not know. Iroquois many tribes big. He chief in big tribe many others! White man kill big many of tribe. A few and chief get away. My father know Chief Golden Eagle. Good friend, he say. Best medicine chief Golden Eagle. Chief Golden Eagle tired. Soon hundred summer, hundred winter live!"

"Chief, what are you going to do with us?" I asked. "Are we captives?"

"No! Good friend of chief. You brave warrior. No captive!" Then he said, "Rain stop now. Soon be dark. Other braves come to watch over settlement. When light comes, we go Cherokee hideout. Get medicine. Maybe Chief Golden Eagle come good, ugh! I go. You need rest more. We make talk more soon!"

The next morning, I was awakened before light and given stuff to eat. Chief Long Feather had Joe sitting up and was giving him broth mixed with meal. After eating, two of the braves brought my and Joe's mules and helped get them packed and ready to go. I wondered how we were going to handle Joe.

Chief Long Feather had it taken care of. His braves had fashioned a carrier, then, wrapping Joe in blankets, they laid him on it. Once the chief was sure everything was taken care of, he taken his horse and one of the braves and led the way. Four braves carried Joe on the carrier. I was motioned to follow, leading my and Joe's mules. The remaining brave brought up the rear, leading their mounts and the two remaining animals.

The chief wound us through a maze of rocks and paths. Finally, we came out on top. Here the land was rolly with very few trees. The chief mounted up and led the way. Everyone followed. The four braves carrying Joe started trotting, and soon were chanting. Every so often, they changed places, never stopping their trotting or chanting, always four on foot, two riding. Hour after hour they did this, only stopping long enough to eat and relieve their bodies. I was hard pressed in keeping up with our four animals.

It was late afternoon when we arrived at their village or hideout, as they called it, and were met by another chief and some of the people as we entered. The other chief said something to Chief Long Feather, then taken a look at Joe. Turning, he said something to the other people standing there, and motioned. Some of the braves came and taken Joe and carried him away. A dozen or so women followed.

I had gotten down from my mule and was standing there, waiting to see what was going to happen. Chief Long Feather talked with the other chief for a while, then walked over to where I stood.

He pointed to the other chief. "Him chieftain, chief over all chiefs of village."

The other chief looked me over, then said to Chief Long Feather, "Boy fine boy. Strong. You take boy. Care for him," then turned and walked away.

Chief Long Feather said, "You come, Na-t-h-a-n. Follow."

I followed with our mules as he led the way. Some small

children and older people stared and a few dogs yapped at the mules' heels. One of the dogs got too close and a mule gave it a kick. The dog went rolling and yelping. The kids that were running beside pointed at the dog and laughed. Most of the kids were naked or close to it. Even some of the grown-up people were mostly naked.

We walked to the far outer edge of the village, where a dozen women were preparing a wickiup by a small stream. Stopping, Chief Long Feather pointed to the wickiup and said, "Chief Golden Eagle stay here till good. You, Na-t-h-a-n, stay here, too, till Chief Golden Eagle good." Putting a big hand on my shoulder, he said, "I get squaws and young braves help you with mules and work." Walking away, he said, "Chief come, we talk more."

I stood there, dumbfounded, not knowing what to do. Looking around, I saw a few of the women had Joe down by the stream and were giving him a bath. When they were through bathing him, they wrapped him in a clean blanket and carried him into the wickiup. Some of the others had already unloaded our mules and carried our things inside and put them along the back wall.

After the women left, I went in the wickiup. Joe was lying on the bed the women had prepared for him. As I sat down beside him, he opened his eyes, then placed his hand on mine. Holding it, after a while, in a very weak voice, he said, "You'll go a long way in life, my son."

I couldn't answer.

It was almost dark when Chief Long Feather came in, followed by two women who brought us some food. I moved to my bed roll and sat. They handed me a bowl of stew, corn cakes and some kind of tea. I sat, eating, and watched as they held Joe up and fed him some stew and gave him tea. When I was through eating and Joe would eat no more, Chief Long Feather motioned them out. He then sat down beside Joe, legs crossed, hands on his knees, looking at Joe. He didn't speak, just looked.

I was sitting on the opposite side, across from him, on my bed roll blanket. As I looked at him, I noticed for the first time he was a good-looking man, tall, thin, very musuclar through the shoulders and arms, dark-skinned, with long black hair that hung in braids. A long feather was fashioned on the headband.

Then, another brave came in and knelt down beside Chief Long Feather, next to Joe. Chief Long Feather spoke. "Chief

Golden Eagle, this is Little Owl, medicine man. Much wise. Make Chief Golden Eagle good … well." The chief then moved over and sat down beside me.

When the chief first came in, he had brought a vessel that contained fat and a chunk of hide and fur for a wick, which he now lit. It gave off a nice light that filled the wickiup. I was able to see what the medicine man was doing. First, he lit some herbs that he had in a vessel. Then, as the smoke rose, he made circular motions all over Joe's body and, at the same time, shook a gourd that made a noise. He never stopped his chanting. He was then joined by two other medicine men, who did their rituals while the first one rubbed some sort of ointment all over Joe's body.

This went on into the night. Finally, they stopped and gathered their things, then left. Chief Long Feather looked at me and said, "Chief Golden Eagle not good. I go. Talk more when sun up." With that, he got up and went out, leaving me alone with Joe.

After he left, I moved close to Joe and put my hand on his forehead. He felt cold. I taken his hand in mine and it felt cold, even though it was very warm in the wickiup. I gathered up everything that would help keep him warm and laid it over him.

17

I had been sitting a long while beside Joe, holding his hand close to me, when a strange feeling crept over me. I realized he hadn't moved in all this time. It sent shivers running up and down my spine. I knew then that Joe—Chief Golden Eagle—would be going soon to the spirit world. Tears rolled down my cheeks as I held onto his hand.

I had no recognition of how long I sat there in that position, when I was jarred back to reality from a noise outside. Getting up, I went to see what was making the noise. When I stepped out, I saw a large, white bird fly from the top of the wickiup.

I stood and watched as it flew off into the darkness. Then, for the first time, I realized the bird had some connection either to Joe or to myself. It was really warm out, and the night sky was clear and filled with stars. Not a sound came from anywhere. I stood, looking at the stars, and thinking of what to do. I decided I would get clean clothes and go bath.

A short while later, as I walked to the stream, a lone owl hooted somewhere off in the distance. I stopped and listened, then wondered if what I had heard about the owl was really true.

Reaching the stream, I undressed and waded in the water, which wasn't very deep, but cool and refreshing. As I scooped it up over my body, I soaped up, then rinsed off, and stood on the bank and let the warm air dry me. After putting my clean clothes on, I returned to the wickiup and dropped my dirty clothes on the ground, and went inside. The little vessel of oil was still giving off light, so I let it burn and checked Joe. He was still cold, and his breathing was very shallow.

I lay down on my bed roll and closed my eyes, not wanting to think about anything. The next thing I knew, Chief Long Feather was shaking me. "Come, Na-t-h-a-n, it's sun up."

I sat up, rubbing my eyes and shaking my head.

"Come, Na-t-h-a-n, you, I talk now."

I got up and followed him outside, where two women

were waiting. They handed me a bowl of mush with some kind of oil over it. I taken it, and followed the chief as he walked to the stream, then up along it. Once away from the wickiup, he stopped and told me to sit.

I sat down by the stream, and he sat a few feet away. For a long time, he sat and looked at me, not saying anything. I had finished eating and reached the bowl into the stream and got some water to drink. Looking over, I saw the chief had a blank look on his face, like he didn't know how to say what he wanted to. He saw I was becoming uneasy, then he spoke.

"Na-t-h-a-n, I think you know Chief Golden Eagle not get good. Medicine man say Chief Golden Eagle much sick inside, not can make good."

I nodded my head yes, and said, "I know."

"Medicine man say you good spirit. People in settlement bad. Army warriors at settlement bad. No like Indian. Hang when catch. We watch over settlement all time. Army take people and make work in mine, I hear. Not know! Braves see you ride out of settlement. Not Chief Golden Eagle. Army not hurt you. Why? You good spirit, maybe make army afraid."

I didn't know what to say. Then we heard the low beating of a drum coming from outside the wickiup.

Chief Long Feather said, "Come."

We ran back to the wickiup. I handed my bowl to a woman as the chief taken me by the arm and led me into the wickiup. He knelt down beside Joe, pulling me down with him. I was kneeling by Joe's side. He opened his eyes and reached his hand out and placed it in mine.

In barely a whisper, he said, "My son, you good friend to Old Joe. Friend of Old Joe, you done right by Old Joe. Now Old Joe give you good medicine."

The medicine man, who was kneeling on the other side, reached down and taken the necklace from around Joe's neck, and handed it to Chief Long Feather. Outside, a drum was being beaten ever so low.

Chief Long Feather reached over and placed the necklace over my head. I barely heard Joe say, "Always wear. Never take it off."

Everyone was silent. Then, we heard Chief Golden Eagle gasp and his hand went limp in my hand. His head rolled to one side. I knew he had gone. The tears streamed down my cheeks. The medicine man started his ritual of chants, to ward off evil spirits. Chief Long Feather stood and taken hold of my arm. He pulled me to my feet, then led me outside.

"Come!" he said. "We walk."

Looking at him, I could see his eyes were filled with tears also. The drums continued their mournful rhythm as we walked down along the stream in silence for a short distance. Then, stopping, he said, "Na-t-h-a-n, medicine men make Chief Golden Eagle for burying. It now time."

Returning to the wickiup, I saw they had moved Joe outside, and had wrapped him in a blanket, along with most of his possessions. Everything was tied, and they had laid him on a carrier. The chieftain and medicine men stood at his head, and two other chiefs stood on each side of the carrier. As we walked up, the chieftain nodded, and the chief bent down, picking up the carrier with Joe on it. The chieftain led the way to the burial ground.

Chief Long Feather had taken hold of my arm as we walked behind. A woman had taken hold of his left hand, accompanied by a boy about my age and a girl a year or two younger. There were many others from the village. Once there, I saw a hole had been scooped out of the ground several feet deep. Joe—Chief Golden Eagle—was laid in the grave and the medicine men did their spiritual burial ritual. The grave was then filled in and stones placed over the top.

Chief Long Feather returned to the village, and I went back to my wickiup and got my things together. I planned on leaving in the morning.

Later that afternoon, I went and checked on my mules, and found them among their horses outside the village in a meadow. Five older boys were watching over them. I went back to the wickiup and sat by the stream. I was thinking about Joe while watching some small fish swimming here and there. I was feeling sad, knowing Joe would no longer be with me.

Thoughts about what I was going to do without him crept into my mind, yet I knew I had to go on. I wondered about the soldiers at the settlement, if they knew, and would they come looking for me. I was deep in my thoughts when Chief Long Feather walked up and sat down beside me. I looked at him, but didn't say anything. Neither did he.

I sat, tossing bits of grass in the water, and watching them float away. He leaned back on one elbow, watching me, chewing on a stem of dry grass. We sat a long time in silence before he spoke.

"Is thoughts troubling my friend?" he asked.

I didn't answer at first, then said, "Yes."

"What trouble, friend?"

I shrugged my shoulders, and said, "I don't know. Maybe. I guess I'm going to miss my friend."

"I know you miss friend. Chief Golden Eagle be with you forever. Take care of friend—*you!* What else on friend's mind?"

I shrugged my shoulders several times, not wanting to talk about it. "Nothing," I said.

"Young friend not want talk. Chief Long Feather know what trouble young friend's mind."

Looking at him, I realized there was no hiding my feelings from this man. He knew, just like Joe knew. Shaking my head, I finally said, "It's what happened on the trail that night that keeps coming back, making me feel bad."

At first, he didn't say anything. For a few minutes, he just sat, staring at the water flowing by in the stream. Slowly turning his head and looking at me, he said in a comforting voice, "My young friend, you feel what you did that night was not right. Spirit say you do right! You do right by Chief Golden Eagle. You, my young friend, do right by you! That night, if soldier army catch you—you, my friend—and Chief Golden Eagle both be dead now! I ask Spirit! Spirit say you do right now. You live on! Na-t-h-a-n, you not feel bad now on."

I sat with my chin propped on my hands, listening and thinking over what he was saying. I realized everything he said was right.

"Chiefs say you, friend, want you stay, not have many young people. My friend, that many tribes here now." He held up six fingers. "Many get lost from tribes when white settlers and soldiers drive from land. Now here!"

"Six tribes? Why six, chief?"

"If chiefs not get land back, they go west sometime."

"All of you'se go west?"

"Sometime, maybe."

"Chief Long Feather, I will be leaving come morning, so as not to bring any trouble or harm to you and your people. And besides, I want to get to the big river."

He nodded. "If that your wish, then you must go as Spirit wish. You stay two more days for Chief Golden Eagle. Yeah, he say before die, yeah!"

"I will stay two more days, as he said."

"Good, my young friend. Tonight not have dance like custom. Make much noise. Hear long, long way. You come chief wickiup. You eat. We sit around fire, smoke pipe, talk."

That evening, I went to Chief Long Feather's wickiup and ate with him and his woman, Shining Flower, and their two children, the boy and girl I saw with them at the burial. Later on, we all went to the main wickiup or lodge, where meetings were held. The other chief and medicine men had gathered, along with some of the other people. The chiefs sat in a semi-circle. The medicine men sat on their right, and everyone else sat in a semi-circle facing them.

A small fire had been lit in the center. I was told to sit by Shining Flower and their two children. After the medicine men did the ritual, the chieftain lit his pipe. It was passed among the chief and medicine men, then another pipe was lit and passed among the rest of the people, stopping several times to be refilled.

When it was passed to Shining Flower, she and the children each had a draw. Shining Flower passed it to me.

"Me?" Hell, I never smoked. I didn't know what to expect. Like a dummy, I taken a big draw and damn near choked and started coughing and couldn't stop.

Shining Flower taken the pipe and passed it on, then handed me a gourd of water. After several drinks, the coughing stopped and everyone shouted and laughed. The talking and storytelling went on. After a while, the pipes were passed around once more. This time I did as Shining Flower told me —just a little. I did, and it worked. She handed me the water anyway.

A little while after I had the second draw, I began feeling a little funny—maybe sick—I didn't know. I was sitting next to Shining Flower. I started to get up. She reached over and pulled me back down. I tried several times, and every time she would pull me back down. Everyone got quiet. The chiefs were staring at me, along with everyone else. The chieftain motioned and said something to Chief Long Feather.

Chief Long Feather stood up and pointed at me. "Young friend. You not like? Maybe young friend have trouble?"

"Yes," I said, "I'm feeling funny. I need to go out—outside!"

Chief Long Feather looked at the chieftain, and the chieftain nodded. Chief Long Feather motioned to Shining Flower. I remember him saying, "Take young friend to wickiup."

As I started to stand up, I fell backwards. Shining Flower and the boy and girl helped me to my feet and led me outside. As soon as I got some fresh air, I felt better. I told Shining Flower

I'd be okay now. "I'm going back to my wickiup."

Taking hold of my arm, she said, "No! You must come to wickiup with me." I didn't protest as she led me to their wickiup. Once inside, she said, "Sit."

I did, while she got a gourd of hot herb tea and handed it to me.

"You drink!"

As I sipped the hot tea, I couldn't help thinking these people seemed to always have a small fire going with a pot of tea or water hanging over it, keeping it hot. The wickiup was dark, except for the small fire that burned, and a clay bowl with oil and a wick that burned low gave off hardly any light at all. I didn't hear any of the children and guessed they had gone to bed.

Then, Shining Flower stepped in front of where I sat and pointed, then said, "You sleep there." She had placed some hides and a blanket close by the doorway.

I finished my tea, then went and lay on the hides, and pulled the blanket over me. I must have fallen right off to sleep, for I never heard Chief Long Feather come in or anything else until morning, when Chief Long Feather said, "Come, young friend, Na-t-h-a-n, sun up, we eat."

I sat up, not knowing for sure where I was, then remembered smoking the pipe the night before that made me feel funny, and Shining Flower and kids bringing me to their wickiup, and the hot tea she gave me, which must have knocked me out.

Getting up, I went outside. The sun was shining brightly, and the smell of food made me hungry. The chief was eating. I sat beside him and was given food. Chief Long Feather said, "You not like smoke pipe?"

"I never smoked before," I said, "and it made me feel funny—like sick."

"Oho! Make funny? Sick?"

"I didn't mean for to make trouble," I said.

"Ugh! Not trouble. Make sick okay."

I told him I would be leaving the following morning.

"When?"

"Early."

"Ugh! You stay, if want."

"Thanks. It's best I go." After I was through eating, I returned to my wickiup, and spent the rest of the day getting my things ready. I checked on my mules, bringing them closer to the wickiup and putting them on the other side of the stream. Later that evening, a couple of women brought me things to eat.

I was up early the next morning, and was getting things packed on my mule, when Chief Long Feather rode up with Shining Flower and three braves, who were leading Joe's mules.

Chief Long Feather said, "Why you not take Chief Golden Eagle's mules?"

While I finished packing my mule, I thought, *What am I going to tell him?* When I finished tying things off, I looked up at the chief and said, "Chief Long Feather, I know Chief Golden Eagle would want *you* to have his mules. Spirit say, 'Nathan, four animals are much too hard for you to take care of.' So, Chief Long Feather, I give them to you."

Chief Long Feather nodded his head in thanks, then motioned the braves to take the two mules away.

"Chief and braves see young friend to river. Make sure no trouble!"

"Thanks, chief, but there's no need. I think I can find my way."

"Chief know! Shining Flower say, 'Chief, go with young friend to river. Make sure safe.' You follow chief. Go now!"

The chief led the way with Shining Flower right behind. I followed.

It wasn't long before the three braves came riding up. Two fell in back of me, and the other rode up with the chief. It was early evening on the third day when we arrived at the Illinois River. The braves scouted around and soon found a nice, safe place to spend the night.

The next morning, we were up early and, after eating, we said our final departing farewells. They wished me the best, and said for the spirits to watch over me, and I wished them the same. I stood and watched as Chief Long Feather, Shining Flower and the braves started the return trip to their village.

After they were out of sight, I started my journey down along the Illinois River, feeling all alone. I was alone now, and I now knew it. I knew things were going to be a lot different now that Joe was no longer with me. I also realized I would have to rely on everything Joe had taught me.

As I rode, I thought about this being my first day alone. I thought about what Joe had taught me—to stay off the main trails, stay away from rivers as much as possible, he would say, but always know where you're at. I rode on, working my way farther south, so that I was off the main trails and away from the river.

As evening came, I looked for a place to hole up and spend the night. I finally found a place that felt safe and was well hidden, with plenty of food for my mules. I made camp, keeping my fire very small, as Joe had taught me. After I was through eating, I put the fire out and bedded down. The night sky was still light enough that I could see my mules from where I lay.

For a long time I lay, listening to every sound, and wondering what it was, and wishing Mr. Joe was still with me, or that I had a dog to keep watch. I thought about what I was doing, where I was going, and would I have made it this far if it hadn't been for Joe? I thought about what month it was. I could see the leaves were turning color, and decided it was getting late in the month of the nut moon, and wondered how long it would be until it got cold.

I knew very little about the weather this far south. I had my long gun laying beside me, under my blanket, and my pistol in my hand as I drifted off to sleep.

18

I got to Starved Rock in the fall of 1818, out of supplies and no money. I knew it was too late to go on without supplies, and getting some was next to impossible. Besides, winter was not so far away. I don't recall what month it was, but it really didn't matter. All I knew was I had to find some kind of work, so I could get something to eat and maybe make it through the winter.

I had located a wooded area with a grassy meadow at its edge, not far from the settlement. I found the thickest place in the wooded area and built a leanto big enough to hold all my things, a few traps, a change of clothes, my winter coat and hat, blankets, musket, pistol, and myself. The tarps that I had everything bundled in to tie on my pack mule I would use to close the front of my leanto, to make it warmer and keep out the weather. The leanto was covered with long, dry grass and cattail reeds lapped over each other, layer after layer, then a layer of leaves, then more layers of grass, until everything was more than a foot thick. The leanto was very warm, and kept out the weather. In the meantime, I would go into town, looking for some kind of work.

After a few days, I found some odd jobs I could do in exchange for something to eat. There were times when the food wasn't too good or I didn't get enough. When this happened, I would rely on the things I trapped or shot, and wild plants, to keep me going.

I don't recall how long this went on, but one day, when I was looking for work, I overheard some men talking about the blacksmith needing a stable man. Before I could ask, the men parted and rode off. My mule was tied to the hitching post across the way. I hurried to the mule, untied it, and jumped onto her back and rode after the one man.

I caught up to him, and rode up beside him. He looked over at me and, before he could say anything, I said, "Excuse me, mister, could you tell me where there is a blacksmith?"

The man just looked at me, then let go with a stream of tobacco juice from his mouth that I thought would never stop. When it did, he spoke in a deep, soft voice. "Due east, son, due east. Not far." Then, he turned his horse to the left, and rode off.

At the time, I didn't know that this man and I would meet again—soon. I kept riding east, and soon I was out of town. I followed the wagon road only a short piece, when I saw what I thought to be the blacksmith shop a half-mile ahead, it was built on a rise, on the south side of the river. As I got closer, I could see it was built mostly of logs and stone laid up for walls. It had a sod roof, and on the one side the roof and ground met. On the other side was a room built on. A house was built on another rise, several hundred feet or so west and south of the shop, and a wagon road went to it.

I didn't see anyone around, so I kept on riding, until I was at the shop. I got off and tied my mule, and then opened the door and stepped in. There was no one around, so I went back out, jumped on my mule, and started down the road when I saw a man and girl come out of the house and stand on the porch. I turned my mule around, and rode up to the house, got off, tied up at the hitching post, and walked over to where they were.

My straw-colored hair hung over my shoulders, and a slight breeze was blowing it across my face. I wasn't wearing my hat, and I knew I didn't look that good. I stopped before I got to the porch, and nodded.

The man said in a sharp voice, "I'm closed on Sunday. What is it you want?"

"I am Nathan," I said. "I need work, so I can make it through the winter. I hear you need someone. Can you help me out?"

He was a short man, maybe five-foot-six, not much more, with brown hair chopped short, and a little on the plump side. The girl stood there beside him, staring at me like there was something wrong. She was about five feet, slim, with long red hair and a few freckles on her face, maybe sixteen or so. Her father looked me over for what seemed a long time, then spoke. "I'm Mr. Henry Jakobes. I own the blacksmith shop. I could use a man, but ... but you're just a boy. Where do your folks live?"

"Near Fort Pitt."

"Where are you staying?"

"I have a leanto out on the other side of town, in the thick woods that I stay in. Nobody knows where it's at."

"How old are you?"

"I'm 15, but I'm big for my age, about six feet, maybe 165 pounds, and I'm strong and can work like any man."

He kept looking at me as though he was thinking. "I don't know, I don't think so."

I turned and walked away, head down, thinking *Oh shit, now what the hell am I going to do?* I needed the work, and was hoping for the job.

I was untying my mule when Mr. Jakobes said, "Hey boy, I think I will give you a try."

I turned and walked back to where he stood. He had stepped off the porch and was looking at me. "Thanks," I said. "When do you want me to start?"

He was still staring at me. Finally, he said, "Tomorrow. Early. Go fetch your things and put them in the stable on the back of the shop. Put your mule in with the horses, back there in the pasture. You get breakfast and supper and whatever you can fix up in the stable to sleep on." With this, he turned and stepped onto the porch.

I was dumbfounded. I just stood there.

"Go, boy," he barked, "before I change my mind."

As I turned to go, I heard the girl say, "No, Daddy." I was on my mule and going.

I spent most of the day getting my things packed up. I was so happy that I whistled all the way back to my new job and a place to be—in out of the weather for the winter, and something to eat.

When I got to the stable, I taken my things in and looked around, then I went out and put my mule in the pasture with the horses. There were four horses there in the pasture. I wondered if they all belonged to Mr. Jakobes. I returned to the stable to find a place to put my things and fix me a bed. I found a place in one corner that had nothing in it, and there was a window on each wall. I could tell the morning sun would shine in the one window. I picked this spot for my bed. The moonlight would also come in when it shone. I would have a good view of the stable doors from this corner.

I taken my time, and gathered up a big pile of straw, and put it in the corner, and with a few boards I made a square to hold the straw in place. I found a horse blanket and spread it out on top of the straw, then spread my blankets over this. It would make a good bed and would be just below the window. For sure, it would be better and warmer than sleeping on the ground like I had been doing for so long.

It was getting late, and the light was fading. I had no light. Now, for the first time all day, I was hungry. I did bring the rabbit and bird I had roasted the night before, and some hard bread that was some days old that I had gotten for some work I did. I went out to the watering trough and got a cup of water and returned to my bed, sat down, and ate the cold meat and bread.

I was so happy as I sat there, thinking how lucky I was to have found work, a bed of straw, and a warm stable to sleep in. I sat there sipping water and thanking the Creator. I soon crawled under my blankets. Gosh, how long had it been that I slept on a bed like this? I wasn't sure. I was soon asleep. I slept the best I had in a long time.

I was up early the next morning, and went to the watering trough and put water on my face and hands, wiped my face on my shirt sleeve, then went back through the stable and into the shop. When I got in the shop, there was a man standing next to the door. The light was dim, so I couldn't see very good. I walked over closer to where he stood. Once there, I saw the man was watching me. Looking at him, I remembered he was the man on the horse that I asked how to get to the blacksmith shop the day before.

He didn't say anything, so I said "I'm Nathan and will be working here for Mr. Jakobes."

"I know! He told me to show you what work you are to do, but now I'm to make sure you get some breakfast." In a low, soft voice I heard him mumble, "Just what I need—a kid to take care of—as though I have nothing else to do around here." Then, he said louder, "Let's go!"

I followed him as we walked to the house. He never said anything. We went to a room that had been built on the back side of the house. He opened the door and went in. I followed. There was a lamp burning bright, and I could see the room was fair sized, longer than it was wide. A kitchen and pantry all in one, I guessed. There was a table close to the door, a dry sink and shelves on the inner wall, a big wood stove with four lids to cook on. This was on the outer wall. There was a door at the other end of the kitchen that went into the other part of the house. I couldn't see what was in there from where I was standing. I stood by the door and waited. The man that I followed sat down at the table. There were three places set.

By then, a woman came through the door, carrying dishes,

and put them in the dry sink. I could see she was a light-skinned colored woman. She looked at me, then at the man sitting at the table. "Good morning, Charley," she said with a big smile. "Who's this young fella?"

Charley just smiled at her and didn't say anything.

She looked at me and said, "What's yo' name?"

"Nathan."

"Nice name. Sit, Nathan, and I'll gib yo' somethin' to eat. I'm Fanny. I do all the housekeepin' here."

As Fanny was filling our plates, I couldn't help but look at her. She was about five-foot-five or so, thin in the waist, with a nice bosom, black hair pinned up in a roll on the back of her head. I guessed she was around 25. She brought our plates filled with eggs and fried potatoes, sausage and bread, and a mug of milk. I started in on my plate of food, and couldn't remember when anything tasted so good. I knew I was hungry—hell no, *starved*. Fanny brought her plate, and sat down. As we ate, her and Charley talked, and I couldn't keep from looking at her. I could see she was a very pretty woman.

We finished our breakfast, and Charley stood up. "Come, boy, let's go."

I headed out the door. I heard Charley say something to Fanny. I heard her laugh. He closed the door, and was right behind me.

Once at the shop, Charley said, "Boy, the boss said your job is to keep the stable and the harness and saddles clean, and make sure the horses have feed, and keep the watering trough clean. Also, keep the ice out when it's froze. You don't have to clean the harness and saddles every day, just when they have been used. And when you get done with that, you are to clean up in here, then help me, if I need you. You hear?"

"Yes, sir. I will remember."

"Don't call me sir. The name is Charley. Now get to work. You'll find everything you need in the stable."

I went into the stable, and looked around. I found the things I needed. I first cleaned the horse stalls. I got a fork and wheelbarrow, loaded the wheelbarrow with manure, and hauled it outside, and dumped it on the pile that was there. When this was done, I worked on the harnesses and saddles. I cleaned them good, then rubbed everything with an old feed sack. When I was done, they shone like new. I went into the shop, found a broom, and started to clean. Charley was working on something with Mr. Jakobes. They never looked up. I cleaned everything up that I thought wouldn't interfere with what the men were working on.

It was way past noon when they finished the work they were doing. They carried everything over by the big doors and set it down, and stood there, looking at what they had finished. They looked around, and I think it was the first time they noticed I was there working. The two men looked at each other, then Mr. Jakobes walked out into the stable. He was gone five minutes or so when he came back in the shop, nodded to Charley, and told him that a man would be coming mid-afternoon to pick up the things they made. Mr. Jakobes told Charley what he was to do, and then went out the door.

I kept on working, and hadn't noticed Charley was gone until I heard a door open. I looked around to see Charley coming through the door that went into another room. It was then that I realized that was where he lived. Charley walked over to me, and handed me a big roll.

"Here, boy. Fanny gave this to me this morning, for your lunch."

I taken the roll, and said thanks, and went out back and got some water, and ate my roll. Then going back in the shop, Charley told me what I was to do. He showed me how to heat flat steel in the forge, then bend it into a round hoop, then heat the ends until they were almost white hot, then overlap them and pound them with a hammer on the anvil, until they were molded together. The hoops were for wagon and buggy wheels.

I caught on fast, and spent the rest of the day making hoops while Charley worked on other things. It was close to quitting when a man with horses and a wagon pulled up outside by the big door and came in. He talked to Charley, and they opened the doors and loaded the things he and Mr. Jakobes had made earlier. I thought to myself, *This is my first day here. Maybe it will be a good place to work.* I was startled out of my daydream by Charley's voice.

"Boy, go wash up. It's time to eat."

I hurried out through the stable to the water trough, washed up, and ran back to the shop. Charley was waiting when I came through the shop. He headed for the house, me following. He taken his place at the table. I did the same. I could hear Fanny talking to someone in the other room. I taken it to be Mrs. Jakobes. Soon Fanny came through the door and saw us sitting at the table. A big smile came on her face.

"How all is you two?"

Charley teased her by saying, "How all is *you?*"

I just smiled.

She soon had our plates piled full of fried chicken, potatoes, gravy, cornbread and milk. Charley and her had coffee. We taken our time eating. Charley and Fanny talked while we ate. Now and then, Fanny would ask me something like, "How old is you?"

"Fifteen," I answered.

"Where is you from?"

"A place called Fort Pitt."

"When dis you leave home?"

"A little after I was 15."

I was through eating, so I got up to leave, and Fanny said, "Wait." She got up and went to the stove, opened the oven, and got a sweet roll and gave it to me. "Dis is for you all later." Then she reached out and pulled me to her, and gave me a big hug. I was embarrassed and turned red. I never had anything like this happen before. I turned and went out the door, not saying anything.

I went back to the shop. Charley had left a lantern burning. I looked all around the shop, to see what all was in there. I could tell that most all the things were blacksmith tools, to work with iron and other things needed to repair things made of iron. I sat there, watching the light from the lantern play shadows on the stone walls. I saw mice scamper along the edge of the rocks. I don't know how long I sat there, lost in my dream thoughts, when I was startled by Charley coming in the door. He didn't say anything and started to his room.

I asked if I could use the light to go get some water. He said, "Yes, but don't go through the stable."

"Okay." I taken the light, and went out front to the watering trough by the hitching rail and got water, then returned and hung the lantern where it was. Charley had a lamp burning in his room.

I outened the lantern, took my roll and water, and went to my bed, sat and ate the roll Fanny gave me, and sipped water. It must have been very cloudy, for it was so dark, I couldn't see anything. The night before, there was a little light coming in the windows from the stars. I soon crawled under my blankets and lay there, listening to mice scamper around, and other night life outside. Off in the distance, I could hear a wolf howl. A little later, an answer came from another direction. That was the last I remember.

The next several days were spent doing the same work, except Charley showed me how to make horseshoes. Hammering iron on the anvil left a ringing in my ears that I heard in my sleep.

It was Saturday evening. The work was done, and Charley and I went for supper. As before, Fanny was her cheerful self and gave me a big hug. "Now all you'se two sit and I'se done goin' feed you'se all."

We sat and soon had our plates full of roast beef and all that went with it. Charley and Fanny talked as usual. I said as little as possible. I finished eating, and got up to go.

Fanny got up and gave me a hug. As I was going out the door, I heard her say "Charley, nows you'se done see dat boy gets a bath tonight and clothes washed, and you'se too, done hear? Or *else!*" At the time, I didn't know what *else* meant. I didn't realize then what the word *else* would come to mean.

As I hurried back to the shop, I tried to remember where I saw a washtub and buckets. We had left the lantern burning, and as I entered the shop, I began looking. I spotted the tub hanging on a peg by the door to Charley's room, and the buckets were stacked upside down below it. I hurried and got the tub down, sat it by the forge, grabbed the buckets, ran out front, got two buckets of water, taken them in, and sat them on the hot coals of the forge. Then, I grabbed the other bucket and went and filled it. I was hurrying, trying to get my bath done with before Charley came back. All this time, I was thinking that Fanny meant for him to give me a bath, and I didn't want no part of that.

Pumping the forge, it didn't take long before the water was hot. In the meantime, I found soap, filled the tub, and was done bathing and had put clean long underwear on when Charley came in. He stopped and looked at me, shook his head, and went into his room. I washed out my clothes, put them up to dry, then put my boots on. Taking the tub out, I emptied it and rinsed it out. I put everything back where I got it, and was about to outen the lantern when Charley came out of his room.

"Boy, leave it on, I'm going to bath."

"Okay," then I went into the stable to bed. I lay there in the darkness, thinking. After a while, I heard Charley go out and close the door. I soon went to sleep.

The next morning, being Sunday, there would be no work in the shop. But I had to take care of the horses, so I was in no hurry. When I finished up, I went into the shop, but didn't see Charley. I headed to the house for some breakfast. When

I walked into the kitchen, Charley was already eating. Fanny looked at me with a big smile.

"Nathan, you'se done bathed and put clean clothes on." She came over and gave me a hug. This time, I could feel her fair-sized bosom pressing hard against my chest. Being a kid of 15, I never thought of anything like this happening. I didn't know what to do. I was embarrassed, and I felt my face turning red. "You'se done sit and I'se get you all somethin' to eat."

I sat down at my place, and Fanny soon came with my plate full and set it in front of me. Charley finished eating, and was drinking his coffee, and Fanny was sipping at hers. I finished my breakfast and got up to leave.

Charley said, "Boy, hitch up the white mare in the buggy, and bring it out front and tie up at the hitching rail."

I ran back to the stable and did as he told me. It wasn't long and I had the horse hitch in the buggy and taken it down to the house and tied it out front. I went back to the stable. My clothes were dry, so I taken them down, and did a few other things.

It was mid-morning when I decided I would go for a ride. I went out back, got Worse, my mule, jumped on her, and headed towards town. When I passed the house, the horse and buggy was gone. I kept on riding. It was about half a mile to town. I wanted to look around. I hadn't been in town much since I got there, just looking for work and doing odd jobs. The road I was on turned out to be the main one through town. I was coming from the east, and once in town, the road widened out. There was a row of buildings on each side, with a path made of wood boards that went from one end to the other. I could see there was a few saloons, a hardware store, trading post, barber shop and another store.

Once at the other end, I swung my mule towards the river, then headed upriver. There was some distance between the buildings and river. I saw several riverboats tied up here, and could see this was where the boats were unloaded. I went about halfways, turned my mule up a narrow road between two buildings, crossed the main road between more buildings, and came to another road. Here I headed east. There were buildings on both sides. I taken this to be wheremost of the people lived. I did see signs. One read CLOTHES WASHED WHILE YOU BATH. Several that read ROOM AND BOARD. I hadn't seen many people as I rode. When I got close to the end of town, I saw a church and a school. I kept riding, and as I passed the church, I could see horses and buggies, a few wagons tied up around back.

It wasn't long and I was at the shop. I put my mule in the pasture, and walked into the shop. Charley was in his room doing something, so I stepped outside. In the distance, I could see a white horse and buggy coming. I figured it to be Mr. Jakobes and his family. When they got closer, I went back inside. I stood so I could see. When they got to the house, they drove past it and up to the shop. Getting out, he tied the horse, then opened the outside door to Charley's room and told him something. This was the first time I saw Mrs. Jakobes. She was as tall as he, and thin, had red hair and was nice-looking. They were dressed in their fancy clothes. They walked around outside a bit, then headed towards the house. Once they were at the house, I went back outside and sat on a bench that was built along the wall facing the house that overlooked the river. The river was close to half a mile—maybe more—north of the shop.

I think it was around mid-November. I'm not sure. The weather was different from what I was used to. Here it would get cold, then warm up, maybe rain, then get cold again. Today it was sunny, a little on the cool side, but nice to be out. In mid-afternoon, Charley came out, taken the horse and buggy, and headed towards town. He wasn't gone long when he returned, stopped at the house, and left a man and woman off, then returned to the shop, tied up, and stomped into his room.

I sat there, lost in my thoughts, until the sun was just about down, then got up and went and taken care of my chores. It was almost dark when I walked into the shop. Charley had the lantern lit and was at the door looking out. I could tell he wasn't happy. He went on out, and I followed. When we walked into the kitchen, I could see Fanny wasn't too happy. I noticed the door that went into the other room was closed. She did come and give me a hug, then put her arms around Charley. He pulled her close. She buried her head in his shoulder. With tears in her eyes, she choked out, "I'se been workin' in dis damn hot kitchen alls damn day."

Charley spoke in a soft whisper, "It will be all right. It won't be long."

She looked up at him and smiled, turned, and went to fill our plates. I was still standing. Charley looked around at me. "Sit, boy!" I sat down as he did. Fanny gave us our food and sat down.

We ate. There wasn't much talk between Charley and

Fanny. When I was through, I got up and put all of my dishes on the sink, then walked over to Fanny and gave her a hug. She was still sitting. I said good night, and went back to the shop.

19

I sat down by a window and looked out into the darkness. I could see a few very faint lights off in the direction of town. A light burned in the upper part of the house, and I wondered if that was where Kate slept. I learned her name when I overheard Mr. Jakobes talking to a customer and referred to his wife, Bertha, and daughter, Kate.

It was now a week that I was working there. I didn't see much of Mr. Jakobes. When we would be eating, I could hear them in the other room. Charley and Fanny never said anything about them at all. I sense it was something they didn't talk about.

Charley hadn't come back from the house yet, so I went to bed. I lay there wondering what was keeping Charley. I drifted off to sleep. It seemed late when I heard Charley bring the horse and buggy and put them in their place, then come into the shop. I went back to sleep.

The weeks went by quickly, and everything stayed pretty much the same. The shop was quite busy now, and Mr. Jakobes was spending more time helping with the work. He even seemed pleased with how I was working out. Every so often, he would give me twenty-five cents. I would thank him, then put it away. I had to save everything. I knew I would need all I could get.

It was close to the end of the year now, and there hadn't been very much snow so far. That was okay with me. It meant I could spend more time outside and away from the shop when I didn't have to work. Every chance I got, I went to town. It wasn't long before I knew where everything was, and where every little road went. I liked going by the river, where the boats were. Some would be having work done on them, others would be unloading. I didn't know anyone, so I spent my time alone when I was away from the shop.

It was the beginning of the new year when, on a Sunday afternoon, I was sitting around the shop, keeping warm and looking out the window, daydreaming about what I was going to do. What all I was going to need when I decided to move on? How was I going to get the things I wanted? A light snow was coming down. The sky was gray and gloomy. Somehow, I knew the snow wasn't going to last. Then I had a thought: *Why don't I make some of the things I will need?* I was saving what little money, hoping to get me a mule or horse before I left. *Hell yes, I have most everything here I need to make a few traps, some snares.* I knew how to use the forge and anvil, and to make the holes I would need.

I got up and looked around to find what I could. Charley's door was open, and as I passed by, I noticed he was working on some kind of a drawing. I had noticed the last week or so he was staying up later than usual at night, doing something in his room. I went about my business. I found some iron that I could use to make some traps. I was hammering some iron on the anvil when Charley walked up beside me. He looked at the piece of iron I had in the forge getting hot. Then he looked at me and shook his head and went back to his room and closed the door.

I worked for a while, then heard Charley come out of his room. "Come, boy, let's go eat."

Fanny was her jolly self as she was most of the time. Right after I was through eating, I got my hug and went back to the shop.

Charley stayed and had more coffee and talked to Fanny. Even though I was young and inexperienced, there were times when I could feel something different about the two of them. As I walked back to the shop, my thoughts wandered back over the weeks that I had been there. I remembered the late nights when I thought I heard the door to Charley's room opening or closing, and the times I thought I heard talking or laughter. I always put it aside as the wind or something else.

Once in the shop, I gathered up the things I was working on and taken them back to my bed, and put everything under the straw. I straightened up my blankets, then crawled in.

I worked almost every evening after supper on the things I would need. It seemed Charley was staying longer after supper lately. When he would come into the shop and I was working, he would come by and look at what I was doing. If I needed any help, he was always glad to tell me how to do it.

One afternoon, Mr. Jakobes handed me a bunch of papers and told me to take the horses and wagon and go to town, where the boats unload, and pick up the things that were on the paper. I was outside, hitching up, when Charley came out and handed me a paper, and told me to see if these things were there, and if so bring them back.

When I got to where I thought I was to be, I asked a man.

"Right over there, son," he said. The man knew the boxes were heavy. "Son, you just wait, and I will help you put them on your wagon."

The first boxes were the ones for Charley. We put them way up front, then put the other boxes on. They were all heavy. I thanked the man.

"Anytime, son!"

I hollered, "Getty-up," and the horses started off. I could tell the way they pulled that the wagon was heavy.

When I got back to the shop, Mr. Jakobes had already gone to the house, so Charley and I unloaded the wagon. We taken his boxes into his room. Then I put the horses and wagon where they belonged, did my chores, and by now it was time to go eat. I walked in through the shop. Charley was still in his room. I stopped by the door and looked in. He had opened a box and was looking at the things that were in it. I saw a dozen or more long, round steel that were hollow inside. At first I didn't know what they were, then I realized they were musket barrels and other parts to go with them. He saw me standing there looking, so he closed the box and came out, closing the door.

After supper, I left, as usual. I wasn't in the shop long when Charley walked in. I was busy working on some throwing hatchets. Soon I heard him working with the boxes in his room. I had four ax blades in the forge, getting hot, so I could shape them to where I wanted them. My traps and snares were done, and hidden under my bed. I had just to finish the axes and a few knife blades. I worked later than usual, and finished the axes. I cleaned up, and put everything away. Charley was still working when I went to bed.

Since the first of the year, I noticed Mr. and Mrs. Jakobes were going away in the late afternoon, two or three times a week, and most every Sunday afternoon. I noticed, too, that he was not the same, like something worried him. He was becoming short-tempered, too, and lately, when Charley was off delivering things for customers, Mr. Jakobes would get mad and take it out on me by beating me with a horse whip. This had happened four or five times. Somehow, I think Charley knew Mr. Jakobes was beating me. But he never said anything. Maybe he saw that I had been crying, but wasn't sure why.

I noticed, too, that Kate was making excuses to come to the shop or stable when her folks would go away. Charley taken notice also. One evening, while we were eating, he asked Fanny, "What's up with Kate?"

Fanny looked at him, then at me, then back at him. "Wells, if you doesn't know, I'se doesn't know."

In the past, the only time Kate ever came near the stable was with her mother, then only when they needed me to hitch up a horse to the buggy or saddle two of the horses. When Mrs. Jakobes did come by the stable, she was very seldom nice. She always had something to bitch about, mostly about Charley and me. Then, she would say something hateful or nasty. When Kate would be with her, Kate would never say anything. Sometimes I would catch her staring at me. There were other times when I knew she would have liked to have said something, but knew better. Most of the time, she just smiled.

Now that her folks were going away more, she would find some reason to come, mostly to the stable, when I was doing my chores, and watch whatever I was doing, wanting to know this, wanting to know that. Every time she came, she asked more questions. It was getting to be that every time Kate got a chance, she would come looking. She knew she would find me either in the shop or stable.

Charley could see what was going on. He never said anything unless it was to Fanny. In fact, he never talked much at all. He was a quiet man with a deep voice, but soft. He wasn't as tall as I, but very husky built with dark hair. I guessed him to be around 30 or maybe 35. I knew he was very strong, and I wouldn't have wanted him getting mad at me. If I happened to see Kate coming, and I could, I would go and find something to work in the stable. There we were alone, and could talk. At first, we both were bashful. That soon changed.

It was around this time, when it was getting a little warmer out, that I decided one Saturday night to go into town, just to see what went on at night. I had heard things and, being young, was curious. So, after I was sure everyone was in bed, I got up, put my coat on, stuck my pistol in the waist of my pants, and opened the back door to the stable slowly and went out, closing it carefully, not to make any noise. It wasn't far, so I walked to town.

Once in town, I stayed in the shadows when I could.

Looking around, I found a place where I could stand without being seen, and yet I would be able to see two of the saloons across the street. I noticed the music was loud, and people were in and out all the time, going from one place to another. I watched awhile, but was getting cold, so I went home.

The next morning being Sunday, I slept a little later, which I did sometimes on Sundays. After breakfast, I went back to the stable and lay on my bed, thinking. It wasn't even noon when Charley came to get the horse and buggy. I got up and helped him hitch up. Then he taken it down to the house. I went back into the shop and looked out the window to see what was going on. He no more than tied up and went around back to the kitchen, when Mr. and Mrs. Jakobes came out and got in the buggy and drove off. They weren't halfways to town, when I saw Kate come out of the house and head for the shop.

It was a sunny day, so I went out and sat on the bench. Kate came up, said hello, and sat down beside me. We talked for a little, when Kate asked if I wanted to go for a walk. I looked at her.

"What about your folks?"

For the first time, I noticed she had green eyes and a small turned-up nose. "They won't be back until dark."

"Okay, where do you want to walk to?"

"Down to the river."

"Down to the river!"

"Yes."

"Are you sure?"

"Yes."

"That's almost a mile."

"I know."

"Are you going like that?"

"Yes, these are my old clothes."

"Okay, let's go."

We headed toward the river. After a little while, we found a path that was wide enough that we could walk side by side. We talked as we walked, and by the time we got to the river we were talking like we were old friends. We spotted a log and went to it and sat down. We talked and watched the river flow by. Mostly we talked about things she liked and things she would like to do, and things she wanted to do someday.

"Why don't you do things you would like to do?"

"My folks won't let me. I would like to go riding by myself, or take the buggy and go to the store for Fanny, or go outdoors to the woods. I would like to go fishing, even if my father went with me, or maybe Charley, like the other kids in school do. The other kids are always talking about the things they do, or the animals they have for pets."

"Don't you ask to do these things?"

"Yes, but my mother—mostly my mother—she says it's not lady like! Blah-blah-blah ..."

"Don't you have any close friends?"

"No! That's why! You are the closest to a friend I have, and I'm not supposed to talk to you, or go near you."

"What would your folks do, if they found out you were talking to me?"

"Mom would have a breakdown!"

"What's that?"

"I don't know. That's what she says. Daddy would make you leave."

I felt so sorry for her. I felt sorry because she wasn't free—free like I was. I was 16 now, and free to do whatever I wanted to—free as the rain, the sun, the wind.

"Kate, how old are you?"

"Why?"

"Because I want to know."

"I'm not telling."

"Why?"

"Because... because I don't want to."

She never would tell me. I guessed she was about 17.

"Kate, we better go back."

"Why?"

"It's getting late."

"Damn! Must we?"

I got up and started off, and she followed. On the way back to the shop, Kate asked me where I was from, and about my folks, how many brothers and sisters I had. I really never told her where I came from. She asked me where I was going to go.

I looked at her. "What do you mean?"

"Where are you going, when you leave here?"

"I don't know."

"When are you leaving?"

"I don't know!"

"Why won't you tell me?"

"I can't tell you something I don't know!" Somehow I managed getting out of telling her. It wasn't because I didn't want her to know. It was because I didn't want her saying anything to her mother or father.

We were about halfway back to the shop, when Kate stopped and turned and looked me in the eyes. "Does my father beat you?"

"Why would you ask me something like that?"

"I want to know!" Somehow she knew, and I didn't want to tell her that her father was a mean, hateful, greedy bastard.

"No."

"Nathan, you're lying. Now tell me the truth!"

I looked down, not saying anything.

"Well! Does he?"

"Yes... sometimes, but it's not bad." I looked at her, and saw the hurt and sadness come over her face, and her pretty green eyes filled with tears.

She lowered her head and, in a low voice, sobbed, "I'm so sorry. I'm so sorry. I wish I could help you. Why don't you leave?"

"Where would I go, Kate?"

"Somewhere!"

"It's winter, and it gets cold at night. There's no jobs around here that would put me up and give me something to eat."

"There must be!"

"No, there ain't!"

"How do you know?"

"I have looked, that's how! Besides, here I have a warm stable to sleep in, a job, and Fanny is very good to me, and gives me lots of good things to eat. She's a very good cook."

"Damn you, Nathan. My father treats his help like all of his animals!"

"Now, Kate! Now quit talking like that. Would you listen to me? It ain't all that damn bad. Besides, it won't be for long!"

"Where will you go?"

"I don't know!" I didn't want to tell her what I planned on doing. She looked at me, still sobbing, and threw her arms around me and sobbed even more. I held her, and pulled her tight to me.

"Now, Kate, it's going to be all right. Stop crying, Kate. We must go home." She stopped crying, and we talked about other things the rest of the way to the shop. Once there, she went to the house.

A few days later, while we were working, Mr. Jakobes

seemed to be mad at everything and everyone, bitching and cursing. I never heard him curse before, but I did this day. He cursed everything in the shop. He even cursed the horses. Finally, noon came, and he went to the house. It was mid-afternoon when he came back, cursing worse than when he left. Charley was not saying anything and staying away. Mr. Jakobes wasn't back half an hour, when he went into a rage, grabbed his horse whip, and started in on beating me. He only hit me three or four times, when Charley grabbed the whip out of his hand.

In a low, soft voice, Charley said, "Don't you ever lay a hand on that boy again ... If you want to whip anyone, start with me!" Charley threw the whip in the farthest corner. Then, turning his back to Mr. Jakobes, went back to work.

Mr. Jakobes just stood there, with a shocked look on his face, turning red. He wheeled around, glaring at Charley, then went out the door, slamming it just as hard as he could.

We didn't see him the rest of the day. In fact, for a couple of days after that, I went to where Charley was working and thanked him. My face was wet with tears.

Charley looked at me and smiled. "Okay, boy," and went back to work.

We finished the afternoon's work, and went for supper. Fanny was her loving, jolly self, gave us each a hug and said "sit."

While we were eating, Charley told Fanny what happened. He spoke quite loud. "Mr. Jakobes taken a horse whip to this boy."

"Charley, yous din't stand there, dis yous?"

"I stopped him." Looking at me, he said, "He won't be hitting you any more, boy. I mean that."

I knew Mr. and Mrs. Jakobes and Kate, who were eating in the other room, could hear everything Charley said. I guess he wanted them to hear.

Saturday came, and Charley and I had finished the work Mr. Jakobes had left us to do. He always had the work we were to do written out on paper, and on the table for Charley at breakfast.

Charley was in his room. I decided to take my bath. I would have enough time before supper. My water was hot, and in no time I had bathed and washed clothes, and hung them to dry, put on all clean clothes, dumped water, and had buckets of clean water heating for Charley.

After supper, I went back to the stable and lay on my bed. I soon heard Charley come in and take his bath and, before long, everything was quiet. I lay there for a long time, and didn't hear anything. Getting up, I stuck my pistol in my waist, pulled my coat on, and quietly went out and headed for town. Once there, I taken up my spot, where I could see what was going on.

It was busy at the saloons. Men and women were in and out all the time. Some were all dressed up. They were in all stages of drunkenness. Me being kind of naive, I didn't understand what was going on. I would see these men and women come out of the saloon, then go into a rooming house. After a while, they would come out and go back in the saloon. Later, the same woman and another man would do the same thing. Some would be so drunk, they both would fall down in the dirt or mud, cursing and hollering, sometimes laughing, then get up and go on. I never knew what they were laughing at. The few times I came here, the same thing was taking place.

Tonight it was louder and busier. I was thinking about going home and didn't notice these two drunken cowboys walk up to me. They taken me by such surprise that I couldn't even run. I just stood there, with my mouth open. I was too scared to reach for my gun. I just froze, waiting for the worst.

"You gots a match, young fella?" one of them said.

"N-nope."

"How's about a drink?"

"N-nope."

He shoved a bottle of some kind of whiskey in my hand, and said in a rough, drunken voice, "Drink, young fella."

I never in my life tasted any kind of whiskey. I didn't know what to expect. I put the bottle to my mouth and taken a big drink. I gasped and just about choked.

One of them slapped me on the back so hard that it knocked the wind out of me. I almost fell down. They each had a pull at the bottle and shoved it in my hand. "Drink!"

This time I didn't take so much. This went on until the bottle was empty. One of them reached in his coat pocket, and brought out another bottle, only half full. We each had a drink. By now, I was beginning to feel a whole lot funny. Not knowing what was taking place, I said, "Man, what the hell is happening?"

The two cowboys said, "Now what?" As they looked at one another, then at me, one of them said, "Young fella, you look like you need laid."

What was going through my mind was *What the hell are they talking about? What do they mean "laid?" What is "laid?"* I didn't want to ask, so I just said in a tone of voice that I didn't recognize, "Yeah, man, indeed I do."

I must have said the wrong thing. They grabbed me by each arm and said, "Let's go." They half dragged me down the street, me walking unsteadily and stumbling. I went with these two drunken cowboys.

"Where the hell are you taking me?"

"To the whorehouse, you dumb ass, to get you laid.'"

"Get laid? What the hell is that?"

"You mean you never been laid?"

"Hell no, I don't know what the hell you are talking about."

One of them said, "Son of a bitch! Some whore is going to get a virgin tonight."

Down the street we went, until we came to the other saloon. We went in this one. My head was a little fuzzy, and I didn't walk too straight, but I didn't give a damn. I could see this place was really nice. There were all kinds of tables to sit at, and there were a lot of people playing cards. I think that's what they called it. And girls brought them drinks. There was a big, long bar at one end, and a lot of men standing there drinking. They were even serving some people food. There wasn't any loud noise here, like the other saloon.

The one man and I stood by the stairway, while this other man went to the bar after a bottle. The bartender said something and protested about me being in there. "Give me a damn bottle, and shut up, you bastard!" The bartender gave him a bottle, and stood there, shaking his head.

The cowboy came over to where I and the other man was standing. In a drunken, loud voice he said, "Come with me, young man, let's go pick one." He grabbed my arm, and up the stairway we went, me not knowing where I was going. I think I must have sobered up some from all the walking and excitement, for my head wasn't spinning any more.

Once we got to the top of the stairs, we went into this room, where four or five girls were lounging around on big, overstuffed chairs, like I never saw before, sipping on some kind of drinks. One woman was sitting behind a table. One of the cowboys walked over to her, and asked her something, and motioned at me. She stood up and looked at me, then said something to him. He reached in his pocket and got some money, and gave it to her. She looked at the girls, and motioned to the one that was the younger looking.

The girl promptly got up and walked over to me, and taken me by the hand, opening the door, and led me out. As we went through the door, the others were laughing, and hollered, "Have a good time."

The other two cowboys were still in the room as she closed it. She kept hold of my hand, and led me down a hall, until we came to a door. She opened it, and we went through into a fair-sized room that had a nice-looking bed, a few chairs, a stand, and a tub. I guess I had come out of my drunkenness somewhat. Things were looking fairly normal.

I looked around, expecting to see the other two, when it hit me. *Hell, they must have gotten a woman and went somewhere. Shit, I don't give a damn.* I was really feeling good. Here I was in this nice room, with a bed, and a tub, and a lamp burning nice and low, a few candles burning here and there. There were rugs beside the bed and tub. I stood there, looking around. I then looked at her, and I could tell she knew I never saw anything like this.

Just then, the door opened, and a little man carrying buckets of hot water came in and filled the tub, then went out and came back with more buckets of hot water. He set them by the tub. He bowed at the girl. She nodded. He then went out.

She walked over and closed the door and put a bar across it, then turned and looked at me.

20

Slowly, she walked over to where I stood, reached up, unbuttoned my coat, and went to take it off. As she looked down, she saw the gun sticking in the waist of my pants, and stepped back and looked at me. At first, I didn't know what she was doing. Then, I saw her looking at my gun. I taken my coat and gun, and handed them to her. She taken them, and laid them by the door. Returning, she stood in front of me, looking up into my eyes. Slowly, she reached up and slid my suspenders down over my shoulders, then undid my shirt and pushed it over my shoulders. Then, off came my boots. Next, my pants were unbuttoned and left dropped.

There I stood in my underwear. I was embarrassed, and too bashful to say anything. Not knowing what to expect, and still drunk enough not to give a damn, she undid my underwear, reached up, and pushed them down over my shoulders, down over my waist, then let them drop to my feet. I stepped out of my clothes, and stood there. She had stepped back, and was looking at me.

Then, she spoke for the first time. "You're a nice built young man." I could feel myself turning red. This was the first I was ever in the presence of a woman, completely nude. I didn't know what to do. I just stood there. Finally, she said, "Get in the tub, before the water gets cold."

I stepped into the tub and sat down. The water was just hot enough. This was the first time I saw a tub this big. She was standing by the bed, undoing her dress, which was very pretty, pulling it over her head and dropping it on the bed. She stood there in all these white undergarments, trimmed in pink lace. Hell, I didn't know what all those garments were called. Slowly, she pulled the top part out, then inched it higher and higher, until her nipples came into view. She pulled it over her head, and tossed it on the bed. Her hands went to her waist, and slowly inched the bottoms down over her hips and stomach, lower and lower, until her dark mound slowly came into view.

Standing there, she slowly moved her hips in a circular motion, teasing, as her bloomers inched their way further down, till they dropped to her feet, then kicking them aside. I couldn't take my eyes off her as she stood there, very slowly turning around in the flickering candlelight as they cast out their radiant yellow glow that played over every curve of her light brown skin. She had dark eyes, hair as black as coal that fell below her waist. She was a very beautiful woman. Sitting there, watching her, I realized she was just a young girl. She looked to be part Chinese or Negro. It really didn't matter. She was beautiful.

She stood only feet from me, and I watched every move as she stepped into the tub and knelt down on her knees, moving closer and closer, until she was almost against me. Picking up a tin cup, she dipped water over my head until I was wet. With her small hands, she picked up some soap and began soaping me, from on top of my head, on down over my shoulders, chest and back. Everything down to where the water was.

"Stand up!"

I was lost in what she was doing, and it taken a moment for me to realize what she said. "You want me to stand up?"

"Yes!"

"No!"

She nodded her head yes.

"No!" I was so taken by this that I didn't know what I should do.

"Please!"

I slowly came up out of the water, and she kept on soaping me. When finished, she handed me the soap. "Now your turn. You do me."

I taken the soap and knelt down. She had tied her hair up and was sitting there, looking at me. I was too bashful to do what she asked. I just knelt there, with the soap in my hand, looking at her. She reached out, taken my hand, and pulled it to her, pressing it between her breasts.

"Now soap me."

I started soaping her wet body. I was really surprised at how smooth and soft she felt. All this was so very new to me. I taken my time, and the longer I soaped, the more I was enjoying it. She never stopped me. Once I was finished, she reached into the bucket with clean water, and dipping it over us, rinsed us clean.

As we stepped out, she picked up a towel and dried us,

then led me over to the bed, folded back the covers, and climbed in. I followed. Everything felt soft and smelled clean and fresh. As she lay there, she looked more beautiful than ever, her long, black hair fanned out over the white linen, the candlelight as it flowed over her nakedness. My heart was pounding as I looked into her eyes. She reached up, pulling my head down. My hand found her smooth, firm breast as our lips met.

Our hands played and caressed with every kiss as our mouths searched, sending new sensations through our bodies. Higher and higher our passion grew.

It was mid-morning when a knock wakened us. She jumped out of bed, pulled her dress on, and answered the door. Someone handed her a big tray of food, milk and coffee. She set it on a stand, and came jumping back to bed and started teasing. It wasn't long before our passion taken over. It was almost noon when we dressed and ate our breakfast, which was good, even though it was mostly cold.

While we were eating, our conversation went to her. Even though she was hard to understand, I was able to make out most of what she was saying. I knew she was only 16, and I wasn't sure, but it seemed as though she was trying to tell me she was either sold or forced into what she was doing. I was hurt with what she was saying. I looked at her.

"You must go," she said.

"What about ..."

"Everything was paid for last night."

"How much?"

"Don't! Plenty. Go now!"

"Will I see you again?"

"I hope, but not here. Maybe some place else. Go! Go to the end of hall. That door go out."

As I reached for the doorknob, she came running, and threw her arms around my neck and pressed her lips to mine, with tears streaming down her cheeks. "You're the nicest man that ever come here."

As I closed the door, I heard her sobbing. I wanted to go back, but I knew I couldn't. I found the door at the end of the hall, and went through it onto a small porch with steps that led to the ground.

It was early afternoon when I walked into the shop. Charley was in his room, working on his things. I went to the stable, to see if the horses were taken care of. They were. I put my coat and pistol on the bed, and went back into the shop. Charley was just going out the door, and headed for the house.

It was a warm day for this time of year, so I went out and sat on the bench in the sun, leaning against the warm boards of the shop. My eyes closed, half dozing, lost in what happened last night and the thoughts of spring, when I was startled by Kate sitting down beside me. She started talking. I was still lost in my thoughts, and wasn't listening to what she was saying. She stopped, and I looked over at her.

"You didn't hear anything I said!"

"What are you talking about?"

"Last night. I'm talking about last night!"

"What about last night?"

"Where did you go?"

"Where did I go?"

"Yes, where did you go?"

"Who said I went anywhere?"

"I did! I just did," she protested with anger. "I saw you heading towards town last night, and you just came home a little while ago."

"If I did, what business is it of yours?"

With this, she jumped up and ran towards the house.

That evening, after I finished my chores, I went in for supper. As I sat down at my place, Charley looked at me. "You missed breakfast, boy."

Fanny spoke up. "Charley, you'se let that boy be."

Charley just shook his head.

I ate and went back to the shop, and was soon in bed. I lay there, thinking of the things I was going to need, besides what I had, and thinking about last night, and those two cowboys, and that girl as I fell off to sleep.

21

It was sometime in the spring of 1819 that I was in town, picking up supplies for Mr. Jakobes, by the boats, when this colored boy happened to walk by. I asked him if he would give me a hand with a heavy box, and learned his name was Cole. He was about my age. We got talking. Then, as time passed, we became friends.

The days were getting longer now. Sometimes, after I was through eating my supper, I would go to town and down by the boats to find Cole.

One of these evenings, while we were walking along the river, talking, I told Cole what I was going to do come next spring.

Immediately he said, "I'se going with you."

"I don't know. I only have two mules," and left it at that.

It was days before I talked to him again. He no more than saw me when he asked if he could go. I had been thinking about Cole going with me since we had talked last. I realized it would be nice to have a companion. I also realized what would happen to him if anything was to happen to me. I knew I could go on. I had traveled a long distance, getting this far mostly on my own, but what about him? Would he be able to make it by himself? I didn't know what he knew about being on his own, especially on the journey I was undertaking, continuing west into a country that few whites have been that I even heard of.

We walked until we found a place to sit. Then I told him he would have to prove to me that he could make it on his own, and tell me what kind of supplies he had.

He looked at me and said, "Nathan, I'se know I'se kin trust you with what I'se hafta say." To my surprise, he said, "I'se a runaway slave. I'se work on dat riverboat down there, and I'se been on my own since I'se was 13. I'se no choice but work on dat boat. Boss man says 'work for me' or him send me back. He never said where back was. I never ask!"

I was thinking about what Cole just said about work. Here he was the second person I had met in a short time that was being forced to work against their will.

"I'se have a pistol, a musket, and lots of powder and balls, and some shot, and some other things. I'se been getting and hiding all this stuff so I'se have it when I'se runs away again. I'se very strong, too, but I'se will need some of those horses." He went on telling me about everything he had hidden out of town somewhere. He said that would be the last time he ever talked about being a runaway, or where he came from, and I wasn't to talk about it either.

We sat for a while, not saying anything. Finally, Cole said, "Will you let me go with you?"

I looked at him, not saying anything, then reached my hand out to shake his. "You're on. But remember, we are in this together, all the way, or not at all. It don't matter what, we must be willing to give our lives for each other."

With that, he pulled out a knife, drew blood on his wrist, then on mine. We pressed our wrists together, and he said, "We'se now blood brothers."

I said, "We will never part, no matter what. We are bonded forever."

We knew we would have to be apart at times, like now. Cole said he must go, and I knew I had a long walk back to the stable also. We parted.

Every Saturday night, I would go to town, to see if I could see the girl from the whorehouse. I knew I wouldn't be allowed in the saloon where she was by myself, so I would stand in the shadows and watch to see if I could see her. Sometimes I would go around the back of the saloon, and up the steps, and peep in the door, hoping I would see her in the hallway, and get to talk to her.

And I would go to town every chance I got and find Cole. He was usually around the boat, or close by. We would then go off somewhere and talk, mostly about the things we were going to need when we decided to leave, such as horses, mules, clothing, and other supplies.

It was around that time when Mr. Jakobes started paying me fifty cents a week. It wasn't much, but it was something. I was lucky and found some work making metal things for the man who owned the harness shop. I was able to make the things in the evening or on Sundays. He furnished the kind of metal I would need, and paid me every time I did a job. It wasn't every evening or every Sunday, which left me time to go find Cole and make plans.

This went on throughout the long, hot summer, fall and winter. The calendar that hung on the shop wall indicated that it was mid January 1821. I had been itching to move on for sometime now.

The next time I talked to Cole, he told me that the boat that he worked on was having some work done on it, and that when it was ready, they would be going upriver. We talked about horses or mules, where we could get some. Cole then told me he heard that there was some wild or stray horses and mules somewhere out of town that were just running wild. We decided to go out some Sunday, and see if we could get some.

Saturday came, and I went to town to find Cole, and we talked awhile. I told him about the girl I met some weeks before. I told him that if I could find her, I was going to ask her to go with us, if that was all right with him. He was all for finding her. It was getting late, and I was ready to go home. We had been standing across from one of the saloons, when Cole said, "Let's go in and get something to drink."

I looked at him. "They won't give us anything."

"We can try."

We crossed the street and walked into the saloon. We looked around, then walked up to the bar. Both of us being young-looking, and him being black, the bartender refused to give us anything, and told us to get the hell out. When I protested, that was all it taken. Now we were about to be thrown out. Then some of the men standing at the bar started yelling, "Serve them." Others yelled, "Throw them out." It went back and forth. Soon, a fight started. It didn't take long and the fight turned into a brawl.

Everyone in the room was in the fight by now, bottles flying, chairs flying, fists flying. A fist hit Cole in the mouth. Up to now, we were left alone, but that did it. He jumped on the man that hit him, and I was right with him. It wasn't long before Cole and I was taking a beating. Only after we handed out as much as we could, we were now both on the floor, being punched and kicked, when a shotgun blasted with a loud roar right outside the door.

Everyone stopped and was looking towards the door. We were still on the floor, and couldn't see who was standing there. The room was quiet. Not even a whisper. We were still on the floor when the man in the doorway broke the silence. In a calm, soft voice, the man said, "Everyone back to the walls. I mean *everyone.*" The crowd of men parted, and for the first time, we were able to see the man standing there with a double barrel musket in each hand, none like I ever saw before. The holes in the ends were huge. I blinked my eyes, to see better. In the same calm, low, soft voice the man spoke. Then I knew who it was. It was Charley. "Come, boys, your fun's over for tonight."

Cole and I were on our feet and beside Charley in a flash. Charley handed me one of the muskets. "Here, boy. The way you're going, you may need this." We backed out the door to the street. Charley had his horse there. Untying it, he led it as we walked Cole down to the riverboat. Then Charley and I headed for home.

As we walked, he put his arm around my shoulder. After a while, he spoke in a very soft tone that sent chills throughout me. "Son, I have been following you every time you came to town at night, from the first. I was there the night the two cowboys took you and went to the brothel. I know my way around, and I saw that beautiful young girl that taken you to her room. I have been watching over you all along. Fanny makes sure of that. Fanny and I know what you and your friend are up to. We will help the two of you in every way we can."

We were back at the shop by now, and I stopped at the water trough and washed the blood that was smeared over my face and knuckles. I had a lot of bruises on my face, and every place I touched was sore.

When I went into the shop, Charley was already in his room.

"Come in here, boy."

I went in his room.

"Sit!"

I sat on a box. He handed me a cup of steaming hot coffee. I taken a sip and knew he had put whiskey in it. I looked at him.

"Drink it, boy. It will make you sleep good." He sat on the bed, sipping some whiskey, and said, "I think we should talk." He told me again how he and Fanny were watching over me, and now my new friend. He told me how delighted Fanny was when I came there to work. "She thinks a lot of you, and so do I. We think any boy your age that has made his way this far, as you did, on his own, is not just any boy, but someone special, and your friend ... what's his name?"

"Cole."

"Yes, Cole. He seems to be a lot like you. I think the two of you will be good companions, if tonight was any example. I told Fanny sometime ago, when you were making traps and the other things, that I thought you would be going when spring came. I want you to know, boy. We will give you all the help we can."

"I thank you very much, Charley. I would like to ask you something."

"Yes?"

"You say you saw me with that girl."

"Yes, I did."

"Do you know what got her?"

"No, but why?"

"I have been looking for her. I wanted to ask her to go with us."

"Go with you and Cole?"

"Yes!"

"Why?"

"Well, I'm not sure, but I think she is being forced to work there. She is just 16, and I would like to help her get out of there."

He hung his head. "Are you sure?"

"I think so. Just like Cole."

"Like Cole?"

"Yes!"

"What do you mean, like Cole?"

"Cole says he has to work on the boat, or the boss man will send him back."

"Back where?"

"I don't know."

After a pause, he said, "I will see what I can find out about the girl. I want you to know, if you were to take that girl with you, they may send men after you to hunt you down."

I thought about that, too.

"Boy, Mr. and Mrs. Jakobes are going away before long. They are going to New Orleans on some business, and will be gone mid-February till mid-March."

"Is Fanny going?"

"No, she must stay here, and see to it that Kate goes to school. If not, she would have to go." Charley stood up and put his big hand on my head. "Go to bed, son."

I got up and thanked him, and went to the stable to bed. I lay awake for some time, and thought over what Charley had told me. *This may be a good time for Cole and I to go, if the boat is going any time then.* Some of the things he told me, I couldn't help but wonder if there was anything going on with him and Fanny. It had been a full night. I was soon asleep.

I was up the next morning and did my chores, then went to the house for breakfast. When I walked in, Charley was already there. Fanny looked at me and said, "What happened to you'se, my boy?" As if she didn't already know. She came and looked me all over, to make sure I wasn't all cut up. Then she gave me a big hug. "I will have your things fixed in a jiffy, son." She brought a big plate of eggs, ham, fried potatoes, milk and bread. I had it all gone in no time. I didn't think I was hungry, but I guess I was. When I was ready to leave, she gave me a big cinnamon roll to take back to the shop for later.

I went back to the shop and did some work I wanted to get done. About noon, Charley came and got the horse and buggy and taken them to the house. Then he stayed with Fanny after Mr. and Mrs. Jakobes left. I was finally finished with the work I was doing, and went out to sit in the sun, for it was a nice day.

I was sitting there, eating and daydreaming in the warm sun, when Kate came from the house and sat down on the ground in front of me, cross-legged, and tucked her dress in all around. I looked at her and wondered why she was sitting that way. But I didn't say anything. We talked and she kept looking at me funny. Then, she asked me when I would be leaving.

"Kate, I told you, I don't know."

"I think you do, but won't tell me, will you?"

"What does it matter when I go?"

"Because I'm going with you!"

"You're *what?*"

"I'm going with you!"

"You are not!"

"Nathan, I want to go with you. I don't want to live here any more. So I'm going!"

"You don't know what the hell you are talking about, girl!"

"I do so."

To get her to shut up, I said I would think about it.

"Do you promise?"

"Promise what?"

"That I can go!"

"Kate, I said I would think about it. And I don't want to talk about it."

"What happened to you?"

"Nothing!"

"How did you get those bruises on your face and the one on your mouth?"

"Who cares?"

"I do!"

"Kate, let me alone."

"Do you want to know something?"

"What?"

"Mom and Dad are going away."

"When?"

"Soon."

"How soon?"

"I don't know."

"Where?"

"I'm not sure."

"Are you going?"

"No! I don't want to go anyway."

"I must go feed the horses before supper."

"I'm going with you!"

"Why?"

"Because I want to learn how."

"Suit yourself." I got up and went to the stable. I told Kate what to do as she helped me take care of the feeding and the other chores. After everything was done, I washed my hands and we started for the house.

"You are going to get in trouble if you keep doing this."

"I don't care, I don't care."

"Kate, I don't want you getting in trouble."

"But ..."

We were at the house now. She ran around to the front and I went into the kitchen. Luckily, Mr. and Mrs. Jakobes weren't home yet.

Fanny said, "What's that girl doing up there at that stable?"

"She wants me to let her help with the stable work."

After I was through eating, I went down to the riverboat to find Cole. I found him sitting not far from the boat, cutting on a piece of wood. I told him about the Jakobses going away, and maybe that would be a good time for us to go.

"When they goin'?"

"I'm not sure. I think in mid-February, some Friday, maybe the fifteenth day."

"How long they be gone?"

"I hear three weeks. I think that would be the first or second Friday in March."

"Boss man's talkin' 'bout leavin' 'round that time. Dat is, if we'se get everything done, and all the things loaded by den."

"Where?"

"Maybe up de big river, and den west. There's talk of goin' downriver, den goin' west, so I doan know for shore."

"What are they going to haul?"

"I hear talk of four people and all they'se things. I hear one fambly is farmers, and dey don't have a whole lot of things to take. And the other... I hear talk the others is goin' as far as boss man will take dem. They want to start a tradin' post of some kind, to trade wid the Injuns, it's said. These people have lots of stuff ... cows, horses, pigs, chickens ... an' a few dogs and cats."

"How many?"

"I'm not shore. Mebbe six horses, four cows, six pigs ... I doan know how many chickens."

"Cole, do you think there would be enough room to put ten animals on there, too?"

"What ten animals?"

"Well, I hope we can go out where you said, and catch a few ... that is, if you can find more out about where they are."

"I will ask around. Yeah, de boat will handle twenty big animals and de small ones. That means we kin get six or eight mules or horses. Yeah! The boat isn't a real big boat, but it's big enough to put everything on."

"I'm thinking if we could get on that boat with all our things, we may save ourselves a lot of time and hard travel."

"Where we goin'?"

"Where are we going? Yes, listen, Cole, we are going west. West—into the country few white or black men has gone, that I know of."

Cole's mouth dropped open. "Y-y-y-ya mean we are goin' somewhere where there is no *persons?*"

"Yes! There are probably Indians."

Cole didn't say anything. He looked at me, wide-eyed.

"Don't you want to go?"

"No ... yes! Yes, I'se wants to go."

"Do you think we can get our things on the boat?"

"I think so."

"Let's get everything ready, so it won't take us long putting it on." We made plans to stash our things close by, in a place he knew of, where they would be safe.

I didn't see Cole for several days. One evening, I went to look for him. I found him by the boat. He was so excited that he came running to meet me. We went for a walk, to get away, so no one would overhear us talking. He told me the crew working on the boat told the owner, John C. Brown, they would be done in a week. That would be next Friday.

"Next Friday! That's when Mr. Jakobes is to leave!"

"They told boss man dey will have it in the water by den. They're planning to take the boat upriver, to try it out, and make shore everything works ba'fore haulin' a load."

This was one of the first steam paddlewheel boats on the river. Mr. Brown had one other boat like this that was used mostly to haul people. Mr. Brown and his crew had worked most of the year getting it ready.

"They said dey would be gone about a week, and if everything worked out, dey hoped to have everything loaded and ready to leave the first Friday in March.

"Are you saying we should be leaving on the day Mr. Jakobes is to get back?"

"Yes."

"That would be great!" I told Cole I would come Sunday morning, and we would go look for some horses and that he was to see if he could find out more about where they were at.

It was dark when I got back to the shop. I went in and straight to bed.

Saturday turned out to be a long day, which made for a late supper, but Fanny was her jolly self, and while we were eating, I asked Charley if he knew anything about the horses that were running wild not far from town.

"I hear talk about them, that's about all. Why do you ask?"

"Cole and I are going tomorrow, to see if we can find them."

"Just you two?"

"Yes."

Charley looked at Fanny, then at me. "How many do you boys plan on catching?"

"We are hoping to get eight."

"Are you planning on leaving here with that many animals?"

"Yes. That would only give us five animals each. Is that too many?"

"No! I don't think so. Would you and Cole mind if I went along?"

"No, that would be great! With three of us, we may stand a better chance. Yes!"

"And I would like to get some for myself."

"You would?"

"Yes."

"What would you do with them?"

"I will tell you when the time is right."

"You will?"

"Yes. Before long. When are you and Cole going?"

"Right after breakfast. Will that be okay?"

"Yes."

I said good night and went back to the shop and was soon in bed.

Right after breakfast, Charley and I returned to the stable. We hitched up the horse and buggy. Charley saddled his horse. I got my two mules. I never had money to buy saddles, so I was used to riding bareback. We taken the horse and buggy to the house and tied it up out front for Mr. Jakobes. Then we rode off to find Cole.

We found him waiting, not far from the boat. When he saw us, he came running. I handed him the reins to one of my mules and he jumped on. Cole told us the horses were maybe three miles downriver. Charley led the way as we headed downriver. I don't know how long or how far we rode when Charley stopped and motioned for us to get down.

We slid off our mounts quietly and went to where Charley was. He pointed to a herd of horses and mules grazing in a meadow several hundred yards ahead. There must have been fifty or more. Charley dismounted and motioned for us to follow him. He saw a place where we could watch the herd while we decided how we were going to catch them. As we watched, we noticed some were branded.

"Hell, we don't want any with brands," Charley said, after spitting a stream of tobacco juice. "Boys, I think if we walk close beside our animals, we may have a good chance of getting near enough to put a rope on some." For whatever reason, the herd didn't seem spooked. "You two go around that side, and I'll go between the herd and the river."

I whispered to Cole that he was to pick out whatever he wanted. I was going to try for some horses. Charley and Cole started out, circling the herd. I waited until Cole was almost in front of the herd. I slowly moved up from the rear. I was surprised when the herd didn't spook. A few of the younger ones became jittery and pranced around some, but soon calmed down. We were able to pick out the ones we wanted, and work our way close enough to throw a rope over their heads without spooking the others.

It taken a long time till we were able to get the ones we wanted. Cole picked out a nice, young, light brown mare and a stallion of the same color, plus three gray mules. Charley had six mares and two stallions of assorted colors. I was able to pick two nice young horses, one a coal black mare with four white feet, and a dark red stallion with white feet, and two black mules.

After making halters out of the rope we had brought, we got them split up in three groups and tied, so we would be able to lead them back home. It seemed like we were strung out a long distance as we wound and threaded our way along the river towards town.

When we got close to town, Charley taken a shortcut, which brought us to a big meadow a half mile or more back of the shop and stable. Charley said there was plenty of grass there, and if we hobbled the horses, they wouldn't go anywhere. After everything was taken care of, we went back to the stable and turned our animals out back.

Cole headed for home, and Charley and I went for supper.

22

The next week turned out to be very busy. Mr. Jakobes wanted to get as much work done as we could before Friday. It was a hard four days, and by early Thursday afternoon, we had everything finished that Mr. Jakobes wanted done. He went to the house, and that gave me a little time to go check on the horses. Charley said we would brand the horses on Friday, so he started making up some branding irons while I was checking the horses.

When Friday morning came, Charley and I taken the buggy and two horses to the house before we went for breakfast. After we were through eating, we loaded Mr. and Mrs. Jakobes' luggage on the back of the buggy. After everything was loaded, I waited while Mr. and Mrs. Jakobes gave Charley and Fanny their instructions for the time they would be gone. They soon climbed into the buggy and were on their way. Charley and I followed as they headed for town.

After we had put everything on board the boat, Charley drove the horse and buggy, and I led his horse beside me on our way back to the shop. After doing the little work we had to get done, we went to the house. Fanny fixed us some lunch, and as we ate, Charley and her talked. The more I listened, the more I thought about them. We finished eating and went back to the shop. Charley went to work, making branding irons, and I went to get some of the horses from the pasture that we were going to brand.

By the time I got back, Charley had the branding irons made. We started branding our horses—a brand for Cole, one for Charley, and one for myself. It wasn't long before we were done. We finished the afternoon grooming the horses and making halters, and returning the horses and mules to their pasture, and did our other work. By now, it was time to clean up and go for supper.

As we walked into the kitchen, Fanny gave each of us a

big hug. I had become used to it, and now looked forward to her pulling me close. As we sat down to eat, I thought maybe Kate would be eating with us. Just then, Charley mentioned it to Fanny, as if he had read my mind. Fanny said Kate had eaten.

I finished eating, then left and headed for the boat to find Cole. He had just got done with his work. There was no one around, so he taken me aboard the riverboat and showed me around. It had more room on the inside than it looked. He showed me where the livestock would be stalled—the feed, supplies and everything that was coming on board. I couldn't help but think, *this is where I will be in a short time.* We talked and made plans that I would start bringing our things on board as soon as the boat got back from its test run.

It was getting late. I told Cole I was going back to the shop. He asked me if we were going into town Saturday night. I thought about it, but decided it would be best if we didn't. For one thing, I didn't want another fight like the last time. We were lucky then. Maybe next time, we would get shot or something worse. We talked a little longer about what we were going to do, once we got under way. We didn't know how far this boat could go, or how far it was going.

"I need to go, Cole. I will see you in a few days." I went back to the shop. I guessed Charley was with Fanny, for he was nowhere around the stable. I went on into the stable and to bed, for I knew we had some work to do on Saturday.

Charley and I were up early Saturday morning, and went for breakfast. Fanny was happier than I had ever seen her. She gave me a big hug and said, "Sit, son, and eat." I could see the sparkle in her big brown eyes when she gave Charley a hug. "Come sit."

Fanny brought our plates piled full, along with coffee and milk.

As soon as I was through eating, I went back to the shop. Charley lingered with Fanny for a time, then came back and went to work without saying anything, except what he wanted me to do. I could tell he had something on his mind. I kept on working, not wanting to interrupt his thoughts.

Mid-day, Fanny brought things to eat and drink. I taken my things to eat and went outside to sit in the sun. I could hear them talking in the shop, but I couldn't make out what was being said.

When I finished eating, I went back to work. Sometime

later, Charley went to his room. When he came back, he handed me a pouch with money and a note, then told me to take one of the horses and go to the Dog Fish Saloon in town. "And give the pouch to the bartender."

I did as he told me. I rode into town, tied up at the Dog Fish Saloon, then went in. There was some people in there. No one even looked as I walked up to the bar.

The bartender came over to where I was standing and said, "What do you want?"

I just handed him the pouch. He taken it and read the note, putting change back in, and handed it and two bottles of whiskey back to me.

"Go now!"

I taken my time getting back to the shop, went in, and gave everything to Charley. He taken it and put it in his room. When he came back, he told me that we were done, and I was to go and check on the horses and mules we had in the back pasture. I walked back to where they were, and looked each one over real good. All were fine. I returned to the stable and taken care of the horses as Charley closed up shop.

After washing up, we went for supper. We walked into the kitchen and Fanny was there to meet us. I was surprised to see Kate sitting there. I sat across from her. She was smiling, and her green eyes sparkled as she said hello.

"Hello, Kate." Fanny brought our plates full of food, then Charley and she sat down and started to eat. Before long, they were too busy talking to notice that Kate and I were even there. We talked while we ate. I finished my supper, said good night to Kate, and picked up my things and taken them to the sink. Turning around to leave, I saw Kate looking at me, smiling. Charley and Fanny were talking and didn't notice as I went out the door.

I returned to the shop, where I had a big tub of water heating for my bath. After all, it was Saturday night. I filled the tub, then put more water on to heat for Charley. After bathing, I washed out my clothes and hung them up to dry. Dumping the water out, I returned the tub and went into the stable to bed.

I was lying there, thinking over the things I had to do before leaving. We would need two days to get everything on board. Cole had told me there would be a crew of five, him and I, and four other people, but he didn't know who. Plus two cows, one bull, some pigs and chickens, and with our horses there would be twenty-five big animals, and a lot of small crates.

I heard Charley come in, making a lot of noise, getting his bath water, then taking his bath. He sounded very happy, singing as he bathed. It wasn't long before I heard him take the bath water out and dump it, making a lot more noise putting things away. It wasn't long before I heard the shop door closing. I got up to see what was going on. As I looked out the window, the moon shone bright enough that I was able to see Charley with a bottle in his hand, heading in the direction of Fanny's room, which was attached to the back side of the main house and pantry.

I lay back on my bed, smiling. What I had suspected must be true between the two of them. I lay there thinking, my bed bathed in the light from the moon as it flowed through the window not far away, when I was startled by the latch on the stable door being lifted, and the door being opened very slowly. I could see the door fairly good. I reached for my pistol that was lying close by. Very slowly, I picked it up and pulled the hammer back into the firing position, not making any sound. Not moving, I just lay there and waited. There wasn't enough light coming in so that I could make out the figure who was in the doorway. Very carefully, it closed the door and latched it, then turning, moved very slowly toward where I was laying. I was puzzled as to who this person was or what they wanted.

They made very little sound closing the distance to where I lay. My heart was pounding as I pointed my pistol directly at this person from under the blankets. The person stopped just off to my left side and stood there. There was enough moonlight now that I was able to make out who it was. Slowly, I uncocked my pistol and laid it down. All the while, keeping my eyes partly closed, so she would think I was sleeping.

I watched as she undid her coat and slid it off. Carefully, she laid it down beside me. Next, she reached down and pulled her dress up and over her head, then laid it on her coat. As she stood there in the moonlight, I could see that she had nothing on. She reached down and lifted up the corner of the blanket and slowly crept underneath. After lying there a few minutes, she moved tight against me. I stirred a little and then relaxed as if I were sleeping. She lay on her right side and slowly placed her left hand on my chest. Carefully, she undid the buttons on my long underwear. Putting her hand underneath, she moved her fingertips very lightly over my chest, down over my stomach. I could feel the softness of her hand and fingers as they moved over my chest and stomach, and just a little below my waist, then up. With eyes barely open, I could see her mouth was only inches away from mine. I reached up with my right hand and pulled her down as her mouth met mine.

Her first reaction was to pull away. My hand was tight on the back of her head, and in less than a heartbeat she relaxed. Then, moving her left leg over on top of me, more or less holding me down as she pressed her lips to mine, I held her tight. While we were kissing, she pushed my underwear down over my shoulders. I sat up as she moved them down around my waist. I lay back and raised my hips as she moved them down until they were at my feet. And off they came.

She was beside me on her knees now. I could see the light from the moon as it came through the window and played over her long red hair that hung down over her left shoulder and partly covered her small but upturned titties. Her right one was not covered as the moonlight filtered across it. I raised up on my left elbow and looked into those green eyes.

In a low voice I asked, "What are you doing here, Kate?"

She just sat there on her knees, looking at me, not saying anything.

"Kate, do you know what you are doing?"

No answer.

"Have you ever done anything like this before?"

No answer.

I reached out and placed my hand on her shoulder and shook her. "Kate, do you hear what I'm saying?"

I must have startled her. She jerked back. This time she answered in a low voice, "No! No! I haven't! No, I never done anything like this ... Believe me ... uh, I just ... I know what you're thinking, but ... but it's not like that. I know it doesn't look good, but I didn't know how else to get you to pay any attention to me. I liked you ever since the day you came riding in here. You were so young, younger than I, and on your own and looking for work. Your long hair flowing over your shoulders, bare chest showing under your open coat. I could see how tall you were, sitting there on your mule, and the necklace you wore ... your necklace ... Did you get it from an Indian?"

"Yes, yes, I did."

"Tell me about it."

"It's a long story. I'll tell you some time. Not now. Kate, if you never done anything like this before, why are you here now?"

"I just told you!"

"What about your parents?"

"What about them? You know they went downriver."

"What would they say?"

"I would never tell them. So how would they know?"

"What about Fanny? What if she goes to look in on you?"

"She won't. Fanny is in her room with Charley."

"How do you know?"

"When I snuck by her room, I stopped and listened. They had a candle burning and were making all kinds of noises."

"Like what?"

"I don't know!"

"Kate, do you know what you're asking... what you are doing?"

"Yes, Nathan, I do. I'm old enough."

I was still resting on my elbow and she was on her knees. The moonlight and shadows played over her nakedness. Her red hair shone, and the dark mound where her legs came together was visible. Her nipples were erect from the coolness of the night. She never taken her eyes off me while we talked. I looked into her eyes and reached out, pulling her down beside me.

Her naked body was cold from sitting there. I pulled the blankets up around us as her head lay on my arm. With my other hand, I pulled her head over to mine and our lips touched and touched again. I was leaning over her, kissing her. Our mouths were locked together as our tongues searched for hidden sensations. Her arms pulled me closer. Her hand was on the back of my head, holding me firmly to her. My fingers were slowly touching her face and running through her long hair, slowly moving down over her neck and onto her shoulders, down her side and on down over her hips, thigh, up the inside. My hand brushed over the softness of her bush, up over a flat stomach and up, until I could feel the slope of her breast. My hand moved over the roundness of her firm tit, then over the other one and down her nakedness. All the while our mouths were searching, my hand was resting on the softness of her bush. Her legs moved apart as my hand slid in between, feeling her wetness.

We never stopped kissing and fondling. Our passion grew and grew. Low moans were coming from within her throat she shoved her hips up against my hand and held it firm with hers. Higher and higher our passion grew, and all the time reaching new heights, higher until our desire overtaken us. As I moved my leg over her, her legs parted, and my hand cupped her firm titties, as she guided me into her.

23

It wasn't light yet when Kate got up, dressed, and went out the door without saying anything. I lay there for a long time, thinking about Kate and what happened, and feeling so wonderful and content. The more I thought about Kate, the more I wondered. I drifted off to sleep.

When I finally got up, I felt rested and happy. I could tell it was late and way past sunup. I thought to myself, *Shit, it's Sunday and this may be one of my last Sundays here.* It was even nicer to think the boss was away. I finally got up and dressed and fed the animals. By now, I was damn hungry. I knew I would be late for breakfast, but what the hell ... I'd go in and see what Fanny had to eat.

As I walked into the kitchen, I got a surprise. There at the table sat Charley, Fanny and Kate. They just started to eat. As soon as Fanny saw me, she jumped up and went and fixed me a plate. I taken my usual place beside Charley. I was facing Kate. Fanny fetched more coffee and milk, setting them on the table, then sat down beside Kate.

Fanny was saying all the while, "Boys, dis you all slept good last night?"

"Yes, ma'am, I did!"

Charley looked over at me, then said, "Boy, ain't you a little late for breakfast this morning?"

"Breakfast is a little late today, so that's why I'm late."

Kate looked at Charley and Fanny and all three burst out laughing. I didn't know what was so funny, but it was great to see them all so happy and laughing. This was the first time I saw anyone laugh while we ate in all the time I was there. I looked up and saw Kate looking at me with those green eyes. Her face was lit up with happiness. This was the happiest I ever saw her. At the same time, she was taking her bare feet and playing with my toes. Then she tried to run her feet up my pants leg. I almost burst out laughing when she tickled the sole of my foot with her toe, but I didn't dare. I was afraid Charley and Fanny may think something was funny and want to know. I kept on eating like nothing was happening. Now and then, I would glance up to see if Charley or Fanny were looking. They weren't. They were too much into themselves. I would look at Kate and she would be all smiles. I thought to myself, *Is this why everyone is so happy, including myself, or is it because the Jakobses are not here?* Or was it a little of both? I thought about it and decided it must be a little of both.

I finished my eating. Getting up to take my dishes to the pantry, I asked Charley if there was anything he wanted me to do. "No, it's Sunday, boy." I told them I would be back sometime in the afternoon. After I taken my dishes to the pantry, I went back and gave Fanny a big hug. Kate was watching and gave me a big smile. I could see she wanted to go.

I didn't say anything and went out the door and headed for the riverboat to find Cole. When I got there, Cole was nowhere to be seen. I went up the gangplank and onto the boat. I didn't see him, so I went down below, where I knew he slept.

There I found Cole, all curled up on a pile of straw with a blanket over him. I saw something was wrong. I sat down beside him. "Cole, what happened?"

Cole tried to sit up and looked at me. "You doan wanna know."

"Yes, Cole, I do. What the hell happened?"

Cole then told me that he didn't get all his work done last night, and that the boss man was drinking and playing cards until daylight and must have lost some money. "Dis mornin', boss man come down here 'fore I was awake and tied my hands, then tied me to de post, then beat me wid a horse whip."

Pulling the blanket back, I could see his back, buttocks and legs were all covered with big welts and cuts. I started to help him get dressed, but could see he was hurting bad. I looked around and found a large cotton sack. I cut a hole in the bottom for his head to go through and one on each side for his arms. This way it would hang on him like a dress and not be tight like his shirt and pants.

"Here, Cole, put this on," I told him.

At first, he balked. I told him it would be better than his clothes. Finally, he put the sack over his head and his arms through the holes. It hung down almost to his feet. I asked him how it was.

"It's much better than my's clothes."

"Let's go!"

"Where're we goin'?"

"You're going with me, back to the blacksmith shop, so I can take care of you."

"No, I'se not!"

"Yes, Cole, damn you, you're going! Don't be that way."

"I'se not goin'!'"

"Look, Cole, if we are going to be together from now on, we are going to take care of each other, do you understand?"

"I'se don't know! Hell! Damn you ... all right! Since you puts it dat way... I'se'll go."

I taken him by the hand and helped him off the boat. We made our way to the blacksmith shop. Once there, I taken him into the stable, where my bed was. I had him take the sack dress off and I laid it out on a pile of straw, then had him lie down on it, on his stomach.

"I'll be right back."

"Where's you goin'?"

"I'm going to get something to put on you, so it will feel better. Just stay here. And be still! All right?" I hurried to Fanny's room. She wasn't there, so I went into the kitchen, and there her and Charley were still sitting at the table. I told them what happened.

They both jumped up and hurried to the stable with me. Fanny knelt beside Cole, and when Cole saw who it was, he started to pull his the sack over him.

Fanny threw it aside. "Now here, boy, you done laid still. I done saw naked persons 'fore I'se seen you. Now I gonna fix you'se all right up. Charley, go out and fetch me some of those aloe plants."

Just then, Kate came in. Now Cole *did* put up a bitch. Fanny pushed his head back down. "Boy, now you'se done be still, else I give you somethin' to holler about."

Cole lay down and was quiet.

"Kate, you'se goes fetch me some warm water, soap and a rag."

Without a word, she went running. She was back in no time with a pan of warm water, soap, a rag and a towel. Kate set it down beside Fanny. Fanny taken the rag and dipped it in the warm water, rubbed it with soap, and very carefully began bathing Cole's back and legs.

I was kneeling on the other side of Cole. Kate came over

and knelt beside me and put her hand in mine. Fanny looked at her, but didn't say a thing.

"Is he going to be all right?" Kate asked.

"He's gonna be all right. He's one tough boy." Fanny just finished patting Cole with the dry towel as Charley came hurrying in with the plants. Fanny taken the plants and washed them in the warm water, then broke them open, telling Charley to wash his hands and to hold the plants over Cole's backside and squeeze them. Charley did as she said. He squeezed the plants, and out came this thick, gooey-looking stuff. Kate and I were dumbfounded as Fanny taken her fingers and spread the gooey stuff all over Cole's backside.

"That sure feels good," moaned Cole.

"Now you'se done lies here all day, you hear, boy?"

"Yes, ma'am."

Charley looked at Kate and I. She was still holding my hand. Then he looked at Fanny. She looked at him and nodded. Neither spoke. He got up and went through the door into the shop. I could hear him in his room. Then I heard him get his horse and ride off.

Fanny stood up, saying, "Boy, you'se just lies here, and I will be back and look in on you." She left, and I thought Kate would leave with her. Instead, she moved closer to me and sat down.

Cole was looking at her and after some time said, "Who is she?"

"This is Kate, the boss man's girl."

No one spoke. Kate and I sat there, watching Cole. Finally, he went to sleep. Kate then put her arm around my neck and pulled me down on top of her, kissing me. I pulled away and told her to quit. She started to giggle. I motioned for her to be quiet and pointed to Cole. I didn't want him to wake up. It was best he sleep.

She got up and taken my hand and pulled until I got up, then led me through the doors and out behind the stable, where she threw her arms around me and kissed me. I returned the kiss, then pulled away.

"Kate, someone is going to see us! Then what?"

She smiled, saying, "I don't care!"

"You will, if your dad finds out."

"Well! Well maybe! Maybe he would be mad. Okay." Then she asked me what happened to Cole. I didn't answer. "Well, what happened?"

"You don't want to know."

"Yes, I do! I must know!"

"You won't like what I would tell you."

"You must tell me, Nathan. I'm big enough, so that I should know! Now tell me!"

"Yes, you're big enough to know what some people do to others, and being black don't help! You must promise not to tell anyone!"

"Okay!"

"You wouldn't want me to tell on you, would you?"

"I promise!"

"Damn it to hell, Mr. Brown boss man tied him to a post this morning and beat him with a horse whip. Cole told me that he was unable to get all his work done that Mr. Brown loaded on him Saturday, and Mr. Brown was drinking and maybe lost some money. So, this morning he taken his anger out on Cole."

"Is Cole going with you when you go away?"

"Why do you ask?"

"I just wanted to know. Besides, I hear talk that you and Cole are close friends. You know, not many white people have Negroes for friends. That's what some people are saying."

"Who?"

"Just some of the people in town. I heard about the fight you and Cole got into at that saloon."

"Who told you that?"

"Just some people. They also are saying you and Cole are hellish good fighters, who would die for each other, and you are blood brothers."

We were sitting out back. I leaned against the warm building as she sat in front, facing me, the warm sun shining on us as the flies and bees hummed around. The birds were singing and doing their mating calls off in the distance. Peepers were peeping. I was enjoying the afternoon sun. And I didn't answer. I didn't say anything. I was looking at her and felt sorrow because she was not allowed to do anything on her own. If her parents knew what she was doing, it would be hard to tell what would happen.

"Well, are you?"

"What?"

"Just what I asked you!"

"Cole and I?"

"Yes!"

"What do you think, Kate?"

She didn't answer. A blank look moved across her face as her thoughts drifted far away. She had been staring into my eyes for several minutes, yet not seeing me. Then, blinking her eyes a few times, she slowly looked around. Then in a low, compassionate voice she said, "I don't care. I don't give a damn if you and Cole are blood brothers, and I don't care if Cole is a Negro. He is your friend. I want him to be my friend. Nathan, when you go away, and I know you will, please take Cole with you, so they won't beat or maybe kill him. Nathan, I want to go with you and Cole."

"Why?"

"This is not a good place to live, like people think it is. There's no happiness. It's just a place to live. My mother and father aren't what people think they are."

"Kate, listen. Do you want to sleep in someone's stable, take handouts, not knowing where your next meal is coming from or when? Do you know what it's like sleeping on the ground when it's cold or rainy, not knowing what's around you or who? Kate, here you have good food, a warm place to sleep, hot water for your bath whenever you want one. Where I'm going there is nothing—nothing like you have here."

"I don't care! I don't want to live here anymore." Her green eyes filled with tears. Her tears spilled over, running down her freckled cheeks. As I stood up, she threw her arms around my waist, holding me tight as her sobs came and came. I lifted her to her feet, looking into her teary wet face and saw so much hurt, so much for a young girl. I kissed her wet eyes, then placed my lips on hers. "Take me, please!" She choked and sobbed as I kissed her.

"Let's go and check on Cole."

Cole was awake and we sat down beside him and asked how he was doing. Just then, Fanny and Charley came into the stable. When Fanny saw Kate, she said, "Kate, what's all you does sittin' out here with these'n boys?"

"I ..."

"What's yo' folks done gonna say?"

"I don't care! And I won't tell!"

"You'se better not!"

"I won't!"

Charley just stood, not saying anything, as Fanny knelt to look at Cole. Then, she rubbed some more of the plant on his back. "There's now, boy, you'se be all better comes mornin'. You'se get dressed and alls you'se comes in and I'se feed you'se supper."

Kate got up and went with Fanny and Charley. I helped Cole get dressed. He was still sore. The whip marks were now more bearable. After getting him dressed, we headed for the house and supper. When Cole and I walked in, Fanny and Kate had the table set and the food ready to be served. This was the first time I saw Kate help in the kitchen.

Fanny said sit and everyone taken their places. Cole sat beside me. Fanny had cooked an excellent supper, and everyone was enjoying the meal and talking. Charley and Fanny were asking Cole about the boat, what his job was on the boat, and so on. Comments were made and everyone would laugh. It was the most enjoyable meal I had eaten there. Everything was so good, the kitchen was filled with happiness. It was like ... well, a home should be! When I would look at Kate, she would be smiling. Her eyes sparkled with the love she was feeling. I could feel the joy, excitement and contentment she was experiencing. The expression on her face told me that the time she spent with us this day and this meal may have been the closest she ever came to having a real family, even though she had parents. I felt so helpless, so sad and hurt, I could feel her pain, yet I knew there was little I could do.

Fanny topped the meal off with a cake she baked that afternoon. Charley said, "I think this is the best meal I ever had," and everyone agreed and thanked Fanny.

It was getting late. I told Cole to come and I would walk him home.

Charley said, "No, Nathan, *I'll* take him back with the buggy. I had a talk with Mr. Brown, and he won't be beating him any more. You can be sure of that, and Cole, you don't have to work until you are healed up. When you're ready, I will take you. Nathan, you take care of the animals and put me some water on to get hot until I get back."

Kate got up and taken my plate and started cleaning off the table. Fanny looked at Kate, then at me, and smiled. Charley and Cole were leaving, so I headed to the shop and put enough water on for Charley and myself. I figured if Charley was bathing, maybe I should also. While the water was heating, I went and taken care of the animals.

It wasn't long before Charley returned. I helped him unhitch the horse from the buggy and put the horse out. While I finished up, he headed for the shop and taken his bath. When he was through, he dressed and went to the house. I knew he was going in to be with Fanny.

After taking my bath, I put everything where it belonged, dressed and pulled my coat on and stepped outside. To my surprise, it was warmer than I expected. I sat down on the bench and leaned back against the shop and watched as the moon, big and orange, peeped over the horizon and shone through the trees far to the east. It was still. I could hear the quacking of ducks and, now and then, a flight of geese honking as they winged their way upriver and north.

I watched as the lamps went out in the down part of the house. A faint one shone through a window in Fanny's room. As I sat there, the stillness of the night grew more intense, and it had cooled. I saw the light in Kate's room go out. It wasn't long before I heard the sound of her coming. She was halfway when an owl let out a hoot not far away. She taken off running and didn't stop until she got to where I was sitting, and sat down tight against me, out of breath, saying, "What was that?"

"An owl."

Sitting there, everything was still and it was getting cooler. Laying her head on my shoulder, I put my arm around her, pulling her close. A faint reply came through the night from an owl far to the south. We sat talking and listening to the sounds of night. A wolf howled somewhere far across the river, or maybe by it. Kate trembled and said, "Let's go in."

"Okay."

Getting up, we made our way through the shop and into the stable to my bed. Moonlight spilled through the window, bathing it in light. Taking my coat off, I threw it on the bed and Kate did hers. I reached for her, pulling her close. Our lips touched and our mouths locked together. We kissed and fondled for some time. With intense passion raging, I pulled away. Reaching down, I taken hold of her dress, pulling it up to her waist, then over her head. I tossed it on the bed. She was naked. I could tell she had just bathed. Her hair was still wet and she smelled so good. Standing there with the moonlight playing over her nakedness, she was very arousing and stirred sensations deep within me. I was out of my clothes and holding her close, our nakedness touching, and feeling the cool night air. Whispering, I said, "Let's get under the blankets."

In no time, we were in each other's arms with the blankets pulled up around us, our arms and legs twisted and entwined around each other. The feel of nakedness to nakedness as we pressed our bodies tight to one another was so stimulating, and with our touching and our tongues playing, it wasn't long before our desire sent shivers of sensation ripping throughout our passionate bodies. She whispered now as she pulled me onto her.

24

Kate was up and gone just as it was getting light. I lay there for a while, then got up and did some of my work before going for breakfast. As I walked into the kitchen, I saw Kate helping Fanny. Charley was sitting at his place and didn't say anything, as usual. While we were eating, Kate and I didn't do much talking. Instead, we listened mostly to what Charley and Fanny were talking about. After a while, Charley did ask me about our horses and mules. I told him I would like to go and check on them after I finished with my work. "That would be good, boy, you go ahead."

Kate looked at me with a surprised look, but didn't say anything. I had finished eating and was about to get up when Kate jumped up and taken my plate and hers to the sink. Then she went into the other part of the house to get ready for school. As I was going out the door, I heard Fanny say to Charley, "I'se wonder what's gotten into that girl."

I went back to the shop and finished my chores, then went looking for our animals. I found them way back in the far end of the pasture. I decided to try to ride one of mine. When I went to jump on the black one, she bucked me off in a hurry. I hit the ground so hard, I saw stars. It knocked the wind out of me for a few seconds.

I jumped up, cursing. Nothing hurt, just my pride. *The hell with it, I'll try the red one.* This one seemed tamer. I petted and talked to him for a while before I tried to get on. Once he settled down, I grabbed hold of his mane and swung up on his back and clung to his mane with both hands. He reared and pranced for a while. Somehow I hung on. Finally, he settled down.

I slid off and walked beside him, sort of leading him in the direction of the stable. As I walked beside him, I couldn't help wondering if he once belonged to someone. He seemed so tame for running wild. The rest started to follow. Once I was closer to the stable, I stopped and petted and talked to him while the rest wandered closer. As I left him and was walking toward the stable, I had a good feeling about this horse making me a fine animal.

When I walked into the shop, Charley asked how the animals were.

"They are doing real good, but they were way back in the pasture, so I brought them closer to the stable." I told him what I did.

He laughed. "Boy, you be more careful around those horses! I have no idea why that one seemed more tame. By the way, this is a list of the work Mr. Jakobes said we were to get done while he was away." Then he read it off.

I looked at him. "Wow! That's a lot of work!"

"Not really. I hope we can get it all done in the next two weeks."

I looked at him. "I know we will have to work hard, and I won't get much time to go see Cole."

"Probably not."

"Charley, I must tell you something."

"What?"

"I will be leaving on the day Mr. Jakobes gets back. That is, if the boat is loaded."

"Where are you going?"

"I'm going as far as the boat goes, or will take me and Cole. I hear that the boat is going downriver, then west on another river, maybe as far as they can go."

"You don't say! Do you know how many other people are going?"

"I'm not sure, but I hear four others and some animals."

"I'm sure the boat will be ready by then. Now, get to work or we won't get it all done."

"Okay."

We worked very hard all week. On Sunday, I went and saw Cole and we spent all afternoon checking over the things we would be putting on the boat. Cole said he hadn't been working so hard since Mr. Brown went with the boat to try it out. He was sure the boat would be back the next Sunday, Monday at the latest. If the boat checked out good, we would start loading Tuesday and should be ready to shove off Friday morning.

"That sounds good, Cole, it's getting late and time for me to get back and do my chores. I'll see you soon!"

I ran most of the way back to the shop and hurried with my work to get it done, then ran to the house for supper, thinking I would be late, but when I went in, Kate and Fanny were just putting the food on the table. As soon as I sat down, I could tell something was wrong.

No one said anything while we ate. Charley and Fanny spoke a few words, and Kate asked me if I saw Cole and how he was doing. Other than that, nothing else was said. I could see Kate and Fanny both were upset. I finished eating as quickly as I could, without looking too obvious. After taking my dishes to the sink, I said good night, and ran back to the shop and started gathering some of the things I wanted to take with me. I had put them on a pile and was about to go to bed when Charley came in.

"Hey, boy, come in here. I need to talk with you."

I walked over to his room and stood in the doorway, not knowing what to expect.

"Sit, boy."

I stepped in and sat on a box that was next to the door. I could see he was pouring some whiskey into a couple of mugs. He turned around and handed me one, then sat on the bed. He looked at me for a while, sipping at his whiskey. I sat there, holding the mug of whiskey, not knowing what to expect. I was feeling a little uncomfortable when he finally spoke.

"Boy, we all have a problem."

Relaxing a little, I started sipping on the whiskey, but couldn't possibly imagine what he was talking about.

"Boy, I don't know where to start and I know you're man enough to understand what I'm about to say. Well, some years ago, I was just drifting and wound up here, was out of work more than I worked, drinking a lot. Mr. Jakobes' blacksmith business had grown to the place where he could no longer handle it by hisself. He had heard talk that I did smithing work. Well, one afternoon, he rode into town looking for me. He knew what my name was, but didn't know what I looked like, so he started asking around, and finally someone told him to check in the Dog Fish Saloon. I was standing at the far end of the bar, having a drink or two, when I heard this man down at the other end of the bar ask the bartender if he knew a Charley Blackstone. The bartender said yes.

"The man then asked if he knew where he could find him. The bartender pointed at me and said 'that's him.' Mr. Jakobes walked down to where I was standing and stood next to me.

'Are you Charley Blackstone?'

" 'That all depends who's doing the asking,' I answered.

" 'Excuse me, mister, I'm Mr. Jakobes. May I buy you a drink?'

" 'That all depends why.'

" 'Well, then, I'll come straight to the point. I'm the owner of the only blacksmith shop around and business has grown to where I can no longer handle all the work by myself. And I'm in need of a good man that can do smith work. It is told that you're damn good at smith work. I would like to hire you, that is if you are Mr. Blackstone and, of course, looking for work.'

" 'Yes, I'm Mr. Blackstone. Just call me Charley. I do need work. I'll take that drink now.' He called the bartender and ordered two whiskeys. The bartender poured, then Mr. Jakobes paid.

" 'Do you mind if we sit at a table where we can talk?'

" 'That's fine.' We sat at one of the tables and I asked Mr. Jakobes to tell me what he had in mind.

"I won't go into all the details now, but we agreed on wages and a place to live and meals. Mr. Jakobes told me to start in the morning. Fanny had been working for the Jakobeses when they came here and started this blacksmith shop. She was somewhat of a slave, if you know what I mean. So they just brought her with them.

"At first, I didn't pay any mind to her. She was just another cook and house cleaner. As time passed, I taken a liking to Fanny, and over the years we have grown very close, and I came to realize what a beautiful, good-hearted, hard-working woman she was. She has taken care of the Jakobeses all these years, and they treat her like dirt, mostly Mrs. Jakobes.

"The more time that passed, the more I knew that I wanted her to be part of my life and a part of me. A few years ago, I told her of my dreams of going west somewhere and building a trading post to trade with the Indians, and anyone else that may happen by. I knew sooner or later people would move farther west. I asked her if she would like to go. She said, 'Are you asking me?' I said yes, I was. She told me she was delighted that I thought enough of her that I would want her to be a part of my life.

"Boy, I knew a lot of women—most in whorehouses—but none that could come close to Fanny. She never had a man in her life before. Fanny never gets paid because of her color, so to help out, she would do sewing in her spare time, mostly at night, and I would take the things she made to town and sell them at the stores. We put our money together and would order things out of the East that we would need to supply a trading post. Everything was shipped in crates. After I would look everything over and make a list, I would put the things back in their crates to be stored. I knew of this fellow who had an old building he wasn't using. I asked him to use it, and we made a deal.

"So, boy, everything that is in that building will be loaded on that boat you're going on."

"The boat with Cole and me?"

"That's right. Most everything on that boat will be mine and Fanny's. We also have the tools to do blacksmith work with. If you and Cole would like to stay on with us, we would be happy to have the both of you. You know how much Fanny thinks of you.

"Boy, don't say anything about this, but for some reason Fanny can't have kids. That's why she taken to you when you came here to work. Now, Nathan, the problem is, today Fanny was in her room, packing some of her things, when Kate came looking for her. Fanny had the door open and Kate just walked in. She looked at Fanny and wanted to know what was going on.

"Fanny wouldn't lie, so she had no choice but to tell Kate that she was packing because she was leaving. I had just walked into the kitchen to see if I could help Fanny with the packing when I heard Kate saying, 'But, Fanny, you can't go! What will Mom and Dad do? You can't go!'

"Fanny said, 'I don't know what they will do.'

"Then I heard Kate starting to cry, 'But you can't go and leave me here just like that!' As they walked into the kitchen, Fanny had her arm around Kate, and Kate was sobbing, Fanny told her to sit down at the table and she would bring her a mug of milk. Kate sat down, tears running down her face. Fanny brought some milk, telling her to drink some.

"Fanny then sat down and put her arm around Kate and pulled her close, saying, 'Now, Kate, it's not all that bad.'

"She lay her head on Fanny's shoulder and sobbed. 'Now, Kate, pull yourself together.'

" 'Fanny, please, don't go. I have known for some time that Nathan was going. That's bad enough. But now you!' She looked at me and said, 'Are you going, too, Charley?'

" 'Yes, I'm afraid so.'

" 'What will I do? Nathan is the only one I had to talk to. Fanny, you have been more of a mother to me than Mom, since Mom and Dad have been away you left me help with the cooking, cleaning and washing clothes. Nathan let me help take care of the animals, and he even took me riding when he had time. All of you treated me like I was one of you! Fanny, tell me you're not going.'

" 'Kate, you must listen. All of us are going to go this Friday. You will be okay, Kate!'

" 'I have been begging Nathan to take me with him and Cole, but all he will say is, 'I don't want to talk about it.'

" 'Kate, listen to me,' I said, 'You must understand where Nathan and Cole are planning on going, not many white or black people have ever been, and Nathan and Cole have been much on their own ever since they were 15. And look how far Nathan has come with just his two mules. Kate, believe me, those two boys are very rough and tough young men. I saw them in a fight one night in one the saloons. I don't think either one is afraid of anything. I think Nathan is 17 now and I don't know about Cole. I would be proud to have either one for a son. I don't know much about Cole, but in the short time I have known Nathan, I must say, even though he is rough, he is one of the most patient and understanding persons I ever knew.'

" 'Are you going with Nathan?'

" 'No, not exactly. It just so happened that Nathan came to work here. He had told me some time ago that he would be leaving come spring. Fanny and I was planning on going the first chance we got, so when Nathan told me about the riverboat, I went to town and talked to the owner and made arrangements for his boat to take us west as far as they would. I don't know how far that will be.'

" 'Does Nathan and Cole know that you're going?'

" 'Yes.' Kate then said she wanted to go and asked for us to take her. She sobbed and cried and pleaded to go. I tried to get her to understand what she would do so far away from everything, and why she would want to give everything up that she has here.

"Then she started telling us, 'Things around here aren't what they seem to be with Mom and Dad. Oh yes, they go to church and all that stuff, and talk about sending me to some special school,' she said, 'which I don't want to go to, and Mom is always bitching that she wants to go back to Philadelphia.'

" 'Kate, what about the business?' I asked.

" 'I don't want it. I see what it has done to them. I hate it! I hate it! I even hate being around them. Besides, I'm going to be 18 before too long, and it's time for me to leave, too. If you won't let me go with you, I can get a job in one of the saloons.'

"After she said that, Fanny and I looked at each other. Then Fanny said, 'Kate, why don't you come and go to bed now? Me and Charley need to talk.' Fanny finally got Kate to bed after giving her some tea made from herbs to help her sleep.

"Nathan, I'm telling you this, so you will know what the problem is. Kate was very upset about our leaving. I'm hoping she will be better come morning. Fanny said she won't let her go to school, so maybe it will do her some good to spend the day helping around here."

I took another sip of the whiskey, then said, "I don't know what to say. Maybe it's best to wait and see what happens. Maybe once she thinks it over, she will change her mind, and if she don't, I guess we'll have to sit down with her and try to work something out."

"Maybe that's the best thing to do. Fanny and I have a question."

"What's that?"

"Do you want Kate to go?"

I was both shocked and surprised. I didn't answer right off. Instead, I sipped on my whiskey, then said, "No! I really don't."

"Why?"

"First, what would she do so far away from home? She's never been anywhere on her own."

"I know."

"And yet, Charley, I don't want to see her stay here, for she just might make good her threat, and she's bullheaded enough to try it, just to get even with her folks." Downing the last bit of the whiskey, I said, "Thanks, Charley, for telling me what was going on. I'll see you in the morning. It's been a long day and I'm going to bed."

The whiskey had made me drowsy and feeling funny. I had no more than crawled in bed and I was asleep.

25

Knowing the next day we had a lot of work to get done, I was up early and did some of my work. Then, when it was time, Charley and I went in for breakfast. We were sitting at the table, eating, when Kate came in. She looked tired and I could tell she had been crying and hadn't slept well. Fanny fixed her breakfast. As she was eating, Fanny told her she wasn't to go to school. She could do anything she wanted to. If she liked, she could help around the house. Kate said thanks.

Charley and I worked all morning, and it was getting close to noon when Kate walked in and asked me if I would help her hitch a horse to the buggy. I looked at Charley. "Go help her, boy." I told Kate to go get one of the horses from out back. She went and led one to where the buggy was kept. I went out and showed her how to hitch the horse to the buggy. She didn't have much to say while I was showing her how to hitch up. Then I helped her in, telling her to tie the horse up at a hitching post if she was going to leave the buggy.

She looked at me as I handed her the reins. I could see the tears swelling in her eyes as she said, "Please," and drove off. I stood there watching her go down the lane. I returned to my work, and by mid-afternoon we had everything done and loaded on the wagon.

Charley said, "Boy, I need to deliver this stuff to the people who ordered it, and help them put it together. While I'm gone, clean up in here, and check on the animals out back. I'll be back in time for supper."

"Okay." I was cleaning in the shop when I heard Kate come back with the buggy. She tied up and came to the door.

"Nathan, would you help me unhitch the buggy?"

"I'll be right out." I went to where she had the buggy, and told her what to do. As we undid the harness, I let her do most of the unhitching, so she would know how. Once done, I said, "Kate, get hold and help push the buggy in its place."

She did it without saying anything.

"That's good. Now take the horse back and put it with the others."

"Okay, I can do that." She led the horse around back and I went back to my cleaning.

It wasn't long before she came in and stood looking at me. I didn't know what to say. I thought she would start in about going. I kept working.

"Do you want some help?"

I stopped and looked at her. "If you want to."

"What do I do?"

"Grab the shovel and hold it, so I can sweep this dirt on it."

"The shovel is full. Now what do I do with it?"

"Take it out around that corner and throw it on that heap out there."

She did and came back for what was left, bringing the shovel back. I taken it and put it and the broom away and closed up the doors. She asked, "What are you doing now?"

"I must go check on the animals."

"Where?"

"Out back!"

"Do you mind if I go?"

"Suit yourself." I went back through the stable and grabbed two bridles on my way and headed for the back pasture. She stayed right beside me.

"What are you going to do with the bridles?"

"I'm going to put them on my horses."

"Oh."

"Did you have any trouble when you went to town?"

"No! I did as you told me, and everything went like you said."

"What did you do all that time in town?"

"Nathan, that's the first time I was ever in a store by myself, so I went in every store I could find. I enjoyed going to town on my own, for once. It made me feel so good, whole, like a woman. Thanks! Thanks to all of you for helping me grow up. Mostly you. You taught me what it's like to be a woman."

By now, we were in the back pasture. I was looking around for the horses and didn't see any of them.

"Where do you think they are?"

"I don't know!"

"Could they have run away?"

"Maybe. But I don't think so."

"Why?"

"I had hobbles on all of them."

"Could someone have taken the hobbles off and taken them?"

"I suppose, but our hobbles are made out of chain and we have links that aren't that easy to open. I think they're here somewhere. Kate, you go along this side of the pasture. I'll cross the creek and take the other side. Look for anything that may tell us which way they went."

"All right."

"Holler if you find anything."

"All right." She started off looking.

I cut across the creek and, looking on that side, I could see her most of the time. After a half mile or so, I lost sight of her. I cut across the creek and headed at an angle so I would come out in front of where I last saw her. It was low here and the bushes were high and thick. I was unable to see any distance.

I was almost to the place I thought Kate should be when she gave out a yell that could have been heard the whole way back to town. I thought, *What the hell happened?* I taken off running as fast as my legs could fly. I don't think my feet hit the ground half the time. She was closer than I thought, and I was to where she stood in no time, and, out of breath I asked, "What the hell happened, Kate?"

"Nothing happened. I just found the horses and mules."

"Where?"

"Up there!"

"Up where?"

"Can't you see? Right up there!" She pointed in the direction they were, then I finally saw them. They were in a little grove of trees on the side of a hill a short distance off.

"God, thanks! I would have looked till dark before I would have found them. How did you find them?"

"I saw tracks back there a little ways and followed them. When I got here, I heard one of them bray. Like you, I had to look and look before I could see them. When I did, I gave out a yell for you."

"I know! The way you yelled, I thought something happened to you. Come, let's go and try to get them."

We hurried to where the animals were feeding.

"I'm going to try and get a bridle on one of mine."

"Which ones are yours?"

"There! You see the dark red stallion with white feet."

"Yes."

"That's one, and look on the far side. The black mare with white feet. That's the other one."

"They're beautiful animals, all of them!"

"You stay here and I'll circle around behind them. When you see I'm back there, you move slowly toward them. Maybe that will distract them enough so I can get close and get a bridle on one."

"Okay, I'll wait here."

I circled around and came in from behind. They were watching Kate as she moved toward where they were. This gave me a chance to move. The one I wanted was off to my right. I moved up beside her and ran my hand down over her side. She jumped a little. I moved on forward, running my hand over her back and along her neck and around her head. With my left hand, I slid the bridle up over her nose and was able to get it in place and buckled. All the while I was petting and talking to her, she started prancing and reared a few times. I finally got her settled down. With all the confusion, the rest moved away.

I led her over to where Kate was. She was all smiles and jumped up and down. "You did it! You did it!" and flung her arms around me and held me tight.

"Come, Kate, let's get going."

"Okay, what do you want me to do?"

"Here, take hold of the bridle and rope and lead her towards the stable."

"What are you going to do?"

"I'm going to get the rest rounded up and hope they will follow you."

Kate started along the pasture and I circled the rest and got them moving in her direction. Luck was with us. They started following her. When I got a chance, I moved up beside the red stallion and did the same to him as I did the mare. He shied away time after time. Finally, he settled down enough for me to get the bridle on him. Then he got a little wild, rearing and bucking. I had him roped in good and was able to keep out of his way. I kept pulling on the rope as hard as I could. After a while, he settled down. Having hobbles on him helped.

Kate was far ahead of me by now and I knew I would have to hurry to catch up. Keeping a short hold on the stallion and pushing him as fast as I could, we were able to keep the other animals moving in the right direction. Kate had gone. It taken some time before I was able to catch up. Yelling, I told her to wait up and let the other animals move ahead. She waited and let the remaining animals move past. Once I was up beside her, I asked her how she was doing.

"I'm doing great and enjoying every bit of this very much. Nathan, thanks for letting me come along with you."

"Kate, let's go. We must move as fast as we can. It's going to be dark soon."

"Yes, I know!"

"And we have a long ways to go yet."

We hurried as much as we could. Kate was leading the way. I brought up the rear, in hopes of keeping them all together and moving. It wasn't quite dark when the stable came in sight. When we were a hundred yards or less from it, I yelled for Kate to stop. I taken the rope off the stallion, leaving the bridle on. Running to where Kate was, I taken the rope off the mare, also leaving her bridle on.

"I think they'll be all right here." I could barely make out the stable because of the darkness. Taking Kate's hand, I said, "Let's get going, or we won't be able to find our way."

We started off trotting until Kate's dress got caught on something and she fell. I grabbed her around the waist and lifted her to her feet.

"Are you hurt?"

"No."

"Then let's go." I taken her hand again. We went on, picking our way the best we could, getting to the stable in the dark. Charley had left a lantern burning in the shop. We went in and I found another lantern and lit it. Taking the lantern, we went out back to the corral. "Here, hold this light, so I can see while I feed them."

"Okay. Can you see now?"

"Yeah, that's fine. Let's see, one more fork full should be enough. There, that's it. Come, let's go for supper."

"I know. Fanny has it ready. Her and Charley are probably wondering what happened to us."

Getting to the house, we hung the lantern on a hook outside that was there for that purpose. When we walked in, Fanny came running and gave us each a hug.

"I'se so happy to see you'se all. Come and sat, and I'se got supper alls ready for you'se, and you'se can tell us where you'se kids has all been."

Kate and I sat down at the table while Fanny filled our

plates and brought them to the table, along with milk and coffee. Her and Charley were through eating, so she poured them more coffee, then sat down. They sat there, looking at us, and waiting for one of us to say something.

Looking at Kate, I saw she was eagerly waiting. I said, "Kate, why don't you tell them what all you did today?" I could see her smiling when I said that.

She giggled a little with excitement as she started telling how she taken the buggy and went to town for the first time, and how that was the first time she was in the stores without her mother, and how she came home and asked me to show her how to unhitch the horse from the buggy and put it in its place, and how she put the horse in the corral, and then helped me finish cleaning the shop, then how we went looking for the horses and mules, and every little detail that went on from the time we left the stable until we got back and fed the animals and came for supper.

I said, "It taken longer than I hoped it would."

Charley then told us that when he got home and didn't see us, he figured we were looking for the animals and maybe having some trouble finding them. We talked for a while about the work we needed to get done and about the livestock.

Finally, I said I was going to bed.

Charley said, "Wait, I'm going, too."

Fanny asked Kate if she would help her do up the dishes, "quickly." Kate said she would. Fanny came and gave us a hug and said, "See you all in the morning."

Going out, I picked up the lantern and Charley and I walked back to the shop, neither saying anything. Once in the shop, Charley went to his room and lit a lamp. I was headed for the stable when he came to the door. "Hey, boy, come in here." I went back to where his room was and walked in. He handed me a mug with some whiskey and said, "Sit. Nathan, as you know, we only have three days left here."

"Yes, I know!"

"We have a little work to do tomorrow in the shop. Then we'll close the doors. On Wednesday and Thursday, we'll move our things out of here and down to the boat and load it. Have you talked to Cole lately?"

"No."

"Maybe you better look him up tomorrow, after we're done here, and see how things are coming along with the boat."

"Okay."

"Nathan, have you given any thought how we're going to deal with Kate?"

"Yeah, I have. But I have mixed feelings. I hate to see her stay here, but what is she going to do if she were to go? Who would take care of her? What happens to her if she stays? There's no way she's going with Cole and I."

"I know. She couldn't endure the hardships. Nathan, this evening, before you and Kate were back, Fanny and I were talking about what to do."

"Yes?"

"We decided Fanny would try talking Kate into going East to school. And if she won't hear to it, we'll take her with us."

"What about Mr. and Mrs. Jakobes?"

"I don't know."

"I don't like it, Charley."

"I know. Kate's soon 18, and if she was to run away, I don't guess there's much they could do."

"I still don't like it! What about the other people that are going? What are their names?"

"Herbert and Gladys Harwood."

"That's it."

"Fanny and I are hoping we can work something out with them, whereabouts Kate could do chores for both of us in exchange for her keep."

"Charley?"

"Yes?"

"What life is that going to be for a young woman?"

"We thought about that. It's better than her staying here and winding up as a whore in some saloon!"

"You may be right. I'm going to bed. See you in the morning."

The next day, we finished all the work there was to do by around noon. I told Charley I was going to look up Cole.

"Go ahead."

After getting my mule, I stopped by the house and had something to eat, then headed for the boat dock to find Cole. I found him loading things on the boat. I talked with him a few minutes, and he told me to get our things to the boat as soon as we can.

I returned to the shop and, as soon as I could, told Charley what he said.

"Go, boy, hitch up the wagon."

I did, and pulled it up to the big door. Charley had a heap of things from his room ready to load. We had it all loaded in no time and was on our way to where the boat was docked. The gangplank was fairly level. Charley was able to get the wagon close, which made it easier for us to unload. We piled everything on a heap. The crew would put it where they wanted it. The boat captain asked how much more. Charley told him. He said he wanted everything loaded by evening tomorrow, except the animals.

We hurried back to the shop and made another load ready to take in the morning. While we ate supper that evening, Charley asked Fanny what they decided. Fanny said, "I'se doesn't like it. Kate say if's we doesn't take her, she's done gonna run away! So I think we's better take her. Charley, look!"

"Well, boy?"

I shrugged.

Looking at Kate, Charley said, "Girl, do you know what you're getting yourself into?"

"Not really, but other women have done it, or we wouldn't be here now!"

"If that's how you feel, then it's settled. Get your things packed!"

Kate smiled and said, "I already did!"

We were up early the next morning and taken a load to the boat before breakfast. By mid-afternoon, we had everything on the boat except for the animals. We had them corraled not far from the boat and were to load them right before we shoved off. Charley and I returned to the shop to make sure we didn't forget anything, and to straighten up the shop.

After supper was over, I told Charley and Fanny I was going to spend the night at the boat, so Cole and I could watch over the animals.

"Sounds good, boy."

As I was leaving, Fanny said, "I'se bring you'se some breakfast in the morning."

"Okay, Fanny," I said.

It was already dark as I rode past the boat and on to where the corral was. Cole had a lantern lit and was sitting there, waiting. As I stepped down, Cole said as he opened the gate, "Kinda dark tonight."

"Yeah, it sure is."

As I put my mule in, Cole asked, "Where're de others?"

"They'll be coming in the morning. Charley didn't want to leave the horses and buggy stand here all night, so he will bring them and the rest of their things early in the morning."

"Is Kate going?"

"Yeah, damn it!"

"Brother, I takes it you would rather she didn't go!"

"Yeah, I sure would! Damn it, Cole. Who and the hell is gonna take care of her?"

"You'se."

"Horse shit to hell if I am!"

"You pokin' her."

"Damn you, Cole! You shithead, don't you realize that girl is gonna want to be with me, no matter what's going on?"

"Yeah. You'se proba'ly right."

"Where's we sleeping?"

"On the boat. I'se put yous'n bedroll and musket alongs with mine, whereabouts we's all be able to hear and see the animals."

"Let's go get some sleep. I have a feeling tomorrow is gonna be a long day. We probably won't get much sleep from now on—at least for a while. Are the Harwoods on the boat?"

"Yeah. Everything on board except the animals and Charleys."

We left the lantern burning that hung by the corral, and bedded down.

It was just light when I heard someone coming on board, hollering, "Nathan!"

Shaking Cole as I sat up, I saw Fanny and Kate coming up the gangplank, each with their hands full. Cole and I were still sitting there when Fanny said, "Good maw'ning, boys," as her and Kate handed us our things for breakfast.

I asked, "Where's Charley?"

"He'll be comin'. He taken the horse and buggy to some man that will take care of them till the Jakobses arrive."

Cole and I ate while they went to look around. When they came back, they said all that was on board was the Harwoods. As Cole and I walked towards the corral, we saw the boat hands come staggering towards the boat. They looked as though they spent the night drinking, along with other things.

We were waiting by the corral when Charley came. "How's everything going?"

"Don't know. Looks like the boat hands spent the night getting drunk!"

"You see the captain?"

"Nope."

"Damn him! Let's start loading the animals. Start with the pigs. Leave the horses for last." Charley hollered at Mr. Harwood. "Come! Let's go find that bastard of a captain!"

We were through loading all the animals and checking to see if we forgot anything when we saw Charley and Harwood coming with the captain.

Captain Fred said, "Did you get everything on board?"

"As far as we know."

"Where are the other men?"

"Don't know."

"Didn't they help you boys?"

"Nope." Charley looked at the captain. "Damn your ass, what kind of a shit crew do you have here?"

Mr. Harwood cut in. "Damn you, Captain Fred! You get that crew of yours and make a quick check of things, and get this boat under way! Do you understand?"

"Yes, sir, Mr. Harwood!"

Then Charley started again. "Captain Fred, I want you to understand something now! After we shove off, there will be no more drinking until we get to where we are going, and everything is unloaded. Second, you nor your crew will give orders to the women or the two boys without going through Mr. Harwood or myself."

"But the black?"

"Him, too. Do you understand?"

"Yes, sir, Mr. Blackstone!"

"Just call me Charley."

"And just call me Herbert! Captain, since we made ourselves clear, now let's get this thing moving—if it will!"

Cole and I sat not far from where the men stood. We couldn't help but hear everything that was being said. I looked at Cole. "I wonder what that was all about."

"I'se doesn't know."

Not seeing anything of the women, I figured they were in their quarters getting things secured away. Cole and I stood at the side, resting our arms on the top rail, watching as the crew pulled the gangplank in and we slowly moved down the Illinois towards the Mississippi.

26

The morning sun was just peeking over the horizon when the boat crew maneuvered us out into the swift current of the Mississippi, and we headed downriver. We crossed the big river and stayed close to the west shore until we reached the mouth of the Missouri. Here, the crew slowly maneuvered the boat up the Missouri.

At the time, Cole and I didn't know that we would be on this river until we reached another river that flowed out of the west that was known as the Platte. Earlier, we were told to stay close by the animals until they got used to the movement of the boat.

It was early afternoon, and the day was still cool and cloudy. Cole and I were standing by the railing, watching the animals, when we saw Kate coming with some rolls and hot coffee. She gave us our rolls and coffee, then walked over to the rail and stood looking over the side.

Amazed to see how we were moving upriver and how wide it was, she didn't talk much, and as soon as we were through eating, she gathered up the things and headed back to the kitchen.

Cole asked, "Why do'an Kate say anything?"

"Don't know."

"Mebbe she's got second thoughts."

"For her own good, I hope so."

"Mebbe things'll work out for her after a while."

"Hope so."

As the afternoon wore on, the boat seemed to have picked up speed and we saw very little of the crew. They stayed mostly up front and close to the captain. It was late afternoon when Charley came to check on us, and to see how the animals were doing. We saw he was carrying his musket, so I asked if he was expecting trouble.

"No, not really. Just in case. I came to tell you we will be stopping anytime to take on wood, and maybe tie up for the night, if they can find a suitable place. Nathan, you and Cole's job is to take care of the animals and nothing else, unless I or Herbert tells you'se different. If we should tie up for the night, we want you'se boys to take the animals on shore and let them feed. Another thing, boys. Starting now, we would like both of you to keep your guns with you all the time."

I asked. "Why?"

"I'll fill you'se in later."

Cole and I went to where we had our belongings piled and dug out our pistols and stuck them in our waist bands.

"I wonder what's up, Cole."

"I'se doesn't know. I'se doesn't like it, but I'se think we's do what boss man says."

"Yeah, I guess we better until we find out what's going on."

"Since it's gonna be our job to look after the animals, brother, whys doesn't we alls move ours belongings to the back of the boat, next to the stable?"

"Sounds good. Let's get at it."

"Okay."

We moved everything next to the stable, and our things would also be closer to the gangplank. We covered everything with one of our tarps, then piled straw over it, keeping everything out of sight. We each hid one of our guns close by the horse stalls, so they would be handy in case we needed them.

We had just finished moving our things when we noticed the boat was slowing down. We stepped over to the side to watch as the crew brought the boat in close to shore. It was a grassy meadow with a few trees. The gangplank was lowered almost to the ground. Then two of the men ran out the gangplank, dragging ropes, and jumped on shore, tying them around the closest trees. The rest of the crew were cranking hand winches that brought the ropes in and the boat closer to shore. The crew soon had everything anchored and secure.

When Charley was sure everything was safe, he and Herbert led their horses off, telling us to stay put until they returned. Mounting up, they rode off upriver. As we stood there, I couldn't help but wonder about Mr. and Mrs. Jakobes. Did they get home? They must have by now. What were their thoughts when we weren't there to pick them up? What would they say when they got home and found no one there? What about Kate?

27

The morning sun was peeping through the late afternoon clouds when the boat returned that carried Mr. and Mrs. Jakobes. They stood by the rail, looking, as the boat slowly glided to a stop at the dock. The gangplank was lowered and, as they walked down, looking for Charley or Nathan, they didn't see neither. Instead, a strange man stood by their horse and buggy that was tied at the hitching post.

They were shocked. Mrs. Jakobes stood at the bottom of the gangplank and waited for their baggage as Mr. Jakobes walked to where the horse and buggy stood. The man asked, "Are you Mr. Jakobes?"

"Yes, I am."

"Charley asked me to bring you your horse and buggy."

"Did he say why?"

"No, only that he wouldn't be able to make it. That's all he said."

"Okay, I thank you. And how much do I owe?"

"Nothing! Nothing at all."

"Thanks." Mr. Jakobes led the horse to where his wife waited and loaded their baggage on the back of the buggy.

As they drove home, he said over and over to his wife, "There must be something wrong, or something happened that Charley couldn't pick us up. That's not like him. He could have sent the boy. I'm worried."

He drove up to the house and tied up, then said, "Bertha, something doesn't seem right." He taken their baggage and they walked to the front door, opened it, and stepped in. The house felt cold, and there was no light, not a sound. They stood looking at each other.

She saw the worried look on his face and became frightened and threw herself into his arms. "Oh, Henry, what is it? Henry, what happened? What's wrong?"

"Now, Bertha, calm down. Damn it, calm down, will

you? I don't know what's wrong." He hollered, "Kate! Fanny, where are you?"

No answer.

"Will you answer! Kate!"

There was no answer, just silence, almost ghost-like. Dark was coming down fast. The house was dark inside now. He found a lamp and lit it as chills ran up their spines. Fear caused their hearts to beat faster and their blood raced. The hair on their necks stood up.

Bertha clung to his arm as Henry Jakobes found another lamp and lit it. Then they moved slowly towards the kitchen. He had already retrieved the derringer from his pocket. As they stepped through the doorway into the kitchen—nothing! It was empty.

Looking around, he found another lamp and lit it. The added light enabled them to see better. It was then that they noticed the papers lying on the table. Stepping closer, they saw one that read "Mr. and Mrs. Jakobes." The other one read "Dear Mom and Dad."

They both pulled a chair back from the table and sat down. Picking up the paper that read "Mr. and Mrs. Jakobes," he asked, "Do you want me to read this?"

"Yes, do!"

He read aloud:

Mr. and Mrs. Jakobes, we thank you for everything you have done for us over the years. We had planned on leaving one day, but didn't know when. It so happened that an opportunity came while you were away that we couldn't turn down. We both thank you.

Charley and Fanny

By the way, we didn't influence Kate in any way, just the opposite.

Picking up the paper that read "Dear Mom and Dad," he began to read aloud, then stopped. "Bertha, do you want me to continue?"

Sobbing, she blubbered out, "Yes!"

He continued:

Dear Mom and Dad,

I'm writing this to let you know how I feel and to say goodbye. Mom, I have known for sometime that you were not happy living here and wanted to go back to Philadelphia. As for being my mother, I love you deeply, but all these years, Mom, you have treated me like I was a little child and never wanted me to grow up, even though I'm almost 18.

I must tell you in the past weeks that you have been gone, I feel like I have grown so much. I feel like a young woman, Mom. I thank you so much for everything you have given me, but mostly I must give thanks to the kind help that you thought so little of and treated so badly. It was them that set me free. I have come to know them and now know they are not the trash you always said they were.

Mom, I have come to love them, for they are the real people. They accepted me as one of them, an equal, not someone that thought they were above them. Mom, in the past weeks they have given me something I had never known before, and that is what it's like to be part of a family, the joy of laughter, the feel of a good morning hug, the heart-warming talks while we ate, the freedom to grow, to help with cooking, doing the dishes, washing clothes, and yes, even the stable work. But most of all, it was the love, the love they gave from their hearts that made me feel wanted, that made me feel grown. But most of all, it made me feel like a woman. It was the love they gave each other that made me realize there was more to life than what you portrayed.

Mom, it was the first time in my life that I can remember that I felt loved and wanted. I know you will be devastated, but this is something I must do.

Love, Kate, and goodbye

Dad,

You have been a good father to me, in a sense, giving me the necessary things I needed in life, but you fell short on the things I needed the most, your fatherly love and some of your time. And you, too, like Mom, would never leave me do the things I would have liked to have done or should have been doing as I was growing up.

You never had time for me when I wanted to go fishing. 'Ladies don't do things like that.' You never let me have pets like others kids did. I was never allowed to go riding on my own, nor take the buggy and go to the store for Fanny. There were lots of things I would have loved for you to help me with, but no! No, it was that damn (yes, Daddy, your little girl said damn!) blacksmith shop. At times, I hated it so damn much that I cried myself to sleep at night.

There were times I knew you wished I would have been a

boy. Daddy, I came to you as a girl and that's something I had nothing to say about. This girl, your girl, would have loved to help her father with the animals and in the stable, and yes, even in the shop.

In these past weeks I have done some of the things that you and Mom should have been letting me do, and I even got to see where Nathan has to sleep, on a heap of straw in the stable like an animal, so you see, Daddy, in this short time they gave me something you and Mom would never give me and that is they let me grow, and now it's time for me to be on my own. I know I have a lot of growing to do, and I will learn with help. Goodbye, Dad.

Love, Kate

Mom and Dad, I love you very much and wish you would have given me the love I needed.

Kate

Dropping the paper, Henry laid his head on his arms and his sobs came loud and deep. He wept uncontrollably, and Bertha was nearly hysterical. It was some time before they got their emotions under control.

Looking up, she blubbered out, "Henry, where did we go wrong?"

"I ... I ... I don't know. I just don't know! What she said in her letter ... maybe it's the truth!"

"Henry, damn you! Are you saying I wasn't a good mother?"

"No! Not at all! I ... just ..."

A big argument started. Finally, Henry got up and went out and taken the horse and buggy to the stable. He stayed, looking around the shop. He found everything was there and the place all nice and cleaned up. After feeding the animals, he returned to the house and found Bertha had settled down some, but was still sitting, sobbing.

Without eating or saying anything, he went to bed. It was hours later that she became so exhausted that she went and flopped in bed, not even undressing.

The next morning, Mr. Jakobes was later than usual getting up. After dressing, he went to the stable and got the animals fed and the rest of the stable work done. Returning to the house, he found Bertha still sleeping. Going into the kitchen, he thought about making something to eat. After looking at the emptiness, and no smell of coffee, no smell of breakfast being made, and worse—no Fanny—he stood by the kitchen window, staring out, staring into emptiness, looking into nothing, his mind going around and around, turning over, trying to focus on what to do, what he should do.

Charley and Hubert came riding in from the opposite direction. We were still standing by the gangplank when they dismounted.

"All right, boys, start bringing them off."

We led the cows off first, then the horses and mules, leaving the other animals on board as the crew cut and hauled wood on board. We hobbled all the animals except our mounts. It wasn't long before the women hollered that supper was on.

Charley told Hubert and I to go eat, that he and Cole would watch over the stock. They had a nice fire going when we returned. Later on, after everyone had eaten, we were all standing around the fire. I asked Charley what they were looking for when they left the boat. He then explained that the captain informed them to be on the lookout for the possibility of rustlers or maybe river pirates, and he would not be responsible for any of the animals taken ashore.

"Boys! Hubert or I will team up with one of you tonight when we're off the boat. That's why we told you to have your guns with you all the time. Besides, we don't know how far we can trust our captain and his crew. Remember, if anything should happen, don't be afraid to shoot to kill. It's them or us! That's it, boys."

The women were told to stay on the boat until we made sure everything was safe for them to come ashore.

Hubert and I was to take the first watch while the other two bedded down. We mounted up and rode the outer edge of the animals, keeping them in close, not letting them stray.

It was a dark, cool night, not many stars. The constant riding kept me alert. The time passed quickly. I saw Hubert ride over and wake Charley and Cole. As I rode over to the fire, they asked how it went.

"Good. No problem."

After throwing more wood on the fire, Hubert and I spread our bed rolls close by and crawled in. It was barely getting light when I was awakened by Cole lightly kicking at my ass.

"Come, brother. Let's get them on board."

By the time we had all the animals on board, it was full light and the crew was ready to shove off. Once under way, Cole and I stood at the rail, talking and watching the shore pass by, when we heard Fanny holler, "How's my boys done doing?

Is you'se all right?"

Looking around, we saw her and Kate coming with our breakfast. We sat down on the deck to eat while they stood by and talked. Kate stood there, looking at me as I ate, then asked, "How come you don't come to the kitchen to eat like the others?"

"We have to stay close to the animals, just in case they get jittery."

"Where do you sleep?"

"Well, last night we slept by the fire on shore and taken turns watching over our stock, and tonight I don't know. Why?"

"Just wondering. That's all."

When we were through eating, Fanny said, "Come, Kate, let's go."

She smiled and left with Fanny.

Cole said, "What was that all about?"

"Your guess is as good as mine."

Finally, Henry pulled himself together and walked to the stable, saddled his horse and rode on into town. Stopping off at one of the saloons, he had some breakfast, then walked up to the bar and asked if anyone knew where he may find someone that could do blacksmithing. No one answered.

Turning to the bartender, he said, "Give me a bottle of whiskey." As Henry lay his money on the bar, the bartender set a bottle in front of him and picked up the money.

Picking up the bottle, Jakobes walked to one of the tables and sat down and poured a glass full and downed it without stopping. Then he sat there, staring blankly at nothing. From time to time, he would pick up the bottle and take a pull. An hour later, the bottle was empty. After making several attempts to stand, Henry finally made it. Steadying himself with the chair and table and looking around, Henry focused his eyes on the door. Staggering, he made his way through it and out into the bright sunlight. Blinking his eyes a dozen or so times, he looked around, trying to locate his horse. Once he located it, Henry made several attempts before he finally staggered over to where it was standing. His horse stood still while he made six or seven tries before making it up and onto the saddle. In his drunkenness, he forgot to untie the reins and the horse wouldn't move.

An old man passing by saw the predicament this man was in and came and untied the reins and handed them up to

Henry. Walking away, the old fellow said, "Young man, you sure must've had one hell of a night."

Henry Jakobes didn't answer. Instead, he turned the horse in the direction of where the boats were. Once he was there, he didn't know what he was looking for, so he rode in circles, hoping to find someone he recognized. Then he saw a young man coming towards him. Henry rode over to the man and stopped.

The young man said, "Hello, Mr. Jakobes. Is there something wrong?"

"Wrong! Something wrong!" Henry said in a slurred tone. "You ask something wrong! Holy hell, man, all my damn help up and left me while I was gone. I have all this damn work to get done. Worse! My damn daughter ran away with that damn, no-good bunch of no-good bastards. If I ever get my hands on them no-good bastards, I'll string them up. Worse than that! That bitch of a wife I have is laying in bed on the edge of a breakdown that she wants. Then you ask something wrong!"

Henry Jakobes blinked several times and looked at the young man through blurred eyes, then asked, "Do I know you?"

"I'm called Jason," the young man replied. "I was standing by with your buggy last night when you and your wife got off the boat."

"You are the man from last night?" Henry Jakobes asked.

"That's right."

"What's you say the name was?"

"Jason. Jason Slaughter."

"Jason, do you do blacksmithing?"

"Yes, Mr. Jakobes, I do."

"Are you in need of work, Jason?"

"Yes, I could use extra work. I only have odd jobs now."

"You say you need work, Jason?"

"Yes, I did!"

"Do you have a horse?"

"Yes."

"Get it and whatever else you have, and come with me."

"Where?"

"I'm putting you to work in my shop, and will give you a place to live."

"Mr. Jakobes, I'll take the job, but I need to find a place to live before my wife gets here."

"You say wife, Jason?"

"Yes, I did."

"Jason, we need a housekeeper also. When will your wife

get here?"

"Three or four weeks."

"I see." He sat, turning it over in his mind a bit, then said, "Jason, I'm making you an offer."

"What's that, Mr. Jakobes?"

"When your wife gets here, both of you can work for me —that is, if your wife wants to—you'll have a place to live and get your meals and wages. Will you accept?"

"That sounds very good, Mr. Jakobes. But there's one thing ..."

"What's that, Jason?"

"Do you get drunk like this often, Mr. Jakobes?"

Henry dropped his head, shaking it. "No, Jason, I don't get drunk. It's what happened with us last night, then this morning my wife ... While having breakfast, I started feeling sorry for myself, and afterwards, I got carried away and, not being used to drinking ... I drank too much. No, Jason, rarely do I ever take a drink."

"Mr. Jakobes, I'll take your word for it. I'll get some of my things and be right with you." Jason gathered some of his belongings and rode off with Mr. Jakobes.

This was our second day and we were headed northwest up the Missouri. The sun barely shone through the clouds. Even so, it was warm enough that Cole and I stretched out on some straw and napped. The next thing I knew, Hubert was standing there, saying, "You boys have a good nap?"

"Yeah. Sure did."

"Sounds good."

"I'll stay here while you boys go eat." I guess Fanny or Kate asked Charley why we couldn't eat in the galley. As we ate, we chatted with the women and they sounded excited as to where we were headed, except Kate. She didn't say much.

Upon returning, we found Hubert and Charley both sound asleep. We let them sleep while we stood by the rail, watching as the boat carried us up the river. The Missouri wasn't near as wide as the Mississippi, and every once in a while we would pass a settlement or some building. The farther we went, the fewer buildings we saw. As Cole and I talked, he told me they had hauled supplies up this river once before to a trading post, but he didn't know where or how far.

It was getting dark now and the crew had made no attempt to find a place to tie up for the night.

"Cole, do you think we will stop?"

"Do'an look like it. Sometimes dey keep moving all night if they know de river."

It wasn't long before the crew lit lanterns and hung them all around the front of the boat. The lanterns had reflectors that reflected the light out over the river. Charley brought a lantern and hung it so it shone over the back part of the boat.

Later on, we checked on the animals, then made up our beds and was sitting there. There wasn't much light, but we saw someone coming as they got closer. We could see it was Kate. She sat down and asked what we were doing.

"Nothing. Just getting our things ready for bed."

"Is this where you sleep?"

"Yes."

"Aren't you scared back here?"

"No. Why would we?"

"Well, I am."

"Of what?"

"I don't know! I just am! I don't see much of you since we left."

"No. We stay back here with the animals except to eat."

"How far are we going?"

"Don't know. Kate, maybe you should go back."

"No! I can't!" Getting up, she said, "I wish I could see you more. I must get back."

After she left, Cole asked, "What did she want?"

"I don't know," and pulled my blanket up around my head.

As the days went by, we would stop every few days to take on wood and let the animals feed. I had lost track of the days, but I think it was around the fifteenth day the crew swung the boat west and up another river. This one I didn't know if it had a name. Later, Charley said the captain told him it's known as the Platte. We only went a short distance when the crew brought the boat in close to shore and tied up. I could see buildings not too far away. Cole said this was the trading post that they came to before.

The captain told us we would be here a day or two while they unloaded a few supplies and did some minor repairs and took on wood. Charley and Hubert went to look for a place to pasture the animals. They stopped by the trading post and asked the owner and was told to take them out back, that they could pasture them there.

After getting them unloaded, we had to lead each one back to the pasture. The pasture was fair sized and grassy. After the animals were hobbled, Cole and I spent the rest of the day cleaning the manure from the deck and hauled it to shore, putting it on a pile for the trading post.

After arriving at his blacksmith shop, Mr. Jakobes showed Jason around the stable, and then the shop itself, and explained what he expected of him and what needed done. Mr. Jakobes then taken him to the house, showed him where the kitchen was, and the things he would need to know, and the room in which him and his wife would be using, and told him they would do a little work in the room to make it more livable for the two of them.

Then, turning to Jason, Mr. Jakobes said, "You will have to do your own cooking until Bertha is able to or until your wife gets here."

Thus far everything Mr. Jakobes told him was agreeable and Jason was pleased with the arrangement.

"Jason," Mr. Jakobes said, "if you agree with everything, you can start first thing in the morning."

"I think the arrangement will work out. I'll start in the morning. Meanwhile, I'll get the rest of my things and store them in the room at the shop."

"Go now."

Jason left and returned to the shop.

Henry walked through the kitchen, through the dining room, and into their bedroom to look in on his wife. He was not at all surprised to find Bertha still lying in bed, fully dressed, just as she was when she flopped herself there the night before. He tried talking to her, but she would not answer. Instead, she just lay there, staring at the ceiling.

After numerous attempts to get her to talk, he finally gave up and left the room. Going back to the kitchen, he started putting something together for supper. When he had it ready, he taken a plate into Bertha, hoping to get her to eat something, but she refused and she wouldn't talk to him.

Henry didn't know what to do except take the plate of food back to the kitchen. After eating it himself, he went to the shop and told Jason to go in and eat, then clean up the dishes. While Jason headed for the house, Henry hitched a horse to his buggy and drove off towards town.

After eating supper, Jason washed the dishes and cleaned up the kitchen, then went back to the shop. Sitting down on the bench outside, he lit his pipe, leaned back against the wall, taking long draws and letting the smoke curl into the air, enjoying the last light of the day. He hadn't been sitting long when he noticed Henry Jakobes coming up the lane with the buggy. He watched as the buggy stopped at the house and Jakobes got down and tied up, then helped a man and woman as they stepped down.

Even with the fading light, Jason was able to recognize the two with Henry Jakobes as the preacher and his wife as they walked to the house. Jason stayed sitting and puffed on his pipe until it was empty. Getting up, he knocked the ashes out and went in the shop and was soon in bed.

The next morning, he was up at the breaking light. Outside, a fine drizzle was coming down as he made his way to the house. Going in, he found the kitchen a little dark. Remembering the lamp sitting on the table, he struck a match and held it to the wick, letting the light come alive. He stood there, looking around, and saw that the door leading to the other part of the house was closed. He listened a few minutes for sounds, but heard nothing. Moving around the kitchen, he looked for the things he needed, and set about fixing some breakfast.

When he was through eating, Jason cleaned up his dishes, and after outening the lamp, stepped outside and found the drizzle had quickened a bit. Then, making a running dash for the shop, once inside he looked over the work that needed to be done. And got right to it.

It was close to noon when Henry walked into the shop. Jason was busy and didn't hear him coming in. Henry was only a few feet away when he said, "How's it going?" Henry knew at once that he had startled Jason and stepped back a few feet just as Jason swung around with a hammer in his hand.

Upon seeing who it was, Jason said, "Good morning, Mr. Jakobes."

Henry didn't answer. Instead, he stood looking at Jason, then went and looked over the work. "Jason, it's looking good." Then he went on to explain what else he wanted done. Henry stayed around the shop, looking over some papers and doing other jobs that needed taking care of.

It was past noon when Henry looked out and saw the rain had slacked off some. Pulling on his coat, he went and got one of the horses and hitched it to the buggy, then drove off towards town.

It was a while later when he returned, bringing with

him Doc Westall. After tying up by the house, they went in. Evening came and it was past supper time, and the doctor was still there.

Jason then realized that Mrs. Jakobes must be sick, if the doctor was still there. Jason thought about going to the house and making something to eat. Instead, he changed his mind and saddled his horse and rode on into town.

After eating at one of the gorge houses, on his way back to the shop, he noticed the horse and buggy were still at the hitching rail, and figured the doctor must still be there. There must be something very wrong. Putting his horse out to pasture, he soon went to bed.

He worked hard for the next several weeks and didn't see much of Mr. Jakobes, except to be told what work needed to be done, or when Mr. Jakobes came to pick up the things that needed to be delivered. Mr. Jakobes said very little to him about his wife's sickness, and Jason had seen nothing of her since his arrival.

With all the work Mr. Jakobes gave Jason to get done, plus doing his cooking and cleaning up, he was kept busy and had little time to himself, which made the weeks pass quickly. Jason was happy with the work he was doing, it was the kind of work he truly enjoyed.

He was in a real good mood, thinking about it being Monday and just five more days before his wife would be arriving—something he had been looking forward to for sometime. He hoped that with his good-paying job and a place for them to live that she would be happy and like it there.

As he worked, his mind wandered and he dreamed of them having their own smith shop and a nice house and even having children. He thought about how nice it was going to be when she got there and he would be able to put his arms around her once again, pulling her close and feeling her breasts pressed tight against his chest, and the feel of her lips as they pressed to his.

He thought about the weekend. He had prearranged with Mr. Jakobes so that he could spend the weekend with his wife. He even went so far as to make arrangements to spend at least one night in town before taking her out to where they would be living. They hadn't been married that long—six months—or was it eight? He didn't recall. How long had it been since he last seen her? Let's see. His mind turned over. This is the fourth week he had been working there. Damn it, must be six or eight weeks.

Thoughts were going through his mind and he wondered what it was going to be like when she got there and what it was going to be like having her again. And now his thoughts were being transformed into pictures in his mind. The image moved in slow motion before his eyes. He saw their first night together, when they were first married. His wedding night passed before his eyes. So real! Real, like it had all taken place the day before. He saw them in their bedroom as they slowly, slowly undressed one another, as each piece of clothing, one by one, came off and was dropped to the floor. In his mind, he could see her upturned firm breasts and how it stirred a sensation in his groin. Then the last piece of clothing dropped to the floor. They were naked! Their eyes fixed on each other. Now, as then, he could see her standing there naked before his eyes and he basked in her beauty. His eyes roamed and finally rested on her dark hairy mount and he grew even harder.

He was startled back to reality when Mr. Jakobes hollered, "Jason! Come out here!"

Laying his tools down, Jason walked out the main door to see what was going on. Mr. Jakobes was standing there with the preacher and the doctor.

Mr. Jakobes said, "Jason, do you think you can fix the loose shoe on the doc's horse?"

Jason taken a look at it, then said, "Yeah, I can fix the shoe."

"Good," Mr. Jakobes said. "When you get it fixed, would you bring the horse and buggy to the house?"

"Yeah, Mr. Jakobes. Will do."

Mr. Jakobes, the doctor and preacher had just started walking towards the house when a muffled gunshot rang out. The doctor grabbed his black bag and all three taken off running.

At first, Jason didn't know what to do. Then he taken off running after the rest. As soon as they reached the house, they saw Mrs. Jakobes slumped against a tree a short distance off the back side of the porch.

Running to her, Henry and the doctor knelt down beside her. They both saw at once the small derringer laying in her open hand. The preacher reached down, getting a hold of Henry's arm and pulling him to his feet and leading him into the house.

Jason helped the doctor lay Mrs. Jakobes on her back. It was obvious to see what happened. Bertha had placed the barrel of the small gun between her breasts and squeezed the trigger, ending her agony.

The undertaker was notified and soon brought a wooden coffin from town. The undertaker then did the necessary things before laying her out in the wooden box. To make matters worse, Mr. Jakobes was notified by the elders of their church that since his wife had taken her own life, he would not be allowed to bury her in the church cemetery.

Mr. Jakobes had given a lot of money over the years to the church, and this angered him very much. He swore he would never again give the church another penny. Now, with his worsened troubles, and in desperation, he turned to the doctor and undertaker and asked if they would make the necessary arrangements to bury Bertha on a small rise that was out away from the south side of the house. They said they would take care of everything.

The coffin with Bertha laying in it was placed in the living room. Since Mr. Jakobes was taking her death kind of hard, the doctor and undertaker decided it would be best if they stayed with him throughout the night. The next morning, shortly after sunrise, she was taken to the burial site. The only ones attending were Mr. Jakobes, the doctor, the undertaker, Jason, and two other men who helped with the grave. Since there was no preacher, the undertaker said a few words, then she was lowered down and the grave filled in.

Jason put up an iron cross that he made with her name on it. Soon afterward, everyone left, and Jason returned to the shop and his work.

It was late Tuesday evening, almost dark, when Henry pulled himself together enough to go to the stable and saddle his horse. Jason was in his room, readying for bed, when he heard Henry ride off. Looking out, he saw Henry headed towards town. He didn't see anything of Henry until Friday afternoon, when Henry returned and stopped by the shop to see how Jason was doing and to give him more work to do. He didn't have much to say as he busied himself around the shop. When closing time came, he paid Jason for the work he did.

Before leaving, he said, "I hope what happened earlier this week won't change anything and you'll continue to work here."

"Mr. Jakobes, what happened changes nothing. I'm sorry for the misfortune that you had, but an agreement is an agreement. Agnes—that's my wife—will be here tomorrow, and I hope we can get settled in the next day. I'm quite sure Agnes will want the job, Mr. Jakobes."

"I hope so," Henry said as he left to go to the house.

Charley came and helped us carry water from the river to wash the deck down. We would let it dry until the next afternoon, when we would put fresh straw down.

Later that evening, after supper was over, we got a fire going at the far end of the pasture. We would take our turns watching over the animals. Hubert and Cole would take the first watch, and Charley would stay on the boat with the women. I would bed by the fire.

When our turn came, Hubert went and wakened Charley, and him and I taken over. The night was peaceful and the animals were quietly grazing. It was sometime toward light when Charley and I met not far from the fire. We were sitting on our mounts, talking, when he said, "Nathan, there is something I must tell you."

"Yeah? What's that?"

"Well ... well, do you remember some time ago, you asked me if I could find out what happened to that girl you spent the night with, and thought she was being forced to work as a whore?"

"Yeah?"

"Ah, well, she was, and she was Chinese. Well, she was trying to run away when her boss caught her. He gave her a beating, then raped her, then he beat her some more. She died the next day. Later that night, he had her body dumped in the river."

"Are you sure?"

"Yes. Very! I knew if I told you then, you would have gone looking for him and I knew someone would have gotten killed, so I decided to wait. Boy, maybe I made a mistake. I don't know. All I can say is, I'm sorry."

He let it go at that and rode off toward the boat. I sat there, my eyes filled with tears as the hurt that I couldn't understand ran wild within me. My mind was numbed with the thought of what this man had done, and no one was going to do anything about it.

I was startled out of my thoughts by Fanny tugging at my arm. "Comes, my boy."

As I slid from my mule, she pulled me close, hugging me. "I'se hurts for you. Come, I'se gives you something to eat."

We walked to the boat, where she fixed me something

to eat. There was no one else around, so she sat and had some coffee while I ate. When I got up to leave, she gave me a hug and said, "Son, I'se hurts with you."

The rest of the day I stayed much to myself or with the animals. The women and Cole were helping around the trading post. Hubert and Charley were helping on the boat. Night came and I went and ate, then taken my turn watching the stock.

At first light in the morning, we loaded the animals and as soon as they were on board, the crew shoved off, chugging our way upriver. Later that day, Charley told us that they talked with the people at the trading post, trying to find out all they could about what lay ahead upriver. The people at the trading post told them that they knew of no other settlers upriver, only the Indians that came to trade, and so far they were friendly.

The captain didn't know the river at all, so the going was slow. We never stopped for three days. It was toward the middle of the fourth day that the captain found a place that was suitable for us to stop at. The banks were low. Few trees and a place where the stock could feed. We tied up, then taken the animals on shore.

Cole and I watched the animals while the rest gathered wood. By now, it was getting late and we could see the captain was becoming uneasy and suggested we bring the animals on board for the night. Charley agreed, so we loaded the animals back on board.

Once it was dark, the crew lit lanterns and hung them overboard, so they shone toward the shore. For some reason that I never did understand, two of the crew stood watch on the front part of the boat and Cole and I were told to take the back half and to keep our guns in easy reach. I had seen no signs that would indicate any trouble.

Cole and I did as we were told. We stood close by the side rail, and watched for anything on shore. Cole told me that the morning before we left the trading post, while everyone was eating breakfast, Charley told him and Fanny and the others there what he told you that morning.

"He said it din't set too well with Nathan. 'Mebbe I made a mistake not telling him them and let him kill dat bastard.' He went on to say dat he felt responsible for what happened, dat he had made de arrangement with de two cowboys to take you there, and from the first time he met you, he had dis strange feeling. And when he came to know you better, he knew there was something about you dat was different. He said you had a calmness 'bout you that affects people, as well as animals, and he never knew anyone so understanding or patient and hard-working. And with such deep feeling for everything. When you told him you and I was leaving, he had dis strange feeling that he should leave when you did, that with you around nothing would happen. And that's why he hurried up and made de arrangements to leave. Then he went on to say there was something about dat necklace you wear, but he was reluctant to ask you 'bout it. To him, it seemed *specter*, or maybe even *spiritual*. And said he had dis feeling dat you wasn't afraid of anything. He went on to say every so often, on a Sunday morning, you would go out back of the shop and shoot your pistol, and a few times he snuck back to see what you was doing. He sat there, shaking his head, den said, 'Dat boy can draw his pistol and fire faster than a blink of an eye. I never saw hands so fast, and it do'an matter which hand he uses. He do'an miss!'

"As Charley was telling us this, everyone was looking at him. Then everything got quiet, so quiet I'se got scared and I'se could see everyone else was scared or worried. Finally, Charley said, 'Now you know and that's all I have to say,' then got up and walked out. Kate got up with tear-filled eyes and said she asked you about the necklace you wore, and all you would say was 'Not now, Kate.' With dat, Fanny jumped up with tears running down her face as she said, 'I'se must goes to that boy now,' and she left.

"Nathan, I'se knows that when we became blood brothers, you'se said you'se would never let I'se down. Does you'se mean that's?"

"Yes, Cole. I never will, and nothing will happen to you. And when it does, it will be time."

We stood there in silence, staring into the darkness on shore, when Charley and Hubert came to relieve us.

"Boys, Hubert's wife has some hot coffee and rolls. Why don't you go have some?"

"That sounds good." We went and had rolls and coffee, then to get some sleep.

Jason's wife arrived Saturday afternoon on a boat that came up from New Orleans. After greeting Agnes with hugs and kisses, Jason gathered up her belongings and taken everything to the room he rented for them to spend their first night together.

After stowing everything out of their way, Jason taken his wife out for a good meal. After eating, they stopped by the Dog Fish Saloon for a drink or two and did a little dancing. It didn't take but one drink for Agnes and she was feeling its effects that sent sensations churning in her lower belly and groin. Pulling Jason close, she whispered in his ear, "Let's go back to our room, darling. I want you."

Looking at her a little surprised, he said, "By all means, let's go, you beautiful woman. I'm also in the need."

They left the saloon and returned to their room.

It was late the next morning when they finally got out of bed and, after a late breakfast, Agnes returned to their room and Jason went and got his horse out of the livery stable and rode back to the shop, where he borrowed Mr. Jakobes' buckboard. He returned to town and their room.

Jason and Agnes loaded all their belongings on the back of the buckboard, then returned to what was to be their home. Before unloading, Jason showed his wife the room they would be living in and the kitchen where she would be doing most of her work. After looking the place over, Agnes told Jason she would be happy to take the job, at least until they could save enough money for a place of their own.

They spent the rest of the day arranging their belongings in their room. Later on, they made supper. Jason then knocked on the door that led to the other part of the house. Mr. Jakobes answered the door and Jason asked if he would like to join them for supper. He said no, that they were to fix a plate and bring it to the dining room.

In the beginning, everything was fairly normal. Then, as the summer slowly slipped by, Jason and Agnes noticed Mr. Jakobes was spending less and less time around the shop and house. It seemed he was spending most of his time in town. The work around the blacksmith shop got to the place where Jason was doing everything. He had to take the orders, do the delivering, and collect the payment, plus do the stable work.

Jason's days began long before light in the morning and ended sometimes way past nightfall. Agnes gave her husband all the help she could, doing most of the stable work and helping with whatever she could around the shop. Now, since they closed the shop on Saturday afternoon, they would have to drive into town, where Mr. Jakobes had arranged at the bank for them to collect their week's pay. Later on, it was up to them to deposit the money they had taken in during the week. Mr.

Jakobes had an account set up at the grocer for them to buy the necessary food for the house.

Even though he was rarely there, Jason and Agnes became very concerned about what was happening with Mr. Jakobes. After talking it over, they decided that on their next visit to the bank, they would ask Mr. Clyman, the banker, if he knew anything about Mr. Jakobes' strange behavior.

On their next trip to town, they went to see the banker. Mr. Clyman looked at them strangely and said, "Please come back at closing time."

Jason and Agnes returned just at closing time. Mr. Clyman asked them into his office and told them to be seated. "Mr. and Mrs. Slaughter, I apologize for not speaking with you sooner. I just kept putting it off." The banker then filled them in on what had been taking place. He told them Mr. Jakobes had, for some reason, put everything in Kate's name.

"That's his daughter," Jason asked.

"Yes. I didn't know if you knew that or not," Mr. Clyman said. He went on to say that if Kate did not return, or could not be found within three years, everything was to be sold and the money given to the town. Mr. Jakobes had also made arrangements for the money that is coming in from his business. "That's the blacksmith shop," he said. "It was be put into an account so that each of you would get the money you agreed on for your work each week. Plus he set two percent of the profits aside for you two. That is, if you stay and operate the business. Money was and will be set aside to maintain and operate the business and, of course, he takes so much for his own living expenses. Any questions?"

"Yes, there is," Jason said. "First, we would like to know what has happened to Mr. Jakobes that he made these arrangements."

"Well, I think it's only fair to tell you," Mr. Clyman said. "Ever since what happened with Mr. Jakobes' wife and with the church not allowing burial for her, and then with his daughter, who just up and left, Mr. Jakobes has not been the same. Mr. Jakobes, I'm told, has turned to drinking and sometimes quite heavily, and it's been said—I don't know for sure—that Mr. Jakobes has been doing a lot of gambling.

"Mr. and Mrs. Slaughter, I'm damn glad he had the common sense to make this arrangement before he gambled it away. Maybe someday he will get himself straightened out and be glad that he still has the business. I don't know if I have the right to say this, but I'm going to anyway. Right before Mr. Jakobes hired you, he and his wife just returned from New Orleans, where she received an inheritance of quite a large sum of money. Mr. Jakobes seriously believes that Kate, his daughter, will return in due time.

"Now, what else can I do for you?" Mr. Clyman asked.

"Oh yes, one more thing," Agnes said.

"What's that?"

"I'm wondering if some kind of an agreement can be put on paper that would protect us."

"I think that would be all right. I'll make a paper up and have Mr. Jakobes sign it, and you are to bring any debits to the bank and the bank will see they're taken care of."

Jason and Agnes left the bank, feeling good about the way things worked out. What the banker told them gave them a lot of hope. They put a lot of hard work in and around the shop to make the business better and it paid off, for in the short time they were there, the business was doing better than when they came there to work.

On one of their visits to the bank, they asked Mr. Clyman if they could hire a young man to help them around the shop. The banker told them he would see what he could do. To their surprise, a young fellow in his mid-teens showed up at the shop the next Monday morning. He went by the name of Royer and that's all.

Jason showed him around and told him what was expected of him, and then put him to work. They saw very little of Mr. Jakobes, and when one or the other did, it seemed to them as though he had lost all interest in the place.

From time to time, they heard stories from the customers about Mr. Jakobes, but paid little mind to what was being said.

It was in the early fall and the leaves were turning color. It was on a Monday morning, and the clouds hung heavy over this little river town. It was cool for this time of year. Jason, Agnes and Royer were busy and with the forge going, it didn't take long before the shop got too warm. Jason told Royer to open the big doors. He did, then turned to Jason and said, "Rider coming," and went back to work.

None of them gave it any thought because they were used to riders coming. They heard the rider dismount, then tie up at the hitching post. When the figure stepped into the doorway, Jason looked up and saw it was a U.S. marshal.

"May I help you, sir?" Jason said.

The marshal didn't answer. Instead, he slowly walked towards Jason, looking all around until he was within ten or so feet. This made Agnes nervous and she moved closer to her husband, putting her hand on his arm. The marshal stood looking Jason over very carefully, then his wife and Royer. He never said his name.

All three noticed the marshal was tall and thin, like a gut with the shit slung out of it, with a straight, tight-lipped mouth, sunken gray, beady, cold eyes, colder than death itself, set in a face that looked like it was chiseled out of stone. His right hand rested on the pistol stuck in his waist band.

"Satisfied," he said in a slow drawl. "Are you Mr. and Mrs. Slaughter?"

"Yeah, we are," Jason answered.

Looking at Royer, he said, "Who's that?"

"Our helper, Royer," Jason replied.

"I rode all the way out here just to inform you that Mr. Jakobes is dead."

"Dead! What happened?" Jason asked.

The marshal ignored the question and said, "I want the three of you to accompany me back to town right now, to identify the body."

Jason said, "Just wait a minute, marshal. Half the business people in town can identify Mr. Jakobes."

The marshal's hand rested on the handle of his gun. Then he said, "Now! And I mean now! Let's go!"

Royer went and hitched up a horse and buggy while Jason and Agnes closed the shop. They all climbed on the buggy and drove to town with the marshal following close by.

Once in town, the marshal taken them straight to his office, where he questioned each one of them separately as to their whereabouts the night before. Finally, after he was satisfied with their stories, he said they could go.

"I thought you wanted us to identify the body," Jason said.

The marshal looked hard at Jason, then said, "I'll be keeping an eye on you." Then he turned and went back into his office.

The Slaughters stood, bewildered, looking at each other. Then Royer said, "I wonder what that was all about."

"I wonder, too," Agnes said.

"Come. Don't worry about him," Jason said. "He looks like one of those government-hired killers I have been hearing about. Come, let's go see Fred at the undertaker's and see if he knows what happened."

After talking with the undertaker, they were told that Mr. Jakobes either hung himself or was murdered.

"Murdered!" Agnes said. "Who would want to do that?"

"Well, I don't know, but I hear tell that Mr. Jakobes was drinking heavy last night and got into a poker game with a couple of men from downriver, and lost a lot of money. I was told that Mr. Jakobes asked the men if they would wait until morning and he would get them the money. They got into a big argument. Finally, Mr. Jakobes left the game and headed for his room, stopping by the bar and getting another bottle of whiskey. That was around eleven last night. As far as anyone can remember, it seems that no one paid any mind to what happened to the other men. It was after three this morning when the bar man closed and was on his way home, when he found Mr. Jakobes hanging off the balcony by his neck. Part of a sheet was knotted around his neck and the other end tied to the railing of the balcony. That's all I can tell you, Mr. and Mrs. Slaughter. I sent two men to dig a grave up beside his wife. I'll bring him out in the morning for burying."

"What about this marshal that's here?" Jason asked.

"Oh, that son-of-a-bitch? He's been pissed off ever since he got here. He has to fill in for a few weeks. Our regular had to go down to New Orleans. He really got pissed this morning when he had to get out of bed to take care of Mr. Jakobes. Ever since, the asshole has been taking it out on everyone, and he's been asking questions around town about a young fellow and an old Indian man. That's all he knows, and he won't say anything more. Very few people around here, if any, ever heard or seen anyone like that. Then the prick thinks everyone is lying!"

"Thanks, Fred, we'll be there in the morning to help bury Mr. Jakobes."

"Thanks, Jason."

Upon leaving, Jason and Agnes thought it best to stop at the bank. After entering, they asked for Mr. Clyman, who soon came out and asked them into his office. After being seated, Jason and Agnes asked the banker what happens now, since Mr. Jakobes was no longer alive.

Mr. Clyman thought for a moment, then said, "As far as this bank is concerned, Mr. Jakobes signed an agreement with you people, and it stands until that time when his daughter returns—if ever—or the time comes that it has to be sold. As far as this bank is concerned, you'll run the business as you have been, and the bank will send someone out to check on the business from time to time.

"Mr. and Mrs. Slaughter, has the marshal been out to see you this morning?"

"Yes," Jason answered. "He made us come into town, where he questioned each of us – even Royer."

"How's the boy doing?"

"Good," Jason said.

"That damn marshal was here as soon as I opened the door, and questioned me hard about Mr. Jakobes and the business, and who all worked for him. I explained to him that the only ones that worked for him, besides you people, were Charley Blackstone and Fanny, and they left here early in the spring and headed west somewhere.

"Mr. and Mrs. Slaughter, this marshal is not a nice man, so be careful around him. Hopefully he'll only be here a few weeks. Are there any more questions that I can help you with?"

"No. I think you made everything clear enough," Agnes said.

Jason and Agnes and Royer returned to the shop and finished up their work.

It wasn't long after light the next morning that Royer came hurrying into the kitchen and told Jason and Agnes that Fred, the undertaker, was coming up the lane with two other buggies following. Agnes had put on a clean dress while Jason changed into other pants and shirt. Royer stayed just as he was. They were waiting when the undertaker arrived, accompanied by Doc Westall and Mr. Clyman, the banker. There were four other people, but they didn't know them. They fell in beside the wagon that carried Mr. Jakobes and walked to the grave site. Mr. Jakobes was lowered into the grave while Fred, the undertaker, said a few words. After he finished, the grave was filled in. Agnes picked some flowers from nearby and placed them on top of the grave. Then the others returned to town.

Later on, Jason would fashion a marker out of iron and put both Henry's and Bertha's names on it, along with the date they were born and the date of death.

Jason and Agnes returned to the house, and Royer became a little befuddled and started for the shop. Agnes saw him and hollered for him to come in with them. Jason and Agnes sat at the kitchen table, having some coffee, and talked about what they should do. Royer didn't say anything, he just listened, but in his heart he hoped and prayed they would stay and continue running the blacksmith shop. He liked this work, and he loved Jason and Agnes even more. For him, these were the first real parents and home he ever had. Jason and Agnes were very good to him, and treated him like their own, even though he was a little slow.

His life before coming here consisted of being pushed from one place to another, wherever there was hard work to be done. He seldom got enough to eat, and never had a real bed to sleep on. He, at times, was severely beaten, for no reason at all. Here, he was treated like a real person. Jason and Agnes never laid a hand on him, and never yelled or scolded him for anything he did, and they explained to him what was right and what was wrong. He had come to love them more than anything he ever knew, and became worried that the Slaughters may not stay and run the business, since Mr. Jakobes was no longer there.

It was a week later, after talking with Mr. Clyman from the bank, that they really made up their minds to stay. Agnes and Jason knew that Royer was very worried about their not staying, so that same night, after they were through with supper, Agnes said, "Royer, Jason and I have something we want to talk to you about."

They could see the worried look on his face as Agnes said, "Royer, you don't need to worry anymore. Jason and I are going to stay, to run the shop, and we want you to stay with us and be part of our family. And Royer, as soon as I can get all of Mr. and Mrs. Jakobes' personal things packed away in trunks, we want you to move your things in here. You can have the room upstairs to sleep in."

Royer became so overwhelmed with joy that his eyes filled with tears and spilled over, running down his cheeks. Agnes put her arms around him, holding him close and comforting him.

As fall turned into winter around this little river town, everything was going good for the three of them. They continued working hard at the business, and were told by the bank that they were doing very well for this time of year.

The winter dragged on, like sometimes they seem to do, and before they knew it, spring was in the air.

28

In the morning, the captain called everyone together and asked what we thought about spending a day or two here and resting. We were all becoming worn out from being on the boat so long that everyone was overwhelmed with the idea. It didn't take long before we had all the animals unloaded and everyone was laying around in the sun, resting. The crew had started a fire, and the women put coffee on.

I was sitting close to Fanny and Charley when I asked Fanny if she would like some fresh meat to cook.

"Boys, would I'se ever!"

"Okay, I'll take Cole and see if we can find some."

Kate heard me and asked if she could go. I looked at Charley and Fanny. They just shrugged and nodded.

Finding Cole, I told him what we were going to do, then whispered to Kate to go get some soap. She looked at me funny. "Go!"

Taking her good old time, she went on the boat and soon returned. In the meantime, Cole and I made the mules ready.

Helping Kate on the one mule, I asked, "Did you get it?"

"Yeah."

We rode a long ways upriver, then came to a stream that flowed in from the north. Looking it over, we decided to follow it. It flowed through a large prairie that extended as far as we could see. After a mile or so, the stream became somewhat smaller with some nice pools. Stopping by one pool, I dismounted and walked over and checked the water. It didn't feel too bad. I started pulling my clothes off, telling Kate to throw me the soap.

Cole hollered, "What are you doing?"

"I'm gonna bath."

"What about her?"

"She can bath, too, if she wants to. And you get yourself in here, too!" I had taken everything off except my long underwear. As I waded in, Kate threw me the soap. The water was cold, *damn* cold. Looking around, I saw Kate's dress coming over her head and dropping to the ground.

Kicking her shoes off, then her stockings, she came wading in, in just her bloomers, the water coming well above her waist. I had finished soaping and handed it to her, pulling my underwear off. I washed and then rinsed.

Cole finally got up the nerve and came in. Kate handed the soap back and then pulled her underwear off and washed them out, then rinsed them. I soaped myself good and looked at Cole. He was standing, twenty some feet away. His eyes were as big as his head and his mouth hung open. He stood there, staring in disbelief.

Wading out, I picked up my clothes and was pulling them on when Kate came wading out. Now Cole *did* get an eye full. I guessed he never saw a woman naked before. Damn, did she look good! She pulled her dress on, then her stockings and shoes. I hung my underwear over a bush to dry, and Kate did likewise. Cole started out, then stopped.

"Come on, Cole, let's go!"

"No! You'se go! Start wherever you're going. Go! I'se'll catch up!"

Helping Kate on her mule, I picked up my musket and jumped on Worse, my mule. We started slowly upstream. I looked at Kate riding beside me and she was all smiles.

"What're you thinking about?" I asked.

"Cole. Poor Cole. He was so shocked."

"Yeah, he was." We continued along the stream, and off in the distance we could see some deer. Stopping, we waited for Cole to catch up. When he finally did, we pointed them out to him.

After watching them awhile, I asked Cole what he thought.

"Wells, there one thing for sure. We can't reach dem from here. I'se been looking. Does you'se see those rocks over to the left?"

"Yeah."

"I'se gonna cross the creek and sees if I'se can get to them. If I'se can, I'se can get a shot. I'se been thinking. If you'se can circle back and around dis clump of trees, and wait till I'se get there, maybe they'se will run towards you'se."

"Okay. I hope it works."

Cole crossed the stream, and I taken Kate and made a

circle, coming in on the back side of the clump of trees. Getting down, I tied our mules to some bushes. Laying my musket down, I reached up to help Kate. As I did, she swung her leg over and slid right into my arms. Her dress went up around her waist and her arms went around my neck.

Pulling me to her, our lips met as we fell to the grass.

Sometime later, I pulled her to her feet. I had just picked up my musket when we heard Cole shoot. Running to the edge of the woods, I saw deer coming straight towards me. Using a tree for a rest, I picked one out and taken aim. When I thought it was close enough, I squeezed the trigger. At the sound of the musket, the deer dropped. Reloading quickly, I ran to where the deer lay. It was dead. I hollered for Kate to bring our mules.

It was a young doe and would make for some good eating. When she brought the mules up, I had already started gutting the deer. She stood there, asking questions, and in no time I was through. Wiping my knife on the grass, I put it back in its sheath. Telling her to bring the mule closer, I slung the deer up on its back and, tying it fast, helped Kate on my mule. I handed her the musket and swung up behind her with my arms around her waist. We rode off in the direction of Cole.

When we rode up, Cole was standing there, looking at the deer. I could tell he was feeling very proud. The first thing that came out of his mouth was, "Brother, I'se kilt my first deer! Now what's does I do?"

Getting down, I put my arm around him and told him what a good shot he made, then told him how and what to do to ready his deer for taking back to camp. It wasn't long before he had it gutted and threw it up on the mule with the other one and tied it down.

Mounting up, we headed for the boat, stopping only to pick up our underwear and put them on. Cole had taken the reins of the pack mule and was headed off, leading the way.

A little past noon we arrived back at the boat. The others came to see if we had gotten anything. We dismounted and was standing there, listening to the others, when Fanny and Charley walked up, saying, "Good work, boys. Did you'se have any trouble?"

"No! Not at all." I saw right a way the smile on Fanny's face as she looked at us. Charley stepped closer, cocking his head, looking. Then he smiled and asked, "Was the water warm?"

Some of the men were already skinning the deer while the others were getting things ready for the women, so we could roast as much as we could. The rest would be made into stew. Roasting was the best way for us to keep the meat for any length of time.

The rest of the day and the next was spent taking care of the meat and making things ready to move on.

The following morning, we headed upriver. Even though the water was deep, the going was slow. I didn't know why, and I had no idea how much farther the captain and Charley had planned on going. The days dragged on. It was now the third day without stopping, and to make things worse, a fine misty rain had been coming down most of the day.

Finally, midday, the captain was able to find a suitable place for us to stop and spend the night. After tying up, there was plenty of time to get the animals on shore and wood cut and brought on board. After we had our evening meal, we got a fire started, even with the misty rain.

Cole and I were told to get some sleep, that we would have the last watch. We found a dry place on board and bedded down. I had no idea what time it was when Hubert came and wakened us. Cole and I went and got our mules and mounted up. As Charley was throwing more wood on the fire, he said, "See you'se in the morning," and disappeared into the dark.

Cole took one side and I the other. A heavy fog hung over the river and surrounding area. It was damp, cold and dark. Visibility was poor. I was glad I had put my heavy coat on, the one Mom had made for me. Pulling the collar up around my head, I nudged my mule slowly into the silence of darkness and fog. The only sounds came from droplets of water falling from the trees, or occasionally a sound from Cole or the animals.

I was feeling all alone and rode aimlessly throughout the silent world of fog and darkness. My thoughts drifted to home. It was only a year and a half ago that I said goodbye and rode away from my family and home. This was really the first time since I left home that, for whatever reason, I was feeling all alone and missed my family and home. I mostly missed Mom and Frances. I wondered how Noel and Abilene were and how they were getting along in school. I thought about Dad and wondered how he felt about me leaving. I thought about Lily and school. I missed school, and wondered if she was still the teacher, and if so, was she spending weekends with Mom? I thought about all the good times all of us had together, and remembering the last summer and fall, the good times Lily and

I had hunting and fishing.

I rode in despair, the cold thick fog tugging at every nerve in my body, making me edgy, and wondered if Mr. Joe's spirit was watching over me. I heard a sound and sensed that something was about to happen. Nudging my mule, I made my way through the darkness a little faster and soon found Cole. He was crouched low on his mule and I could tell he was trying to see something.

Crouching low, I eased my mule up close beside him. Neither of us spoke. He just pointed. We listened. We could hear something or someone moving near the edge of the trees. He motioned there was two or three. Sliding down from our mules, we stayed on the blind side and nudged several of the animals towards the edge of the trees, where we thought someone or something may be, and stayed close to them.

Cole was kneeling under the head and neck of his mule, as I was mine, waiting and listening. The tension grew. After several long minutes, we saw movement.

Not more than twenty feet away, we saw a crouched figure running towards us, then another. The first one was closest to Cole and when it was within reach, Cole stood up, swinging his fist, hitting the figure square between the eyes. It dropped like it had been kicked by a mule. Just then, the second one was right there. I gave a leap and tackled it. As it was getting up, I planted my fist with all I had into its stomach. I heard the wind go out. It folded and hit the ground. Kneeling down, I felt for a weapon and got a hand full of tit and realized this one was a woman. Dragging her to her feet, I shoved her over to where Cole was. Cole was kneeling, checking the other person over. I asked the woman who he was.

"My man," talking very broken.

I asked her who else was in the woods.

"Our kids."

It was now starting to get light enough so that we could see. The man was coming around. Cole helped him to his feet.

"What's happened?"

"You got hit! That's what!"

"And who is in the woods?"

"Our kids."

"Okay, call them. If it's anyone else, they will die before they get halfway here."

"Oh, no! It's our kids!"

They called, and two kids came out from where they were

hiding, carrying what little belongings they had. Cole looked at me and said, "What're we gonna do with dem?"

"I guess take them on board and see what the rest say."

The kids were crying and clinging to their mother. Cole and I each picked up one of the children and told the man and woman which way to go. After getting them on board the boat, we taken them to the kitchen, where the women were already making breakfast.

As we walked in, they stopped and looked with such surprise, Fanny told Kate to get the captain. We were able to get a good look at these people now. I guess the man and woman were in their 30s, and the boy and girl around 8 and 10. Their clothes were next to rags and dirty. They stank like hell.

Fanny and Gladys fixed them each a plate of breakfast and had them sit at the table. You could see they were half starved, the way they were gorging their food down.

The captain and Hubert were trying to get them to tell where they came from, but their English was so bad, it was hard to make out what they were saying. Charley had motioned Cole and I outside, where he asked us where we found them. We told him everything, just as it happened.

Going back in the kitchen, it sounded like Hubert and the captain were finally piecing together what they were trying to say. It sounded like they got across the Missouri River somehow with their horses and wagon, and were headed west to homestead, and had traveled a week or so when some outlaws caught up with them one afternoon and accused them of having stolen animals. They were no match for the four outlaws, so they didn't try to put up a fight. The outlaws burned the wagon and shot the two cows and dog. They taken the horses and rode off, leaving them.

They tried to salvage what they could, which wasn't much at all. A few things that were packed in trunks didn't burn too bad. They did save their coats and a few pieces of clothing, and the things they were wearing, a hatchet and knife. The loss of their guns was the worst. This left them literally helpless. They told how they spent the next few days butchering the cows and drying as much meat as they could carry. After that, they started walking and somehow got turned around until, finally, they had no idea which way they were going. They just walked and hoped they would find a settlement or help. They saw numerous Indians, but would hide due to fear.

They had no idea how long or how far they had walked.

All they knew now was they were happy we captured them, for if they had gotten away with the horses, they would have had no idea what direction to go. They told how they almost froze some night due to fear of building a fire, and when their dry meat began to run out, they only ate a little in the morning and sometimes at night, and some plants when they found them. But this time of year there wasn't that many. Mostly, they drank water and as much as they could.

They went on to say how they had stopped to get out of the misty rainy weather. They were wet, cold and hungry and close to giving up. As it grew dark, they finally saw a ray of hope, our campfire maybe a half mile away. Talking it over, they decided he would sneak down and check to see what was going on. When he saw the horses and four men and didn't see the boat, he thought it was the outlaws and got out of there as quick as he could. Once back with his family, it was decided they would strike in the early morning, when they were sure everyone would be asleep, then sneak in and take some horses and be out of there before they were missed. But it didn't work out, and they were glad we caught them.

Hanging his head, the man asked, "What do you plan on doing with us?"

The captain looked at all of us, then said, "Nothing. What do you want us to do?"

"If you could give us some food and get us started in the right direction, we can be gone. We don't want to be any bother," the man said.

"No, I can't let you do that. There's no way you can take those kids and go and expect to make it. Look at you. You're in no condition to go on. I don't know how much farther we'll be going. If you want, you can get yourself cleaned up and rested, and help out on our return trip back to Starved Rock. Think about it. Now we must get under way."

Once everything was on board, we shoved off and headed upriver.

29

For the next four days, we slowly made our way farther upriver, only stopping once. Deeper and deeper into an unknown wilderness, we continued. Several times we saw Indians making their way along the river. None showed any hostility towards us.

It was early evening on the fourth day that we came to a fork in the river. The captain slowed the boat almost to a stop while him and Charley looked the situation over. They quickly decided on the north fork of the river. We continued on, and after about another mile, the crew pulled the boat in close to the shore on the south side.

After finding a place to dock and tie up, we got everything secured, and by the time we got the animals on shore, there wasn't much light left. Someone got a fire going while the other men gathered wood for the fire and the boat. Supper was called, and after everyone was through eating, we all gathered around the fire, including the new people—Adolf and Alfreda, their kids, Alma and Abel—and talked, mostly about how much farther we wanted to go.

Kate had taken the two kids, Alma and Abel, and was playing with them. I sensed the captain and his crew were getting edgy and concerned about going on. And the new people ... Hell, I think everyone was wondering if maybe we came too far. Everyone except Cole and I. Maybe we were just too damn dumb or didn't give a shit. I didn't want to hear any more, so I motioned to Cole. We went and got our mules and rounded up the stock, bringing them in closer.

It was a clear night and a little cool. Cole and I sat on our mules, talking and gazing at the stars, when we saw Charley walking up. He asked how the animals were.

"Fine," we replied.

He looked at me. "Nathan, I want to know something."

"Yeah?"

"What do you think about tonight?"

"What are you asking?"

"I'm asking, do you think we'll have any trouble tonight?"

I looked at him a few seconds. "No, Charley. No trouble this night."

"You sure?"

"Yes."

Then he turned to Cole and said, "I know I can depend on you. I'm asking you to take Hubert and the new man, and take the first watch. Would you do that?"

"Yes'm, Charley!"

"Nathan, you and I will take the last watch. Will that be okay?"

"Yeah, sure."

"Before we turn in, I would like to ask you two something."

"Okay."

"How come you're not uptight like all the rest of us have gotten?"

"There's no reason to be. That's why we left and came out here."

"Okay, boys."

The lanterns had been all lit and hung around the boat. It wasn't long before everyone turned in. Handing the reins of my mule to Cole, I told him to keep it with him at all times. "That way, I will know where it is, just in case."

Charley and I spread our bed rolls by the fire. Hubert wakened us when it was our turn. Getting up, we threw more wood on the fire, then drank some leftover coffee. By then, Cole rode up, leading my mule. Charley looked at me and asked, "What's Cole doing? Why does he have your mule?"

"For the same reason I will have his."

"And that is ...?"

"If I need him, he will know where his mule is."

Charley shook his head and mounted up. "You take that side and I'll be over here."

The rest of the night passed quickly, with only the occasional howl of a wolf or the hoot of an owl or some other night animals that broke into the solitude of the darkness. It was getting light in the eastern sky as I rode up to the fire, dismounted, and turned the mules loose.

As Charley was putting wood on the fire, he said, "I'm damn glad that night's over!"

"Why?"

"Oh, I don't know. I guess I let the others get me a little

jumpy last night. Boy, let's grab a few hours' sleep, then I would like it if you and Cole would ride with me today."

"We're not moving?"

"No, not today."

"Where are you riding to?"

"Just to scout around, to see what this place looks like and what it has to offer."

"I would be glad to, and I know Cole would be, too."

After eating and getting a little sleep later that morning, the three of us mounted up and rode out to take a look. We rode west along the river a short distance when we came to a steep incline, but not that steep that it couldn't be traveled with horses and wagon.

Swinging south, we rode along the bottom of this ridge that rapidly became a cliff that was more than fifty feet high and straight up. Here we were high enough that we could look out over the whole area. To the east, we could see where the two rivers came together. A mile to the south was the south fork of this river. The land lay in a triangle, with the cliff to the west and the rivers on each side. The land was rolly and covered with thick grass. There were clumps of trees scattered throughout, and both river banks looked like they were heavily wooded, with open spots here and there. Where we were standing was a huge spring or water hole that bubbled up from under the rock cliff and formed a stream that flowed southeast.

We continued south to the river and found it to be swift and full of rapids. The cliff ended at the edge of the water, then continued on along the other side. From here, we made our way east, the biggest part of a mile, to where the rivers joined together. We looked the land over good as we zig-zagged our way back.

Before reaching camp, Charley stopped and got down. Cole and I did, too. He walked around, looking and looking, then finally turned to us and asked, "What do you think?"

I didn't say anything. Instead, I let Cole answer.

"Wells," he said, "I'se thinks it's looking good." After a little while, he said, "What about you, Nathan?"

After a few moments, I looked him in the eye and said, "Charley, last night I knew most everyone was afraid, and I didn't know of what or why. So, on our watch, I rode out of camp."

"Out here? You did."

"Yes, and I talked with the spirits, and the spirits said this is a good place. I think you'll do very well here, Charley. Look around you. The cliff to the west, the two rivers, trees and rocks to build with, a good spring, and the ground looks good for planting. You must decide."

For a few moments, he stared at me as though he thought I was crazy or something. Then he shook his head and started off, leading his horse back to camp.

We walked in silence, except for Cole saying, "I think Nathan's right."

We got there just in time for supper, and after it was over and everything cleaned up, Charley called everyone together and explained that we looked the area over and it looked really good, and he would like to stay here and give it a try. Tomorrow he would like it if everyone who wanted to would go out with him and see for themselves what it's like.

The captain said he was willing to set a few days until a decision was made. The new people said right away that they wanted to return with the captain, if the offer still stood. Captain Fred said it did.

That left Fanny, Kate and the Harwoods.

The next morning after breakfast, Charley asked me if Fanny and Kate could ride my mules.

"Sure, Charley," I said. "I'll go fetch them. As you know, I have no saddles."

"I know."

Hubert and Gladys had already mounted up when I returned with the mules. While Charley got Fanny on the black one, I helped Kate on the other. As they rode off downriver, the captain said, "I think I'll go, too." Asking Cole to use a mule, he mounted up and rode off after the others.

The new woman, Alfreda, and her kids, Alma and Abel, stayed in the kitchen while the new man, Adolf, helped the crew cut wood and haul it on board. While they were doing this, Cole and I hauled the manure off the boat and piled it on a heap so it could be used later. Next, we cleaned and scrubbed the deck. It wasn't long after we were through that the others came riding back.

After helping Fanny and Kate down, Charley asked if Cole and I could put the horses and mules with the others. The women had gone on board. I guess the new woman had already made something for lunch. By the time Cole and I got back, the women were bringing lunch to shore.

While everyone sat around the fire eating, Charley said,

"I'm sure glad you boys got the boat cleaned up." Before long, the conversation changed to the land. Everyone was talking about the land. Cole and I stayed out of it and just listened. While Charley and Hubert were talking it over with the women, after a while, Charley looked at Cole and I, then said, "You boys are right. This *is* a nice piece of ground. Do you boys think we should settle here?"

I looked at Cole and he looked at me, neither one of us saying anything. Finally answering, I said, "It's not what Cole and I think, it's what the five of you think and decide. It's *your* decision, not ours. But there's one thing."

"What's that?" Charley asked.

"I think this is where you're to build."

Every head turned, staring at me.

I looked at Cole and he mumbled, "Don't look at me, brother. I'se doesn't know."

Then Charley asked, "Are you sure?"

Hesitating a little, I said, "Yes, yes. Very sure."

The others looked at each other. Charley sat, staring at the ground. Finally, he looked up. Then he looked at each of the others, then at me. By the look on his face, I knew he was very concerned. A slight smile crossed his face as he said, "Son, I'll take your word for it. I say we stay!"

A sigh of relief came from the rest as each one agreed. The captain said, "I think you'll do all right here. Let's start unloading."

Getting up, I turned and walked to where the animals were. The midday sun was warm on my face as a cool spring breeze tugged at my long hair. Putting my arms around my mule, I lay my head on its neck and held it, wondering what made me say things like that and why.

"Why?" I held my mule for a few minutes, then swung up on its back and rode off. I rode towards the west, along the river and up the grade, not knowing why. Stopping just before reaching the top, dismounting, I stood looking back over the way I came, and I could see over the whole area and for miles beyond.

Turning to the west again, I led my mule the short distance to the top. Looking out ahead from where I stood, I could see a large prairie that extended as far as the eye could see. As I stood there, taking in the beauty, my eyes caught the movement of something far off in the distance. After watching awhile, I could make out that they were some kind of large dark animals. Not ever seeing a buffalo before, but hearing about them, I just knew that's what they were.

I was about to head back when I saw a fairly large white bird fly across in front of me. It was too far off for me to make out what kind it was. As I watched it, it flew south towards the river, circling around to the east, then on around to the north of me and on back towards where I saw the animals. Then, it disappeared just as quickly as it appeared.

As I turned to leave, I could feel the presence of the almighty spirits all around, and then I knew this was the right place. Kicking my mule into going, I rode back to the boat and found everyone busy, getting things ready to take on shore.

Hubert and Charley were busy putting one of the wagons together. I looked for Cole and found he had gathered all of our things together and was about to start carrying them off the boat. With my help, we had everything packed off and stowed in no time.

We had selected a spot under a large evergreen to pile our things until we could get a shelter built. Then, we helped the others until the women hollered that supper was on. They had prepared the meal over the open fire, and it smelled so good. As the women filled our plates, everyone found a place to sit around the fire or close by, talking.

Cole and I were sitting somewhat alone, listening to the others talk, staying out of the conversation, when Kate walked up behind us and asked if we minded if she sat with us.

"Oh no, sit," both of us said.

For what all of us had been through for the past month, and for someone who never experienced hardship before, Kate looked very good. Her long red hair was combed and tied back. Her cheeks looked smooth and rosy, and those green eyes of hers sparkled as only hers could. As she sat down between us, a heart-warming, pleasant smile crept across her face as she said, "I don't get to see much of you two, that you aren't working or off somewhere."

"We'se doesn't sees you much either, that you all not doing work," Cole answered.

"How long will it take before the boat is unloaded?" Kate asked.

"Two days."

"Once the boat leaves, where will we sleep?"

"I don't know what Charley has in mind," I said.

"What about *you* two? Where are *you* going to sleep?"

"Cole and I plan on building a leanto as soon as the boat is unloaded, and in the meantime we're hoping it doesn't rain until we can get one built."

We were caught not knowing what to say when she looked at both of us and asked, "If I help you build the leanto, can I share it with you?"

Cole and I were dumbfounded.

"What kind of a question is that?" I asked.

"Well ... Well ... I'll need a place to sleep, and I *don't* want to sleep in the same place as Charley and Fanny." She went on and on as to why.

"I'se doesn't like this," Cole said.

"Kate," I said, "do you know what you're asking?"

"Yes! I'm asking to share the leanto with the two of you."

"Kate, what do you think the others will think or say?"

"I don't know, and frankly I don't give a damn. I need a place to sleep."

Finally, I said, "Kate, it's not up to us. It's up to Charley and Fanny, and I think we should wait and see what they plan on doing."

"Damn you, anyway! I guess I have no choice but to wait and see." Getting up, she said, "Give me your damn plates!" Taking them, she went stomping off to help the other women.

Charley hollered, "Come on, boys, there's a little light left. Let's make some use of it."

Going on board, Charley taken the captain and his crew and got to loading the wagon while Cole and I helped Hubert put the wheels on another wagon. As daylight ran out, the captain lit lanterns, so we could see. Hubert and Charley picked out the boxes and crates they wanted first, while the rest of us loaded them on the second wagon. In no time it was loaded.

Looking at Charley, Captain Fred said, "That's it for today."

About that time, Gladys hollered, "There's coffee and rolls. Come have some!"

Cole and I, being the first in the kitchen, picked up a couple rolls each and a mug of coffee, then stepped outside to stand by the railing. It was quiet and peaceful here, except for the little talk and now and then laughter that drifted out from the kitchen. The sound from the river smothered most of that. The night was cool and the sky was clear and starry. We were leaning on the railing, munching on our overdone rolls and sipping hot coffee, neither one saying anything, just listening to the night sounds and our thoughts, when they were broken by the sounds of Hubert and then Charley.

"What's you boys doing out here?" Hubert asked.

"It's too damn noisy and crowded in there," Cole answered.

After that everyone was quiet for a spell, then Hubert asked, "Do you'se think there's need to stand watch?"

"I don't know," Charley said. "What do you boys think?"

Taking another sip of coffee, I looked over at Cole, who just shrugged. Turning to Hubert and Charley, I said, "I think everything will be just fine. So, if you'se want, the two of you can sleep on board tonight, and we'll sleep out there by the animals. Is that okay with you, Cole?"

"Yes'm, brother, yes'm, but make sure if you hear any shots, you'se come running."

"Will do," Charley said.

"Charley, come as soon as you're up and waken me."

"Why?"

"I would like to show you something."

"Nathan, we have work to be done in the morning."

"I know, Charley, but it's important that you see this."

"All right, boy, but it better be good!"

Cole and I left and went to where the animals were feeding. Gathering wood, we built a big fire and sat a long time, watching it burn. The night was very still and silent, and the fire had burned down. Putting more wood on, Cole asked, "Brother, what's we all gonna doo'se about Kate?"

I sat staring into the fire, not saying anything. Cole was quiet. He knew I didn't have an answer. Finally, I said, "Cole, let's let Fanny and Charley take care of her."

"I'se thinks, too, brother." We talked about our leanto and where to build it. I told him about my ride earlier that evening and what happened. The look on his face told me he didn't like it. I think it spooked him somewhat.

I asked him if he would ride with us in the morning.

"Will do, brother. It's getting late. I'se thinks I'se gonna put more wood on de fire ands beds down."

"Okay." I waited until he got settled down, then I lay down and pulled my blankets over me.

30

It was just breaking day when I heard Charley hollering, "Get up, boys!"

Jumping up, I rolled up my bed roll. So did Cole. Catching our mules and throwing our bed rolls on, we tied them down. Mounting up, we rode to where Charley and Hubert were waiting.

"Where to?" Charley asked.

Pointing west, I said, "Just a little beyond that rise. Not far."

"That's it?"

"Yes."

"Let's go."

We rode in that direction and, in no time, were ascending the steep grade. Dismounting, we led our animals, stopping for them to rest, and at the same time looking back over the way we came.

The others were taken back by the vast view that surrounded this area. Once reaching the top, I led the others to where they had a full view of the vastness of the prairie that lay ahead. Spellbound, they stood, holding onto their animals, with a look of disbelief for what seemed an eternity.

"Is this what you wanted us to see?" Charley asked.

"Yes."

"Thanks. Now let's go."

"No! There's one more thing the two of you need to know."

"What's that?" Hubert asked.

"Do you see that big rock with the trees, just to the left of that herd of buffalo?"

"Yes," they both said. "What about it?"

"That's as far west as you'se may claim as your land."

"What do you mean?" Hubert asked.

"As long as neither of you try claiming land beyond that rock, I think you'll be safe."

Charley and Cole stood, staring out over this vast prairie. Neither one spoke. Then Hubert started to protest, but Charley cut him off.

"Nathan, that's fair enough. Now, I think we should be getting back." He turned and started leading his horse back. Hubert followed.

Cole was still planted there, gazing out over the vastness.

"Come, Cole, let's go get some breakfast."

Only then did he break his gaze. "Alls right, brother."

Once back at camp, we found breakfast ready. After eating, it was back to unloading the boat. Charley taken Fanny and Gladys to help him cut poles and erect frameworks to support the canvas that he brought along to make shelters. The two smaller ones would be for sleeping, one for Charley and Fanny, the other for the Harwoods. The kitchen one was the largest. It would house the stove, dry sink and table.

While Cole and I worked, unloading, we wondered if they were making a place for Kate to sleep. Later, when we stopped to have something to eat, they had the shelters all erected and the canvas stretched and fastened, so the sides could be rolled up, if needed. Kate and the two younger kids, Alma and Abel, had the job of watching over the animals and making sure they didn't wander too far. By late evening, they had everything set up, and we ate our first meal in our new kitchen.

While we ate, Cole and I noticed they had fixed a place at one end for Kate to sleep. We were more than happy.

After supper, we continued unloading until it was too dark to work. The way the unloading was going, we would be done sometime the next afternoon. Again, the women had rolls and coffee waiting. After everyone had something to eat, they soon turned in.

I noticed Charley and Fanny and the Harwoods were most anxious to turn in, and wondered if it was because they had their own sleeping quarters. Kate had her place in the kitchen tent. I must say, Charley and Fanny had fixed up a nice bed for her, with a canvas type drapery for privacy.

The crew had gone back to the boat to sleep. Cole and I bedded down, as usual, close by the animals, always taking care not to bed down too close to one another, just in case of trouble.

Since we left Starved Rock, we had been very lucky. The nights that we slept on shore, under the sky while watching over the animals, we stayed mostly dry, but there were several nights that we were awakened by rain or a heavy downpour beating on our faces. We would be soaked through to our hides in no time, and be cold or chilled to the bone. Usually, we were able to get a fire going as soon as the rain stopped, and dry our clothes. Other times, we stayed wet until they dried.

The next morning, we awakened to a cloudy, overcast day. After breakfast was over, it was back to the job of unloading, and we were through with the unloading long before I had figured. The women had an early lunch ready, and afterwards Captain Fred and his crew, along with Adolf and Alfreda and their kids, made ready to start their return trip.

Everyone shook hands, and Captain Fred said he would see us sometime before snowfall with new supplies. We all stood on the bank and watched as the crew slowly moved the boat out from shore into the current and headed downriver. I think, at the time, all of us had—to some degree, an insecure feeling—a feeling of being abandoned. We watched until the boat was no longer in sight, then it was back to work.

Charley and Hubert started putting up another shelter to cover the huge stack of crates. The women were busy moving everything undercover that needed to be out of the weather. I had no idea that Charley and Fanny had so much stuff packed in crates, until I taken a good look around and saw that most of the crates were theirs.

Hubert and Gladys had a lot, but nothing in comparison. As for Kate, she had nothing except her clothing and a few personal belongings. Cole and I had a hard time agreeing on a place to build our leanto, but finally we found a place we both liked. It had good drainage and was the right distance from the others.

While the others were busy, we went along the river and cut the necessary poles we would need to build our leanto, and dragged them back with the mules. After the framework was up, it was back along the river, looking for cattail reeds. After going some distance, we found a nice plot.

We had a few huge piles cut when Kate came looking for us. We talked her into helping us tie them in bundles and load them on the mules, and all the while we were working, she never stopped talking. Finally, we figured we had enough and headed back to our leanto with the reeds. After unloading, we turned the mules loose. Kate pitched in and helped as we laid layer after layer of reeds until they were more than a foot thick over the entire framework.

We had worked up a good sweat and must have smelled pretty damn bad, for Kate asked, "When was the last time you two taken a bath?"

"Why?" I asked.

"Nathan, you mean you don't know?"

"Well, no. What you trying to say?"

"You and Cole smell so damn bad, it's like you haven't had a bath in a month."

"You mean that, Kate?"

"Yes, I do, Nathan."

"Hey, Cole!" He was on the other end, working, and didn't hear what she said.

"Yeah?"

"When was the last time you taken a bath?"

"Doesn't know for sure. Maybe when we all done bathed in that creek some weeks ago. Why?"

"Kate just told me we stink a damn side worse than our mules."

"I'se be damned. I never would'a thought a nice girl like her would say somethin' like that. You'se means she's saying we should go take a bath?"

"She's shaking her head yes!"

"Tell her it's too cold."

"You tell her, Cole!"

I went and caught our mules and hitched them to one of the wagons. While Cole gathered up our shovels, throwing them on the wagon, Kate climbed up and sat down, so I handed her the reins and told her to drive. Cole sat on the back while I walked alongside the mules to lead the way down along the river, until we found a nice place to cut sod. Kate stayed on the wagon while we cut sod and loaded it.

We were close to having enough when I looked at Cole and winked. "Cole, Kate thinks we stink."

Cole stopped and looked at me and winked. "Brother, you'se tells that lily white-assed woman if she doesn't like the way we'se all smell, she's can makes sure that's we'se alls dones get a bath."

"Did you hear that, Kate?"

"Yes! I heard what the hell that black ass said."

"Now, Kate, that's not …"

"Don't Kate me, you! He called me a lily white ass first."

We had finished loading sod and started back. On the way, Kate said, "I'll dare you—both of you—to come over to the kitchen tonight after everyone's in bed. I'll have water hot and ready, and I'll give your dirty hides a damn good scrubbing."

We were back at the leanto now, and started to lay the

sod on the sides, forming the walls. Kate climbed down from the wagon and headed for the kitchen. Then, stopping, she hollered, "I dare you!"

Cole and I kept on working, not answering. The shelter was sturdy enough that we were able to walk on it to finish putting the sod in place. On the top, we left a hole in the center and laid sod up to form a chimney. Later, we would gather clay from the river and coat the inside and outside. We had left a few holes in two sides for light to come in and a doorway, which we would fashion some kind of closure later. We planned on keeping a small fire burning inside until it dried out good.

We were looking for anything we may have missed and were fixing it when Charley came to see how things were coming along. He looked it over, inside and out, then said, "Looks real good, boys. Looks real good. I'll see if I can fashion something that you can use to heat with, later on. Okay, boys, after we're through eating supper, I want all of us to sit down and discuss plans on what we need to be doing first. And yes, I want you two boys to bath more often and wash your clothes. And that's an order. Do you hear?"

"Yeah, I hear."

"Where are we to bath?" Cole asked.

"I don't give a damn. Just bath! Come, let's have some supper."

It was a little after dark that evening when we all gathered around the table in the kitchen with milk, coffee and rolls, to decide what needed done next.

Hubert and Charley did most of the talking. Cole, Kate and I just listened. Fanny and Gladys did express their needs and desires. The first thing that was agreed on was the need for getting the ground ready for planting. Second was to build the necessary buildings, since the Harwoods wanted their own living quarters. Everyone agreed it would be a good idea to build two separate dwellings to live in, in case anything should happen to one. The third was a place for the livestock, and the last was where to build, close to the river or up higher, next to the spring.

After some discussion between the Harwoods and Fanny and Charley, they all agreed it would be best to build closer to the spring, even if it meant hauling supplies a little farther. Closer to the spring would mean fresher water. Being higher, they had a better advantage.

Everything was agreed on, and everyone agreed Charley should be the one in charge, seeing to the work that needed done.

"Well, since you put it that way," he said, "tomorrow we'll get the plows ready, so you boys can start plowing, and get the things ready that we're going to need to build, and decide just where we're going to build. I think that's all for one day. Come, Fanny, it's time for bed."

As the rest were leaving, Charley looked at Cole and I, and said, "Boys, I see there's plenty of hot water on the stove. Now get bathed, and I mean bathed!"

Kate had already gone behind the tarp partition to her bed. Cole said, "Brother, I guess we'se better gets bathed, if boss man Charley says we better."

"All right."

We went to our belongings and dug out some cleaner clothes. Returning, we saw everything was dark, except a dim light burning in the kitchen tent. Going in, we found Kate had filled a tub with hot water and was sitting at the table. "It's about time you got your asses over here!"

"What's all you doing up?" Cole asked.

"Waiting for you, so I can give you a damn good scrubbing."

Looking at Cole, I said, "You're first, so get undressed. I can't wait to see Kate give you a bath," I teased.

"Nots I, brother, I ain't gettin' in theres. She ain't bathing me. No, not I, brother, not I!"

After trying to persuade him, we saw he wasn't about to let her bath him.

"Okay, Cole, you don't know what you're missing. Nathan, get undressed and get in there, before the hot water gets cold."

Undressing, I stepped into the tub, sitting down. The water was still hot, but not too bad. Kate started scrubbing on me, and when she said a "scrubbing," she meant it. When she was through and I got out, my hide was as red as a beet.

Sitting there at the table, Cole never taken his eyes off of us. Dressing, I taken the water out and dumped it. Bringing the tub back, Kate filled it.

"Now, Cole, it's your turn."

"No's way, Kate, I'se do'an want you'se scrubbin' on me. I want you'se to go someplace so I cans bath. Will you'se, Kate?"

"All right, Cole, *be* that way!" Taking my hand, she said,

"Come, Nathan, let me show you where I sleep."

We went behind the partition. She had fixed up a nice bed for herself. A mattress filled with dry grass was placed on top of empty crates that Fanny gave her. She had an empty crate beside her bed for a nightstand. A candle was placed on it, along with her hair brush and an assortment of other articles. A nice, warm-looking down quilt cover was spread out over the bed and a small throw rug was on the floor. It looked like she must have brought these things from home.

The room was small, just big enough for her bed, stand and a place for her clothes and a mirror that sat on the stand. She sat down on her bed while I stood looking around at everything. My eyes went back to her. She reached up and pulled me down on top of her. Our mouths met as she pulled me close, whispering, "Nathan, it's been so damn long, so damn long, take me! Take me now."

"Not now, Kate! Cole!"

"Now, damn you! I don't give a damn about Cole! I need you now! I don't give a damn if he hears, sees or what."

Pulling her dress up over her head, she was naked.

I don't know how long we had been there. When I started getting up, she whispered, "Thanks, I needed that."

Standing, I turned to get dressed and saw Cole standing there, watching us. I didn't know how long he had been watching.

As I finished dressing, he stood looking at her, lying there on her side, the dim candle light flickering over her nakedness. To this point, she made no attempt to cover up. I saw Cole couldn't take his eyes off her. I left him and stepped out into the kitchen, gathered up my dirty clothes, and blew out the lamp.

As I was stepping outside, I heard Kate say, "It's all right, Cole. Come lie down."

Even though the stars were shining, it seemed dark and cool. I made my way back to our shelter. There was still a lot of red embers left from our fire. Throwing some wood on, it flamed up, giving off enough light that I could check on the animals. They seemed all right. Rolling out my bed roll, I lay down, pulling my blankets up over me, and listened to the crackling of the fire, wondering about Cole as I drifted off to sleep.

31

In the morning, when I saw Cole, I put my hand on his shoulder and asked how his night went. He looked at me strangely, and I could tell he was blushing. He put his arm around my waist, then said, "Thanks, brother. We need to get to work, putting those plows together."

After everything was together, we hitched a team of horses to each plow. Charley came along to show us where he wanted plowed. At first, I had a little trouble showing Cole how to handle the horses and plow. Most of his trouble was due to the heavy sod we were plowing. After an hour or so, he caught on, and the rest of the day went fairly well.

We didn't stop at noon to go eat. When we didn't show up, Charley came with fresh teams, and Kate brought something for lunch. While Cole and I sat down to eat, Charley and Kate hitched up the fresh teams. Charley then walked around and looked over what we had plowed, then said, "Not bad, boys. For the first time, not bad."

"Charley, we will plow as long as the animals hold up," I told him.

"All right, but don't overwork them, boys. Come, Kate, bring the other team, will you?"

It was a beautiful spring day, sunny and warm. I had my shirt off most of the afternoon. The sun had dropped out of the western sky when Cole and I unhitched and headed back to camp and turned the horses and mules out to pasture.

While Cole and I were washing up for supper, I asked him if he was going for a bath later on.

"No's, not I, brother, I'se too damn tired."

We finished with the plowing the next day, then with the help from the three women, we were able to get the planting done by week's end. With the planting done, all our energy was put into helping Charley and Hubert with the building.

Each had leveled a spot where they would build. Charley had chosen a place that would be close to the spring, yet not too far from the river, for his trading post and house. Hubert had picked a place on the opposite side and yet close to the spring.

They would make sure that all the buildings were far enough apart that, in case of a fire.

Everyone worked hard. Stones had to be hauled for the back walls, which were dug into the bank. Trees had to be cut and hauled to the building sites, then they had to be notched. Clay was dug from the river banks and hauled to be mixed with dead grass and used for caulking and also to be used on the floors, where it was tamped and leveled and then left to dry.

Kate was in charge of doing most of the kitchen work. Fanny and Gladys would help with the evening meals and did the milking, along with taking care of the other animals. Besides the building, there was the taking care of the things that we had planted.

It was late June now, and the weather had turned hot. Everyone was working hard from first light until dark, which left very little time for anything else. Even the night that Cole or I would spend with Kate came to almost an end.

As the weeks dragged on, it got to the place that I no longer knew what day it was. The hot weather and hard work was taking its toll on everyone, and it didn't help any that Kate couldn't understand what the matter was. She became irritable and shunned Cole and me. Even Cole and I were feeling the effects of all this, and had drifted somewhat apart, neither one having much to say to the other, and it didn't help any that all of us were filthy most of the time, with the exception of Kate. Somehow, she managed to keep herself looking nice and clean. The rest of us smelled worse than the damn pigs.

It all came to a boiling point one afternoon, while Cole was working with Hubert and Gladys. Hubert started in on Cole, cursing him and telling him he was no damn good. Cole didn't say anything. Instead, he just turned and walked away, got on his mule, and rode off.

I saw him ride away, but didn't say anything. We had just sat down to eat when Cole walked in and taken his place at the table. Right off, Hubert started in on him, cussing him. Charley hadn't said much, but Hubert kept on. Cole sat, taking it. Fanny and Kate both started hollering at him to stop, but he didn't. He kept on.

Finally, Cole had all he could take. Jumping to his feet and stepping back from the table, his hand hung over the gun in his belt. Hubert and Charley were both on their feet now.

"Which one of you bastards want to be first?" I heard Cole say.

I hollered at Kate. Even before it got out, she had jumped in front of Cole, throwing her arms around him. I was already on my feet, my hand on my gun, facing Hubert and Charley, and hollered, "Don't even think about it! Neither of you'se will make it!"

Charley knew that, and taken his hand away from his gun, and hollered at Hubert, "Sit down!" Dropping his head, he sat back down, and then Hubert did, too.

Kate still had her arms around Cole, holding him tight. I stayed standing, and said to Cole, "Come, brother, I guess the time has come for us to move on."

Gladys was standing with her arm around Hubert's shoulder, not saying anything, but looking as horrified as hell. Then Fanny lit into all of us and hollered at Kate, Cole and myself to "sit y'all damn asses down ... ya'll hears me, I'se ain't gonna tells ya'll again. First, ya'll gonna eat y'all supper, then ya'll will talk about this!"

Everyone sat and finished eating, mostly in silence. When we were finished, Fanny stood and said, "Now, ya'll gonna listens to me. What happened this here night was uncalled for. Someone could've gotten killed. And second, Hubert doesn't ya'll ever curse that boy or any of these kids again, and that goes for y'all as well, Charley Blackstone."

Hubert yelled back at her. "Whenever I tell that black bastard to do something, I want it done!"

With that, Cole jumped to his feet. Kate was sitting on one side and I on the other. We grabbed him by the arms and pulled him back down. He was pissed. I had never seen this side of him. Kate got up and stood behind Cole, putting her arms around his shoulders, more or less holding him down. Then she said, "I'm with Fanny. There is no need for all this."

Cole then said, "I'se want to say some-sun. I'se came with my brother here. I'se help ya'll work hard just for what you feed me, but I'se not ya'll's slave, and I'se not to be treated likes one neither. If y'alls not like my work, I'se ride out of here."

"That goes for me also," I said, "and besides ... anyone picks on Cole or Kate, picks on me."

Kate stood behind both Cole and me, with tears rolling down her cheeks. She had an arm around each of us. Except for Kate's and Fanny's sobs, everything got quiet.

Finally, Charley stood. Looking at each of us, he said, "Fanny and Kate are right. What happened here tonight was uncalled for! I take the blame. I saw it coming, but I didn't do anything. I should have ended it right then. But I didn't! I was too wrapped up in work to give a damn, and hoped it would pass. But it didn't! Now, we have to find a way to keep anything like this from happening again. We all came here as one big family, to make a new life for ourselves. The life we wanted! And that's what I want most of all."

Gladys, being very religious, who didn't want to get involved, said, "I agree with Charley. We must find a way. I myself think everyone is working too hard. We have no time to ourselves."

Fanny and Kate both agreed with Gladys. And so did Charley. Looking at Cole and me, he asked, "What about you, boys?"

Knowing Cole was pissed, I put my hand on his arm, hoping he would be quiet. Then, I said, "It's not up to us! As you'se well know, Cole and I can ride out of here anytime we want. It's your choice."

Stillness fell over the tent. Kate's fingernails dug deep into my shoulder as I knew they did Cole's.

Then Hubert piped up and said, "That won't be necessary, boys. You both are damn hard workers, and so is Kate. And I'm ashamed of myself for what I said to you today, Cole. I'm the one who left my temper get out of control and brought this down on us tonight, and I'm truly sorry about all this. Gladys here, bless her soul, tried to tell me earlier to lay off, but I was too damn bullheaded to listen. I agree with the women and Charley. Since we have been talking, I came to realize we all need some time for ourselves, and we are not having it. I think the building is coming along real good. What do you think, Charley?"

"I think so, too. What would the rest of you say if we only worked six days, then taken Sunday to do whatever we wanted … except for the necessary chores?" Charley added, "I think we can finish the building by late summer or early fall, and still have time to take care of our crops. Our animals are in need of more care than we are giving them now—mostly the horses and mules. What do the rest of you say?"

Everyone agreed that having Sundays to ourselves was just what we all needed.

As the summer slowly passed, Cole and I spent our Sundays riding west along the rivers—either the south or north fork—looking for places to trap, and to learn all we could about what lay ahead, for we planned on striking out on our own, and going farther west.

32

It was early fall now. The buildings were all up, and Charley and Fanny had moved into their cabin, which would serve as their living quarters and trading post. The Harwoods also moved into their cabin, which was smaller. Kate remained in the kitchen tent as it would be used for eating, until it got too cold. All the food and crops were stored for the coming winter. The hay had been put in big stacks outside of the small barn that was to stable the few milk cows. The grain had been put into a makeshift shelter right next to the barn until next summer, when something better could be built.

Over the summer, the women had canned most of the vegetables that we had grown and what could be stored was put in the underground root cellar we had built. During the summer, there hadn't been much excitement, except for a few Indians passing by on the north bank of the river. For some reason, none came over to our side that we knew of. Occasionally, a rattlesnake or some other small animal would wander into camp. When they did, they were dispatched quickly and prepared for food.

It was late in the fall, and all the trees were bare of their leaves, and the weather was getting colder—cold enough that meat could be hung for a long period of time without spoiling.

One evening, while we were eating, Charley asked Cole and I if we would do the hunting for winter meat. To say the least, we jumped at the chance that would mean getting away for a while.

The next day, Cole and I readied the things we would need, and a few days later, we set out on our first hunt, taking the mules we would be riding, and two pack animals each. We headed west along the south fork of the river. As we rode, we talked about the hunt and decided we would ride for several days and scout for game, and then hunt on our way back.

At the end of the fourth day of riding, we had seen plenty

of game and knew if everything went right, we should have no trouble getting enough meat. That night, as we sat around our small campfire, roasting meat from a deer we had killed, we decided we would wait until we were closer home before killing any big animals.

The sun was setting on the fifth day when we spotted a herd of elk. After tying our animals up in a small wooded area, we were able to stalk within good shooting distance. The spirits were with us. Cole and I managed to bring down four young elk. After dressing and quartering them, we hung the meat high in the trees, above where we had the mules tied.

After filling ourselves on fresh roasted elk, we settled in for the night. Early the next morning, we headed for home. After riding for some time, we spotted something white off in the sky, some distance ahead. We kept watching it. As we drew closer, we could see it was a large white bird. It wasn't long after that, we bagged a large doe. After cleaning, quartering and loading it on the pack animals, we continued on home.

It was late that evening when we rode into camp, and everyone came to see if we had gotten anything. They were surprised when they saw the load the pack animals were carrying. Hubert and Charley looked the meat over, then said, "Boys, you did a damn good job."

Fanny said, "You boys come and Kate and I'se fix you some supper. The others will take care of the meat."

While we were eating, the others came in and sat down at the table. Kate poured tea for everyone. Charley said they had hung the meat and turned the animals out to pasture. Then, everyone wanted to know all about the hunt and what it was like farther west, and what all we saw. We told them how we rode west for four days and saw a lot of game, then decided to hunt on the way back.

While we were talking, I noticed Kate had put two wash boilers of water on the stove to get hot. After telling everything we could think of, it wasn't long before the others said they were turning in. As they were leaving, Charley said they had made us a stove for our hut. We thanked them.

Getting a lantern, we headed to check out the new stove and get clean clothes. Returning, we found Kate had readied two tubs of water for our bath. It didn't take long and we were out of our clothes and in the tubs of hot water.

After our baths, she wanted to see our new stove. Once in the hut, we got a fire started in the stove. It wasn't long before it was nice and toasty. The candle we had gave off very little light, but enough. In no time, Kate had her hands on both of us.

It was sometime later that I stepped out of our hut to walk Kate to her bedroom. I could tell by the moon that it was way past midnight. An owl hooted, then somewhere off in the distance the sound of coyotes were howling. Kate said that reminded her of the time we were sitting outside the blacksmith shop and the coyotes or wolves were howling.

Cole and I would make several hunts before winter really set in. We had no trouble finding game. On the last hunt, we found a herd of buffalo and were able to get three yearling cows. This would make enough meat to do us through the winter.

When winter really did set in, it got cold, colder than any of us were used to, but we managed. Kate slept most nights with Cole and I in our small hut. It didn't take much firing for it to stay nice and cozy. Nothing was said by the others that Kate was sleeping with us.

Cole and I continued trapping, despite the bitter cold weather, and did quite well, catching fox, skunk, muskrat, but mostly beaver. Come spring, we would have a nice amount of fur to sell. Despite the cold and long winter, and the hard work it brought, everything and everybody fared very well.

It was late February and spring was coming on fast. Captain Fred and his crew had just tied up at the bank of the trading post after bringing supplies that were ordered on his last trip. We all pitched in and helped unload the supplies. When everything was on shore, Captain Fred handed Kate an envelope that had her name on it.

I was walking away when he hollered, "Nathan! Here's a letter for you. It's from home."

I thanked Captain Fred for the letter, then went off by myself to read it. I had written only once since I left home, and that was right before we left the Jakobses'. At that time, I had told Mom everything that had taken place from the day I left and up to the time we were getting ready to get on the boat, leaving Starved Rock.

I had walked up along the river to a nice, quiet place, to sit and read my letter. When I opened it, it read:

Nathan, my son …

Tears filled my eyes as she went on to say …

We all miss you so very much. Your father blames himself for you leaving, and worst of all, the way he treated you. Since you left, things have changed around here. One thing, your father has quit his drinking and has taken up reading the Bible. He reads it almost every night and reads to your sisters and brother, and we go to church every Sunday. Your father has since leased out the mill and now stays home and does all the farming.

We now have several more milk cows. Your father and Frances take the extra milk into town and sell it. Your brother and sisters have grown so much since you last saw them. All three of them are doing good in school, I must say! I think Frances misses you the most of all the children, but your mom misses you most of all.

Remember your teacher, Miss Martin? Well, she still comes every two or three weeks to spend the weekend, but I can see she is not the same person as she was when you were here. I can tell she misses you so much, as much as we all do, I think.

The letter you wrote us was the most wonderful letter we have ever gotten. It was read over and over by everyone. When Miss Martin came by, I showed it to her and said she could read it. When she was reading it, tears filled her eyes and she got up from the table and went outside, where she finished reading it. Finally, I went out to see if she was all right, and found her crying. Sitting down beside her, I put my arms around her and pulled her close and let her cry as she buried her face on my shoulder.

My dear son, we all pray that one day you will come home.

Your loving mother, father,
Frances, Noel and Abilene

After reading it, I sat and stared at the water as it rushed by. My thoughts turned over and over in my mind, faster than the water in the river. This was the first time, in a long time, that I missed home and everyone there.

That evening, as we were having supper, Kate informed us as to what her letter said, then asked us what we thought she should do. After we all talked it over, everyone agreed it would be best that she return and take care of the business that was left her. Then, if she wanted to come back to the trading post, it would be up to her. (At that time, she had no idea how wealthy she would be.)

Captain Fred had planned to lay over one day, to take on wood. That would give Kate plenty of time to pack her few belongings, and also gave her two nights to spend with Cole and me.

On the morning the boat was leaving, Cole and I carried her bags on board and said our last goodbyes. She had already said her goodbyes to the others. As we all stood there on the bank, watching as the boat made its way down the river.

33

It was March and spring filled the air in the little river town that lay on the south side of the Illinois River, not far from where it emptied into the Mississippi. A riverboat was just returning, after delivering supplies up the Missouri and Platte rivers. It was midday, warm and sunny. A young woman stood on deck and watched as the riverboat glided to a stop at the dock. A warm, gentle breeze ruffled her long red hair as she waited patiently for the gangplank to be lowered.

Once in place, she bent over and picked up her two pieces of baggage and slowly walked down the gangplank, looking all around. Even though it was only a year ago that she had last been here, everything seemed strange. Stepping off the gangplank, the young woman hurried to a tree that stood nearby. Setting her baggage down, she stood there in the shade, bewildered, not knowing which way to go. All these years she had lived here, she was never to this part of town, except for the day she left, and then it was early morning and barely light, and now she couldn't remember exactly which way to go to the main part of town.

Picking up her baggage, she had just started walking east along the dusty road when an elderly man and woman stopped with their buckboard and asked if she needed help. The young woman replied, "Why, yes, I could use a ride."

"Where to?" the man asked.

"Why, I'm looking for the bank, and I'm not sure if I'm going in the right direction."

"Throw your things on and climb aboard. We're going right past there, young lady," the man said.

Putting her baggage on the back, she sat down beside it, letting her legs dangle over the back. It wasn't long before the man hollered, "Whoa," and the horses came to a stop. "This is where you get off, and right over there is the bank."

Jumping off, she picked up her baggage, and thanked the

man and woman. The woman never said anything. She just stared, stone-faced ahead, as though she didn't approve of Kate.

Looking around, everything was familiar now, and she knew where she was. Crossing the dirty, dusty street to where the bank stood, she stepped up on the plank walkway, setting her baggage down, then dug in one of her bags until she came up with the letter. The letter that Captain Fred had delivered to her. The one from the bank.

Standing there, she ran her fingers through her hair, trying to smooth them down, then brushed the dust from her dress and straightened it the best she could. Taking her baggage, she walked into the bank. She noticed that no one else was there, except the man behind the window. She sighed with relief. The man immediately asked if he could help her.

"Why, yes. I would like to speak with Mr. Clyman."

"Please be seated, madam, and I'll check and see if he will see you now."

Before she had a chance to sit down, the man had returned and said, "Madam, Mr. Clyman will see you. Just go back into the hallway. It's the door on the left." He pointed.

Picking up her baggage, she thanked the man and walked to the door on the left. It read OFFICE. She stopped at the doorway and knocked. Mr. Clyman looked up from his work, then stood for a few moments, staring at this beautiful young woman with long red hair, standing in the doorway.

Mr. Clyman caught himself staring and, with a red face, quickly said, "Come in and be seated."

She stepped in and placed her things beside the chair in front of his desk, then sat down.

"How may I help you, madam?"

Looking him straight in the eye, she said, "I'm Kate Jakobes, and this is the letter you had delivered to me at Charley Blackstone's trading post up on the Platte." She handed it to him and he opened it. It was the letter he had written, explaining the circumstances surrounding Mrs. Jakobes' and then Mr. Jakobes' death and the blacksmith shop, plus all the other property. "You say you're Kate Jakobes?"

"That's right."

"Did Mr. Jakobes have anyone working for him that you know of?"

"Yes. Fanny was our maid and Charley Blackstone was my father's blacksmith, and a young man by the name of Nathan also worked for my father."

"Miss Jakobes, I want you to take me to where you lived. I'll get my buggy and meet you out front. You can leave your baggage here."

"Mr. Clyman, what is this all about? Don't you believe me?"

"Miss Jakobes, I must make sure you are who you say you are, and we must find at least two people who can tell me if you are who you say. Identify you as Miss Kate Jakobes."

"That will be fine, Mr. Clyman. We can stop at the church. The preacher can tell you that I'm Kate Jakobes. Then at the school, the teacher also knows who I am."

"We'll do that, Miss Jakobes. Now, I'll get my horse and buggy and meet you out front." He quickly told his teller where he was going, then went out through the back and got his horse and buggy and drove around to the front, where Kate was waiting. Kate climbed on board. Mr. Clyman hollered for the horse to get up and headed off in the direction of the preacher's house.

Once there, he told Kate to stay in the buggy. Mr. Clyman went the short distance to the house and knocked on the door. When the door opened, he saw it was the preacher.

"Yes, Mr. Clyman, what can I do for you at this time of day?" They hadn't spoken to each other since Mr. Jakobes' burial.

"Well! Preacher! I need you to take a look at this young lady who is sitting there in the buggy. She says she is Kate Jakobes, and said that you could verify who she is."

"Well, I don't know!"

"Preacher, I know we have our differences. But would you please, for her sake?"

" But ... I'll do it."

"Thanks." The preacher walked to where the buggy stood and looked at the young woman sitting there. Kate smiled at him, but he didn't say anything to her. He just looked, then turned to Mr. Clyman and said, "That's Kate. Now get her out of here." And he walked back to his house.

Mr. Clyman climbed back on the buggy and drove off. The next stop was the school. It so happened the teacher and children were outside for their afternoon recess when Mr. Clyman drove up. Right away, the school master came to see what was wrong. He looked at Mr. Clyman and said, "Good afternoon, Mr. Clyman, and good afternoon, Kate. It's good to see you again. What brings you here on this nice sunny afternoon?"

Mr. Clyman said, "I wanted to know if you knew this

young lady, so I can settle some business."

"Why, yes! I know her. She's Kate Jakobes. She was a very good student. Smart *and* pretty, if I may say so."

"Thank you," Kate replied.

Mr. Clyman said, "Thank you, that is what I needed to know," then drove off. Turning to Kate, he said, "I don't see any need in going anywhere else. We'll go back to the bank and I'll make up the necessary papers and everything will be yours. I do hope you will continue to do your business with my bank, Miss Jakobes."

Kate had taken notice that Mr. Clyman couldn't keep his eyes off of her and seemed to take a special interest in her, even though he was probably in his early 50s. "Why, yes, Mr. Clyman, I do want to continue doing business with you."

They were back at the bank now, and he didn't stop out front. Instead, he drove around to the back, where he kept his horse and buggy. Getting down, he said, "Miss Jakobes, just wait until I tie up, then I'll help you down."

Kate liked all this attention he was giving her and stayed seated until he came around to help her down. Mr. Clyman taken her hand and, as she was about to step down, she pretended to slip, letting herself fall into his arms, almost knocking him off-balance. She looked up into his eyes and smiled. "Thank you. I'm so sorry. I'm such a clod."

He blushed when he realized his hand was still covering her breast. "I'm so terribly sorry," he apologized.

"Don't be. It's all my fault."

Taking her by the arm, he led her into his office. "Please be seated, Miss Jakobes, while I put the necessary papers in order."

She waited patiently, watching every move he made, and turning it over in her mind.

Finally, he said, "Miss Jakobes, if you will put your name right here, the property and bank account will be put into your name. If there is anything else at this time I can help you with, Miss Jakobes, I would be pleased to do so."

"Why, yes, yes! Mr. Clyman, you did say, didn't you, that you had someone living in the house and taking care of the shop?"

"Yes, I did."

"So, I'll be needing some money so I can get a room and something to eat. I want to rest for a few days and think things over before I make any decisions."

"Yes, of course, and I apologize, Miss Jakobes. I should have realized you will be needing these things."

"Just call me Kate, would you, please?"

"Yes, Kate. Now how much do you want?"

"Well, I don't know. I have no idea what a room with meals will cost, and also I would like to buy a good horse and buggy."

"But, Kate, you already have horses and a buggy out at your place."

"I know. But I don't want to take them away from the people that are living there. Mr. Clyman, do you know someone who would be willing to help me pick out a good horse and buggy? I would be glad to pay them."

"Why, yes. If you need help with these things, I can find time, and would gladly help you."

"Thank you. If you don't mind, I would like that. Mr. Clyman, if you will take some money out of my account, whatever you think I will need, and give me directions to a good place for me to stay at, I'll be running along."

"Kate, since you don't seem to know the town very well, why don't you wait a few more minutes? We will be closing before long. Then, I will drive you to what I think is the best boarding house in town. The owners are real nice, and it's very clean, and they have good meals. They tolerate no roughness nor drunkenness. I think you will find it to your liking."

"Mr. Clyman, thanks, but I don't want to take advantage of your generous hospitality."

"You're not! Kate, it's the least I can do for you."

"I do appreciate everything you are doing for me, Mr. Clyman, but ... I ... I don't know how I'll ever repay you."

"We'll discuss that later."

"Well, if you think it's all right, I will wait."

"It's all right, Kate." Then he handed her several hundred dollars. "Here, this should tie you over for a while."

"Thanks." Kate waited while he and his teller put everything in order and closed. After letting his teller out the front door, and locking it, he turned to Kate with a big smile and said, "Come, my dear." With one hand, he scooped up her two bags, and with the other, taken her by the hand and led the way out the back door to where the buggy stood.

Throwing the bags in back, he taken her left hand in his and put his right one over her buttock to help her into the buggy. He untied his horse and climbed on and drove off.

It was a warm late afternoon, and the sun was already setting. The sky was a scarlet red as they drove toward the boarding house. He commented how beautiful the sky was, and her, too. She blushed and was silent. As he drove he told her about the boarding house and that it lay on the banks of the big river. It was on the outskirts of town, away from the noise and busy part of town.

Reaching their destination, Mr. Clyman drove up to the hitching post and Kate looked at the sign that read "Adam and Ruby's Boarding House. Hot meals, hot baths, rooms, clothes washing." Then she said, "Looks real nice."

After helping her down and picking up her bags, he led the way to the main entrance and opened it, letting her go in first. Several lamps burning lit the room nicely. A small counter stood in one corner, several chairs and a fainting couch were placed at various locations around the room. A tall, thin man who appeared to be around 70 walked into the room and stepped behind the counter, squinting his eyes. He said, "Good evening, Mr. Clyman. Who is this young lady you bring?"

"This is Miss Kate Jakobes, Adam. Kate, this is Adam Fry. He and his wife, Ruby, are the proprietors of this fine establishment."

"Thank you, Mr.Clyman. Now what is it I can do for you, Miss Jakobes?"

"Well, I'm in need of place to stay for a while, and it doesn't have to be much."

Mr. Clyman winked at Adam, and he nodded.

"Miss Jakobes, I think we have just the room for you. Just come this way, please." Adam led the way up the stairway to the second floor. Kate followed, and Mr. Clyman fell in behind with her bags. Adam led the way down the hallway to its end. There, he unlocked the door and opened it. The room was dark. Adam struck a match and lit one of the lamps, then pulled the curtains open that covered the two windows. Now Kate could see, and she was amazed at how nice the room was. There was another door and Kate asked where it went. Adam opened it, so she could see. Kate looked out and was surprised to see there was a small porch with stairs leading to the ground, and the river wasn't far away.

Turning back to Adam, she asked him, "How much is the room?"

"Fifty cents a day, or one dollar with three meals."

"Kate," Mr. Clyman said, "you can well afford that much.

I think you should take it."

Kate didn't know exactly how much money she had, but she trusted Mr. Clyman and said she would take it. Adam handed her the key and said, "Please come down to the desk."

They followed him downstairs, where he made up the proper arrangements, then asked her how long she wanted the room.

"I'll pay for two months now." She handed him the money, then thanked him and Mr. Clyman, and walked over to the steps.

She already had one foot on the stairs when Mr. Clyman said, "Wait, I want to talk to you."

She stopped to see what he wanted. He stood close to her, leaning on the banister. In a low voice, he said, "Kate, I'll see you ..." Then he stopped as if to think. After doing some quick mental calculating as to what day his wife would be tied up with her church and social gatherings, he said, "I'll see you in three days. Then we will see if we can find you a horse and buggy. It will be best if I come up the back stairs."

Then she nodded. "I'll see you then."

The next day, Kate walked to the main part of town to shop for some new dresses, frilly undergarments, new shoes, and whatever else she thought she may need. On the day Mr. Clyman was to pick her up, she was up early, bathed, powdered, then put on all new clothes, then went downstairs and had her breakfast.

After eating, she went back to her room, milled around, and paced back and forth to the window, watching for Mr. Clyman. Several times she had an uneasy feeling that he wouldn't show up, and she was beginning to worry. It was midmorning when she heard footsteps coming up the stairs. After he knocked, she waited a few moments before she answered.

"Yes, who is it?"

"It's me, Grover."

"Okay, just a minute." She stepped in front of the mirror, to see how she looked. Not bad. She knew she looked her best. Opening the door, she said, "Please come in, Mr. Clyman."

"Just call me Grover, would you, Kate?" He reached his hand for hers. Instead, she put her arms around him, pulling him close, giving him a nice long hug, then asked him to be seated on a chair that was next to her bedstand.

"Would you like a cup of tea?" she asked.

"Why, yes, that would be fine."

After pouring them each a cup of tea, she sat on the bed. They talked and sipped tea, and talked some more. Horses and buggies weren't on their minds. Setting his cup down, he moved over onto the bed beside Kate. Leaning back, he pulled her down on top of him. Their lips met, and his hands worked at her dress. It had been a long time for her, and she was more than willing. In no time, they were both naked.

It was several hours later before they got dressed and went down the back stairs to where the horse and buggy stood. Getting in, they drove off in the direction of the livery stable. Neither one spoke for a long time. Just before they reached the livery stable, he said, "You are very good."

She blushed and smiled, then said, "Thanks, it was good, I needed that!"

At the livery stable, they found the horse and buggy to her liking, and the price was right, so she bought them, then made arrangements to have them stabled there. After paying the boarding fee, Mr. Clyman drove her back to her room.

"Would you like to come in for a while?" she asked.

He knew what was on her mind, and said, "I can't, Kate. I have to get back to the bank, and get some work done before closing time. I'll stop by in a couple of days."

As the days passed, Kate thought more and more about her old home place, until finally she got up the courage to drive out to where she once lived.

It was on a Sunday afternoon when she drove up to her old home. It looked just like it did when she left, more than a year before. Funny feelings stirred inside her as she tied up at the hitching post.

As she walked to the front door, she felt weak in her legs. She kept her wits as she knocked on the door. The Slaughters and Royer had just finished their midday meal. Jason answered the door. "May I help you?"

"Yes. I'm ... I'm Kate Jakobes. May I come in?"

Jason felt as though he was just kicked by a horse. After gaining his poise, he said, "Yes, yes, please do." He held the door for her to enter.

As she stepped into the parlor, he asked her to be seated, then returned to the kitchen to get Agnes. Jason and Agnes introduced themselves and invited Kate to the kitchen for coffee or tea. She accepted, and the three of them sat at the kitchen table, making small talk. After the awkwardness passed, and

Kate made it clear that she had no intentions of living there, they became comfortable with each other.

Kate told them she was happy with the arrangement, and hinted she may be interested in selling them the place.

Over the next weeks, she made several trips to visit the Slaughters and visit the site where her parents were buried. Mr. Clyman would stop by once or twice a week, and they would make love. Most of the time, it was fair to good, but she didn't love him, never would, and he didn't love her, and never would.

Sometimes they just sat and talked. Other times they would walk to the river. One day, on one of those walks, he told her that the owner of one of the better saloons had passed away, and it was being sold, and asked if she would be interested in purchasing it.

"I ... I don't know. I know nothing about managing something like that."

"Kate, I can give you all the help you may need. Besides, you're a very intelligent person, and I know you have the ability to do it."

"I don't know. I have been thinking about returning to Charley and Fanny at their trading post."

"Kate, you can't return! That's no life for a beautiful young woman like you. You belong here. You deserve better than a life in a trading post."

"But ... .they're my only friends."

"I know, but this is a good opportunity, and you'll make friends here. Can't you see that?"

"But my heart is at the trading post with them."

"Kate! Please listen! You will get over them in time, so don't pass up this opportunity to better yourself. Please take your time and give it some serious thought."

"Okay, I'll think about it. But I make no promises."

"That's fair enough."

"How much is this place?"

"I'm not sure. No price has been set as of yet. But I'm sure it will be something you can afford, and it may be a month or more before I know. You'll have time to think about it."

As the weeks passed, she gave it a lot of thought as to what Grover had told her. She lay awake at night, turning it over and over in her mind as what to do. But her mind always went back to the trading post and what she left behind. But most of all, she thought about Nathan and Cole, and what the three of them had together, and it weighed heavily on her mind. Buy the saloon, or return? She knew if she was to return, the chances of Cole and Nathan being there was next to nothing. And the chances of them returning was even less. Yet her heart yearned so much for them. Even worse was the fact that her body ached with a burning desire even more.

Finally, she made up her mind, and sold the blacksmith shop and the rest of the property to the Slaughters. Then, within six weeks, she was the new owner of the saloon. By fall, she had it all redone to her liking, and everything else was put in order. She also renamed the saloon. It would now be known as Kate's Place. From opening night on, business was very good, far beyond anything she expected. Her girls were paid well, and so were the rest of her help.

The marshal stopped by the first night she was open for business. He asked for the owner, and introduced himself as Marshal Lee Dawson. Kate told him her name, and asked him to be seated at her private table, which was situated so that she could see everything that went on. They talked and talked, and as the night faded away, he was impressed with the way she ran her business, and not only that, but the way she dressed and the way she talked. It was very late when he finally said he had to get back to his office. They shook hands.

"I hope you will be stopping from time to time."

"Kate, you can bet on that."

Mr. Clyman would drop in every few days to check on how business was doing. He was her guidance of sorts, and was impressed with how well she was running the business. They always went to her private quarters, which was off one side of the main building and consisted of a nice bedroom, kitchen and parlor. Most of the time, they went to bed to satisfy their needs, which on Kate's part was becoming more and more demanding, to the point where she no longer was being satisfied. Her fantasy left her cold and empty. Her heart was broken, and her body ached for Nathan and Cole. Mr. Clyman was the only sexual partner she had since returning. She was not one to drag just any man to bed. She had to like them first, then learn to know them. They had to be more than just the rough and dirty riverboat hands or cowboys that patronized her place.

Marshal Lee Dawson would stop by sometimes after work and have his evening meal, and since he lived alone, he never was in a hurry and would sit and talk with Kate. She didn't mind, for his presence kept any trouble at bay.

As time passed, she began looking at him in a different manner. He was at least seven years older. He was fair to good looking, tall and thin, with a good build, educated with good manners. It wasn't long before he was stopping in daily to eat, and it wasn't long before Kate saw to it that he was having his meals in her private quarters, and then most of the time, after a few drinks, they would bathe and spend most of the night making love.

One night, he asked her to marry him. Without any hesitation, she said, "No!" Despite the fact she knew he was a good lover, she didn't love him, she couldn't love him, she never would love him.

She filled her days, her nights and her lovemaking with fancies and images of what she once had.

34

For the next several days, Cole and I turned the soil over and made the ground ready to plant. One evening, after the planting was all done and supper was over, Cole and I were out checking on the animals when he said, "Nathan, when you think we'll be heading west?"

"I don't know. I have been looking around, and realized there's more work than Charley and Hubert can handle this summer."

"What's you sayin', brother? That we'se not going!"

"No. What I'm saying is, I want to know what you think about us staying and helping them out the rest of this year. Then, early next spring, heading west."

"I'se do'an know. It's not the same without Kate being here."

"I know."

"I'se can see there's all kindsa work to get done. Mebbe that'd be the best thing for us to do. I'se knows they needs the help."

"Think it over, Cole."

"I'se has. I'se say we do the right thing and stay."

One morning, some weeks later, while having breakfast, Fanny said, "When's you boys plans on goin'?"

Cole looked at me, waiting for me to answer.

"Fanny," I said, "if it's all right with you and Charley, Cole and I would like to stay the rest of this year and plan on leaving early in the spring."

Her mouth dropped open and there was a surprised look on Charley's face. "What changed your minds?" Charley asked.

"You. Fanny. The Harwoods. Mostly you two. Cole and I talked it over, and realized there was more work than you'se can handle."

"How well I know that," Charley said. "Thanks, boys. I was hoping you would change your minds. I know Hubert and Gladys will be also."

Fanny came around the table, her eyes filled with tears, and gave us each a long hug. "My boys, my boys, how happy I'se that you boys think enough of my Charley and me that you'se is gonna stay and help."

Cole and I worked hard through the long hot summer, way into the winter. I was very pleased with what all of us had got accomplished, adding a room to the trading post for more storage, work on the barn, a place to store hay and straw, among other things that needed done. Every chance Cole and I got, we would go fishing or hunting. Sometimes I would fish while Cole hunted. We kept Fanny and Gladys well supplied with fresh meat.

When the last supply boat left that fall, I sent two letters along with it, one to my family, and one to Kate, along with a bundle of fur and instructions for her to sell the fur and buy Cole and I each two shirts, one pair of pants, one pair of shoes and one set of long underwear, along with the sizes each would need.

The winter seemed long and cold. It didn't stop Cole and I from tending our traps and hunting for necessary meat for the winter. Charley and Fanny had Cole and I sleep in the new room for the winter. The room had one window and two doors, one going to the outside, and the other to the main part.

From time to time, a few Indians would stop and trade, mostly for coffee, salt, sugar and bright-colored cloth and beads. Occasionally some hearty souls would stop by on their way upriver, usually by canoe. Rarely did we see anyone return. I wondered at times whatever got them, or where they had gone. The ones that stopped would never say where they were headed to.

I guess it was late February or early March 1822 that the boat made it back with supplies. After everything was unloaded and put away, Cole and I opened the package from Kate. We were surprised that she had sent three of everything we ordered, except shoes. There were two pairs each, and a note saying how much she missed us all.

After the boat left, Cole and I began readying everything we owned for packing on our pack animals. We had spent one hell of a lot of time over the winter working with and training our animals. I knew they were ready and would work well. Charley and Fanny saw what we were doing and tried their best to talk us into staying longer. The Harwoods didn't say much. They knew. They all knew.

One morning a few days later, we loaded our belongings

on our pack animals and wished everyone the best, and that we would see them in due time, jumped on our mules, and headed west.

We were traveling along the south bank of the Platte's north fork, and had been riding for more than eight days, when we realized our animals were in need of rest. After checking the animals over, we decided it would be better for us and the animals if we worked only three or four days, then lay up for a day or so, letting them rest and feed.

Thus far in our moving, we had encountered no signs of any human beings, only wildlife. We realized how fortunate we were as we moved on west, staying far enough away from the river so as not to be easily seen, yet knowing where we were.

We had been on the move for more than a month, and things had been going good. Then, one afternoon, we stopped for the day and tied the animals up in a grove of cottonwoods. We were making our way toward the river that lay several hundred yards away. I was a short distance in front of Cole. The prairie grass was head high. Visibility was very poor. I was concentrating on rattlers, for we had seen quite a few earlier, and hadn't given any thought about any other animals, until a bear charged from my right.

There was no time for me to shoot before being knocked to the ground with the bear on top of me. Cole rushed to help. As soon as the bear saw him, it raised its head, mouth open, snapping its teeth. That's when Cole shoved the muzzle of his gun in its mouth and at the same time pulled the trigger.

The blast tore most of the beast's head off, but not before it tore me up pretty good. Cole, shaking like a leaf, rolled the beast off me. I was shaking worse. Then, he helped me to sit up. I sat there, looking at myself, and couldn't believe what happened. I was covered with blood, my own and that of the bear.

Helping me to my feet, he led me the rest of the way to the river, then had me sit in the cool water. Taking his hands, he dipped water over my head. "Brother, you'se got a gash that starts at your hairline and goes down over your eye to the corner of your mouth and chin. Brother, can you see out of your left eye?"

After washing more blood out of it, I said, "Yes, I can see."

"Nathan, you'se damn lucky you didn't lose an eye."

"Yes!"

"Here, let me help you get your shirt off."

"No, I'm okay."

"You're *not!* Now let's get it off!"

Once it was off, Cole checked me over and found puncture wounds in my left shoulder, and four or five claw gashes on the back side of each shoulder. There wasn't much he could do, except keep putting cold water on until the bleeding stopped.

Once back at camp, he got a needle and thread, then sewed my face the best he could, then made several hot poultices from plants and put them on my wounds.

"I think we's better stay here a few days, brother."

On the evening of the fourth day, my wounds showed signs of healing good—good enough that I would be able to ride.

It was ten days later. We broke camp early one morning and had been riding several hours. We could see a great distance in all directions, and could see no signs that would indicate there were Indians about.

Cole had just said how nice it was that we hadn't seen any Indians, when eight Indians appeared, two on the right and two on the left, two rear, two out front. We stopped to see what would happen.

The two in front motioned us to follow. We kept riding and they stayed with us, not getting any closer than twenty yards. We rode a long distance like this, even though we had our long guns at the ready. I knew we would never stand a chance if we made a run to get away. This made me very nervous.

Finally, the two in the lead veered north toward the river. Cole and I kept on going straight, but were cut off by the two on our left. We shook our heads no and pointed straight. They had other ideas, and made it clear that we were to follow the leaders. We had no choice.

Cole and I were now riding side by side, with our pack animals strung out behind.

"What do you think they will do with us?" Cole asked.

"I don't know. I don't know. There's one thing ..."

"What's that?"

"There's something very wrong. These Indians aren't acting anything like the stories we have been told."

"What's you mean?"

"Just look. They haven't gotten any closer than twenty or thirty yards to us. To me, that means there's something not right. Don't you think?"

"Yeah, yeah, sure. Look, that way!"

They led us across the river and up a long narrow valley. Sage and brush covered both sides. We saw several lookouts stationed high above the trail. The trail kept on rising and finally broke out into a small meadow, surrounded on three sides by a heavy forest. We could see an encampment of several dozen tepees scattered about.

We were escorted to the far end, where a longhouse stood next to the woods. Since we had entered the village, the braves had moved in closer to us. The two leading stopped a short distance from the longhouse. As they dismounted, two young boys came running and taken their horses, leading them away. The two braves then walked to the longhouse and entered.

Cole and I stayed sitting on our mules. A crowd had begun gathering around. Not knowing what to expect, we became very uneasy. Just then, an elderly man with long white hair emerged from the longhouse, wearing his brightly colored headdress and nothing else, except for his loincloth. It was obvious that this man was indeed the chief. He and the two braves walked within ten feet of where we sat.

"I don't like this," Cole said.

"I don't either. I think the best thing for us to do is stay calm and show no fear. That's the only choice we have."

The chief looked us over good, then motioned us down from our mules. We did and stood in front of our animals, keeping our long guns cradled in our arms. He taken a few steps in front of his braves and raised his hand, a sign of peace.

Cole and I returned the sign. My friend, Chief Golden Eagle, had taught me enough so that I was able to understand most everything he was saying. I would translate to Cole. He said he was Chief Buffalo Man, a chief of one of the Sioux clans that I don't recall. He asked where we came from. I told him. Then he wanted to know what we were called.

I said, "He is called Cole," pointing at Cole. "And I'm called Nathan. We're just passing through your land and would like to be your friends."

He nodded his head, then walked off to one side, so he could see Cole's back. Neither of us had shirts on. He then came around to me and, looking at my back, stopped right in front of me and pointed with his stick at the gash on my face. Then he asked, "What happen face? Pawnee?"

"No." I explained to him that I was mauled by a bear.

"Bear? Brave man! You and friend many battle scars for

young warriors."

Cole's back had far more scars from the beatings he had taken than I had. I tried to explain to him what the scars were from, but I don't think he understood.

He just smiled. "Brave warriors!" Touching the necklace I wore, he then said, "Chief Golden Eagle! Chief Golden Eagle show me and my people you be coming, bringing black man friend with you, and show me you blood brothers. Chief Golden Eagle show me big bird and say good spirit follow you and watch over you and friend, keeps away bad spirits. You have fine animals. Squaw take care of. You come with Chief Buffalo Man." He motioned, and four women came and taken our animals.

We, not knowing what lay ahead, didn't protest, and followed the chief. The one thing that made no sense was the fact that they didn't take away our guns and knives. Chief Buffalo Man led the way to the longhouse and entered. We followed.

Once inside, we saw it had a fair-sized opening in the ceiling and walls to let in light. A small fire burned at the far end. We were escorted to where the fire burned. The chief motioned for us to sit. He then went around on the opposite side and sat down. A medicine man then sat on each side of him. The eight braves that brought us here sat four on each side of the medicine men, to form a semi-circle. Eight women sat behind the braves.

Looking around, I saw the space behind Cole and me had filled with people. They were in all stages of dress, most naked from the waist up. Cole and I sat, cross-legged, with our long guns laying across our laps. I looked at Cole, who was showing no fear now, and said, "It looks like we are guests instead of being held captive."

"I believe so."

The chief held up both hands. Everything got quiet. He then said to Cole and me, "You are our guests. We knew long time you would come. That why I had braves watch for you and bring you to Chief Buffalo Man. Chief Golden Eagle of Spirit World show me you two 'good medicine.' "

Then the chief began asking questions. "Where you and friend come from?"

I told them where we came from.

"How come you friend of Chief Golden Eagle?"

I decided then it may be best if I tried to explain everything to them, even if they didn't understand. I began with where I was born, and how old I was when I first came to know

Chief Golden Eagle, and all the events that occurred from the time I left home with Chief Golden Eagle and what happened to him, and everything up to the present.

Every time I answered the questions they asked, or told of an event, the chief would nod. The others merely uttered a grunt. Some nodded. It was late afternoon when he finally called a halt and asked for food to be brought. This gave an opportunity for me to ask if Cole and I could go relieve our bodies. The chief nodded, and two braves promptly got up and led us outside and showed us where to go.

When we returned, we saw most everyone had left except for the chief and his council. It wasn't long before food was brought. Everyone gathered in a circle around the small fire. The chief then did a ritual over the food. The food was then passed around. To our surprise, the food was very tasty compared to what Cole and I were used to eating.

While we ate, there was little conversation. By the time we finished, it was dark. Cole, not wanting any more talk, leaned close to me and told me to ask the chief if we could get our bed rolls so we could get some sleep. I asked the chief and he nodded. We were shown to a wickiup, where our belongings had been neatly stacked. We were told this was where we were to sleep.

Over the next few days, we were asked to sit in council, which we did, and we were asked many questions, such as how many whites were there where we came from, and could we get guns, horses and so forth. In the short time we were there, we learned a lot about these people and how they lived.

Cole and I were very honored to have had the opportunity to be accepted as friends, and told Chief Buffalo Man and his council how honored we were.

The morning of the sixth day, Cole and I packed our animals and bid our friends farewell, then continued on our journey west. Our plans were to trap a few years and, if we had a fair amount of fur put up, we would return to Charley and Fanny's trading post and sell our fur. But little did we know what lay ahead.

It was some weeks after we left Chief Buffalo Man and his village that we made camp under a rock ledge in a stand of cottonwood trees with a nice rushing stream nearby. It will still early evening. I was gathering firewood when I heard Cole holler, "While you get a fire going, I'll go see if I can catch some fish and bring water."

I had just gotten a fire going when Cole gave out a shrill scream. Grabbing my gun, I went running. When I got to where Cole was, I saw in horror what was taking place. A huge mountain lion had jumped on Cole and had him down and was really mauling him. Cole, being one hell of a fighter, was no match for a cat this huge.

I quickly moved to a point so I was facing the cat. When it realized I was there, it reared back, ready to pounce, and let out a bone-chilling scream that sent shivers running up and down my spine. At the same time, it gave me my one chance. Shoving my gun close to the cat's face, I squeezed the trigger. Its head exploded as the blast flipped it off of Cole and to the side, where it lay limp. I knew the cat was dead, so kneeling beside Cole, I was able to see how bad he was mauled.

He was out. I could see he was tore up bad enough, but it could have been worse. I shook him and he didn't respond. I shook him more, this time harder, and for a moment I thought I had lost him. Finally, I could see he was breathing. Running to the stream, I got some cool water and put it on his face. Slowly, he opened his eyes and looked at me strangely. I didn't say anything, just let him come back on his own.

Checking him over, I found he had some bad bites and deep slashes from the cat's claws. I kept on putting water on his wounds while he collected his wits and his general feeling and awareness of what had happened.

After resting awhile, he said, "How bad?"

"Not bad, Cole, not bad. When you think you can walk, I'll help you get back to camp and get you fixed up."

"I sure will try, Nathan."

After getting him to his feet, I picked up our guns and, with him hanging on me, we made it to camp, where I got him to sit and lean back against some rocks. After getting the fire built up, I taken my gun and returned to the stream and got more water. When it was hot, I washed his wounds and sewed up the worst one, then put poultices on them.

It was past dark by now. A slice of the moon hung low in the western sky. A pack of wolves let out a howl not far in the distance. I knew what had to be done. I told Cole I was going to go skin the cat and save some of the meat before the wolves got to it.

"I'm going with you!" he cried out vehemently.

"No, Cole! No, Cole, you need to rest, you hear? You can keep the fire going."

After putting a heap of wood within his reach, I made a torch and lit it, and grabbed my gun and made my way to where the cougar lay. After I had the cat skun, I saved as much of the meat as I could. Wrapping it in the cat skin, I went to camp. Cole was waiting and had the fire blazing.

"I see you got it."

"Yep! As much of the meat as I could."

"How's about roasting up some?"

"Yeah, sounds good. You lay back and take it easy, you hear?"

"Yes'm, I hears you."

After hanging a few chunks over the hot embers, I settled back beside Cole to wait for the meat and check how he was doing.

"Nathan, where we headed tomorrow?"

"Don't think anywhere. Cole, I think we're better off staying here and let you heal some."

"I think I can make it."

"We'll see tomorrow."

That night it rained, and it rained for the next four days. A steady rain came down. This was just what we needed. It would give Cole time to rest and heal, and the animals needed some rest. It would give me time to go over our equipment and repair what needed to be fixed. I made sure Cole stayed out of the rain by giving him the job of cutting up the meat and drying it over the hot coals. I did some fishing, even if it was raining. At least it would give us a change in our diet.

On the afternoon of the fourth day, the rain stopped and the sun came out, nice and warm. By now, Cole was feeling good and his wounds were healing nicely.

"If you think you can ride, we'll pack up in the morning and move on."

"I can do it, Nathan!"

"Okay, tomorrow we move."

35

Two moons later, we found ourselves deep in Indian territory, at the foot of the big mountains. We were moving south along the foot of these mountains and looking for a place that we might cross that wouldn't be too difficult—valley, river gorge, something. The going had been fairly good—open meadows and nice streams flowing from higher up. By now there was a little nip in the early morning air, and each day we made our way farther south.

Little did we know we were on Crow land. One early afternoon, without knowing it, we rode too close to a Crow village and, before we knew, were surrounded by twenty or thirty whooping, yelping, hollering Crow warriors, some waving lances, some bows. They rode in a circle, closing in closer and closer, with each circling, yelling something we could not understand. We were riding side by side and kept on moving.

Cole said to me, "Brother, if this be the end, I wants you to know I could'a never asked for a better brother than you been to me. I want you to know dat."

"Thanks, Cole. I, too, couldn't have asked for a better brother, and I want you to know that also."

The yelling kept on. We thought for sure they were going to kill us. I said, "Let's stop, Cole, and see what happens. We have nothing to lose, brother, except our lives!"

We stopped and the circling stopped. We knew better than to try and make a break. This would have been suicide. We were taken to their village that lay miles away, and then in front of their chief, who looked us over good.

Raising our hands in peace, the chief just looked.

Cole said to me, "Make sign." I did, and told him that I was Nathan and this was Cole. He must have understood, for he nodded. Then, with his hands, he told us he was Chief Standing Bear, then said something to his warriors.

We were yanked from our animals and dragged to a tepee and roughly shoved inside, whereupon our hands were lashed behind our backs, then our feet. We were bound to a post that was in the center of the tepee. They left, closing the flap behind them.

At once we heard a lot of commotion outside. We couldn't understand what was being said, but we could tell one was the chief talking. Then everything got quiet, except for some animals. We wondered if they were ours.

Darkness fell and we were all alone in this prison of darkness, not knowing what to expect, and with nothing to drink nor food. Cole and I struggled to free ourselves until we were exhausted. Making matters worse was the fact that we both had knives tucked in our belts under our shirts that hid them. They hadn't checked.

We sat in silence. My thoughts were running wild, not knowing what was to happen to us. I thought about home, Charley, Fanny. Cole, not know what he was feeling. A while later, he asked, "What's you think?"

"Don't know. How's about you?"

"Does'n know either. I guess we pray for the best."

"I think you're right." I tried keeping Cole talking, to help the night pass quicker. We talked about Charley, Fanny and the trading post, most of all about Kate and what she was doing.

Exhaustion taken its toll. We fell asleep.

Sometime after sun up, the flap on the tepee was opened and four warriors stepped in. Two of them untied us from the post. We were dragged outside, feet first. I was momentarily blinded from the light. A slight mist was coming down and, when my eyes adjusted, I saw we were surrounded most of the village.

No one came by, except four warriors that stood some feet away, their bows drawn. Chief Standing Bear stood next to them. He said something in Crow and motioned. Two warriors promptly came forth, untied our feet, then dragged us to a standing position. Chief Standing Bear then started yelling and waving his hands.

We had no idea what was being said. When we didn't respond, he viciously yelled louder, hands waving wildly.

Not knowing what else to do, I turned my back and moved my hands as if to say "Untie me."

Two warriors came forth and cut my hands loose. I stood, rubbing my wrists. Then the chief started making signs with his hands. I understood most of what was being said, and shook my head no. He yelled loudly. I pointed to Cole's hands. The chief shook his head no. I yelled, "Yes!" and sat down, cross-legged, folding my arms across my chest, figuring if we were going to die, it might as well be now. I shook my head yes, and two warriors jumped in front of me, knocking Cole off his feet next to me. A brave made a lunge for Cole, and Cole kicked out with both feet, which landed square on the brave's nuts. He folded as other braves rushed forward.

Before they could reach us, the chief stepped in front, raising his hands, yelling something to ward them off. I helped Cole to his feet and untied his hands. He stood there, rubbing his wrists, and Chief Standing Bear said something to his people in Crow, and some of his people started forming two lines.

I knew what was coming. I then tried to reason with the chief, but he just shook his head no. Now we were shoved to the head of the two lines that were maybe twenty or so yards long, but looked a mile. Everyone in both lines had some kind of a club. Chief Standing Bear motioned for us to run.

We shook our heads no. A few braves gave us a shove. Now we had no choice. I was held back as they gave Cole a shove between the two lines. I hollered to Cole, "Run fast! Zig-zag from side to side!" I watched as he zig-zagged his way between the two lines of club-swinging people, and I wondered if he would make it or be clubbed to death.

We both were used to running hard and fast. I could see the blows landing hard on him. Knowing how tough a man he was, I had no uncertainty about him making it now.

When they saw Cole made it, both lines raised their clubs in the air and cheered. Now came my turn. Getting ready, I looked at the chief and said, "You asshole," and I was off running, running harder than I ever thought I could, zig-zagging back and forth. Yet the blows came and landed hard on my back side. With the mist coming down and the ground being slippery, I almost fell several times.

Despite all of this, I made it. We both made it. This didn't set well with some of the warriors, for when Cole grabbed me and we started to walk away, we were surrounded by warriors. When their chief came, they demanded that he have us fight each other to the death. When Chief Standing Bear told us this, I shook my head no and said, "If you'se want to see us die, then go ahead and kill us. Cole and I are blood brothers. We taken a sacred oath that we would always take care of one another. So, you see, we will not fight each other just for your bloodthirsty pleasure!"

Chief Standing Bear stood staring at us, then said, "You fight best two warriors."

I said no. It was too late. The people had already formed a wide circle around us. Two warriors came into the circle waving knives. We were handed each a knife. Cole, standing close, said, "I don't want to kill anyone."

"Me either."

Instead we went to where the chief stood and threw the knives at his feet. He snarled as we turned and faced the two knife-waving warriors. They stood looking at us in disbelief. A moment later, they charged.

Cole and I had done a lot of practicing in hand-to-hand fighting, just in case we should encounter something like this. The two warriors stopped ten feet away, then charged again. This gave us a chance to size up our opponents.

Cole shouted, "Let's take them!"

"Okay, brother!"

The one charging Cole had his knife in his right hand. Cole sidestepped the charge to the left and, with his left fist, planted it square between the warrior's eyes. His lights went out as he collapsed to the ground.

I also was able to sidestep the brave charging me and tripped him. He landed hard and as he rolled over, he swung high with his knife, ripping through my pants, slicing my upper thigh just enough to draw blood. I saw the terrified look on his face as I kicked the knife from his hand as he struggled to gain his feet. He no more than stood when my fist caught him in the gut. He folded over, and I grabbed him by the hair and yanked his head down hard as I brought my knee up, smashing it into his face. Blood gushed from his nose. He went limp, collapsing on the ground.

Going to where the chief stood, we told him we would be on our way. He shook his head no, and once again we were surrounded and shoved to a tree that stood nearby. Asking the chief what he intended on doing with us, he replied, "You dishonored and disgraced two of our best warriors. Now you die."

We were made to take our shirts off, then our hands were tied to a limb that Cole and I were barely able to reach. We were tied face to face. The braves that tied us told the chief to come look. He came over from where he stood and the brave motioned toward Cole's back side. Chief Standing Bear stepped even closer and rubbed his hand over Cole's back that was covered with horrible-looking scars and welts. Then he did the same to me. Then he noticed the necklace that hung around my neck.

He stepped back and was about to say something when a large, white bird swooped low over the circle of people and vanished as quickly as it appeared. A muffled mutter came over the crowd of people. Chief Standing Bear stood, head tilted back, arms stretched skyward, chanting.

"Brother, what's they doing?" Cole asked.

"I don't know, but I think it has something to do with that white bird swooping low over us. Did you see it?"

"Yeah, I did."

Chief Standing Bear motioned us to be cut loose. Some squaws handed our shirts back to us and while we were putting them on Chief Standing Bear was saying, "My people believe you are some kind of spirits. They don't want you put to death."

Both Cole and I bowed to the chief and the circle of people, then thanked them for sparing our lives. We asked the chief what they did with our animals. He pointed to a meadow at the edge of the village. There they stood, just the same as the last we saw them. We thanked the chief again and told him we would be on our way.

Shaking his head no, he said, "You must stay. My people want a feast to honor your spirits. Next sun."

Looking at Cole, I asked, "What you think?"

"Don't know. I think we'll be safe now."

"Yeah, I guess."

The chief was saying, "You put things in tepee. Sleep in tepee." Then he said, "I have squaw take care of you." He walked away, leaving us standing.

Cole looked at me and shrugged his shoulders. "Let's go catch our animals." We did and brought them to the tepee, and just started to unpack them when two women brought us each a basket of things to eat, then left.

We finished putting our things in the tepee, then sat down outside and ate most of what was given us. That was the first we had anything to eat since sometime the day before.

As soon as it got dark we went to bed, putting our bed rolls close to the center of the tepee. On each side of us lay our two long guns, one a double-barreled gun, and beside that we each had three pistols and kept at least one hand on them.

I slept good and Cole said he did also. It was late when we got up. Upon going outside, we found food that had been left. We went to the nearby stream to wash up, then returned and ate.

After checking on our animals, we casually moseyed throughout the village, stopping briefly to talk and watch what was going on. After a while, the chief spotted us and came to talk and invited us to be his and his wife's guests for the celebration that was to start in late afternoon.

We accepted and were told where to meet them. After thanking them, we went and dug out some clean clothes, then went to the stream and taken a bath.

It was late afternoon when the feast got under way. Cole and I met the chief and his wife. As we sat and talked his wife made sure we had more than enough to eat. The celebration was getting into full swing and a nice fire was burning in a clearing.

Beating of the drums filled the night air as people danced around the fire. The chief lit up his pipe, taking a long draw, then passed it to Cole, who also took a long draw. Then it was passed to me. I taken a long draw and passed it back to the chief.

As we talked and watched the others dancing, the pipe was passed back and forth I don't know how many times. All I knew was I was feeling lifted up strange, like I could walk on air.

While the chief and his wife were getting up, I asked, "Chief, what kind of tobacco do you smoke?"

"Ugh? Many spirit kind. Now smoke good medicine." Then they disappeared into the circle of dancers.

Looking at Cole, I asked, "How are you feeling?"

"Damn good, brother. Wow! Wow, that smoke is ..." He never finished. A young maiden grabbed him by the hand, pulling him to his feet, and led him toward the fire. Then they disappeared into the crowd of dancers.

I sat looking into the circle of dancers, hoping to see Cole and a little bewildered. Yesterday they were filled with killing us, and now, a day later, they were feasting in our honor. Suddenly, I felt someone running their fingers through my hair that hung loosely down over my shoulders. Turning, I looked into a dark face with dark eyes, long coal black braids that hung over her shoulders.

Smiling, I asked her what she was called. She moved closer and sat down beside me, handing me a gourd of some kind of drink. Again I asked what she was called.

To my amazement, she said in very broken English, "I called Morning Star. You?"

"I'm called Nathan. My friend is called Cole." I asked,

"What was in the gourd?"

She shrugged and motioned for me to drink. I did. Whatever it was tasted damn good. Handing it back to her, she put it to her lips and taken a drink. Handing it to me, I finished what was left. As we watched the circle of people dancing, my head was feeling the effects from the smoke and now the drink, kind of funny, you know ... weird!

Looking at her, I could see the drink was having its effect on her. Smiling, she jumped up, grabbed me by the hand, and pulled me to my feet. I asked, "Where are we going?" She giggled and kept pulling me along. I tried looking for Cole, but wasn't successful in seeing him. As she pulled me along, the spirits inside me told me not to worry, that Cole was in good hands.

I asked again, "Where are we going?" She just smiled and giggled, leading me through the crowd of people into the darkness and away from the light of the fire.

Soon we came to a tepee. She opened it and stepped inside. I followed. A small vessel sat close to the center that contained some kind of oil and a wick that was giving off a nice yellowish glow. Looking around, I saw Cole and my bed rolls spread out on top of buffalo robes, one on each side.

Sitting on the one that was mine, she motioned me to sit beside her. I did, and I could see she was quite attractive. But first I wanted to know what she was up to. After making several attempts at what I was asking, she said, "You. You friend in no danger. Chief Standing Bear tell my sister, Evening Star. I Morning Star see you get lots to eat. Be you companion, warm bed in night. Chief say you. You friend Great Spirit. Chief say he give spirit special gift."

"Morning Star, how old are you?"

Shaking her head, she said, "Don't know. Maybe seventeen winters, seventeen summers."

"Your sister?"

"Same."

Just then Evening Star came in through the opening, leading Cole by his hand.

"You all right, Cole?" I asked.

"Wow, brother, is I ever!"

"What have you been doing?"

"Wow, this little squaw had me in that circle of dancers. Then when we left, we stopped and get gourd full of drink. We drank all. Wow! Yeah! Gosh! Gosh, yeah, feel like I could fly."

Evening Star then pulled him down on his bed roll and

started taking his clothes off. Cole giggled.

Morning Star leaned over and blew out the little light, then pulled her clothes off and pulled me down beside her, undoing my clothes and pushing them to the side. Pulling the blankets over us, moving closer, wrapping her naked body around mine, our lips found each other's. I pulled her even closer, feeling her young tits pressed hard against my chest. The playing went on and on. My hand cupping her firm breast, my lips found the other as my hand moved slowly over the flatness of her stomach resting there.

Taking my hand in hers, she placed it over the mound between her legs, pressing it firmly to her. Her wetness was intoxicating. Firmly taking hold of my hardness, she urged me between her spread legs, moans coming from within her.

It was mid-morning when Evening Star and Morning Star wakened us up, telling us they were bringing something for us to eat. Dressing, Cole and I stepped outside. It looked like a nice day, but not much sun. The two women were soon back with things to eat. They sat down with Cole and me, in what little sun there was coming through, while we ate. We talked, trying to understand each other the best we could. By now, Cole was doing good using sign language.

In our communicating with these girls, we came to know a lot about the Crow nation, also about their main concerns, which was about settlers coming. Coming with them would be soldiers. This in itself was why they were hostile toward the white man.

That night the feast went on, and the girls spent the night with us. The next day it was raining. Cole and I and the two girls were sitting inside the tepee, talking, when the flap opened and the chief and four warriors stepped in without acknowledgement. Taking us by surprise, Cole and I stood and motioned them to be seated. They accepted, sitting around the small fire we had burning in the center of the lodge. Earlier, the girls had put a pot of some kind of tea over the fire to steep. It being ready, the girls set about pouring us each a small clay bowl of hot tea.

While we were sipping our tea, the chief and warriors asked Cole and me a lot of questions pertaining to what they could expect by the coming of the white people. We told them what they could expect the best we could. With the settlers would come the soldiers—white man's warriors. The tea we were sipping must have been very potent, for it didn't take much, and we were all feeling the effects. In a way this was good, for it loosened the tongues of our guests, and let Cole and I communicate with them more freely. And it gave us an opportunity to learn more about these people and learn some of the things that we would need to know if we headed south.

We were told where to cross over the mountains, to the western side, and how long it would take us to get there, and what to expect once we crossed over to the other side.

"You be in Shoshone land. Good people, but stay high in mountains many days. You go south, come to Ute land. Look for where river start. Follow river many days more. You come to deep canyon. Go through, find where water come up from ground hot. Utes make winter camp close to hot water. Many good beaver in mountain, good!"

One of the warriors pointed at me and asked, "Where get necklace?"

I explained how I came to obtain the necklace, meeting Cole, how we came to be there.

Another asked, pointing at Cole, then at me, "Many battle marks on back. You great warrior. Like me."

The questions went on for some time. We answered the best we could. Chief Standing Bear, satisfied, nodded. "We smoke now." He broke out his pipe, put tobacco in it, lit it, and passed it all around.

When they were ready to leave, two of the warriors handed Cole and me each a leather pouch that had a nice braided strap for hanging around one's neck. The chief then said, "Good medicine. Hang around neck all time. Keep bad spirit away. We go now."

Several days later, Cole and I packed our animals and wished the chief and his people the best of spirits and started our trek south.

36

For the next two moons, the going was slow. The mountains were rough and at times downright treacherous. It was down in the fall by now as we made our way over the mountains. The mules and horses at times were plowing through snow more than halfways to their knees. We knew we had to get to lower ground soon or risk being trapped for the winter.

As we made our way down the west side of the mountains, we would see from time to time the large white bird, and I knew the Great Spirit was guiding us. We had encountered very few problems, finding the headwaters of the river the Crow told us about.

After following the river for several days, we found the valley widening and the river meandering through meadows of tall grass that had turned brown, along with trees and bushes that had shed their leaves from the passing of summer. The going was easy now, compared to coming off the snowy part of the mountain.

With our string of pack animals, we had been following the river for days when we finally heard a roaring of water in the distance that must have been coming from the gorge the Crow talked about.

It was mid-afternoon when we dismounted. Looking the place over, we decided to pitch camp and take our time checking out the canyon. After camp was set and the animals turned loose to feed, we each grabbed our long guns and pistols and set out on foot to explore the canyon.

At the beginning, it didn't look that bad, but as we made our way deeper into the canyon, it changed dramatically. The roar that was coming from the raging water as it tumbled, churning its way over large rocks that created these awesome rapids, was all but deafening. The trail narrowed and appeared to be quite treacherous in places.

Seeing what we wanted to know, we returned to camp

just in time to get a fire going before darkness settled in. While our meat was cooking, we discussed what we needed to do to get us through the canyon.

After we had rested a few days, we packed up, and by mid morning were headed for the Gorge. Cole was in the lead. I stayed back a safe distance, in case of trouble. When the trail narrowed some, we dismounted and led our pack string through the worst parts. The sun was setting when we broke out the other end of the canyon.

Right off, we looked for a spot to spend the night. It wasn't long before we came upon a wide draw that offered an ample supply of food for the animals and a nice outcrop of rocks to spend the night under. We had long since dug out our heavy coats, for it had been getting colder for some time. Tonight the cold seemed more intense, maybe due to the nearness of the river, causing dampness. I knew tonight that my heavy sheepskin coat Mom had made for me would be a most welcome blessing.

The next day as we followed the river, we encountered a Ute encampment not far from the river. As we cautiously rode by, we were confronted by three Ute braves, one the chief. Were we surprised when he spoke in English, wanting to know what we were doing there, and where we came from.

We explained our whole journey, including the fact that we had spent some time at a Crow village as their guests, not too long ago. We knew that they were impressed by the gibbering that went on. They knew very well that not many crossed Crow territory and lived to tell about it.

They invited us to their village. We accepted, and found them to be most pleasant people. They told us where there was a good place for us to spend the winter. They said the water came out of the ground hot, with good shelter. We thought it over and, knowing winter would soon be coming, decided to take their offer and make camp.

Cole and I made camp out away from the village, by a place where the water was bubbling up out of the ground hot. We pitched our shelters, one on each side of the spring, far enough apart, just in case of trouble.

As the days passed, we started digging out a shallow hole a short distance from the spring, in order to dam up the hot water for bathing and soaking. When a few of the early teenaged boys saw what we were doing, they pitched in and helped. Little did we realize it would draw so many from the village, mostly young braves, sometimes the chief and his elders.

A few squaws, mostly young or widows, would frequent the pool. Even though there were several around the village, it looked like a couple squaws and their sons had taken a liking to Cole and me. They would come and help work or just talk and bathe. At first, Cole and I didn't know what to expect, but as time passed, we came to realize no one seemed to notice or care.

It had been getting colder for some time now. And we figured the beaver pelts would be prime. We had been making things ready. One day, when two of the young boys, Running Dog and Swift Fox, asked where we were going, I told them we were going upriver to trap beaver. The boys had been fascinated with our steel traps and wanted to know if they could go with us.

I told them it was up to their mothers. They left and it wasn't long before they were back, telling us they could go, only if their mothers went with them. I told them we would think about it. Cole and I talked it over, and decided it might not be a bad idea. The squaws could help take care of camp and help with the beaver pelts if we caught any. In turn, we would teach the boys how to trap.

Later that morning, when the two boys returned, I asked them if they had horses. They said they did. We told them if they could have everything they wanted to take and packed come morning, we would take them with us.

Early the next morning, as Cole and I were saddling our mules, Running Dog and Swift Fox rode up with their mothers, Snowflake and Dawn.

"You have everything you need?" I asked.

Both squaws said they did.

I was already in the saddle when Cole yelled, "I'se bring up the rear."

As I started up along the river, Swift Fox and Running Dog and their mothers fell in behind me, forming a single file. Cole brought up the rear.

Three days later, we found a stream that had a good amount of cottonwood trees along both sides before breaking into a large meadow that extended for miles. The meadow was dotted with beaver ponds and dense willow thickets. The stream was about twenty feet wide and shallow in some places.

We found a place for our camp on a knoll that was heavily wooded and overlooked the stream and meadow, giving us a view of the surrounding area. We spent the rest of the day making camp and taking care of the animals, and putting up our shelters.

Running Dog and Swift Fox gathered in enough firewood that would last several days, while Snowflake and Dawn were preparing our evening meal.

The next day, Cole and I taken the two boys and traps and made our way to some of the closer ponds. Cole and I kept the boys close to us as we made eight sets, then returned to camp. We would check them before nightfall. As time passed, Swift Fox and Running Dog caught on how to set the traps, and were catching a few beaver and muskrats.

Then, one morning, while we were checking our traps, I was between the boys and Cole, maybe fifteen yards or less from where the boys were. I could hear them talking and going on. Then everything got quiet for a second. Then came screams of horror.

Grabbing my gun, I taken off running as fast as I could, the alders towering overhead and visibility poor. With Cole right on my heels, we broke through the alders just in time to see this big warrior ascending down on the boys, tomahawk waving.

The boys had backed to the water's edge. The one holding the trap that they had just set waited until the warrior closed within five feet or so, then gave it a sling, hitting the warrior square on the face, pan first, which triggered the jaws, causing them to close on the warrior's face. I never heard such screaming. Dropping his tomahawk as he fought to remove the trap, one of the boys grabbed the tomahawk and the other had already drawn his knife and moved in close to the warrior, sinking his knife just under the warrior's chest bone. We saw the boy with the tomahawk swing it hard, coming down on the back of the warrior's head, sinking it in his skull as far as it would go. Blood gushed out, spilling down over the warrior's shoulders and back as he slumped to the ground.

Running Dog and Swift Fox stepped back, shaking like willow leaves in a wind storm. Then the boys got sick and threw up. A few minutes later, Cole and I heard the pounding of hooves coming in our direction. Shoving the boys out of the way, telling them to hide, we could see two warriors towering over the alders as they made their way toward us.

Cole yelled, "Brother, take the one on the right!" Cole had ripped the heavy trap and chain from the warrior's face. I picked up a piece of green driftwood the beavers had cut, as thick as my wrist, five feet or so long. When the two horsemen were almost even with Cole and me, we sprung from our hiding place. Cole swung the heavy trap by its chain, smashing it into the side of the warrior's head. At about the same time, I swung my heavy club with such force that when it struck the warrior under the chin and broke his neck.

The two warriors no more than hit the ground when we pounced on them, sinking our knives deep into the warriors' hearts. Running Dog and Swift Fox, seeing it was all over, came running, throwing their arms around us.

Not saying anything, I understood what they were telling us. Cole and I were sure there were more, but how many? Tying the dead warriors' horses to some willows, I told the boys to get mounted and follow Cole and I to camp.

Long before reaching camp, Cole and I could hear the two women screaming. Reining up a short piece from camp and tying our mules in the stand of cottonwood, we made our way slowly into camp until we were close enough to see that there were just two warriors. We couldn't tell exactly what the warriors were trying to do. One thing was for sure. They weren't trying to kill the women. Whatever it was, the women were putting up one hell of a vicious battle, legs and arms flying, screaming, kicking, biting, scratching, pounding with their fists.

The warriors were so busy with the women, they never heard or saw Cole and I walk right up to them. Cole taken the one, giving him a hard whack over the head with the barrel of his gun. He toppled forward, falling off the squaw. As the other warrior looked up, I slammed the butt of my rifle right between his eyes. I knew the warrior must have saw all kinds of stars shooting through his head before everything went black and he fell backward.

The squaws scrambled to their feet, bawling and cursing like hell, in Ute. Checking the women over, we found the women weren't hurt all that much. Lots of scrapes, mostly on their backs, bruised arms and legs, bloody and swelling lips, cloth torn.

"You'se put up a damn good fight," I said as Cole went to get some rope to tie those two sons-of-bitches thieving bastards up. I told the women to go find the boys while I watched the two warriors. Soon they were back with the boys, and Cole returned with several pieces of rope from our packs and tied the warriors' hands and feet while I kept watch with my rifle.

Once the women saw Cole had tied the warriors good, they said they were going to the stream and wash the crud off them. Cole looked around from what he was doing and motioned with his head for me to go with them. "I'se and the boys keep watch on these two squaw thieves."

I followed Dawn and Snowflake to the spot along the stream that we used for bathing. After looking around, I found a place where I wouldn't be easily seen, in case more Arapaho were lurking about. Settling down against a large boulder, I was able to see and hear if anyone came near. Snowflake and Dawn shucked their clothes and waded into the cold water. They rinsed out their clothes and hung them over some bushes.

At first light, there was a heavy frost blanketing everything. Now, the sun was high enough that it was casting its warming light that encircled everything around, and the frost had done melted. The sun had since warmed the air some. The two women stood knee deep in the cold water while I sat, ears strained, to the utmost sounds that were not familiar, eyes straining at any movement that wasn't natural. I glanced at the squaws from time to time as they taken handfuls of fine sand and scrubbed their bodies. I marveled at their smooth, honey-colored skin. The droplets of water that formed on their brown bodies sparkled and shimmered in the sunlight, and caused things to stir deep within my own body. It wasn't like I never saw them naked before. This was something different, maybe the Crow women were better looking, but in my mind the Utes had a nicer, richer-colored skin.

A shadow crossed between me and the women, interrupting my thoughts. Looking up, I saw the big white bird circling overhead. Experience told me that danger lurked somewhere. Maybe in the dark shadows across the stream. Straining my eyes and ears, I watched. Minutes passed, then I caught the movement of a branch, then another.

I made a chirping sound like that of a ground squirrel. The women left the water at once, without looking in my direction. As soon as the women left the water, the movement on the other side taken form. I held the rifle sight on the center of the figure's chest and squeezed the trigger, and then heard the ball make a *thump* sound as it hit the warrior some fifty yards away. I saw him step backwards, then lunge forward face down in the water.

The squaws scrambled for cover when another figure came into view. This one was aiming a gun, what looked like in the direction of the squaws, or maybe myself. All I could see was the right side of this figure. Dark shadows covered the rest. I leveled my rifle so the sight was right on the man's right shoulder. As I squeezed the trigger, I heard the man's own gun explode and the ball hit the rock where I sat, no more than six inches off to my left, and heard my own ball make a thumping sound as it hit flesh.

Cole, hearing the first shot, grabbed two of his guns and came on a dead run. I was already at the creek when Cole caught up and yelled at the women to go to the boys. We crossed the stream in leaps and bounds, just in time to see the figure heading downstream. Giving it our all, we closed the distance in seconds. I gave a flying leap, grabbing the man around his legs, bringing him down. Cole was on him in a flash, grabbed a handful of hair, pulling the man's head back, and at the same time pressing his skinning knife against the man's throat. Yelling over his shoulder, Cole said, "I'se be damned, brother, this son-a-bitch he's a *white* asshole!"

"Are you sure?"

"Damn right I'se sure."

Pulling him to his feet, Cole and I stripped him of any weapons. We knew by this man's dress this shitbrain wasn't just any trapper or mountain man. Wool shirt, wool pants, heavy blanket coat, black boots that came almost to his knees. *Hell, no, who was he?* When Cole and I went to remove the man's coat, he resisted at first, but then changed his mind. After getting his coat off his right shoulder, we saw his blood-soaked shirt. A closer look showed the wound wasn't all that bad. The ball from my gun ripped a gash through the outer flesh of his shoulder. With care it would heal in no time.

We asked him his name and where he came from. He refused to answer. He stood fast, eyes filled with rage. I asked, "Are you gonna tell us your name?" He shook his head no. Cole reached out with his big hand, grabbing the man's wounded shoulder, and squeezed. At first this stubborn son-of-a-bitch tried to prove how damn tough he was. After a little more pressure, he sank to his knees, tears filling his eyes.

Finally, he choked out, "Okay! Okay! The name is Mr. Lloyd and I'm with the English Fur Company."

"Are you English?"

He nodded his head that he was.

"Get up and I'll go get your horse," Cole told him as he headed in the direction the two horses were tied.

"Where are you taking me?" he asked.

"To our camp, so we can get your shoulder patched up," I told him.

"You mean you're not going to kill me?"

"No, Mr. Lloyd, we're not going to kill you, you stupid shit brain."

A look of relief crossed his face. Cole returned with the two horses. It was plain which one was Mr. Lloyd's. His had a fancy-looking saddle and saddlebags. Cole had already looked through everything of Mr. Lloyd's, to make sure he had no weapons. Cole helped Mr. Lloyd onto his horse. I led his horse and Cole followed with the other one.

We stopped by the creek, where the dead warrior lay. Picking him up, we threw him across the back of his horse. The horse snorted and bucked a little, but soon calmed down. After lashing the body to the horse, we headed for camp, Cole leading the way.

Our camp was situated around some very large boulders and big evergreens, which offered good protection against the weather and any intruder. The women and their sons each had their shelters close to one another. Cole was off to the one side, and mine some thirty feet back among some large rocks and trees, with a lot of thick brush overhead.

We tied the animals a short ways outside of camp, then led Mr. Lloyd to where the women and boys were watching over the two Arapaho warriors. When Mr. Lloyd saw the two warriors' tied hands and feet, the look on his face was one of much disappointment. Later, Cole and I discussed the idea that maybe Mr. Lloyd was counting on the two warriors lurking about, just waiting for the right opportunity to attack and free him.

I had just told Mr. Lloyd to sit down when the white bird glided a few feet overhead. Perching on a snag protruding out from the rocks, Snowflake, Dawn, and their two boys knew nothing about the white bird that watched over Cole and me whenever danger was present. Mr. Lloyd's mouth dropped open and the two warriors began to chant immediately.

Cole, being the closest to Mr. Lloyd, asked him what they were saying.

"I don't know," Mr. Lloyd answered.

I, knowing Snowflake could talk a little Arapaho, then asked her what the warriors were saying.

Listening closely, Snowflake finally said, "Warriors sing a

chant. Ask Great Spirit to protect warriors."

The warriors looked at the white bird, then at Cole and me.

Snowflake then said, "Warriors tell friend white bird watch over white man and black man. Much big spirit. Warriors then say to friend they hear big talk from Pawnee, Shoshone, Sioux, Cheyenne, Flathead. Say black man and white man and white bird much big medicine. Crow say much brave, much big spirit. Talk say some Blackfoot warriors not make fight with black man or white man. White bird watch over. Arapaho not make fight. Arapaho say white man and black man good spirit."

While the squaws worked on Mr. Lloyd's shoulder, cleaning and applying poultices, Snowflake had spoken mostly in Ute when she translated. So Cole asked Mr. Lloyd, just to see what he would say, what the braves told him.

He took a long time studying Cole before answering. "I see and hear now that most of these savages hold high respect for the two of you."

Dawn and Snowflake were listening to everything that was being said as they finished tending to Mr. Lloyd's shoulder. Once they were finished, Cole and I questioned Mr. Lloyd more about why he was out riding with Arapaho.

After some time passed, I said to Mr. Lloyd, "Well, what do you have to say? Are you going to tell us why you are riding with these assholes?" Pointing to the warriors.

"What do I get if I tell you why I'm here?"

"Maybe your freedom. And if you *don't* tell us, well, we'll have no choice but to take the three of you to the Ute village and let *them* make you talk."

He thought for a few minutes, then said, "Myself and four others live at one of the Arapaho villages. We work for this English fur company. Our job is to stir up trouble among the different tribes, in hopes they will turn against the white trappers. They want control of all the fur trade. They hired us to bribe the Arapaho with cheap trinkets and a few things that were of good—blankets, pots, knives, hatchets, and so on. I hope what I have told you will give you some idea of what you may be up against."

Cole looked at me and motioned for me to follow. The two of us then walked off a few steps from the others to talk it over and decide what would be the right thing to do. After talking it over and coming to a decision, Cole and I shook hands, as we always did after agreeing on any important matter.

Turning back to where Mr. Lloyd was sitting, I asked him, "What do you have in mind on doing if we were to set you free? Would you and your friends over there try to kill us like you'se did before?"

"No! No! I have no intention of being so stupid as to try to kill the two of you. No! Not after what I witnessed this morning … the two of you and that supernatural entity." He pointed at the white bird. Mr. Lloyd then went on to say it must be one hellish good feeling knowing that something or someone is always there watching out for you.

"Thank you. Mr. Lloyd, we want you to ask your two friends what they intend on doing if we were to spare their lives."

Cole, Snowflake and Dawn made sure they were close to listen when Mr. Lloyd asked the two warriors what they would do if the black man and white man let them live and set them free. Both warriors tried to talk at once, but Mr. Lloyd told them just one at a time.

"The warriors both said," Mr. Lloyd replied, "they say white bird give much big medicine to white man and black man. Necklace on white man give him great power from spirit." Mr. Lloyd went on to say, "the warriors want no trouble, only to go back to their people."

Cole then asked Snowflake and Dawn if that's what the warriors said. They nodded their heads. I then told Mr. Lloyd in order for the three of them to go free, they had to agree to take the four dead warriors with them and return to the Arapaho village.

Cole turned to Mr. Lloyd and said, "You tell those two assholes if they ever cross our paths again, their blood will be spilled all over the ground."

Mr. Lloyd repeated it and the two warriors nodded that they understood. Cole held two of his guns on the warriors while I untied them. At first, they looked like they might try to run, but changed their minds.

Dawn and Snowflake and the two boys went and brought the warriors' horses back to camp, along with their own, where Cole and I were holding the three captives at gun point. I told Mr. Lloyd that he and the two warriors were to lead their horses and the one with the dead man up the valley to where the other three dead warriors lay.

Mr. Lloyd started to protest, but when I hollered, "Get moving!" he motioned for the two warriors to follow as he headed in the direction he was told to go. Cole and I then climbed on our mules and followed the three, hollering for the squaws and boys to come on and bring the horses.

When they reached the place where the dead warriors lay, Mr. Lloyd was instructed to tell the two warriors to wrap the bodies in their bed rolls and tie them and then place them over their horses' backs and lash them down good. The two warriors seemed reluctant to do this and didn't move. Mr. Lloyd spoke to them again. When they turned to face Mr. Lloyd, they saw Cole's rifle leveled at their heads, and got to work wrapping their comrades in their bed rolls.

After that was finished, they placed them over the horses' backs and lashed them down. The women and their boys sat on their horses a short distance in back of where Cole and I sat on our mules. Cole barked for Mr. Lloyd and the warriors to get mounted.

Instead, Mr. Lloyd turned and faced Cole and me, the women and boys, raising his hand. I said, "Get moving."

"No, please, hear what I have to say first."

"All right, let's hear it," I said.

"You could have very easily killed me and the two braves. But you didn't. Instead, you did everything to see that this stupid ass lived. I've watched the two of you ever since you took me prisoner early this morning and came to realize how stupidly wrong I was to think what I was doing for the fur company was right, trying to start trouble among the different tribes of Indians and white trappers. So, maybe they would kill one another. For what?" Mr. Lloyd said. "Just so the fur company can gain control of the fur business and the damn money that can be made? So what I'm telling you is, I will have no part of this kind of business. I was a stupid asshole for not seeing what the fur company was doing. Now I'm asking the two of you to let me stay here with you. I see now and I know I'm not anything like what the two of you are, but ... but ... I would like to try, if you would give me a chance."

Cole said, "Brother, what's you done thinks on this?"

"Don't know," I replied. "I only know in these mountains a man is free, free to do as one chooses. Mr. Lloyd, as long as one don't bring hardship or harm to anyone else, unless one is defending oneself or friends like we did this day. So you see, Mr. Lloyd, Cole nor I cannot give you advice one way or another as to what we think you should do."

"I'se thinks all along you wants to make it back to your friends at de Arapaho village," Cole said.

"No! No! I don't want to go back."

"What about your belongings?" I asked.

"There probably isn't anything left. Those thieving bastards more than likely took everything."

"I'se makes you something to think about, Mr. Lloyd," Cole said.

"What's that?"

"Mr. Lloyd, you take them there two red-ass bucks and them four dead-ass bastards back to that Arapaho chief, and you tells that son-bitch if'n he's ever sent his warriors to make trouble or war, you tells him, Mr. Lloyd, white man Nathan, black man Cole they'se come riding out of de night like a winter blizzard through Arapaho village. Kill every damn brave or warrior they finds. And you get alls yours things and anything else you can get from your partners."

"Like what?" Mr. Lloyd asked.

"Lead, powder, shot, knives, coffee, salt, sugar, tobacc'ee, blankets, robes, traps and whatever else you can get from them there English friends of yours, and anything you can get from them Injuns," I said.

"And brings them four Injun horses with yours, and yes, pack saddles for all of dem," added Cole.

"Damn it," Mr. Lloyd said, "that's quite a bit of stuff you expect me to get."

"Maybe it looks that way, Mr. Lloyd," I said. "If you are serious about living here in these mountains, and surviving ..."

"Yes, yes," Mr. Lloyd broke in.

"Then you will need to do everything you can to get things you're going to need, if you expect to survive."

"How do I know you will be here if I do come back?" he asked.

"You can count on us being somewheres in these parts, until de ice gets too thick or de snow too deep," Cole said.

I told Snowflake and Dawn to take the boys and ride back to camp and bring a front shoulder and the hind quarter off one of those deer, and bring Mr. Lloyd's guns and anything else belonging to them. While Cole and I waited for the women to return, we explained to Mr. Lloyd what would be expected of him when he came back.

"One other thing," I said.

"What's that?" Mr. Lloyd asked.

"If you or your friends should decide to bring any of the Arapaho down on the Utes or us, you'll die a very slow, agonizing death at the hands of the Ute squaws. The two of us will see to that."

"I'll see to it that it doesn't happen," he answered.

The women and boys soon returned with everything that belonged to Mr. Lloyd and the warriors. Cole and I seen to it that everything was in place and secure on Mr. Lloyd's horse, and helped him get mounted, then told him he might be smart if he kept all the weapons with him.

Mr. Lloyd nodded and said, "Thanks for your advice."

"You have only fifteen, maybe twenty-one days, to make it back here before the snow gets too deep."

"I'll do my best. And, by the way, just call me Les. Short for Lester."

"All right, Les," I said. "Now get your damn asses moving. You still have a lot of the day left. You can make a hell of a lot of miles before stopping."

Les lay his musket across his lap, in spite of his shoulder, then spoke in Arapaho to the two warriors. They looked at Cole and I, raised their hands in peace, then dug their heels into the ribs of their horses and moved out at a good pace.

Cole hollered after Les, "Keep them there red-assed bastards moving. If's you intends to make it, don't take your eyes off dem."

We, along with the women and boys, watched as Mr. Lloyd and the warriors rode out of sight. Turning to Cole, I said, "What you think, brother?"

"Doesn't know! I'se guess we'se wait and see, Nathan."

"I guess you're right. We'll have to be on the lookout at all times. So let's get back to tending our traps."

"What about de boys and women?" Cole asked. "They don't look like they are going back to camp alone."

"No, don't look so. How about you taken one of the squaws and her boy back to camp. I'll take the other two with me and check traps."

"Right by me I'se can do some needed repairs on our tack. The boy can help me. I'll have the squaw keep watch and listen."

"Good. Which ones you want?"

"I'se take ... don't matter. Come, Dawn and Swift Fox, we'se going back to camp."

I, Snowflake and Running Dog set off to finish tending to our beaver sets. Running Dog stayed close to me and helped with the setting of traps and the skinning of what we caught. The temperature was dropping as it grew later in the day. The sun had already dropped behind the mountains off to the west.

I noticed Running Dog was shivering from the cold. Looking around to find Snowflake, who was keeping watch from on top of her horse, I motioned her over to where Running Dog and I stood.

Lifting the boy up on her horse in front of her, I saw that Snowflake was shivering also. Going to my mule, I got the robe and blanket I always carried behind my saddle. Taking the robe, I threw it over the horse's back, in front of Running Dog, then pulled it back tight around their waists so it would cover Snowflake's legs, and secured it around her back, then through the blanket, up over the back of her shoulders, pulling it around the front of her and the boy. The heat from the horse would help warm them.

Returning to my traps, I soon had them all checked. Taking the last four beaver and the six hides that we had already skinned, I tied them together and hung them over Running Dog's horse. Tying his horse to the rear of Snowflake's animal, and grabbing the reins to hers, I climbed on my mule, leading them.

Arriving back at camp past dark, Cole and Swift Fox, who had been sitting close by the blazing fire repairing packs and pack saddles, came to help. After getting Snowflake and Running Dog down from the horse and close to the fire, Cole and I unsaddled the animals and picketed them, so they could feed.

Returning to the fire, Cole got at skinning the remaining beavers with the help of Swift Fox. I settled down by the fire and watched as Dawn ladled hot elk meat and broth into a big wooden bowl and handed it to me. Snowflake and Running Dog already had theirs and were eating. Cole, Dawn and Swift Fox had eaten before the rest of us returned.

Life here in the mountains and among the Indians was nothing like it was back where Cole and I came from. Saloons, gorge houses, whores, dry goods stores. Back East one could stop by a store or saloon and get something to eat or clothing. In the mountains, one was almost always looking for food or making clothes. Sometimes one could trade with the Indians for clothes. One didn't have many extras, if any. Then again, you had to always be looking over your shoulder or wondering what lay ahead or around the next bend, or what was waiting across the river, over the next knoll, hill, what lay in wait as one rode past the next thicket. This was the way of life for most Indians, and the mountain men who came West to trap mostly beaver and be free—free like Cole and I—ones who befriended many of the Indian tribes by treating them fair, sometimes spending a whole winter with one tribe or another, and sometimes even having to fight the ones that were hostile to other tribes and most all whites.

Cole, sitting by the fire across from me, lacing a beaver pelt on a green willow hoop, looked up from his work, then said, "It's high time yous'n gots here. I'se thinking maybe ..."

"No, Cole, everything went fine," I interrupted, not wanting to cause any unnecessary concern.

"You did right today," Cole said.

"Yeah," I replied, "you, too."

While Dawn and Snowflake went to make sure the boys got themselves tucked in their buffalo robes and blankets for the night, everything was quiet except for the crackling of the fire. Cole was still working on beaver pelts.

I, chomping down the last of hot juicy strips of deer meat and sipping hot coffee, looked over at Cole and said, "Want some coffee?"

"Nah, maybe later."

"Cole, it brings to my mind that maybe we should move a few miles up the valley, trap some new creek and ponds a few weeks or so before it gets much colder. What's your thought on this?"

"Sounds good to me. I'se thought on this myself."

"You did?"

"Yeah. Only one thing."

"What's that?"

"What if that Mr. Lloyd come back?"

"Well, I thought about that, and figured he'll find us or we him."

"What about ...?" Nodding his head toward the women and boys.

"We'll ask them. They can either go with us or return to their village."

When asked, the squaws said they wanted to go with us.

"We pack everything in the morning?" Cole asked.

"I think that would be the best. We can pack our animals first, then go and pick up our traps and any catches on the way past."

I took the first watch, even though I wasn't too worried that Mr. Lloyd and the Arapaho warriors would return. It would be more peace of mind, but ... just in case, after all the others were bedded down for the night, I heaped a bunch of wood on the fire, then picked a place where I could see and have the advantage. Cole had moved his bed roll into the shadows, away from the light of the fire and the women and boys.

I picked the large boulder that we had built our fire close to. It was close to nine feet high. There were two evergreens on the back side that towered high above this boulder and the branches reached out over and above the rock, making it an ideal place to watch from. Taking my two double-barreled muskets, two pistols and a heavy robe, I made my way up the back side of the rock.

Looking it over, picking a place that gave me the best view, I pulled the buffalo robe over my shoulders and wrapped it around myself, then settled down for the long cold watch.

As the dark of night dragged on, from time to time I would catch a glimpse of the moon, just a sliver peeping through. The heavy clouds rolled in. My mind rolled like the clouds, rolling from place to place, time to time, back over the years to when I was still at home. My mother's love and her cooking. The beatings my father gave me. The sisters and brother that I had left behind. I wondered if my sister was married and had a family by now. The preacher, his wife and daughter who came every few months or so for Sunday supper. Their daughter, who always managed to get me alone for some kissing and poking. Later on, she was sent to a convent in Philadelphia to become a nun. I never mentioned her to anyone. The schoolteacher who came every other week to spend the weekend and always made sure to sleep on the loft between me and my brother and sisters.

37

My mind went back to the times she would lock her legs around my back, holding me tight to her as she bucked up and down like a bucking mule and I rode her like one. My fantasy was shattered when I felt something cold and wet on my hands and face. Looking up, I saw big fluffy snowflakes falling, and the clouds were parted just enough that I could see the slice of moon hanging directly overhead.

I let the big fluffy flakes of snow caress my bearded face with their coolness. As I sat there, gazing into the darkness, I realized how still and quiet it was. I could actually hear those big fluffy flakes landing. Gathering up my guns, I made my way down the back side of the rock.

Coming around to the front where the fire was, I found Snowflake already putting wood on the fire and arranging the coffee pot over the red hot coals. Several slices of deer meat hung roasting.

I put my guns where they would stay dry, then returned to the fire, wrapped in my buffalo robe, and found a good spot by the fire, then sat down, letting the robe hang open so the heat from the fire could enter. Reaching for the tin cup of coffee that Snowflake was pouring, my eyes met hers and the expression on her copper-colored face was blank.

As I picked up the tin cup of coffee, Snowflake never taken her eyes off mine. I wasn't sure, but I could see there was something different in those eyes. She never moved until I said, "I'm going to wake Cole."

Snowflake immediately stood, then said, "No, you eat and drink hot coffee. I know you must be cold. I go." She turned away before I had time to say anything, and went and wakened Cole. Returning, she piled more wood on the already blazing fire, then disappeared into the shadows where her bed was.

I was sitting there, chewing on the hot strips of juicy meat and sipping coffee, when Cole walked up, rubbing his eyes.

"What goes, brother?" He sat down close to the fire to get warm.

"Nothing, Cole, except it's starting to snow, as you can see."

Cole and I sat, sipping coffee and eating, without saying anything. No sounds except the crackling of the fire and from time to time, and the sound of us slurping hot coffee.

After a while, I said, "I don't think there's anything to worry about, but keep the fire big anyway. Maybe you might want to stay in the shadow some."

"All right."

"It looks like we'll have snow by morning."

"Yeah, looks so."

"I'm going to bed." I tramped off to where I slept, gathering up my guns on the way and placing them within easy reach. I undid my bed roll, spreading the tarp and blanket out, then put the buffalo robe over the top. Then I crawled under the blankets and heavy robe.

Despite feeling a little cold, I soon drifted off to sleep. It was sometime after I'd laid down that I felt someone crawl under my robe and blankets and skooching tight up against me. Then Snowflake said, "Come warm friend, yes!"

Getting to her knees, she began stripping my duds off, one piece at a time, until I was completely naked. Then she quickly shucked out of her clothes, then lay down, wiggling herself tight up against me. Resting her head on my left shoulder, her left leg over my belly, pulling herself as close as she could, her head mashed tight against my beard. Her hair smelled of wood smoke, her body smelled of sage and wood smoke combined, a very arousing smell.

It had been some time since any woman held me like this. It felt so good, so cozy and warm, that I almost drifted off to sleep. I would have if it hadn't been for Snowflake's hand slowly moving up and down my shaft. Her lips brushed mine slightly as she slowly moved over on top, straddling me, keeping the blankets pulled tight up over her shoulders. Then, in slow motion, her hand wrapped around my hardness and she guided it into her, slowly down until she could go no farther. She sat there, rocking back and forth, feeling every sensation within her come alive. Then, slowly, she moved up, then down. Over and over she moved until she began to shimmer and quake like aspen leaves in a wind storm, leaning forward, putting her hands on each side of my head, putting her breast within easy reach of my mouth.

Sucking one of her honey-colored nipples in between my lips made her move all the more, and digging her fingers into the muscle on my arms, scratching, bucking like some wildcat in heat, moans coming from deep inside her. As she reached her climax, she bit into my shoulder until she almost drew blood. Her climax was so intense, and she never once stopped moving until she felt my hardness erupt. Only then did she stop moving and stayed, sitting, panting like a runaway mule until her breathing became normal. Moments later, she moved off, grabbing her clothes, and got dressed.

I asked, "Where are you going?"

"Back to bed. Can't stay here."

"Why?"

She didn't answer.

"Okay, if you say so ... thanks." Pulling the blankets and robe up over myself, I was soon asleep.

It wasn't light yet when Cole came and awakened me. I could smell coffee cooking while I was getting dressed. By the time I got to the fire, I saw the others already eating.

After pouring myself a tin cup of coffee and settling down close to the fire, Dawn handed me a bowl of hot broth and a trencher full of roasted beaver tail.

"Is we now moving, brother?"

"Yeah, as soon as everyone has something to eat, we'll pack and get moving." I noticed when I looked at Snowflake, she dropped her head and busied herself with the fire. Cole and I continued talking, discussing our plans for the day, and I noticed Snowflake no longer looked away whenever I happened to glance at her. Instead, she simply smiled and went on with what she happened to be doing.

Before going for the animals, I asked Dawn and Snowflake how much time before the snow got deep. They looked at each other, shrugged, then Dawn said, "One moon and maybe one half. Ute never know when big snow come."

"That leaves us four to six weeks, Cole,"

"Yeah, maybe, brother."

Taking Swift Fox and Running Dog, we went and caught our animals and brought them to camp. With the help from the two boys and their mothers, we were able to get all the animals saddled and packed in no time.

"Is we ready, brother?"

"Yeah, Cole." I swung into the saddle on Old Curse as Cole climbed on his brown mare, then said, "You'se lead, Nathan. I'se bring up the rear, just in case."

"Okay." I led, stopping only to pick up our traps, and

anything we caught we threw on top of one of the pack animals, to be skinned later. From that point on, Cole and I rode side by side, so we weren't strung out so far. We each had five pack animals and the squaws each had one, then the two boys.

After several hours, we came to a nice stream that flowed into the river from the northwest, that looked like it had a number of beaver ponds. From here on, we started looking for a place to set up camp. As we pushed on along the stream, another mile or so, we came to a nice stand of cottonwood that was quite large on a knoll west of the stream. The stand of trees was quite dense and would offer both shelter and protection from anything unwanted. The area around the stand of cottonwoods was open for hundreds of yards in any direction, except for the willows that grew along the banks of the stream and ponds. There was plenty of dead wood for fires and plenty of young saplings and blowdowns to erect shelters.

Cole and I had the women and boys pick the place to put their shelters. After they decided on the spot, I put my shelter back some ten yards and off to the left of where the women were. Cole did the same, except front and to the right. This gave Cole and I the advantage of anything unwanted. I noticed Snowflake and Running Dog put their shelter on the side mine was. Cole and I seldom put up shelters except in rain or snow. Other times we preferred spreading out bed rolls under bushes or deadfall, among blowdowns. This gave us the advantage of not being spotted easily and harder to get to without making noise. This setup worked and was very efficient.

Over the next four weeks, the taking of beaver was far greater than our expectations. Dawn and Snowflake, Running Dog and Swift Fox were kept busy scraping and stretching. Cole and I helped as much as time permitted. Some days we checked the traps just after light and again just before nightfall. When the two boys weren't too tired, they would tag along, but mostly they watched over our animals and tended to their dozen or so snares that we had given them to use.

Running Dog and Swift Fox kept the rest of us well supplied with grouse and rabbits, which was greatly appreciated. While checking their snares, they were always on the lookout for any signs of hunting or war parties. The squaws always had some kind of meat cooking over the fire while they worked on pelts, whether it be sage hen, deer or rabbit.

Early one morning some weeks later, just after light, I was standing knee deep in the ice cold water just off the bank. Cole looked down from where he stood on the bank, dripping wet from above his knees down. I could see his elk hide leggings beginning to freeze, and he said, "Brother, I'se thinks we'se need to get our asses out of here before we'se can't."

I threw a beaver up on the bank at his feet and looked at him. "I think you're maybe right. So what you say we pull up our traps today and get the hell out of here? Maybe in the next two or three days, before we get more snow or colder."

"I'se damn well ready. We'se need some meat before we go."

"Yeah, we need to do that. What you say tomorrow one of us go do some hunting and the other stay in camp and get some of our things packed?"

"All rights by me."

"Which do you want to do?"

"I'se tells you what," Cole said.

"What's that?"

"De one who catches the most beavers as we pull our traps stays in camp tomorrow and helps squaws with de pelts and what else."

"I'll go for that."

"You do's?"

"Yeah."

"Why? You'se already gots two beaver more den I! Dammit to hell, I'se doan think about dat!"

We always shared any work equal and that also applied to tending our traps and pelts. The pelts had to be scraped, stretched, then dried, then sorted according to size, and tied in bundles of fifty to seventy pounds.

At the end of the day, when Cole found out I had caught one more beaver than him, a smile spread across his face from ear to ear. I knew for some time he was getting eager to get out and do some hunting. I felt a sense of happiness for him, knowing he would be doing what he liked to do.

Later that evening, while sitting around the fire having rabbit stew and roasted grouse, Cole asked the two boys if they would like to go hunting with him in the morning and look for some deer, maybe an elk. The boys jumped at the chance.

"Good," Cole said. While they ate, he told them what all they were to get ready before turning in for the night.

First thing in the morning, they were to get their bed rolls rolled up and tied good.

"What for?" Swift Fox asked.

"Listen what he say," Dawn scolded.

Cole looked at him, then said, "The first thing is, I'se said. The second is, if we must spend the night, you'se will have something to help keeps you warm."

Swift Fox dropped his head, then said, "I not no more say dumb things, I listen!"

"As soon as you're finished eating, we'se goin' to catch the animals we'll be needin' and bring thems close to camp. Then hobble dem. That way we'se can find dem when it's still dark in the morning."

Swift Fox and Running Dog now listened to everything Cole was telling them. Just as soon as they finished their food, the three of them hurried off to look for the animals before it got too dark. I stayed sitting and finished my stew. Looking over the rim of my tin of coffee I was sipping, I noticed Snowflake watching me.

"Yes, what is it, Snowflake?"

"You not go hunt?" she asked.

"No, I stay tomorrow. I pack, make ready to go back to the village."

"Back to village?" Dawn asked.

"Yes, back to your village."

"When?"

"Soon." Nodding my head.

"Soon two day, maybe three. That why you not hunt?" Snowflake asked.

"Yes." I saw she was smiling as she looked away. I knew what was going through her mind. Ever since we had set up camp, Snowflake would come to my bed in the wee hours of the night, every three or four nights, whenever she was certain all the others were asleep.

It was dark when Cole and the boys returned with the animals they planned on using the next day. I went and helped hobble and picket the animals. While Cole and the boys had some hot broth, Cole told Swift Fox and Running Dog it was time to get to bed, that he would be awakening them early, and he was going to bed, too.

Dawn and Snowflake were already in bed. After throwing more wood on the fire, I sat back down and sipped at a cup of hot broth. While finishing stretching the last pelt from the catch that day, after going and relieving myself and getting undressed, I crawled under the blankets and heavy robe on my bed, knowing that sometime during the night Snowflake would be coming.

It wasn't light yet when I was awakened by Cole and the two boys stirring about. I lay there, staring into the darkness, trying to clear my mind, recalling Snowflake coming to my bed, yet couldn't remember her ever leaving. It really didn't matter. That's the way it always was. As soon as our copulating was over, she went back to her own bed. I didn't want to get up, but knew it was best that I did and give Cole a helping hand. I knew he would do the same for me.

Cole, Running Dog and Swift Fox were sitting by the fire when I got there, chewing on chunks of meat and sipping some hot broth that Dawn and Snowflake had already made. Pouring myself a tin of steaming hot broth, then sitting down close by the fire, Dawn then handed me a big slice of juicy hot meat.

In between chewing on the meat and sipping the hot broth, I asked Cole if he could think of anything else they might need.

"No, brother, I'se has my three long guns, and dem there three pistols."

"Enough food?"

"Yes'm. The squaws done filled us a big pouch of roasted meat."

"Good."

"Brother, we'se better gets on our way."

"I'll give you a hand saddling the animals."

"Sures, would thinks well of dat, brother."

Swift Fox and Running Dog carried everything that was to be loaded for us. When everything was loaded and secured, I wished them a good hunt and watched them mount up. As they rode off into the cold gray dawn, I hollered, "Keep your powder dry, brother!"

"Will do," came the echo of his voice drifting back through the cold graying dawn as they faded out of sight.

Returning to the fire, I saw that Snowflake and Dawn had already crawled back under their robes. Finishing my mug of broth, then throwing some wood on the fire, I went back to bed, pulling the blankets and robe up over my head.

Before I knew it, I was awakened by the sounds coming from the women. I ambled out to the fire, where Dawn and Snowflake were busy preparing food for the trip back to the Ute village, which might take two or three days. Settling down by the fire, I dug deep in my possibles pouch until I came up with my pipe and tobacco. Filling my pipe, I picked up a small burning twig and lit it, then poured a tin cup of coffee and settled back to enjoy my smoke—the first in many a day.

I spent the rest of the morning sorting beaver pelts to size and quality and primness, then tied them in bundles of fifty or so pounds, and readied everything I could for the trip, then scrounging around until I found our short-handled spade. I told Snowflake and Dawn to grab a couple hides or canvas bags and come with me to dig some cattail root bulbs. We found a large patch of cattails not far from camp that would be easy to get to. I dug the plants out of the somewhat soggy wet ground, throwing them to the women, where they cut the bulbs from the stalks, cleaning them, and putting them in the bags until they were full.

Back at camp, the women filled a pot with the bulbs and water, then put the pot over the fire to simmer. It was getting on toward evening. Snowflake and Dawn were out gathering wood when they spotted four riders way off in the distance coming out of the northeast.

Dawn and Snowflake came rushing back to where I was sitting by the fire, working on some elk hide panniers. They were all excited. Looking up from my work, it was plain to see that something was wrong. They both tried telling me at once.

Finally, Snowflake calmed down enough to tell me. Holding up four fingers. Come this way. From north. Pointing, four? You sure? They both shook their heads yes.

Gathering up three of my guns, shooting pouch, and sticking four pistols in the pockets of my sheepskin coat, the one my mother had made, telling the two squaws to come. I led the way to the far end of the wood plot from where the women saw the four riders.

Sure enough, through the dimming light, I could make out four riders coming our way. Cole had indicated that he didn't plan on coming back the same day, so who were these four riders? Leaning my gun against a fallen tree, I told the women to get down as I crouched low behind the tree and waited.

When the riders were fifty yards away, through the dim light, I was able to make out that the riders were Cole and the two boys. But who the hell was the fourth one?

Telling Snowflake and Dawn, "Come, let's get back to camp," putting my guns out of sight except two pistols, which I always kept in my coat pockets, I racked my brain trying to figure out who in hell would be riding in with Cole.

I had long past forgotten about that asshole Mr. Lloyd

until they rode up to camp and he slid down from the saddle.

Clamping a hand on Mr. Lloyd's shoulder, I said, "Damn it to hell, I done gave up on you sometime back, you skinny asshole. But ... but ... I'm glad to see you made it, I guess! Cole, how was the hunting?"

"Good, brother, good. Come see."

Going to where they had tied the pack animals, I was surprised to see they had killed two buffalo calves and one cow elk and a deer. "Damn it to hell, Cole, you'se sure did good. Never figured on you'se getting this much meat."

Darkness had settled in. I told Swift Fox and Running Dog to go tell their mothers to bring some torch lights and help with this meat. We made torches by soaking the brown spikes of the cattail plants in hot fat until thoroughly soaked. When lit, these torches gave off good light and lasted a long time.

The squaws came with the torches and held them while Cole and I secured the meat high enough in trees so no animals could pull it down, first cutting enough steaks to fill everyone's bellies.

Once back at the fire, the women put the meat over the hot coals to cook slowly. Meanwhile, Cole and I helped Mr. Lloyd unload his pack animals and set up his shelter not far from where Cole had his.

Going back to the fire, I settled down in my favorite spot between the fire and the big rock, to wait for the meat to get cooked. As we waited, Cole told how he, Running Dog and Swift Fox came across fresh tracks of six horses. Cole said the tracks told him that there were six riders or the horses were load heavy. He figured it would be best to follow and see who it was. Cole said they hadn't gone more than a mile or so when they caught sight of the horses and only one rider. He decided to kick up their pace and overtake this lone rider. When they got closer and could see better, he figured out the rider was Mr. Lloyd. Cole said he figured if he fired a shot into the air, it would bring Mr. Lloyd to a stop and also let him know they were friendly. When Mr. Lloyd heard the shot, he wheeled around, gun ready, then saw it was a black man, and waited until Cole caught up.

"Cole, that you?" Mr. Lloyd asked.

"Yeah, it's Cole, Mr. Lloyd."

"What are you doing out here?"

"We'se out hunting, getting meat to take back to de village."

"Where's Nathan?"

"He's at camp, making ready to move day after tomorrow."

"How far's your camp?"

"Not far now."

Cole said he decided it would be best if they came back to camp, since it was getting on toward evening and camp wasn't that far.

"I'm glad you did." Hooking one of those hot, juicy steaks with the point of my skinning knife and settling back against the boulder, I said, "You'se'd better snatch one of those chunks, Cole. You, too, Mr. Lloyd."

Cole settled down close by me. Mr. Lloyd waited until Snowflake and Dawn handed Cole and me a trencher with a pile of hot steaming cattail bulbs that were simmered in hot fat. I flopped my chunk of meat on the other half of the trencher as Dawn handed me a tin of fresh steaming coffee.

Mr. Lloyd picked a spot close to the fire and sat down with his trencher of food. While we ate, Mr. Lloyd began unraveling his tale of how he and the two warriors returned to the Arapaho village, how the two warriors went to the chief, telling him everything that happened.

The next day, the chief and elders had Mr. Lloyd taken to the meeting lodge, where he was asked all about the white man and black man and their white bird. The chief said, "Our two warriors say white bird have much big spirit, watch over white man and black man. You talk," the chief said.

Mr. Lloyd said he explained to the chief and elders everything that had taken place ever since he and the warriors came across the camp of the two squaws and two boys, not knowing the white man and black man were with them. "Three warriors died, I was wounded, and they spared the lives of the two warriors and mine. The white man wears a necklace—around the neck—given to the white man by a great medicine man far away in the east, just before he died. The necklace and white bird are of great spirit from the spirit world. They protect and watch over the white man and his blood brother, the black man," Mr. Lloyd went on to say.

"I told the elders that if the Arapaho start wars on the white trappers or any others, like the English ask, so they can have all the fur, the white man and black man will come riding through your village like a furious winter storm coming out of the north, and they will destroy every lodge in your village and that any warrior that tries stopping them will be eliminated."

Mr. Lloyd went on to say that what he and the two warriors told them brought much commotion and concern among the chief and elders. "The chief summoned a dozen of their braves and had them bring the four Englishmen to the lodge. When the four of them entered the lodge and saw the chief and elders all sitting, and me sitting in front, they looked at me and wanted to know what was going on."

The chief motioned them to sit. "I tried my best to inform them as to what the two warriors had told the chief and elders what had happened on the raid we went on. The elders then asked each one if they came to the Arapaho village to talk the Arapaho warriors into starting war with other tribes. I punched the one closest to me in the ribs with my elbow, hoping no one would notice, and whispered to him, 'You better explain the true reason why we came here. If not, it's all over for us.'

"After the chief and elders listened to them tell their story, the chief motioned for the braves to take the four of them out." Mr. Lloyd said the two warriors and himself were told to stay sitting while the elders and chief discussed what must be done.

Some of the elders wanted to put them to death. Others wanted to keep them as slaves. Mr. Lloyd said, "Finally, one of the elders—by his looks he probably was the oldest of them all —so wrinkled and frail, nothing but skin and bones—raised his hands upward and spoke. All the others stopped and listened. He spoke very softly and distinctly and to the point. 'Spirit World say to Elder Killdeer to kill the four English only bring more whites. Spirit World say to Killdeer send the four whites back to their chief. Give four English men three days of food, one horse, cloth and blankets. Spirit say they take message to white chief. Arapaho people not want them in village. If Englishmen come back, they be put to death,' Elder Killdeer said, pointing to me, 'You Englishmen can stay and be Arapaho, or you can go from village. You have till four suns to make up mind what Englishmen do.'

"For a few minutes there was mumbling among the others, then it was all quiet. The four English were brought back in. As they stood before the elders, the chief explained the decision the elders came to and told the four they could thank the spirits for their lives. 'You will leave at first light. Ten braves will ride with you till night of day three. Then you are on your own. Tell your chief not to send any more. If so, Arapaho make war.' "

Mr. Lloyd said he made his decision right then, thanked the chief and elders, and went back to their shelters, hoping to find the other four and talk with them, but found none of the others. "It was getting dark. I knew it was no use looking for them. Instead, I ate something, then tried to get some sleep, hoping I would be up before it was light."

Mr. Lloyd said he was up before light, had a fire going, and waited and waited. No one showed. When it was fully light, he went looking for them, walking around, hoping to find them. Then he went on to say he walked almost to the other end of the village where he spotted them. They were all mounted up, and five braves were leading them out of the village. Five braves followed close behind.

Mr. Lloyd said he yelled after them, hollering their names, but not one of them turned his head to look his way. He went on to say he could see they had their bed rolls and other belongings tied behind their saddles. Mr. Lloyd said he watched as they rode out of sight, feeling very disappointed and hurt, knowing he was the one who brought this down on them, knowing it was for the best.

Wiping the tears from his eyes with the back of his hands, he said he hurried back to their shelters before the villagers converged on their leavings. Mr. Lloyd said when he returned to their shelters, he gathered up everything out of the other four shelters and piled it in his, then hurriedly tore the other four shelters down, knowing the heavy oiled hemp canvas that was shipped from England would be of good use sometime in the future.

After sorting things in piles he would take with him, Mr. Lloyd said he began the hard task of packing things in panniers or canvas bags that hung on the pack saddles. He also said he didn't feel safe being alone and wanted to get as far away from the village as soon as he could by nightfall. He began to load the pack and the animals, which took longer than he figured. Finally, he got all the animals loaded and their packs lashed down.

From where his camp was, Mr. Lloyd said he had a good chance of getting out of the village without anyone hearing or seeing him leave. He waited until the village became quiet except for a dog barking here and there, and the whinny of a horse now and then. It was a cold night, and he knew everyone would be in their lodges early. "I had the two horses saddled and the pack animals all lined up. After piling more wood on the fire to make it look like I was around, I led the five pack animals and the two I would be riding out and away from the village, letting the animals get used to following one another. After what seemed a mile, I climbed in the saddle and kicked my horse into moving at a good pace. I rode throughout the night, only stopping to give the animals a short rest or to drink when I came across a stream. I rode until midday before I found a place that I felt would be safe, and the animals out of sight. I built a small fire and made coffee and something to eat. After putting the fire out, I settled down and tried to sleep. When it was getting dark, I drank some cold coffee and dug out of one of the packs a big handful of dried meat, climbed back in the saddle, and pushed on throughout the night with a half moon and starry skies. I did this day after day."

He told how one day one of the pack animals slipped somehow and broke its legs very bad, giving him no choice but to put it out of its suffering. Getting the packs and pack saddle off, and not wanting to make noise by shooting, he taken his knife and cut the horse's jugular vein and throat. "I continued riding until Cole and the boys picked up my tracks and finally caught up to me."

Mr. Lloyd finished his story by saying, "I'm very tired and think I'll turn in. I thank you for taking me ito your camp." With that, he got up and started for his leanto.

Cole stopped him by asking if he wanted to join him and the boys in the morning, to go look for more buffalo. Taking a few minutes to turn it over in his mind, he finally said, "Wake me in the morning."

Turning to Cole, I said, "You going to look for more buff tomorrow?"

"Yeah, I'se think I'se and them there two boys can gets a few more."

"You sure you want to?"

"Yes, brother, I'se think we'se gonna need alls we'se can get."

"Yes, you're probably right. I'll stay here and cut up the meat and get Dawn and Snowflake to dry as much as they can. Cole, you know we have to get out of here."

"I'se know!"

"So we leave here the day after tomorrow, early."

"Can do, brother." Cole, Running Dog, Swift Fox, along with Mr. Lloyd, struck out early in the morning to look for buffalo. I, along with Snowflake and Dawn, cut up the meat and dried as much as we could, and readied it for packing back to the village.

The squaws put some of the bones and meat in two big pots, along with several hands full of beans Mr. Lloyd supplied before he left.

Mid afternoon, Cole and the others came riding in, loaded down with two more young buffalo and two more elk. Cole told me he figured this would be all we would be able to pack. Looking the animals over, we decided to quarter the animals and pack the meat that way. The next morning, we lit out for the village.

Mid morning of the third day, I was leading as we drew deeper into the canyon. I had a strange feeling, and the farther we rode, the more the eerie feeling crept over me. It kept getting colder and colder. It wasn't long before we rode into a frigid snowstorm. The cold was so frigid that the breath from my mule turned to ice crystal.

The snow was coming down so heavy that visibility was next to nothing. We were deep into the canyon, and there was no turning back. The eerie feeling was clawing at my mind. I was wondering if the others were feeling the same.

The canyon had narrowed to the point that it was just the trail and the river. We hadn't gone far when an eerie, ghostly sound came up the canyon. On the wings of the wind, through the blowing snow, I saw what looked like figures sitting on a bluff, overlooking the trail and river.

I immediately brought Curse, my mule, to a stop, pulled my gun from its cover, and made sure it was ready. I sat there, in the numbing cold, wondering if my eyes were frozen and playing tricks on my mind.

Cole, who was riding in the middle of our train, came running, hollering into the storm, "What's happened, brother? What's happened?"

I couldn't hear him until he was beside me. I could see them more clearly now, and pointed to the two dozen or more warriors, some sitting on horses, and some standing by their mounts. Squinting to see through the blowing snow, teeth chattering, Cole finally said, "Damn it to hell, brother, nows what!"

"Hell, brother, we have no damn chance against that many."

Snowflake and Dawn had dismounted and came running, asking what was wrong. I pointed to where the warriors were. Dawn and Snowflake began rattling something off in their tongue. I had just told them to talk slower when the white bird came flying out of the snow storm, crossed right in front of us, then was gone.

Lost in the blowing snow, I turned back to Dawn and Snowflake, who were shivering, teeth chattering, and scared to hell. "What were you going to tell us?"

Snowflake then said, "That people from village see these warriors from time to time. Elders claim they are spirit or ghosts. The elders claim these warrior are ones who died in battle or were lost, one way or another, when out hunting. Elders say these spirits watch over Ute people and Ute village. Ward off evil."

"You mean, they are ghosts?" Cole asked.

"Yeah, much spooky, brother, much spooky!" Dawn then said, "Warriors, they make no battle."

"Are you saying it's safe for us to go on?" I asked.

"Yeah," Snowflake answered.

"If you say so, then mount up and lets' get the hell moving, before we freeze. Cole, maybe it would be best you wait until Mr. Lloyd passes, so he don't do something stupid."

"Will do, brother."

I kicked Curse into moving as the others fell in behind. We hadn't gone a mile when the frigid cold storm stopped and we were in a warm, bright, sunny day. It was like riding out of hell and into another existence. I kept riding until I found a large, wide place along the trail, and stopped and slid down from Curse. I waited until everyone caught up and dismounted.

Just as Cole slid out of his saddle beside me, the white bird circled overhead, then was gone. Mr. Lloyd was very shaken at what he had witnessed, and just stared at me. When he quit shaking, he said, "Nathan!"

"Yeah?"

"Just what the hell went on back there? I damn near froze. Damn near shit myself."

I just shrugged.

Cole broke in. "That's was damn spooky. I'se not know what happened, but I'se was damn scared. I'se knew you, brother, not get spooked."

Snowflake and Dawn stood there, holding their boys tight to them. All four stared at me. None of them said anything, just looked. I watched their reaction, and wondered what was going on in all their heads, and yet somehow I guessed I really knew.

Turning to Cole, I said, "We're not far from the village now. Will you lead?"

"Yes'm, can do."

"Cole, go straight to the squaws' lodge."

"Can do."

"I'll bring up the rear."

"All's right!"

Cole and I picked our way through the village to the

squaws' lodges. Both Dawn and Snowflake's mates had gone hunting one day, many winters ago, when their sons were only two and three summers old. Their mates hadn't been seen since. Both their parents were getting along in years, so after some time had passed, Snowflake and her son moved in with her parents. It wasn't long before Dawn and her son did the same.

When we reined on the backside of their parents' lodges, that were only forty feet or so apart, both their parents came rushing out. Running Dog and Swift Fox jumped off their horses and tied them, then went running, throwing their arms around their grandparents. Dawn and Snowflake were right there, hugging their parents.

Cole and I stayed sitting on our mules. Mr. Lloyd sat some distance away on his horse and looked on. Once they were reacquainted with their family, I looked down from where I sat into the copper-colored faces of Snowflake and Dawn, that were all smiles, and asked, "Where do you'se want your meat put?"

Snowflake said, "It's not our meat, it's *yours*."

"No! No, Snowflake. Each of you get one and a half buffalo, and one and a half elk, and half of all the deer meat."

They stood there, mouths hanging open, then turned and translated to their parents. Their fathers stood in awe and the mothers with hands over mouths and eyes filled with tears. When Snowflake and Dawn turned to face us, Cole and I saw eyes filled with tears, flowing down copper-colored cheeks.

We slid down from our mounts and were standing there. They both looked at us a long moment, then came running and gave us each a long hug. When Snowflake gave me a hug, she looked up into my eyes, smiled, then said, "I now understand, I think."

Cole and I got the meat hung high, so it was out of reach of dogs. I gathered up the rope to my pack animals, grabbed my reins, and stuck a foot into the stirrup and swung my ass onto the saddle on Curse. Cole was already mounted as I pulled on the reins to swing Curse around.

All of them were standing, watching. I stopped and held up three fingers and said to Dawn and Snowflake, "Three days, bring the boys and come to our camp, and we will divvy up the hides and plews[1]."

Snowflake covered her mouth with a hand as tears ran down her copper-colored face.

[1] *French for pelts*

Kicking Curse into moving, I followed Cole and Les out of the village and down the river to the place that we had chosen to winter.

Late morning on the third day, Dawn, Swift Fox and Snowflake, Running Dog, came riding into camp. As Dawn slid down from her horse, she asked, "Why so far from village?"

"We're not," Les answered. He hadn't all that much to talk about, since we arrived back at the village, staying mostly to himself.

Cole and I couldn't figure what was bothering him, and left him to himself.

The boys and their mothers gathered around to watch Cole and I divvy up the plews so that each squaw and her son got the same amount as each Cole and I did. The squaws were overwhelmed that we would share so much with them.

As they were leaving, Swift Fox and Running Dog yelled, "Come see you soon."

Over the course of the winter, the men of the village invited us to join them on hunts. Cole and I would always accept. Mr. Lloyd, on the other hand, never joined in on the hunts. He preferred staying in camp.

Winter had dragged on, and as close as I could figure, it was somewhere in mid February. as we had been getting the itch to mosey on north for sometime now, and had been repairing anything that needed fixed, sorting things to be packed.

Running Dog and Swift Fox had been coming by every day to help, but mostly they watched and talked. One morning, they were early. I asked, "What brings you early?"

"Our mothers sent us to tell the three of you to come to our lodges for to eat this afternoon, before sun go away."

"Cole, what you think?"

"I'se going!"

"How about you, Les?"

He shrugged. "I don't know."

"Well, are you or aren't you?"

"I guess," Les said.

"Go tell your mothers that we will be there."

That afternoon, when we rode up to the back side of their lodges, Swift Fox and Running Dog came running out and taken our animals and put them in a makeshift corral they had made. Dawn and Snowflake were busy cooking over a hot fire and motioned us to come over, telling us to sit.

We found a chunk of log and placed it close to the fire and

sat. They had roasted elk and buffalo, along with other things. While we ate, Cole and I complimented Snowflake and Dawn on how wonderful the food was. I added that this was the best meal I had eaten since we left Fanny and Charley back on the Platte. Cole agreed.

As soon as Les was finished eating, he asked Swift Fox and Running Dog if they would bring him his horse. Cole asked, "Where's you going, Les?"

"Nowhere, I just need to get back to my camp and get some things done."

The boys brought him his horse. He thanked them and the squaws, mounted up and rode off. The others looked at Cole and I.

I shrugged and said, "Don't know."

We talked with Dawn and Snowflake and their parents. Their parents wanted to know everything about where we were from. Snowflake and Dawn had to translate most everything we said.

The sun had disappeared and dark was closing in. Cole said, "Brother, we'se better be going."

Dawn said, "Wait!" Her and Snowflake disappeared around the tepee and soon returned, each with a bundle what looked like tanned hides. They handed Cole and I each a bundle.

Looking up at them, I asked, "What's this?"

Their parents nodded and motioned for us to open them. We untied the bundles and spread it out over our laps, finding a tunic-like shirt trimmed with fringes, leggings, and loin cloth, made from deer hides they tanned, moccasins made of elk hide and lined with beaver. Then Running Dog and Swift Fox came, each carrying a buffalo robe, and handed us each one.

To say the least, we were taken back and so very grateful that tears came to my eyes. Looking up into the faces of Snowflake, Dawn and the boys, I asked, "How can we ever repay you'se?"

Dawn and Snowflake both shook their heads no. "You owe not—think! We owe *you*," Dawn said. "You save our and boys' lives, and all the meat you give our people. Parents say need give gifts, so all us work to make gift for white man and black man. Parents say hope like."

We told Snowflake and Dawn how much we appreciated the gifts and they were to tell their parents we liked the clothes and robes very much. We thanked all of them, bid them good night. As we rode down along the river toward camp, the stars shone bright overhead. The only sound was the sound of the animals' hooves on the hard, rocky ground, and the water rushing by in the river.

We were getting close to camp when Cole asked, "Brother, what's you thinks chewing at Les?"

"Don't know. But I have this feeling we might better keep a close eye on him."

"I'se feel too something not right."

"Maybe we should have a talk with him before heading north. What you think?"

"Maybe so."

A day or two had passed when I asked Mr. Lloyd if there was something not to his liking.

"No! Not really."

"Then, what?" I asked.

"Ahh! Just been missing home. Sometimes I think maybe I should have just went on home."

"Just wondering, Les," I replied.

When Cole and I were alone, I said to Cole, "I think we still need to keep an eye on him."

"I'se thinks you'se right."

During the long, cold winter days, there were some from the village who would come to our camp to talk and bathe in the hot water we had dammed up. Chief Red Rock, chief of the clan of Utes, would come often to talk and bathe. His name came about from the red rock in the area.

38

It was early spring and we figured it to be late February, maybe early March. Cole and I decided it was a good time to mosey on our way north. We never did ask Mr. Lloyd if he was going with us. We just assumed he would. Early one morning, Cole and I loaded our pack animals, then I swung my ass onto the saddle of Old Curse, my mule. Cole and Les mounted up, and we rode by the village, stopping by Snowflake's and Dawn's lodges. As we reined up at their lodges, Swift Fox and Running Dog came running, followed by their mothers and grandparents.

I slid from my saddle, as did Cole. Les stayed mounted. He never felt at ease around the boys and squaws. My feet no more than hit the ground when one of the boys threw his arms around me, holding me tight. The other one Cole. Dawn came, throwing her arms around me, then pulling me to her.

"Stay here," she whimpered.

"No, Dawn, it's time we move on."

She looked up at me, her eyes wet with tears, then stopped and turned to Cole. Then Snowflake pulled me close to her, wrapping her arms around me, squeezing me so hard, I could hardly breathe. Pressing her face tight to my chest, between sobs, she muttered, "You greater hunters. Great warriors, too! My people want you stay. I want you to stay. Snowflake know in her heart you want to go. You must go then. I think I understand."

Releasing her hold, she looked up into my eyes, the early morning sun bathing her copper-colored face as tears flowed from her dark, pleading eyes, making my own fill with tears.

Looking at her a long moment, I then said, "Snowflake, you are a good woman, as is Dawn. You both have sons to be proud of. You'll fare well. May the Great Spirit watch over you'se and your people. As you know, it's time for us to be moving on."

Gathering up the reins and the lead rope for the pack string, I climbed back in the saddle on Old Curse, urged her into moving, waved one last time, and followed Cole and Les out of the village. We followed the river[1] in the direction that Cole and I came from.

Day after day, we followed the river as it wound its way east by northeast. From time to time, we would stop to rest the animals for a few days and do some trapping. Then we would move on. By the time we got to where the Muddy Creek[2] entered the river, we had a fair number of pelts. Heading north northwest, along Muddy Creek, Cole and I both noticed Mr. Lloyd wasn't showing much interest in trapping, staying in camp much of the time.

Finally, we made it to the pass. After crossing over the pass, we found Grizzly Creek, which led us to the headwaters of the North Platte. We had been traveling along the Platte for several days when, off in the distance, we spotted movement on the crest of a rise, moving in our direction. Even at this distance, we could tell they were Injun.

Cole reined up beside me. "What you think, brother?"

"Don't know, but I think we oughta high-tail it over to those trees and those rocks when those Injuns drop out of sight into that ravine."

"I think that would be wise," Les said. From where we were at, we were concealed fairly good by the tall willows that grew along the stream. When the last Injun dropped out of sight, we skedaddled for the trees and rock cliff, which was a good quarter mile away.

Once there, we tied our pack animals in groups of five, head to head. That way, they couldn't run off. Each one of us grabbed our guns. Cole and I each had two double-barreled muskets, two single-shot muskets, and four pistols each. We didn't really know what all Les had, besides his two muskets. Each one of us picked a good vantage spot and made ready.

The Injuns came down to the creek and let their animals drink, then crossed over that when they saw the fresh tracks. From where we were, we could see them waving their arms and pointing in our direction. The way it looked, they were deciding if they wanted to follow our tracks, which would lead them right to where we were.

When the Injuns were a hundred yards out, Cole and I counted fourteen in all. That wouldn't be too bad of odds with

[1] *The river would later be known as the Colorado*

[2] *Near present-day Kremmling*

the fire power we had, plus whatever Les had. I whispered to Cole to hold his fire until they were fifty yards away, and to tell Les. At that distance, we would have a damn good chance if those red-ass bastards made a full charge.

We watched as those red asses tied their horses not far from the creek, then, advancing toward us on foot, taking advantage of the few trees and rocks that separated us from them, Cole and I were about to blow the hell out of them, when Les yelled out, "There are four white men out there! Damn it, they look like the four I was with!" Jumping up, Les began hollering their names, waving his arms, and started walking toward them.

"What's dat stupid shitbrain doing?" Cole asked.

"Don't know. But get ready."

"That brainless asshole won't make it very far." Cole no more than said it when three arrows slammed into Les's chest. Then came a loud boom from one of their muskets. We saw Les's hat fly off as the ball from the musket smashed him in the face, knocking his head backward as it ripped out the back.

I hollered to Cole, "Give it to them!"

"I'se will."

Using our single-shot muskets first, we left four red bastards lifeless. We were hoping these Injuns would think we would have to reload and charge. They didn't know we each had eight shots left before we needed to reload. That meant we had to make every shot count. The red asses must have thought what we hoped, for they made a full head-on charge right out in the open, yelping and yelling their war cries.

They had only a few guns among them, the way it sounded. When they were about thirty yards away, we opened up, letting four more bastards plow up the dirt.

Looking to where Cole was hunkered down behind some large rocks, I saw him struggling with an arrow protruding from his left thigh. Looking around to see if I could see anyone, I started inching my way over to where Cole was, when a ball from one of their muskets ricocheted off some rocks, slicing a gash through the outer edge of my right shoulder. It stung like hell and made me even madder at the assholes.

Blood oozing down my arm, making my hand slippery, I grabbed my two muskets and four pistols, and made it the rest of the way to where Cole was, and settled in beside him. He asked, "How many thems dirty red bastards out there?"

"Don't know. I think six at the most. How bad the leg?"

"Not too bad. Broke the staff off. Get de rest out after

we'se finished with dem red basters. How's 'bout you'se arm?"

"Ah, just a scratch. Bleeds like hell, though." Gathering up my shooting pouch, I poured a charge of powder down the barrels of each of our muskets and rammed a ball, then made sure they were primed, while Cole kept watch.

"Cole, can you see any of them?"

"No. Wait, I just saw someone moving, brother. What dey doing? I think it's one's of dems English men. He's on his hands and knees, trying to drag one of the wounded."

"How far?"

"I'se guess sixty yards!"

"Damn it to hell!"

"What?"

"One of those red-assed bastards is dragging the other white man."

Getting up on my knees so I could see over the rocks, we watched as the one Englishman moved into a spot that left him visible. Soon the Injun dragging the Englishman came into view. Resting our muskets over the top of the rocks, we placed the front blade of our guns high on the two men's chests and at the same time squeezed the triggers. The Injun and English both flopped over backwards, hitting the ground, not moving.

Cole and I watched as the tense minutes slowly passed, for any trace or indication of movement. None! I just stood up when we heard the shrill, shrieking, piercing sound of four warriors charging out of nowhere. The one was almost on me when I leveled my pistol and fired. The heavy ball caught the warrior mid-chest, knocking him back on his ass. He didn't move.

Out of the corner of my eye, I got a glimpse of one of the warriors giving a flying leap over the rock Cole was still crouched behind. Cole rolled to one side and the red-assed bastard went head first among the dirt and rocks, giving Cole enough time to bring up his musket as the warrior turned in a low crouch, shrieking, knife in one hand, tomahawk in the other.

Cole fired point blank. The ball ripped through the Injun's chest, knocking him back. Blood ran from the ugly hole and oozed from his mouth. As I kept watch while Cole recharged his musket, I saw the other two trying to sneak away. I knew we couldn't let them escape. They would bring the entire tribe after us. I hollered to Cole, "Grab your gun. There are two trying to get to their horses!"

We each grabbed two muskets that were already loaded, and took after them. We caught up to where they were, just in the nick of time. We were ten or fifteen yards away when we saw the two Injuns trying to mount their horses, which were prancing all around, making it difficult for them.

Flopping to a sitting position to steady our weapons better, we each picked one red devil and fired. The balls found their mark. Two more Injuns lay lifeless.

Reloading, we slowly moved to where the two lay, to make sure they went under. Then, covering each other's backs, making sure there was none just laying, waiting to attack. After checking each one, we felt sure we had gotten all of the bastards.

Returning to our pack animals, we dug out our medicine bags. I removed the arrowhead from Cole's thigh. For some reason it hadn't penetrated very deep, which made it easier to dig out. As for my shoulder, just a groove where the ball ripped through the outer part, not doing any serious damage.

After getting our wounds taken care of, we knew there was no way we could bury all of the bodies. Instead, we decided to drag them to a large, bare spot next to the creek and put them on a pile. We stripped every body of anything that would be useful in trading, even the arrowheads, after the shafts were broken off. The only guns were those of the Englishmen. There were six muskets in all. The Englishmen had good shoes and clothing, which we salvaged before putting their bodies on the pile.

We drug all the tree branches and brush we could find, piling it on top of the bodies. Then rounded up all the animals of theirs that we could find. With our own, we had close to forty. We knew that would be a lot of animals just for the two of us to handle. There was only one thing to do, try and hope for the best.

Cole was already in the saddle, watching over the animals and waiting for me to set fire to the heap of brush that covered the dead Injuns and Englishmen. Once the fire was blazing good, Cole yelled, "Come, brother, let's get the hell out of here!"

Grabbing the reins, I jammed my foot into the stirrup on Old Curse and flopped my tired ass onto the saddle.

"You'se leads!" Cole shouted.

"All right." Giving Old Curse a pat on the neck, I then nudged her into moving, following the North Platte as it wound its way north. Cole and I rode through the night. Stars filled the sky, giving us enough light that we were able to keep track of the animals and each other.

The eastern sky was turning a pinkish glow when we

finally came across a grove of trees not far from the river, with plenty of grass, and it looked like it offered a fair amount of concealment and good visibility.

We decided to hole up here, at least for the day, maybe two. The animals needed rest, and so did we. After getting the animals all unpacked and a large area roped off for them to feed in, it was decided that one of us would be on lookout at all times. We chose the highest tree that would be easy to climb and would provide a good view over our back trail and the surrounding area.

I taken the first watch, and was high in the tree when I spotted the white bird silhouetted against the clear blue sky, circling overhead. I knew then we would be safe. I had seen it the day before, when we were being attacked.

The next evening, we packed up and headed north along the river. We traveled north night after night, until the Platte headed eastward. Here we headed northwest until we came to the south fork of the Powder River.

Here we felt more safe and traveled by day, following the Powder until it headed in a northeast direction. Leaving the Powder and striking out northwest until we came across the Rosebud, following it north until it emptied into the Yellowstone. From here we would be on the lookout for signs of a Crow village. We moved west along the Yellowstone, then on to the Musselshell, stopping for a few days at a time, to rest the animals and mostly ourselves.

Checking the animals, we found we still had the same amount we started with, mostly horses, some mules. We were between the Yellowstone and Musselshell when we came across a box canyon far off the beaten path, with high cliffs and a very narrow opening. We rode up the canyon for what seemed close to two miles. It was very rugged country all around. We decided to take a chance and cache most of our belongings in several different locations, to be more safe and leave most of the animals.

After everything was cached, the only thing to do was figure out a way to close the entrance so it wouldn't be noticeable and yet keep our animals in and out of sight. We once again hit the saddles and set out looking for Chief Standing Bear's Crow village.

Some days later, we located it on the Sweetgrass. Before we got to the village, we were confronted by a half dozen Crow warriors. Cole and I recognized two of the warriors as the ones we were made to fight when we first encountered the Crow people. We had several antelope, a couple deer, and an elk we had taken while looking for their village. The two warriors also recognized us. They tried talking the others into taking the meat, then killing the two of us.

We had picked up enough Crow talk to make out what was being said. I guess the two thought we didn't understand what was being said and kept on taunting us. The other four didn't say anything. Finally, I had enough and said in Crow, "We come to Crow village to pay honor to Chief Standing Bear, and bring meat for Crow people."

We started to ride on, but the two warriors swung their horses around about ten yards, out in front to block the way. I said to Cole, "I guess these two want to fight," and swung my double-barreled musket up at the two of them.

Cole doing the same, I said in Crow, "Make one move and four die," and I set the hammers on my musket. Then, one of the other four rode in between and held his hand up and said, "No shoot. We not make fight. We take to Chief Standing Bear lodge." The four other warriors made the two ride out front, staying in between.

We spent the next four days with Chief Standing Bear and the Crow people, making lots of talk with the chief and council, and gave them lots of foofaraw. On the fifth morning, we packed and pulled out for where we had our supplies cached.

Retracing our way back, we kept vigilant at all time to make sure those two red sticks weren't trailing. After making certain no one was trailing us, we made our way into the canyon, checked on the animals, then made camp.

That evening, while sitting around our small fire, roasting antelope and sipping coffee, Cole said, "Brother."

"Yeah, what is it?"

"I'se been thinking. What's your thoughts on goin' to dis here rendezvous?"

"I don't know, it's a long ride. What you say?"

"I'se not know. Might be good! We'se trades horses for supplies."

"Yeah, we could do that."

"Get some tobaccy and other staples."

"Cole, how many Injun horses do you think we would need for trading?"

"Brother, I'se thinks ten be enough."

"Maybe so! When you think we should make it out of here?"

"Maybe day after tomorrow."

"Sounds good. Then we'll do it."

After some hard riding along the Green, we finally smelled smoke and heard the shooting long before we could see anything of the rendezvous. After another mile or so, it came into sight. Dozens and dozens of tepees and leantos of all description scattered here and there along the Green River and cottonwoods.

Cole and I went upriver a hundred yards or so from the closest camp, and found a spot amongst some cottonwood, and put up camp. After making a makeshift corral and picketing some of the animals, it was time to make a fire and roast something to eat. It had been a long, hard day, and it would feel good to crawl in my bed roll.

It was mid morning when we decided to stroll down to where the trading was going on. We slung our shooting pouches over one shoulder and the medicine bags the Utes made for us over the other, shoved two pistols in our belts, and skinning knives and tomahawk. Cole and I then made our way down along the river, passing all kinds of Injuns, bearded buckskin-clad trappers, some half naked, going here and there. Shelters were strung everywhere. We knew we looked kinda rough and woolly, probably some of the youngest trappers there. It was a hot morning, so neither of us had our shirts on, instead carrying them. When anyone would look at the two of us, and see the many scars we carried, most gave us a wide berth.

We found the main tents where all the trading taken place. I noticed the clerk behind the counter, but didn't pay him any attention as I was looking at the trade merchandise when I heard the clerk say to Cole, "Hey, black man, you a runaway?"

I quickly turned, facing the clerk, hand on pistol, and said in a very stern voice, "He's my brother."

Cole hadn't answered. The clerk looked at me a long moment, then said, "I apologize, sir. Is there anything I can do for you?"

"Well, we come here looking to talk with the man in charge."

"I don't think that's possible, sir."

I placed both big hands on top of the counter, leaned over and put my face only inches from the clerk's, and before I could finish, Cole taken hold of my arm and pulled me around.

"Take it easy, brother. No harm done!"

When I turned back to the clerk, he was gone. A

few minutes later, the clerk and another man came from somewhere out of the back. He was a short, squatty man with spectacles and beady eyes. He looked Cole and me over, then said, "I'm Mr. Clark." He was very calm and courteous. "I heard what my clerk said, and I apologize. Now, what can I do for you gentlemen?"

I said, "I'm Nathan, and this is my brother, Cole. We have been riding hard for a number of days. Maybe I'm a little edgy."

"I understand. What is it I can help you with?"

"Well, Mr. Clark, I heard you may be in need of some good horses."

"Yes, I may be! What you got?"

"We have ten good horses that pack and ride."

"How much you want for them?"

"You come and take a look at them, Mr. Clark. Then we talk price."

"Fair enough. Where you fellows camped at?"

"The last camp upriver."

"How would it be if I stop by about midday tomorrow?"

"That will be good."

"Anything else?"

"Well ... Mr. Clark, how much for a gourd of whiskey?"

"Five dollars."

"Can you give us a little credit, Mr. Clark?"

He looked at Cole and me a few moments, then said, "Give the clerk your names and he'll put it on your tab." Then he turned and left.

I looked at the clerk and said, "Mr. Clark said you will put a gourd of whiskey on our tab."

With contempt he snarled, "Name!"

"Nathan and Cole." I watched as he wrote whiskey after our names and nothing else.

"Mister," I said, "would you put five dollars after the whiskey?"

The clerk looked at me sharply, then wrote five dollars after the whiskey in the ledger. "Anything else?"

"Yes, write me a slip that says one gourd, five dollars, and your name."

He hesitated a few minutes, then wrote it out on a slip of paper, then went and filled the gourd, and handed it to me. I thanked him.

Cole and I turned our attention to looking over the merchandise that was for trade. After looking at everything, we returned to camp and brought all the horses in closer, to make sure none would come up missing.

With the animals taken care of, I decided it was about time to wash what little clothes I had, and maybe even bathe. I taken everything I had and strolled down to the river and washed them. Then I taken a good sand bath.

It was almost dark when I returned to camp. Cole had a hind quarter of antelope roasting over the fire. After pouring each of us a tin cup of whiskey and slicing off a big chunk of antelope, I leaned back against a tree, sipped my whiskey, and chewed on the meat. Cole was sitting on the opposite side of the fire, chewing a slab of meat and sipping his whiskey. As we talked, it wasn't long before I noticed the whiskey was getting to Cole. Not long after he finished his whiskey and meat that he said, "I'se think I'se goin' to bed." Getting up, Cole stumbled his way to his leanto, which was about fifty feet from mine, on the opposite side of the fire.

Finishing my meat, then rinsing it down with some black coffee, I headed into the bushes to relieve myself, and after throwing more wood on the fire, I crawled into my leanto and lay down, leaving the flap open. I lay there, watching the flickering of the fire and crackling sounds it made as it burned.

In my foggy state of mind, I saw the white bird sitting on a branch not far from the leanto. Then I saw Charley and Fanney come out of the flickering flames. Then came Kate, Old Joe, Chief Golden Eagle, Chief Long Feather. Then came Mom, Dad, Frances, Noel, Abilene and baby Jeanette. They all floated off into the darkness.

Mr. Clark was true to his word and showed up when the sun was high overhead. The first thing he asked was, "What are your names again?"

"I am Nathan, and this is Cole."

"I take it you're trappers?"

"That's right," Cole replied.

Then he introduced himself again and his three employees. "Where's the horses you want to trade?"

We led the way to where the horses were, and told Mr. Clark which ones were for trade. He looked the animals over really good, then came to where we were leaning on our muskets, looking us up and down.

"You have some fine-looking animals. I'll take nine of them, and pick the ones I want, and give you seventy dollars each."

Cole, not knowing much about money, looked to me to answer.

Lowering my head, I spat a stream of tobaccy juice on the ground and turned to leave.

"Hold on," Mr. Clark said. "I see you know what you have. So ... how much *you* think you should have?"

"One fifty each," I replied.

"I'll give one."

"Make that one twenty-five, and you got a deal," I said.

"One fifteen and no more."

"You got a deal. Write a credit statement out for Nathan or Cole, Mr. Clark, in the amount of one thousand thirty-five dollars for nine horses."

Mr. Clark dug a small tablet from his pocket and wrote a credit statement in the amount agreed on, in our names, and signed it. Handing it to me, he looked at me, then said, "I see you can cipher numbers also. Would you be interested in working for me?"

"No. Not really."

"But maybe, sometime off in the future, if you ever do, look me up."

I thanked him and he had his men cut the horses that he bought, then they rode off. Cole and I knew that good horses and mules brought big money, especially when someone was in bad need.

Later, we moseyed on down towards where the trading was taking place. Cole stopped and looked at me, and said, "Nathan, you'se not thinking to works for that Mr. Clark, is you?"

"No, Cole, you're stuck with me. Don't you remember, we're blood brothers, and that means we take care of each other."

"Yes, I remember. Good. I'se don't know if I'se could make it on my own."

"Come, Cole, let's go see what we're going to spend our money on."

When Cole and I walked into the trade tent, we noticed that the same clerk was there, and so was Mr. Clark. When he saw us, he came over and said, "Nathan and Cole, please feel free to look."

Then he turned to his clerk and said, "Cecil, you treat Nathan and Cole fair and square, you hear?"

"Yes, Mr. Clark."

After looking over the trade goods for a while, Cole and I left and meandered throughout the camps, stopping often to talk with the many trappers and Injuns, the ones we could understand, finding most in groups.

Dark was coming down, so we made our way back to camp. Later that evening, while sitting around our fire, we decided on the supplies we would need to see us through the coming winter. We talked over the idea of buying our supplies as soon as we could, and pulling out for the Yellowstone, and look for a good place to trap and spend the winter.

It was midday when Cole and I made our way down to where all the action was. Stopping off at the traders' tents, putting two two-gallon kegs of whiskey on our tab, we then strolled on past various camps, where groups of men milled about, talking, laughing and cutting up. As we walked past one group that had a hot fire going under two back quarters of some kind of meat they were roasting, one of the buckskin-clad men yelled, "Ol'coons! Come on over! Trade meat for whiskey!"

We wandered on over closer to their fire and stood looking this bunch over. One of the leather-faced, bearded men said, "Ol' coons, what's you called?"

"I'm called Nathan."

"And I'm called Cole. What's yours?"

"I'm John. Some call me the Hatchet. That one over there is Whiskey Joe." He pointed to one of the others and said, "That's Windy Bill. This is Eagle Eye Sam." Pointing with his knife at the Injun, he said, "This is Crooked Stick, Lame Deer and Red Antelope. They's Flathead," Hatchet said. "Find a place and sit, and pour up some of that whiskey. Dry we are!"

Cole and I poured everyone a tin cup of whiskey. Windy Bill cut a slab of meat off of a hind quarter and handed us each a slab. We spent the rest of the afternoon eating, drinking, smoking, and listening to their tales that each one spun. It was getting late in the afternoon and most everyone was feeling the whiskey, some letting out hoots and howls. One coon was pounding out a rhythm on an old beat-up pan. Another one was trying to squeeze out a tune on somewhat of a squeeze box.

Hatchet and a man named Gordon, the leader of the other group, formed contests to see which group was better at knife and tomahawk throwing, pistol and musket shooting. Thus far, Cole and I taken our share of winning. I was sweating like hell from the whiskey and hotness of the day. Gordon was standing a little off to my left and a few steps back when I pulled my tunic over my head. I wasn't paying him no mind when he said, "Damn it to hell, coon! What the hell happened to you?"

I turned to face him and asked, "What? What the hell you talking about?"

"Your back. All them scars! And the necklace."

Some of the others close by heard him and gathered around to see what Gordon was talking about, and looking at.

Whiskey Joe, who was standing by, looked at my back, then said to Cole, "Come over here!"

Cole came to see what he wanted. "What's you want?" Cole asked.

Whiskey Joe said, "Cole, would you mind pulling your shirt off?"

Cole, feeling the whiskey, said, "Cole not mind," and pulled his shirt off.

Hatchet, Gordon and Whiskey Joe all crowded around to look at Cole's back.

Hatchet said, "What the hell happened to you coons?"

I walked over to the fire, sat down, and poured myself a tin of whiskey, and Cole one. Cole sat next to me. "What's you think, brother?"

"Don't know, Cole."

Whiskey Joe, Hatchet and some of the others gathered around, poured themselves some whiskey, then sat down.

"Where you fellows from?" John asked.

Cole nudged me with his elbow. He, not being one to make much talk, let me make most of the talking. I started by telling them, "I was born outside of Pittsburgh, 1803. I left home when I turned 15. Made my way to a place called Starved Rock, worked there for a blacksmith, maybe one year and a half. That's where I met Cole."

"Where was Cole from?" Eagle Eye Sam asked.

"Hell only knows," I replied. "Cole was being held a slave on a river boat where the owner beat him every time things didn't go right."

John said, "What about the welts and scars on *your* back?"

"My father used to beat me every time he got drunk, and sometimes he beat my mother. One night, when I was in bed, he started slapping my mother around until he heard the cocking of my pistol, which he didn't know I had. I leveled it at him from up on the loft where I lay. That's where I slept. I said to my father, 'If you ever again beat my mother or any of us again ... I'll blow a hole in you.' It was shortly after that I left home.

"My father never hit any of us, that I know of, after that.

The answer to one of your other questions is, I was mauled by a bear on our way out here. Cole was attacked by a very large cougar late one afternoon."

We talked way past dark. They told how this first rendezvous was made possible and who owned it. They told of Jed Smith, Meek, Bridger, Beckwith, Fitzpatrick, to name a few, and said we had to meet some of these coons.

I was tired and guess Cole was, so we excused ourselves and thanked them all for such a nice afternoon and evening and all the palavering. Then we gathered up our muskets and whatever else we had, and started to leave, when one of them asked, "Are you two the coons that every Injun tribe far and wide talks about?"

I didn't answer.

"If you are, you'se better watch yours hair. Every buck Injun be lookin' to hang it on his lodge."

I stopped and looked at them for a second, then said, "I don't know what Injuns talk about. As we told you'se, we wintered with the Utes and the only trouble that came about was with some white Englishman bossloper[1], go under to[2] they did. My brother here and I wouldn't let a dozen or so red sticks be much of a concern. And that's the way my stick floats[3].

Silence fell over the ol' coons sitting around the fire as Cole and I made our way toward camp. When we got close to camp, we could see our fire blazing bright. Cole said, "What the hell?"

We hunkered down to wait and see what was going on. Some minutes had passed when we heard someone coming from the direction of the river. As they drew closer to the light of the fire, we could see there were two of them. Each had a blanket over their head and wrapped around them.

We stayed hidden, to see what they were up to. They stood by the fire, holding the blanket open a few moments, then draping them over their arms. We could see now. They were two squaws and they were completely naked. They said something to each other, then one of them went to Cole's leanto and crawled in. The other one stood by the fire a few minutes longer, then headed for my leanto, lifted the flap and crawled in.

Cole and I waited a while longer before walking into camp, like we didn't know anyone was there. I sat down by the

[1] *trapper*

[2] *died*

[3] *That's the way I feel about it*

fire, poured a tin of cold coffee, drank some, then said to Cole, "I'm goin' to bed."

"Brother, I'se done goin', too."

I watched as Cole went to his leanto. "Make sure you don't lay on something pointy," I said.

"You'se too."

I lifted the flap to my leantop, placed my musket and pistols in easy reach, shucked out of my clothes, and crawled into my bed roll. I could tell she was as far back as she could get. I had been laying there for a few minutes before I felt a hand moving over and touching me. Grabbing it by the wrist, I twisted the hand upward and asked, "Who are you? And what are you doing in my bed?"

She chattered something off I didn't understand.

"You talk white man talk?"

"Little."

"Who the hell are you?"

"I Flathead."

"You come from way up where it gets cold?"

"Yes."

"What's you doing in my bed?"

"My man drink much whiskey with you and other white man, then sleep, then drink more whiskey, get sick, sleep more, not wake, sleep! Hear much talk about you and black man. I talk friend to come find you camp. We find. We wait. When see you soon come, I tell friend, 'Come, we go. We hurry to you camp.' Go to river, bath, come back. I go in you bed, wait. Friend go to black man's bed."

Letting go of her arm, she moved her hand, letting her fingers move up and down over my nakedness. Reaching my manhood, her fingers closed around it. Then she moved on top, straddling me, taking my hardness in her hand and guiding it into her wetness, moving so slowly down.

Rocking back and forth, letting her tits brush lightly over my chest, taking one in each hand, I massaged her erect nipples while she moved up and down. It wasn't long before sounds within her were coming. I knew she was about to go over the top. I backed up against her, going over the top at the same time.

When it was over, she rolled off and curled up beside me, resting her hand on my chest. In a blink of an eye, she was asleep and I was, too.

The next thing I knew, she was arousing me once again. This went on throughout the night. I was beginning to wonder if she never got enough.

Night was beginning to fade the last time. Getting up, she hurried into her clothes and stepped outside, gave a whistle. Her friend came out of Cole's leanto, dressing as she walked over to her friend. They both disappeared into the semi darkness toward the river.

I was completely drained, to say the least, and went back to sleep.

The next thing I knew, Cole was hollering, "Lave Hoi![1] It's early afternoon." He had just gotten up himself.

I finally crawled out from under my blankets. The sun was torture on my eyeballs. After a few minutes, I gathered up my clothes and headed to the river and waded in up to my waist. Scooping up several hands full of sand, I scrubbed myself over and over, hoping to wash the whiskey hangover and the squaw away.

Returning to camp, I saw Cole had built the fire up and put coffee on. Cole said he was going to the river and bathe. Looking at him, I said, "Brother, you look like you had one hell of a rough night."

"I'se sure did. Brother, you'se not looks any better. Likes you'se done been really worked over!"

"Yeah, you're probably right. I feel like shit, too. That damn rotgut whiskey was bad enough. Then that damn squaw in my bed wouldn't let me alone! She wanted poked just as often as she could get it up. You?"

"That bitch sure as to hell gaves me one hell of a work over. I'se damn glad when she left. Brother?"

"Yeah?"

"Does you know who they was?"

"Flathead, she said. That's all I could get out of her. Oh, yes! One thing she did say... that her man was drinking all afternoon and got so drunk, he passed out."

"You mean, one of those we were drinking with?"

"Yeah."

"Damn! Now I'se knows I'se goin' to the river."

While Cole went to bathe, I cut several slabs of meat from the deer we had hanging, sticking them on pointed sticks and placing them over the hot coals. When Cole returned from the river and while we were eating, he asked, "Whats you thins on we oughts to do? I'se thinks we ought to get some of the supplies traded for. What you think, brother?"

[1] *Get up!*

"Sounds good to me, Cole."

"I'se likes gets outta here in a coupla days."

"Yeah, I think we should. Let's get what supplies we can today. What you say?"

"I'se with you, but … no more whiskey."

"Yesterday and last night was enough for this coon."

"Me too."

Taking several pack animals, Cole and I led them down to where the main trading tents were. Tying our animals off, we moseyed on in and looked everything over. The talk was that Rocky Mountain Fur had brought 30,000 dollars' worth of trading merchandise all the way from St. Louis and started this, the first rendezvous, in 1825, on Henry's Fork of the Green River.

We began the difficult task of deciding what supplies we would need to see us through most of another year. Cole, not being able to cipher numbers all that good, left that part up to me. The first thing was to purchase some paper to keep tally on. Deciding what was needed, we started with staples first.

Sugar	25 lbs.	@ 1.50 a lb.	47.50
Flour	50 lbs.	@ 1.00 a lb.	50.00
Coffee	75 lbs.	@ 1.50 a lb.	112.50
Pepper	2 lbs.	@ 1.75 a lb.	3.50
Rice	20 lbs.	@ 1.00 a lb.	20.00
Plug tobaccy	10 lbs.	@ 1.50 a lb.	15.00
Smoke tobaccy	25 lbs.	@ 1.00 a lb.	25.00
Powder	25 lbs.	@ 2.00 a lb.	50.00
Lead	20 lbs.	@ 1.00 a lb.	20.00
Musket balls	40	@ 1.00 a lb.	40.00
Pipes	4	@ 1.75 each	7.00
Traps	12	@ 9.00 each	108.00
Woolen underwear	4	@ 9.00 each	36.00
3 pt NW blankets	4	@ 15.00 each	60.00
Fire steel	10	@ 1.00 each	10.00
Corn meal	30 lbs.	@.50 a lb.	15.00
Flint	1 dozen	@ 1.00 a dozen	1.00
Fish hooks	1 dozen	@ 1.00 a dozen	1.00
Salt	10 lbs.	@ 1.00 a lb.	10.00
Rum (2) 2 1/2 gal. kegs		@ 10.00 a gal.	50.00
Shot	10 lbs.	@ 1.25 a lb.	12.50

Soap	10 lbs.	@ 1.00 a lb.	10.00
Gun locks	2	@ 8.00 each	16.00
Percussion caps	1,000	@ 5.00 a hundred	50.00
Copper kettles	4	@ 11.50 each	46.00
Red & black flannel shirt	2	@ 2.50 each	5.00
Green & black flannel shirt	2	@ 2.50 each	5.00
Gun warms	10	@.75 each	7.50
Playing cards	2 decks	@ 1.00 each	2.00
Files	4	@ .75 each	3.00
6″ butcher knife	4	@ .75 each	3.00
Tin pans	4	@ .75 each	3.00
Pistols	2	@ 45.00 each	90.00
Iron kettle	1	@ 5.00 each	5.00
Iron skillet	1	@ 5.00 each	5.00
Tin cups	6	@ .25 each	1.50
Beans	40 lbs.	@ .50 a lb.	20.00
Beads	5 lbs.	@ 1.00 a lb.	5.00
Looking glass	5 dozen	@ 1.00 a dozen	5.00
Needles	5 dozen	@ 1.00 a dozen	5.00
Thread	5 dozen spools	@ 1.00 a dozen	5.00
Rope	500 ft.	@ .20 a ft.	100.00

39

It had taken Cole and I three and a half days before we had all the supplies bought, mostly due to others coming by wanting to palaver, or drag us off to meet some other coons[1]. There was no need to worry about anyone stealing our supplies, for among these people there was a Code of Honor. And as far as we knew, everyone honored it. We knew if anyone didn't, they would probably get hung. Most of the coons worked for the Rocky Mountain Fur Company or some other. Anyone working for a fur company had to sell their fur to the company, sometimes at a cheaper price than the free trappers got. Cole and I were free bosslopers, answering to no one.

The rendezvous was coming to an end. We had all the supplies our credit would allow. After saying so long, with slaps on the back or bear hugs to all the ol' coons we'd made friends with, all the others we met, the squaws that went to our robes night after drunken night, it was time we made tracks toward where we figured would be good wintering. We had stayed longer than we originally had planned. It wasn't all that bad, for we came away not at all disappointed. We had learned a hell of a lot listening to the stories and the tales from the many trappers and Injun bucks.

We weren't the only ones making ready. Many others, some in groups, some with squaws, others with papooses and squaws, were heading somewhere to their favorite haunts. It was early morning when Cole and I swung our asses into the saddles on our favorite animals, and pointed their heads east-northeast, winding our way over the South Platte, then north until we came to the Yellowstone River and Crow Country.

It had been many weeks since we left the rendezvous and it looked like many more before coming across Chief Standing Bear's village. We knew it was getting late enough in the fall that Chief Standing Bear probably would have moved his village to their wintering grounds. We figured that to be somewhere close to the Yellowstone.

1. friends (what the mountain men referred to one another)

Some days earlier, Cole and I had stopped at the canyon where we had our animals and some supplies cached. The animals all looked in good shape and everything else was just as we left it. After several days of going through supplies and caching what we didn't take with us, we mounted up, putting our noses to the wind in search for Chief Standing Bear's village. And, at the same time, keeping our eyes open for good beaver signs, checking every feeder stream flowing down from the high country to the Yellowstone River.

From where we were, the Yellowstone flowed through a valley sixty or more miles long. Valleys like this were sometimes referred to as Holes by the mountain men who traveled there. Like many others, they were good places to hole up for the winter, usually with plenty of feed for animals and wood for fires, and lots of water, and protected some by the high mountains from winter storms.

Working our way up the west bank of the Yellowstone, we came across a small stream, maybe a foot and a half wide, that seemed to have a lot of water flowing in it. After getting down from our mules and letting the animals drink, then ourselves, I asked, "What you think?"

"I doesn't know, brother."

"You think we should go check it out?"

"Mights be a good idea."

From where we stood, we could see the stream was coming from the west somewhere off toward the towering mountains.

"Cole, do you see out there, maybe a mile or so, the stream seems to disappear around some low buttes?"

"Yeah. I'se can see whats you say. I'se think you'se and I'se should rides out there, maybe see where it's coming from."

"Let's go." Crawling back on our mules, we rode off along the small stream. After riding some distance, the stream beared off to the right around the butte. A short distance farther on, the stream swung to the left and headed toward what looked like the beginning of a small valley.

"What's you thinks, brother? Goes on?"

"Yeah. So far it looks like it may turn out to be something we're looking for."

"Shore hopes so."

The stream flowed out from between two small hills that were not visible from the Yellowstone more than three miles away. The valley between the two small hills was no more than fifty yards wide. As we rode beyond the small hills, we could see the valley opening up, and the farther we rode, the wider the valley got. It looked like it may be three-quarters of a mile across.

Stopping, we sat and looked in disbelief at what we were seeing. The valley looked like the ideal place to trap. It was skirted by a heavy growth of aspen and dotted with evergreen. Looking at Cole, I asked, "What do you think?"

"Brother, this is one hell of a good-lookin' valley. You looks at all them there beaver ponds. How's much far you'se think to the other end?"

"Don't know. It could be two miles or more to that rock cliff."

"Back there."

"Whadda you say you ride along the north side and I'll take the south side?"

"Let's do it."

"Stay close to the tree line."

"Yeah. Wills do."

We could see one another except for the occasional clump of cottonwood trees scattered here and there through the valley. As I rode along the south side of the valley, I noticed how many springs there were flowing into the beaver ponds. As I rode up closer to the cliffs, I noticed how much higher the land was here than the rest of the valley.

I whistled for Cole. He came over to where I was standing, in a cave-like opening in the rocks that went back in a good fifteen feet, and with a ceiling several inches over my head and close to twenty feet wide.

"Brother! Ain't this somethin'?"

"Yeah, sure the hell is."

"What you thinks?"

"Well, Cole, like the coons back at the rendezvous would say, 'This child likes it!' It has a good feeling about it, and it looks like there may be a good number of beaver, a sufficient supply of wood, and water."

"Yeah, I'se think it's good! Over wheres I was, there's a nice meadow that goes to de north, grass belly high to my horse. I'se thinks a good place for us to spend the winter."

"Yeah, I say we stay. Maybe we should stay here for several days before we go dragging our supplies here. What you think, Cole?"

"I'se think we should, and learns to know our way around."

"Maybe have time to start closing some of the openings in."

"That sounds good."

"And maybe go cut for sign of the Crow."

"Yeah."

After unpacking the animals, we set to work scraping the loose dirt and rocks out from under the overhang, making a place for our supplies and ourselves.

Early one morning several days later, we set out to cut for tracks of the Crow. We had been riding two-thirds of the day when we cut signs. We knew it to be a large party on the move, by the signs they left. We could see they were following a stream west toward the mountains. We had rode a mile or more when we rounded a bend, and there it was, spread out over one half of a large meadow and surrounded on most of its sides by heavy woods. We knew at once this had to be Chief Standing Bear's village.

Riding slowly toward the village, we fired our muskets to let the village know we were coming in peace. Four or five warriors came galloping to meet us. The first to reach us was Lame Leg and Long Knife. The first thing they wanted to know was where White Man and Black Man go for so long. "Chief Standing Bear say maybe happened you not come back."

"We go far south, to rendezvous," I told them. "We now come to visit Chief Standing Bear."

While we rode, I asked Long Knife, "How chief?"

"Chief good, bring village here five suns past. Good place for winter animals for meat, much wood. I, brave Long Knife and brave Lame Leg, find place when hunting."

Riding up to Chief Standing Bear's lodge, the chief and his wife were waiting. They had already heard we were coming.

Cole and I slid down from our animals, me from Old Curse. Today was Old Worse's day to pack. After much palavering with the chief the rest of the afternoon, dark was coming down fast. The chief said, "My friends, stay night, talk more." He told us to bring our bed rolls into his tepee, which was quite large.

Following the chief in, we put our bed rolls next to the entrance. The chief motioned Cole and I to come sit by the fire, where his wife and two daughters were cooking over a small fire. The women had roasted boudins, cooked buffalo tongue with wild rice, and mint tea. All the while we were eating and talking with the chief, I noticed his two daughters watching Cole and me from the shadows, where they were sitting with their mother, eating.

After we were all through eating, Cole and I presented the chief with a new shining knife, a pouch of smoking tobaccy and pipe, and presented his wife with a cast iron kettle and tin skillet, and a pouch of foofaraws, beads, finger and ear rings, to each of his daughters.

The chief thanked us, then motioned his wife to bring more tea. We settled back and talked more, smoked our pipes, and sipped tea way into the night. With the dim light, I was barely able to make out the three women still sitting in the shadows. I guess they were listening to what we were palavering about. From time to time I saw Cole nodding off.

Finally, I said to the chief, "I think we need to get some sleep."

The chief nodded, then asked where Cole and I would robe when it was winter. Cole looked at me and shrugged.

"Chief," I said, "we found a place that is a little more than a half a day's ride from here. It's up a small valley and far enough away from the river, so anyone traveling by won't be able to see or know we are there."

"Chief see. Talk more when light." The chief then disappeared behind his partition. We unrolled our bed rolls, one of each side of the entrance, and crawled in. As I lay, thinking about the things we palavered about and listening to the wind whispering its song as it moved through the tops of the poles on the outside of the tepee, I could feel an energy force, an energy so strong and wonderful that I could see it. It filled the inside of the tepee.

As I lay there with my blankets pulled up around my head, hearing the snoring sounds from the others, I came to realize there was a higher force that watched over each and every one, and it didn't matter whether Injun, Black, White or what, and I knew then that the white bird was part of it.

It was mid morning when Cole and I saddled up after telling the chief how to get to where we were camped. We thanked him and his wife for welcoming us into their lodge and for the food they shared.

It was almost dark when we rode up to the place we were preparing to make ready for the winter.

The next morning, gathering just the necessary things we would need and readying the pack animals, Cole and I crawled back in the saddle and headed for the box canyon where we had supplies cached. It was late evening on the third day of hard riding that we rode into the canyon. The sun was overhead on the second day, when we heard the whoops, yelping, yelling as the sound echoes up the canyon, of Injuns coming a good mile away.

I realized at once that in our tired state of mind the night before, when we rode in, we had neglected to cover our tracks. Knowing now some Injun came across tracks of horses and were coming to look for them, we made ready by positioning ourselves so that if anyone came, they would be caught in somewhat of a crossfire. We also realized by the sounds of them that we would be outnumbered.

The wait wasn't long before the sound of beating hooves grew closer. We always made sure the animals were back in the farthest end of the canyon. That meant the red sticks would have to pass us in order to get the animals.

We were waiting when the Injuns came galloping around the bend. We each had four muskets cocked and waiting, plus four pistols each. We hadn't figured on there being as many as there were. It was our intent to shoot only to wound, if possible. Now I didn't know. After wounding several, we thought it would take the fight out of them. No, these red-ass Injuns kept on coming. They were a fearless, bloodthirsty bunch of bastards.

I didn't know how many were left when Cole yelled, "I'se needs help, brother!"

I taken off running, and before I could reach him, a ball from one of their muskets raked across my ribs, just under my left arm, causing me to stumble. Before I hit the ground, I yanked one of my pistols from my waist, landing on my left side just as that red stick charged. Swinging his gun like a club, I had just enough time to pull the trigger. The ball smashed into the bastard's chest.

Before he hit the ground, I was on my feet, running like hell toward where Cole was. I got to Cole just in time to see an Injun swing his club down hard toward Cole's head, and I saw Cole move to one side with his left arm up to ward off the blow. The club hit Cole's forearm. I heard him give out a yell as the bone in his arm broke. Cole's knife was already sunk in up to the handle in the warrior's lower stomach. Yanking upward, blood and guts spilled out from the warrior.

Dropping his club, both of his hands grabbed at his stomach, slumping to the ground, mouth moving, nothing coming out.

Before I had time to reload my musket, I heard the shrieking of another red ass charging toward us. Crouched low, war club in one hand, knife in the other, I waited until he was close enough, but not too close. Stepping a little to one side, I swung the gun with all I had, catching the red stick on the bridge of his nose. He stumbled back, then hit the ground hard.

Cole yelled, "Behind you!"

Turning just in time to see another one almost on me, tomahawk raised to strike. I raised my gun with both hands just as the warrior came down with his tomahawk, hitting the barrel just back of the blade, snapping it off. When he went for his knife, I brought the butt of my gun up, hitting the bastard hard under his chin. His head snapped back. Swinging the stock of my gun hard against the side of his head, this time his knees buckled and he went down to stay.

I looked the surrounding area over really good, to make sure there weren't any waiting for a chance to attack. Not seeing anything, I turned my attention to Cole, to see how bad his arm was. He was on his haunches, trying to tie the one up that was knocked out. Cutting some strips from the red ass's clothes, I tied this one's hands and feet. Checking on Cole again, I could see his arm starting to swell. Feeling along his arm, I could feel the bone was out of place. I explained to him what had to be done, so his arm would heal right.

"Let's do it!" Grabbing his shooting pouch and folding it in half, he then bit down on it. Gripping his arm just above the break and with my other hand on his wrist, I jerked slightly. I could feel the bone moving back into place. Looking at Cole, he had his eyes squeezed tight shut, sweat pouring down his face, still biting down on the pouch.

"Cole, you sit here, and don't move that arm. I'm going to look around and make sure there are no other Injuns that can sneak up on us."

"Yeah."

After loading all of our guns and shoving three of the pistols into my waist band, and a musket in each hand, I went in search of anyone that might be able to put up a fight. Finding none, I gathered up all the weapons of the wounded and taken them to where Cole was. Then, turning my attention to Cole's arm, I wrapped it with a piece of soft deerskin, then placed sticks on all sides. Wrapping them with long strips of leather, and cutting a long strip of leather from one of the dead Injun's legging, I fastened it just below his elbow, the other end was tied around the sticks just above the wrist, so Cole could put the strap around his neck and shoulder to keep his arm from hanging down.

"Brother, what can I'se do?"

"See if you can get a fire going, and maybe cut some meat and get it roasting."

"I'se can do that."

"While you do that, I'm gonna get the wounded close to the fire before it's too dark."

"Yeah, all right."

Dragging the wounded, two at a time, I lay them close by the fire. But little did I realize there would be seven wounded and five dead, plus the two we had tied up.

After patching up the wounded the best I could, I then gathered up the bed rolls and blankets from their horses and threw each one a blanket. It didn't matter at all to me whose was whose.

Sitting down close to the fire, Cole said, "Brother, those two tied up, they come around now."

"Did you ask if they understood white man talk?"

"No, I'se didn't. I'se saw they watch every move you done make."

"All right."

Dragging the two of them to a sitting position close by the wounded and the fire, I asked if they talked English white man talk. They didn't answer. I had already given the wounded something to eat and drink. As I turned to leave, the one said, "*Hun*-gry."

I said, "What you say?"

He again said, "*Hun*-gry."

"So you *do* talk white man talk?"

Shaking his head up and down, he said, "Som-me lit-tle."

I got him a chunk of meat and some coffee. He shook his head. Getting more meat and coffee, I handed it to the second warrior. This one just sat there, looking intent. Looking him directly in the eye, I said, "I know you red-ass stick bastard knows what the hell I'm saying, don't you? I brought you something to eat and drink, so *eat* it! I want you to listen to what I say. When first light comes, you two will get your wounded warriors on their horses, and the dead on theirs. Then the two of you will see that they get back to your village. What tribe are you from?"

They just sat, chewing on the meat I gave them. I reached around, pulling my knife from its sheath, and pointed it at them, then said, "I'm going to start scalping the wounded until one of you two tells me!"

I turned and started to walk away when the one said, "No, not scalp! We Cheyenne warriors!"

"What the hell are Cheyenne doing in Crow country?"

"We come looking for horses. See tracks, follow. Not know white man horses."

After giving each one more meat and coffee, I poured myself a tin of coffee and sliced a chunk of roasted meat and sat down beside Cole and started to eat. That's when I realized how completely drained I was. I had already placed the wounded around the fire so the light would allow us to watch over them.

"Brother," Cole said, "you get some sleep. I'se take de first watch. My arm, it hurts too much for me to sleep."

"All right, Cole. Wake me when it's my time."

"Okay, brother."

"And, Cole ..."

"Yeah?"

"Keep your guns on your lap, and if any of these assholes go to give you any trouble, blow a hole in them!"

"Will do."

I bedded down not far from Cole. It was getting close to light when I awakened. Looking around, I saw Cole still sitting by the fire. "Cole, how come you didn't get me up?"

"My arm bothered me too much for'se to sleep."

Getting up, I put a pot of coffee over the fire to cook and some meat to roast. I noticed Cole had laid down. Daylight was beginning to break with a hint of reddish sky peeping through far off somewhere in the east.

When the meat was ready, I saw to it that the wounded each got a chunk of meat and made sure they had something to drink, and also the two that were tied up. Cole had drifted off to sleep. I knew he was worn out and was in need of sleep and rest. Figuring I could handle this bunch of red sticks on my own, I let him sleep.

Cutting two 10-foot lengths of rope, I tied one piece around each Injun's ankle, and the other end to two of our mules, then untied their hands and their feet. They knew the game all too well to try anything. I told them to get their wounded loaded on their horses. They just stood, looking at me, until I swung my double-barrel musket up and leveled it at them. They got the message, and made short work of getting the wounded and dead loaded on their horses and the dead tied down.

Cole had awakened and saw I was holding my musket on the two of them that were tied to the mules. "Whats you wants I'se to do?" he asked.

"Hold your pistol on them." I then told them to untie the rope from their ankles and get mounted. The last thing I said to them was, "If we ever come face to face again, and you start any trouble, I will cut your black hearts out and feed it to the magpies, and cook your livers and eat them! Now, get these wounded back to your village as soon as you can. Get moving!"

Not a word was said as they single-filed away. Cole and I watched until they were out of sight.

40

Four and a half days later, through a misty rain, much of the time we made it with our supplies to where we planned on spending the winter. It felt good to be here as we unloaded the pack animals and set up camp. Cole, with his broken arm, did the best he could. One morning, a few days later, we were getting things arranged and some supplies stashed in several caches, when Cole said, "Brother, did you see that white bird when dems Injuns was comin' at us?"

"Yeah, I saw it. Why?"

"It stayed close the whole time we were there."

"I know."

"Nows it sits on that snag across the creek, like it's watchin' us."

"Yeah, I see it." The trees and underbrush had long since turned color, and after a willow killer came, most of the leaves had fallen off the cottonwoods, aspen and the willow that grew thick along the stream and ponds. Few remained on the scrub brushes that grew closer to the evergreen. The many ponds were now home to ducks and geese that stopped on their way south.

Cole and I labored, getting traps ready and in order, so we could start trapping beaver and anything else that we might catch. From time to time I would stop working and look out over this small but abundant valley, and I could feel this wonderful energy that surrounded it. I had a feeling of being secure and content.

If the coming winter wasn't too harsh, there would be plenty of forage for the animals, and from what I could see, there would be plenty of beaver to keep Cole and me busy. It taken several weeks before Cole's arm got back to normal. By now, we had the front of the overhang closed in, except for an entrance. With the abounds of flat rock that lay around, we were able to construct a fire pit with a chimney that would carry most of the smoke outside. It was time to hunt for our winter meat, since the days were cold enough now that we could hang it and it would last a long time.

One day, while Cole and I were hunting, we came across a Crow hunting party from Chief Standing Bear's village, who said they were going after buffalo and asked if we would hunt with them. I said we would be honored to hunt with the Crow. They knew we had much better weapons and would be able to help them get the meat they needed.

Cole and I had been riding with the Crow for two days when they spotted a fair size herd of buffalo half a mile off in the distance. There were close to thirty Crow. It must have been most of the braves and squaws from their village. Each had a pack animal and some had two. The valley was mostly barren except for knee-high grass and scattered clumps of sage. There were several washes here and there. I taken up a position in one of the washes that was deep and narrow. Cole was off to my right. I could see him , but when the hunt started, with all the yelping from the Injuns and the pounding of hoofs from the buffalo stampeding by, I couldn't hear a damn thing he was saying.

The hunt was very successful and came off without an incident. We had no idea how many buffalo we killed, but it didn't matter. The Crow braves were more than happy. They had all the meat their animals could pack. Cole had taken a calf born that spring and I killed a yearling cow.

Everyone spent the rest of the day and some of the next cutting up the meat and packing it in the green buffalo hides, so they would be ready to load on the pack animals when it was time to move on. The night following the hunt, everyone pitched in and we had a feast, roasted hump ribs, liver, buffalo cider, and boudins, roasted, until it was good and crisp and sizzling. Although everyone was very friendly, praising us for helping them with the hunt, we were not all that comfortable being outnumbered so badly.

When it came time to bed down, we picketed our animals in a circle, so we could bed down in the middle, keeping out weapons in our bed rolls. We were up just as it was getting light. After eating something, we pitched in and helped with loading the animals. By midday, the Crow were all packed and on their way back to their village.

Cole and I rode off in the direction we needed to get to our wintering place. The young buffalo, along with the meal we already had, would see us through the winter. Arriving back at our shelter, we found everything the way we left it, and the animals we didn't take all looked fine. The meat we hung at the far end of the overhang, where it would stay cold.

Over the next few days, I staked out most of our traps while Cole kept watch toward the lower end of the valley and hunted ducks and geese, taking most of two dozen ducks and half that many geese. Snow had started to fall now, coming down heavy at times, and the snow made me feel a lot better, knowing it would cover any tracks that we may have left coming into the valley. I figured with no tracks coming in or going out, no one would know anyone was in this valley. Our camp was far enough away from the main trails along the Yellowstone that any smoke would not be seen, and probably not smelled. But I also realized smoke could be smelled a long way.

We were taking a fair amount of beaver now. By skinning most on the spot, we were able to cut down on the weight we had to carry. Then, fleshing and stretching the plews by the light from the fire and several bitch lamps, sometimes way into the night, sipping hot broth, coffee or tea, made the work more enjoyable.

By now, winter had fully settled in. The snow wasn't all that bad, but the bitter cold that came with it froze most everything solid, and had a way of creeping through every little opening. Our animals fared quite well. They seemed to find enough to forage on

It was late winter and the end of our third winter of trapping. Cole and I had put up as much fur as our pack animals could carry and were preparing for the trip East to see Charley and Fanny, where we hoped to sell our fur. We had only a few days' work left and we would be ready, when an unexpected snow eater swept through, dumping several feet of snow and accompanied by extremely frigid weather, which lasted several days.

After the worst of the storm passed, Cole and I ventured out of our cozy, warm shelter and found that the furious wind of the past several days had swept away a lot of the snow. After looking things over, we decided to put on our snowshoes and see if we could dig out the remaining traps.

I was breaking trail and a short distance in front of Cole when suddenly I broke through some rotten ice that had been covered with drifted snow over a beaver pond.

I went in over my head. I could see the huge opening and was struggling with all my strength, but was unable to reach the top. My heavy clothes and snowshoes were holding me down.

I then saw Cole shove his long walking stick down in front of my face, where I was able to grab it. When he felt I had a hold, he gave a big heave upward with all his strength and I shot to the surface, where he grabbed me by the hair and was able to keep my head above water until he was able to get a firm grip on my coat collar and drag me to safety.

As I was choking and gasping for air, at the same time coughing and spitting out water, Cole crouched beside me and asked in a shaky voice, "Nathan, is you all right?"

"I think so."

He rolled me in the powdery snow, in order to soak up as much water from my clothes as possible, and helping me to my feet, he said, "Come, I'se needs to get you back to camp."

Still dazed and my head spinning, I said, "I think I can make it."

"Let's get moving before you freeze."

We headed for camp. Once I got moving, I gained some of my strength back and was more steady on my feet. He was leading the way, taking a shortcut, which saved time. The going was rough. I was numb with cold.

In what seemed a loud voice, I heard Cole say, "We're here. Let me get those snowshoes off and get you inside."

Once inside our shelter, I could feel the warmth on my face and hands. While Cole added wood to the fire, I stood as close as I could. My clothes, along with my hair, were frozen stiff. My hands were so stiff, I couldn't undo the fastening of my coat. Cole saw and came and undid them and helped me out of my frozen clothes. He got my wool blanket and wrapped it around me, and one of my buffalo robes.

I sat as close to the fire as I dared and, after my teeth quit chattering, I told Cole how grateful I was to him for saving my life. "If you wouldn't have been there with me, I wouldn't have been able to get out on my own. I just want you to know how thankful I am to have a brother like you."

"Oh, gosh, gosh! I'se knows you would do the same for me. Like we said from de start, we'se must take care of each other if we'se gonna survive."

Staying as close to the fire throughout the rest of the day

and night, I felt I was never able to get warm. By the next morning I was feeling hellish, burning up with fever.

"Is you all right, brother?" Cole laid his hand on my forehead. When he removed it, I saw the worried look on his face.

After putting wood on the fire and piling a heap nearby, he turned to me and said, "Nathan, I'se gonna ride to de Crow village and see if I can get help. I'se be back." With that he left.

The day would diminish by the time Cole would return. As I lay on my bed that day and into the night, in a feverish state of mind, I saw come before me the white bird. As it came to me, it brought with it an Indian maiden who would heal my sick body and make it whole. It was told to me by the white bird that the Indian maiden from this time forth would be known to me as Bird of Night.

"She, in time, will become your soul companion," it told me.

Finally, I heard Cole come in, bringing someone with him. In the subdued light I was unable to see who. I was close to being unconscious. Nothing seemed able to make sense. Vaguely I remember hearing someone say, "Let's get him outside and lay him into snow until his fever comes down."

I had no idea how long I was left lying in the snow. The next thing I can reckon, I was lying on my bed, thinking I was hearing a woman telling Cole to make some hot water while she wrapped blankets and my buffalo robe around me.

Faintly, in my feeble state of mind, I recall Cole saying, "The water's hot."

Soon I was being force-fed some kind of brew that tasted horrible, then some broth. It was even worse. After swallowing all I could, nothing seemed to matter. I guess I passed out.

At times throughout the night, it felt ... or maybe I imagined it ... but I thought someone was in bed beside me, keeping me warm, and would get up often and force more tea and broth into me until I would gag. Then they would stop.

This went on throughout the night and for the next two days.

On the morning of the third day, I opened my eyes and was able to grasp what was going on for the first time in days. Realizing a heaviness over my legs and hips, I remembered what had happened and I couldn't help but wonder.

I raised myself up on my elbows in order to see why I couldn't move my legs, and was astonished to find myself looking into the sleeping face of a woman. She was curled up beside me, her head cradled in her arms that lay over my upper legs.

Struggling to free myself wakened her. Opening her eyes, she saw I was half sitting and a look of disbelief settled across her face. A warm smile of happiness swept over her. Reaching over me, she wakened Cole with such a hard shake that brought him to his feet, as if he was struck in the ass by a nest of bumblebees.

Cole yelled, "What! What! What's wrong?"

Seeing her pointing at me, he then noticed I was sitting up. Kneeling on one side of me, with her on the other side, they clasped my hands in theirs. Cole was mumbling, "You'se come back. You'se come back … come back … from the dead! Brother, you'se back from the dead!"

The Indian woman was taking this all in. Fear filled her shining dark eyes as she listened to everything that Cole was saying. I thought she was about to bolt, but instead, in a tongue that was unknown to me, she began to chant, a chant that stopped Cole and I cold, and sent shivers running up and down my spine.

Cole had already stopped what he was talking about and placed his hand on hers. She looked at him in bewilderment, but stopped her chanting. "Nathan needs to eat. Will you see what you can find?"

She nodded and got up.

Later that afternoon, while I was lying on my bed recuperating, Cole and the Indian maiden came and sat beside me. Cole then began filling me in on what had happened. He went on to say that I became very sick. He did everything he knew to do, but it didn't seem to help. He then became worried and, not knowing what else to do, decided the best thing was to ride to the Crow village that lay more than a half a day's ride away.

Upon arriving, he went straight to Chief Standing Bear's lodge. The chief greeted him and asked him to come in and sit. Cole said he did, then the chief asked, "What bring friend in big hurry?"

Cole then said he told the chief, "White brother very sick. Need medicine and medicine man."

He said he was in a hurry, "then the chief told me his people had a bad winter. Many more than half sick. Not enough to eat. Medicine man, they sick, can't help white brother. Chief have no help for his people."

Cole then said he told the chief he understood, and now he must return and do what he could for his white brother. "Chief nodded, we shook hands, and I left," Cole said.

After gathering up his mules and leading them toward the edge of the village, he heard someone yell at him to wait. Turning to see what they wanted, Cole saw this young maiden come running from among a row of tepees. "I waited to see what she wanted. She was bundled in several blankets with three pouches hung over her shoulders," he explained. "I asked, 'What you want?' She say, 'I heard you ask Chief for medicine man, and medicine for sick brother. All our medicine men sick. I say to chief I can go. Chief say no. I say I go help. Chief bow head like he think, then say go see if you can help. I get good medicine and run after you. I help!' Well, I had nothing to lose, so I said yes."

Cole continued, "I ask her what she was called. Nesshyah, she reply. I help her on de other mule, and wrap all de blankets and a buff robe round her to help keep her warm, and den led de mule as we rode away from de village. Nathan?"

"Yeah?"

"You know that large white bird we see from time to time?"

"Yeah?"

"Wells ... wells, it ..." His voice became a little shaky. "It's ... it's come out of nowhere, swooping low over our heads, and flew just far enough in front so we can always see it."

From time to time I would glance at Nesshyah. She would nod in agreement at what Cole was saying.

"I'se swear that when daylight faded into dark, and I'se mean dark! Brother, so damn dark that I'se could only see that white bird flying only feet in front of my black mule. I'se tell you, Nathan, I'se ... I'se ... sure to hell was spooked. Not know about her. I'se to hell knows she held onto that muley like she frozen to that damn thing. All de time white bird stay out in front like guiding our mules all the way. Damn to hell, it was so spooky, I'se was scared shitless. I'se feared that bird and my mules, theys was talking! Shit, you'se know, Nathan, what's I means ... communicating! Shit, you'se knows not saying a damn anything! Nathan, that bird, it's flown right up to our cave! And brother, when that bird flies right on in, I'se got even more spooked, and I'se thinks Nesshyah she gotten much spooked as I'se. We's not know if we's should come in. We's thought maybe ..."

"Cole! Cole! What happened to the bird?"

"It's ... it's ... still setting over there. Hasn't moved since ... just sits there! Spooky! And watches us every time one of us goes out or comes in. Sometimes it makes a noise like maybe it's wanting to tell us something. I'se doesn't know."

"Cole, do you know what kind of bird it is?"

"I'se don't know. Squaw, she say it's a White Raven. She say much spirit! She say White Raven good, very sacred."

"Cole?"

"Yeah?"

"Do you think you'se can help me to my feet?"

"Why? Why you wants do that?

"I would like to see this White Raven before it flies away."

"Wells ... okay. I'se think we's can."

After they helped me to my feet, I realized just how weak I was. With their help, I made it the short distance to where the bird was perched, just as they said it was. With the light from a lamp, I was able to see it more clearly. It was a beautiful bird, "snow white." I expected it to fly, but it didn't. It just stayed perched on the ledge and would cock its head to one side, then to the other.

From the very moment I looked into that bird's eyes, something from deep within told me that this White Raven would always be close by to watch over me, just as Chief Golden Eagle had told me.

As the days passed, I regained enough strength that I was able to help Cole. Then, one day while we were making our things ready, four braves from the Crow village showed up, looking for the squaw, then informed her she was much needed at the village.

Quickly she gathered her possessions and climbed on the pony the braves brought, then waved and rode off. Cole and I watched as she rode out of sight, then turned back to our task of concealing our cave, making it look as natural as possible.

My strength had fully recovered by now, so we decided before going East we would do some hunting, and if we got some meat, we would swing by the Crow village and give it to them. Cole had said they were short of food.

Over the next few days, we were able to bag seven deer and an elk. Arriving at the Crow village with our kill, we tied up as close to the chief's lodge as possible. By now a bunch of kids had gathered around, along with a few squaws looking at our kills, gibbering among themselves.

"Now what?" I asked Cole.

"I'se don't know! I think I best stay here while you go see de chief."

"Well, all right, I guess that will work." I went straight to the lodge and found the chief and his wife sitting outside. She was working on some hides with him just sitting there. When he saw me coming, he stood up, looking at me strangely. I greeted him with, "How Chief this fine day?"

His reply was, "What bring friend?"

"We brought Chief and his people some food. Come, I show you."

He and his wife followed as I led the way to where Cole was waiting with the animals. We showed the chief and his wife the seven deer and the large elk. While they were looking the kills over, they gibbered back and forth, which made little sense. Finally, he looked at us and said, "What you want in return?"

"Nothing. The meat is our thanks to you and your people for letting the medicine woman come to our camp with good medicine to make me well."

"Squaw good medicine woman."

"I'm strong now. Cole and I are riding East to sell our fur."

"You bring Chief many guns?"

"How many guns Chief want?"

"Many!"

"How many?"

"Many guns for my warriors. You show warriors how to use, then hunt like you." He held up his ten fingers ten times.

"That many? That's one hundred guns." I looked at Cole. He was looking at me. "What you think?" I asked.

"Don't know."

"I think we would be taking a big chance."

"I think you're right." Then he added, "I think we can do it, Nathan."

I looked at Cole, bewildered for a few minutes, then said, "If you think so, then we will try. Chief, we will do our best to get the guns you want."

The chief nodded, then said, "Come, we smoke. Squaws take care of meat."

We went with the chief to his lodge and followed him in.

We were told to sit as he lit his pipe and passed it around. "You good friends. You bring guns."

"We will try, Chief. If we can't get guns, we're still friends?"

He nodded.

We shook hands, gathered up our animals, and set out on our journey East.

About the Author

Ethan Miller was born in Somerset, Pennsylvania on March 2, 1934. He worked various jobs until the age of 21, when he moved to northeastern Ohio, to work for Ford Motor Company.

His passion for the outdoors led him to spend leisure time hunting and trapping. His dream of moving to Alaska, and living in the wild never manifested. After retirement, he spent time in Arizona and Colorado, and eventually settled in the small town of Paonia, Colorado, in the Rocky Mountains. He enjoyed the solitude of being in the mountains with his wife, Annie, and their dog, Ranger, and three mules.

He had started working on the sequel to *Night of the White Raven* when he became ill in 2006. He returned to Ohio early in 2007 with his wife and his dog, and was still writing *The Return of the White Raven* when he passed away in September 2008.

He is survived by two sons, three grandchildren, and three stepsons. His widow, Ann Ulrich Miller, an author and editor in her own right, has decided to finish the sequel, in response to her husband's wishes, which will be published sometime in 2018.

"***He was a mountain man at heart***. Ethan was a remarkable man, loved by all whom he met, and he had a very generous heart for someone who grew up poor during the Depression. He is remembered lovingly by people in his community who would always get this response when asked how he was doing: *'I'm absolutely marvelous!'*"

—***Annie Miller***

www.ingramcontent.com/pod-product-compliance
Lightning Source LLC
LaVergne TN
LVHW041924090826
845145LV00015B/296

9780944851241